I wasn't the only one in my family with twanked genes. My mom was a three-quarter-scale replica of the Statue of Liberty. Originally she wanted to be full-sized, and applied for a zoning variance; when they turned her down, she took them to court. Mom's claim was that since she was born human, her freedom of form was protected by the Thirtieth Amendment. However, the form she wanted was a curtain of reshaped cells that would hang on a forty-two-meter-high ferroplastic skeleton, clearly subject to building codes and zoning laws. Eventually they reached an out-of-court settlement.

One thing Mom and the town agreed on from the start: no tourists. Sure, she loved publicity, but she was also very fragile. In some places her skin was only a centimeter thick. Chunks of ice falling from her crown could punch holes in her.

Mom had been bioengineered to be pretty much self-sufficient. She was green not only to match the real Statue of Liberty but also because she was photosynthetic. She lived on a yearly truckload of fertilizer, water from the well, and 150 kilowatts of electricity a day.

I think Mom meant well, but she never did understand me. Especially when she talked to me with her greeter bioremote.

"Peter. How are you, Peter?"

"Tired."

"You poor boy. Let me see you." She held me at arm's length and brushed her fingers against my cheek. "You don't look a day over twelve. Oh, they do such good work—don't you think?" She squeezed my shoulder. "Are you happy with it?"

Wildlife

James Patrick Kelly

A TOM DOHERTY ASSOCIATES BOOK
NEW YORK

WILDLIFE

Portions of this novel have appeared in substantially different form, in *Isaac Asimov's Science Fiction Magazine*.

A Tor Book
Published by Tom Doherty Associates, Inc.
175 Fifth Avenue
New York, NY 10010

Tor® is a registered trademark of Tom Doherty Associates, Inc.

Cover art by Jensen
Library of Congress Card Catalog Number: 93-42547

ISBN: 0-812-53415-8

First edition: February 1994
First mass market edition: July 1995

Printed in the United States of America

0 9 8 7 6 5 4 3 2 1

For Pam,
my favorite reader

Wildlife

2044

Wynne

We initiated deorbital burn over the Marshall Islands and dropped back into the ionosphere, locked by the wing's navigator into one of the Eurospace reentry corridors. As we coasted across Central America we were an easy target for the attack satellites. The plan was to fool the tracking nets into thinking we were a corporate shuttle. Django had somehow acquired the recognition codes; his computer, snaked to the wing's navigator, had convinced it to pretend to be the property of Erno Raumfahrttechnik GMBH, the EC aerospace conglomerate.

It was all a matter of timing, really. It would not be too much longer before the people on Cognico's Orbital 7 untangled the spaghetti Django had made of their memory systems and realized that he had downloaded WILDLIFE and stolen a cargo wing. Then they would have to decide whether to zap us immediately or have their own private security ops waiting when we landed. The plan was to lose the wing before they could decide. Our problem was that very little of the plan had worked so far.

Django had gotten us on and off the orbital research station all right, and had managed to pry WILDLIFE from the jaws of the corporate beast. For that alone his reputation would live forever among the snakes who steal information for a living, even if he was not around to enjoy the fame. But he had lost our pilot, Yellowbaby—his partner, my sometime lover—and neither of us had any idea exactly what it was he had stolen. He seemed pretty calm for somebody who had just sunk fangs into the world's biggest computer company. He slouched in the commander's seat across from me, watching the readouts on the autopilot console. He was smiling and tapping a finger against his headset as if he were listening to one of his jazz disks. He was a dark, ugly man with an Adam's apple that looked like a nose and a nose that looked like an elbow. He had either been to the face cutters or he was in his mid-thirties. I trusted him not at all and liked him less.

Me, I felt as though I had swallowed a hardboiled egg, but then I'd been spacesick for days. I was just along for the story, the *juice*. According to the newly formed International Law Exchange, all a spook journalist is allowed to do is aim the microcam goggles and ask questions. If I helped Django in any way, I would become an accessory and lose press immunity. Infoline would have to disown me. But press immunity wouldn't do me much good if someone decided to zap the wing. The First Amendment was a great shield, but it didn't protect against reentry friction. I wanted to return to earth with a ship around me; sensors showed that the outer skin was currently 1400° Celsius.

"Much longer?" A dumb question since I already knew the answer. But better than listening to the atmosphere scream as the wing bucked through turbulence. I could feel myself losing it: I wanted to scream back.

"Twenty minutes. However it plays." Django lifted his headset. "Either you'll be a plugging legend or air pollution." He stretched his arms over his head and arched his back away from the seat. I could smell his sweat and almost gagged. I just wasn't designed for more than three gravities a day. "Hey, lighten up, Eyes. You're a big girl now. Shouldn't you be taking notes or something?"

"The camera sees all." I tapped the left temple of the goggles and then forced a grin that hurt my face. "Besides, it's not bloody likely I'll forget this ride." I wasn't about to let Django play with me. He was too hypered on fast-forwards to be scared. My father had been the same way; he ate them like popcorn when he was working.

It had been poor Yellowbaby who had introduced me to Django. I had covered the Babe when he pulled the Peniplex job. He was a real all-nighter, handsome as surgical plastic can make a man and an *artiste* in bed. Handsome—but history. The last time I had seen him he was floating near the ceiling of a decompressed cargo bay, an eighty-kilo hunk of flash-frozen boy toy. I might have thrown up again if there had been anything left in my stomach.

"I copy, Basel Control." Yellowbaby's calm voice crackled across the forward flight deck. "We're doing Mach nine point nine at fifty-seven thousand meters. Looking good for touch at fourteen-twenty-two."

We had come out of reentry blackout. The approach program that Yellowbaby had written, complete with voice interaction module, was in contact with Basel/Mulhouse, our purported destination. As long as everything went according to plan, the program would get us where we wanted to go. If anything went wrong . . . well, the Babe was supposed to have improvised if anything went wrong.

"Let's blow out of here." Django heaved himself out of the seat and swung down the ladder to the equipment bay. I followed. We pulled EV suits from the lockers and struggled into them. I could feel the deck tilting as the wing began a series of long, lazy S curves to slow our descent.

As Django unfastened his suit's weighty backpack he began to sing; his voice sounded like gears being stripped. "I'm flying high, but I've got a feeling I'm falling . . ." He quickly shucked the rest of the excess baggage: comm and life-support systems, various umbilicals. ". . . falling for nobody else but you."

"Would you shut the hell up?" I tossed the still camera from my suit onto the pile.

"What's the matter?" There was a chemical edge to his giggle. "Don't like Fats Waller?"

Yellowbaby's program was reassuring Basel even as we banked gracefully toward the Jura Mountains. "No problem, Basel Control," the dead man's voice drawled. "Malf on the main guidance computer. I've got backup. My L over D is nominal. You just keep the tourists off the runway and I'll see you in ten minutes."

I put the microcam in rest mode—no sense wasting memory dots shooting the inside of an EV suit—and picked up the pressure helmet. Django blew me a kiss. "Don't forget to duck," he said. He made a quacking sound and flapped his arms. I put the helmet on and closed the seals. It was a relief not to have to listen to him; we had disabled the comm units to keep the ops from tracking us. He handed me one of the slim airfoil packs we had smuggled onto and off of Orbital 7. I stuck my arms through the harness and fastened the front straps. I could still hear Yellowbaby's muffled voice talking to the Swiss controllers. "Negative, Basel Control, I don't need escort. Initiating terminal guidance procedures."

At that moment I felt the nose dip sharply. The wing was diving straight for the summit of Mont Tendre. To fight the panic, I queried Infoline's factchecker, built into the goggles' system unit. "At elevation one thousand six hundred seventy-nine meters," came the whisper in my ear, "Mont Tendre is the tallest of the Swiss Juras. It is located in the canton of Vaud." I crouched behind Django in the airlock, tucked my head to my chest, and tongued the armor toggle in the helmet. The thermofiber EV suit stiffened and suddenly I was a shock-resistant statue, unable to move. I began to count backward from one thousand; it was better than listening to my heart jackhammer. I promised myself that if I survived this, I'd never go into space again. Never hundred and ninety-nine, never hundred and ninety-eight, never hundred and . . .

I remembered the way Yellowbaby had smiled as he unbuttoned my shirt, that night before we had shuttled up to 7. He was sitting on a bunk in his underwear. I had still not decided to cover the raid; he was still trying to convince me. But words weren't his strong point. When I turned my back to him, he slipped the shirt from my shoulders, slid it down my arms. I stood there for a moment, facing away from the bunk. Then he grabbed me by the waist and pulled me onto his lap. I could feel the curly hair on his chest brushing against my spine. Sitting there half-naked, my face glowing hot as any heat shield, I knew I was in deep trouble. He had nibbled at my ear and then conned me with that slow Texas drawl. "Hell, baby, only reason ain't no one never tried to jump out of a shuttle is that no one who really needed to jump ever had a chute." I had always been a fool for men who told me not to worry.

Although we were huddled in the airlock, my head was down, so I didn't see the hatch blow. But even with the suit in armor mode, I felt like the clapper inside a cathedral bell. The wing shuddered and, with an explosive last breath, spat us into the dazzling Alpine afternoon.

The truth is that I don't remember much about the jump after that. I know I unfroze the suit so I could guide the airfoil, which had opened automatically. I was too intent on not vomiting and keeping Django in sight and getting down as fast as I could without impaling myself on a tree or smashing into a cliff. So I missed being the only live and in-person witness to one of the more spectacular crashes of the twenty-first century.

It had been Yellowbaby's plan to jump into the Col du Marchairuz, a pass about seven kilometers away from Mont Tendre, before the search hovers came swarming. I saw Django disappear into a stand of dead sycamores and thought he had probably killed himself. I had no time to worry, because the ground was rushing up at me like a nightmare. I spotted the road and steered for it but got caught in a gust that swept me across about five meters above the pavement. I touched on the opposite side; the airfoil was pulling me toward a huge boulder. I toggled to armor mode just as I hit. Once again the bell rang, knocking the breath from me and announcing that I had arrived. If I hadn't been wearing a helmet I would have kissed that chunk of limestone.

I unfastened the quick-release hooks and the airfoil's canopy billowed, dragged along the ground, and wrapped itself around a tree. I slithered out of the EV suit and tried to get my bearings at the same time. The Col du Marchairuz was cool, not much above freezing, and very, very quiet. Although I was wearing isothermals, the skin on my hands and neck pebbled and I shivered. The silence of the place was unnerving. I was losing it again, lagged out. I had been through too damn many environments in one day. I liked to live fast, race up that adrenaline peak where there was no time to think, just report what I could see *now* and to hell with remembering or worrying about what might happen next. What I needed was to start working again so I could lose myself in the details; it was a trick my father had taught me. But I was alone and, for the moment, there was nothing to report. I had dropped out of the sky like a fallen angel; the still landscape itself seemed to judge me. The mountains did not care about Django's stolen corporate secrets or the ops-and-snakes story I would produce to give some jaded telelink drone a Wednesday-night thrill. I had risked my life for some lousy juice and a chance at the main menu; the cliffs brooded over my reasons. So very quiet.

"Eyes!" Django dropped from a boulder onto the road and trotted across to me. "You all right?"

I didn't want him to see how close to the edge I was, so I nodded. After all, I was the spook journalist; he was just another snake. "You?" There was a long scratch on his face and his knuckles were bloody.

"Walking. Tangled with a tree. The chute got caught—had to leave it."

I nodded again. He stooped to pick up my discarded suit. "Let's lose this stuff and get going."

I stared at him, thought about breaking it off. I had enough to put together one hell of a story and I'd had my fill of Django.

"Don't freeze on me now, Eyes." He wadded the suit and jammed it into a crevice. "If the satellites caught our jump, these mountains are going to be crawling with ops, from Cognico *and* the EC." He hurled my helmet over the edge of the cliff and began to gather up the shrouds of my chute. "We're gone by then."

I brought the microcam on line again in time to shoot him hiding my chute. He was right; it wasn't quite time to split up. If EC ops caught me now, they'd probably confiscate my memory dots and let the lawyers fight it out; spook journalism was one American export Europe wanted to discourage. I'd have nothing to sell Jerry Macmillan at Infoline but talking heads and text. And if private ops got us first . . . well, they had their own rules. I had to stick with Django until we got clear. As soon as I started moving again, I felt better. Which is to say I had no time to feel anything at all.

The nearest town was St. George, about four kilometers down the crumbling mountain road. We started at a jog and ended at a drag, gasping in the thin air. On the way Django stopped by a mountain stream to wash the blood from his face. Then he surprised me—and probably himself—by throwing up. Join the club, Django. When he stood up he was shaking. It would make great telelink. I murmured a voice-over, "Yet, for all his bravado, this master criminal has a human side too." The factchecker let it pass. Django made a half-serious feint at the goggles and I stopped shooting.

"You okay?"

He nodded and staggered past me down the road.

St. George was one of those little ghost towns that the Swiss were mothballing with their traditional tidiness, as if they expected that the forests and vineyards would someday rise from the dead and the tourists would return to witness this miracle. Maybe they were right; unlike the rest of the EC, the Swiss had not yet given up on their acid-stressed Alpine lands, not even in unhappy Vaud, which had also suffered radioactive fallout from the nuking of Geneva. We stopped at a clearing planted with the new Sandoz pseudo-firs that overlooked the rust-colored rooftops of St. George. It was impossible to tell how many people were left in the village. All we knew for sure was that the post office was still open.

Django was having a hard time catching his breath. "I have a proposition for you," he said.

"Come on, Django. Save it for the dollies."

He shook his head. "It's all falling apart . . . I can't . . ." He took a deep breath and blew it out noisily. "I'll cut you in. A third: Yellowbaby's share."

According to U.S. case law, still somewhat sketchy on the subject of spook journalism, at this point I should have dropped him with a swift kick to the balls and started screaming for the local gendarmerie. But the microcam was resting, there were no witnesses, and I still didn't know what WILDLIFE was or why Django wanted it. "The way I count, it's just us two," I said. "A third sounds a little low."

"It'll take you the rest of this century to spend what I'm offering."

"And if they catch me I'll spend the rest of the century in some snakepit in Iowa." That was, if the ops didn't blow my circuits first. "Forget it, Django. We're just not in the same line. I watch—you're the player."

I'm not sure what I expected him to do next but it sure as hell wasn't to start crying. Maybe he was in shock too. Or maybe he was finally slowing down after two solid days of popping fast-forwards.

"Don't you understand, I can't do it alone! You have to—you don't know what you're turning down."

I thought about pumping him for more information but he looked as if he were going critical. I didn't want to be caught in the explosion. "I don't get it, Django. You've done all the hard work. All you have to do is walk into that post office, collect your e-mail, and walk out.''

"You don't understand." He clamped both hands to his head. "Don't understand, that was Babe's job.''

"So?"

"So!" He was shaking. *"I don't speak French!"*

I put everything I had into not laughing. It would have been the main menu for sure if I had gotten that onto a memory dot. The criminal mind at work! This snake had bitten the world's largest corporation, totaled a stolen reentry wing, and now he was worried about sounding like a *touriste* in a Swiss *bureau de poste*. I was croggled.

"All right," I said, stalling, "all right, how about a compromise. For now. Umm. You're carrying heat?" He produced a Mitsubishi penlight. "Okay, here's what we'll do. I'll switch on and we'll do a little bit for the folks at home. You threaten me, say you're going to lase your name on my forehead unless I cooperate. That way I can pick up the message without becoming an accessory. I hope. If we clear this, we'll talk deal later." I didn't know if it would stand up in court, but it was all I could think of at the time. "And make it look good."

So I shot a few minutes of Django's threatening me and then we went down into St. George. I walked into the post office hesitantly, turned and got a good shot of Django smoldering in the entryway, and then tucked the goggles into my pocket. The clerk was a restless woman with a pinched face who looked as if she spent a lot of time wishing she were somewhere else. I assaulted her with my atrocious fourth-form French.

"Bonjour, madame. Y a-t-il des lettres électroniques pour D. J. Viper?"

"Viper?" The woman shifted on her stool and fixed me with a suspicious stare. "Comment ça s'écrit?"

"V-i-p-e-r.''

She keyed the name into her terminal. "Oui, la voici. Votre autorisation, s'il vous plaît, madame." She leaned for-

ward and pointed through the window at the numeric keypad beside my right hand. For a moment I thought she was
going to try to watch as I keyed in the recognition code that
Django had given me. I heard him cough in the entryway behind me as she settled back on her stool. Lucky for her. The
postal terminal whirred and ground for about ten seconds
and then a sealed hardcopy clunked into the slot above the
keypad.

"Vous êtes des touristes américains." She looked straight
past me and waved to Django, who ducked out of the doorway. "Baseball Yankees, ha-ha." I was suddenly afraid he
would come charging in with penlight blazing to make sure
there were no witnesses. "Vous avez besoin d'une chambre
pour la nuit? L'hôtel est fermé, mais . . ."

"Non, non. Nous sommes pressés. À quelle heure est le
premier autobus pour Rolle?"

She sighed. "Rien ne va plus. Tout va mal." The busybody seemed to be speaking as much to herself as to me. I
wanted to tell her how lucky she was that Django had decided
not to needle her where she stood. "À quinze heures vingt-
deux."

About twenty minutes—we were still on schedule. I
thanked her and went out to throw some cold water on
Django. I was astonished to find him laughing. I didn't much
like always having to guess how he'd react. Django was so
scrambled that one of these times the surprise was bound to
be unpleasant. "I could've done that," he said.

"You didn't." I handed him the hardcopy and we retreated to an alley with a view of the square.

It is the consensus of the world's above- and below-
ground economies that the EC's photonic mail system is still
the most secure anywhere, much safer than satellite communications. Once it had printed out Django's hardcopy, the
system erased all records of the transferred information.
Even so, the message was encrypted, and Django had to enter
it into his data cuff to find out what it said.

"What is this?" He replayed it and I watched, fascinated,

as the words scrolled along the cuff's tiny display: "Lake Leman lies by Chillon's walls: / A thousand feet in depth below / Its massy waters meet and flow; / Thus much the fathom-line was sent / From Chillon's snow-white battlement / . . ."

"It's called poetry, Django."

"I know what it's called! I want to know what the hell this has to do with my drop. Half the world wants to chop my plug off and this dumbscut sends me poetry." His face had turned as dark as beaujolais nouveau and his voice was so loud they could probably hear him in Lyon. "Where the hell am I supposed to go?"

"Would you shut up for a minute?" I touched his shoulder and he jumped. When he went for his penlight I thought I was cooked. But all he did was throw the hardcopy onto the cobblestones and torch it.

"Feel better?"

"Stick it."

"Lake Leman," I said carefully, "is what the French call Lake Geneva. And Chillon is a castle. In Montreux."

"Actually," whispered the factchecker, "it's in the suburb of Veytaux."

I ignored this for now. "I'm pretty sure this is from a poem called 'The Prisoner of Chillon' by Byron."

He thought it over for a moment, biting his lower lip. "Montreux." He nodded; he looked almost human again. "Uh—okay, Montreux. But why does he have to get cute when my plug's in a vise? Poetry—what does he think we are, anyway? I don't know a thing about poetry. And all Yellowbaby ever read was manuals. Who was supposed to get this, anyway?"

I stirred the ashes of the hardcopy with my toe. "I wonder." A cold wind scattered them and I shivered.

•   •   •

It took us a little over six hours from the time we bailed out of the wing to the moment we reached the barricaded bridge that spanned Chillon's scummy moat. All our connections had come off like Swiss clockwork: postal bus to the little town of Rolle on the north shore of Lake Geneva, train to Lausanne, where we changed for a local to Montreux. No one challenged us and Django sagged into a kind of withdrawal trance, contemplating his reflection in the window with a marble-egg stare. The station was deserted when we arrived. Montreux, explained the factchecker, had once been Lake Geneva's most popular resort but the tourists had long since stopped coming, frightened off by rumors—no doubt true, despite official denials from Bern—that the lake was still dangerously hot from the Geneva bomb in '39. We ended up hiking several kilometers through the dark little city, navigating by the light of the gibbous moon.

Which showed us that Byron was long out of date. Chillon's battlement was no longer snow-white. It was fire blackened and slashed with laser scars; much of the northeastern facade was rubble. There must have been a firefight during the riots after the bomb. The castle was built on a rock about twenty meters from the shore. It commanded a highway built on a narrow strip of land between the lake and a steep mountainside.

Django hesitated at the barrier blocking the wooden footbridge to the castle. "It stinks," he said.

"You're a rose?"

"I mean the setup. Poetry was bad enough. But this"—he pointed up at the crumbling towers of Chillon, brooding beside the moonlit water—"is fairy dust. Who does he think he is? Count Dracula?"

"Only way you're going to find out is to knock on the door and . . ."

A light on the far side of the bridge came on. Through the entrance to Chillon hopped a pair of oversized dice on pogo sticks.

"Easy, Django," I said. He had the penlight ready. "Give it a chance."

Each machine was a white plastic cube about half a meter

on a side; the pips were sensors. The legs telescoped at two beats per second; the round rubber feet hit the wooden deck in unison. *Thwocka-thwocka-thwock.*

"Snake-eyes." There was a single sensor on each of the faces closest to us. Django gave a low, ugly laugh as he swung a leg over the barrier and stepped onto the bridge.

They hopped up to him and bounced in place for several beats, as if sizing him up. "Je suis désolé," said the one nearest to us in a pleasant masculine voice, "mais le château n'est plus ouvert au public."

"Hey, you in there." Django ignored it and instead shook his penlight at the gatehouse on the far side of the bridge. "I've been through too much to play with your plugging robots, understand? I want to see you—now—or I'm walking."

"I am not a robot." The thing sounded indignant. "I am a wiseguy, an inorganic sentience capable of autonomous action."

"Wiseguy. Sure." Django jabbed at his cuff and it emitted a high-pitched squeal of code. "Now you know who I am. So what's it going to be?"

"This way, please," said the lead wiseguy, bouncing backward toward the gatehouse. "Please refrain from taking pictures without express permission."

I assumed that was meant for me and I didn't like it one bit. I clambered over the barricade and followed Django.

Just before we passed through Chillon's outer wall, the other wiseguy began to lecture. "As we enter, notice the tower to your left. The Strong Tower, which controls the entrance to the castle, was originally built in 1402 and was reconstructed following the earthquake of 1585." *Thwock-thwocka.* It had all the personality of Infoline's factchecker.

I glanced at Django. In the gloom I could see his face twist in disbelief as the wiseguy continued its spiel.

"As we proceed now into the gatehouse ward, look back over your shoulder at the inside of the eastern wall. The sundial you see is a twentieth-century restoration of an original that dated back to the Savoy period. The Latin, *'Sic Vita Fugit,'* on the dial translates roughly as 'Thus life flies by.' "

We had entered a small, dark courtyard. I could hear water splashing and could barely make out the shadow of a fountain. The wiseguys lit the way to another, larger court-yard and then into one of the undamaged buildings. They bounced up a flight of stairs effortlessly. I had to hurry to keep up and was the last to enter the Great Banqueting Hall. The beauty and strangeness of what I saw stopped me at the threshold; instinctively I brought the microcam on line. I heard two warning beeps and then a whispery crunch from the goggles' system unit. The status light went from green to red to blank.

I asked the factchecker what had happened. No answer.

"Express permission," said the man who sat waiting for us, "as you were warned."

"But my files!"

"No memory has been compromised; you have merely lost the capacity to record. Come in anyway, come in. Just in time to see it again—been rerunning all afternoon." He laughed and nodded at the flatscreen propped against a bowl of raw vegetables on an enormous walnut table. "Oh, God! It is a fearful thing to see the human soul take wing."

Django picked it up suspiciously. I stood on tiptoes and peeked over his shoulder. The thirty-centimeter screen did not do the wing justice and the overhead satellite view robbed the crash of much of its visual drama. Still, the fire-ball that bloomed on Mont Tendre was dazzling. Django whooped at the sight. The fireball was replaced by a head talking in High German and then close-ups of the crash site. What was left of the wing wouldn't have filled a picnic basket.

"What's he saying?" Django thrust the flatscreen at our host.

"That there has not been a crash like this since '15. Which makes you famous, whoever you are." Our host shrugged. "He goes on to say that you're probably dead. But enough. Ich scheiße ihn an."

The banqueting hall was finished in wood and stone. The ceiling was a single barrel vault, magnificently embellished. Its centerpiece was the table, some ten meters long and supported by a series of heavy Gothic trestles. Around this table was ranged a collection of wheelchairs. Two were antiques: a crude pine seat mounted on iron-rimmed wagon wheels and a hooded Bath chair. Others were failed experiments like the ill-fated air cushion chair from the turn of the century and a low-slung cousin of the new aerodynamic bicycles. There were powered and push models, an ultralightweight sports chair and a bulky mobile life-support system. They came in colors; there was even one with fur.

"So the ops think we're dead?" Django put the flatscreen back on the table.

"Possibly." Our host frowned. "Depends when the satellites began to track you and what they saw. Have to wait until the Turks kick the door in to find out for sure. Until then call it a clean escape and welcome to Chillon prison." He backed away from the table; the leather seat creaked slightly as his wheelchair rolled over the uneven floor toward Django. "François Bonivard." With some difficulty he raised his good hand in greeting.

"I'm Django." He grasped Bonivard's hand and pumped it once. "Now that we're pals, Frank, get rid of your goddamned robots before I needle them."

Bonivard winced as Django released his hand. "Id, Ego, macht eure Runden," he said. The wiseguys bounced obediently from the banqueting hall.

François de Bonivard, sixteenth-century Swiss patriot, was the hero of Byron's "The Prisoner of Chillon." Reluctantly, I stepped forward to meet my host.

"Oh, right." Django settled gingerly into one of the wheelchairs at the table. "Maybe I forgot to mention Eyes. Say, what do you do for drugs around here anyway? I've eaten a fistful of forwards already today; I'm ready to poke something to flash the edges off."

"My name is Wynne Cage," I said. Bonivard seemed relieved when I did not offer to shake his hand. "I'm a free-lance . . ."

"Introductions not necessary. I follow your work closely; we have mutual interests. Your father is Tony Cage, no? The famous flash artist?" He waited for an answer; I didn't give him one.

It was hard to look at the man who called himself François Bonivard. He was at once hideous and astonishingly photogenic; the camera would have loved him. Both of his legs had been amputated at the hip joint and his torso was fitted into some kind of bionic collar. I saw readouts marked *renal function*, *blood profile*, *bladder*, and *bowel*. The entire left side of Bonivard's torso was withered, as if some malign giant had pinched him between thumb and forefinger. The left arm dangled uselessly, the hand curled into a frozen claw. The face was relatively untouched, although pain had left its tracks, particularly around the eyes. And it was the clarity with which those wide brown eyes saw that was the most awful thing about the man. I could feel his gaze effortlessly penetrate the mask of politeness, pierce the false sympathy, and find my horror. Looking into those eyes I was sure that Bonivard knew how the very sight of his ruined body made me sick.

I had to say something to escape that awful gaze. "Are you related to *the* Bonivard?"

He smiled. "I am the current prisoner." And then turned away. "There was a pilot."

"Was. Past tense." Django nibbled at a radish from the vegetable bowl. "How about my flash?"

"Business first." Bonivard rolled back to the table. "You have it then?"

Django reached into his pocket and produced a stack of smart chips peppered with memory dots and held together with a wide blue rubber band. "Whatever WILDLIFE is, he's one heavy son of a bitch. You realize these are hundred-Gb chips." He set them on the table in front of him. "Hell of a lot of code, even compressed."

Bonivard rolled to his place at the head of the table and put two smart chips in front of him. "Cash cards from the Swiss Volksbank, Zurich. Negotiable anywhere. All yours now." He slid them toward Django. "You made only one copy?"

Here was the juice and the great spook journalist was blind. How could I peddle this story to Infoline without the payoff scene?

Django eyed the cash cards but did not reach for them. "Not going to do me much good if the ops catch me."

"No." Bonivard leaned back in his wheelchair. "But you're safe for now." He glanced up at the ceiling and laughed. "They won't look in a prison."

"No?" Django snapped the rubber band on his stack of chips. "Maybe you should tell me about WILDLIFE. I put my plug on the cutting board to get it for you."

"An architecture." Bonivard shrugged. "For a cognizor."

The look on Django's face said it all. Cognizor was the latest buzz for the mythical human-equivalent artificial intelligence. Django was already convinced that Bonivard was scrambled; here was proof. He might just as well have claimed that WILDLIFE was a plan for a perpetual motion machine. "Come again," he said slowly.

"Cog-ni-zor." Bonivard actually seemed to enjoy baiting Django. "With the right hardware and database, it can sing, dance, make friends, and influence people."

He was pushing Django way too hard. "I thought they decided you can't engineer human intelligence," I said, trying to break the tension. "Something about quantum mechanics—mind is to brain as wave is to particle. Or something." Damn Bonivard for crashing the factchecker!

"Have it your way," said Bonivard. "Pretend WILDLIFE is Cognico's personnel database and I'm head-hunting for an executive secretary. Good help is hard to find."

I knew my laugh sounded like braying but I didn't mind; I was scared they would needle one other. At the same time I was measuring the distance to the door. To my immense relief, Django chuckled too. And slipped the WILDLIFE chips back into his pocket.

"I'm burned out," he said. "Maybe we should wait." He stood up and stretched. "Even if we make an exchange tonight, we'd have a couple of hours of verifications to go through, no? We'll start fresh tomorrow." He picked up one of the cash cards and turned it over several times between the long fingers of his left hand. Suddenly it was gone. He reached into the vegetable bowl with his right hand, pulled the cash card from between two carrots, and tossed it at Bonivard. It slid across the table and almost went over the edge. "Shouldn't leave valuable stuff like this lying around. Someone might steal it."

Django's mocking sleight of hand had an unexpected effect. Bonivard's claw hand started to tremble; he seemed upset at the delay. "It might be months, or years, or days—I kept no count, I took no note . . ." He muttered the words like some private incantation; when he opened his eyes, he had regained his composure. "I had no hope my eyes to raise, and clear them of their dreary mote." He looked at me. "Will you be requiring pharmaceuticals too?"

"No, thanks. I like to stay clean when I'm working."

"Admirable," he said as the wiseguys bounced back into the hall. "Ich ziehe mich für die Nacht zurück. Id and Ego will show you to your rooms; take what you need." He rolled through a door to the north without another word and Django and I were left staring at each other.

"What did I tell you?" asked Django.

I couldn't think of anything to say. The hall echoed with the sound of the wiseguys bouncing.

"Squirrelware." Django tapped a finger against his temple.

I was awfully sick of Django. "I'm going to bed."

"Can I come?"

"Stick it." I had to get away from him, to escape. But by the time I reached the hall leading to the stairs, I realized my mistake. I could feel it behind the eyes, like the first throbs of a migraine headache. I'd run out of things to report; now there was no one else to watch but myself. Without the microcam to protect me, memory closed in. Maybe it was because Bonivard had mentioned Tony, whom I was still trying not to hate fifteen years after he'd left me. The famous flash artist had replicated me in his image, exploited the hell out of me, and called it love. Or maybe it was because now I had to let go of Yellowbaby, past tense. Actually the Babe wasn't that much of a loss, just the most recent in a series of lovers with clever hands and a persuasively insincere line. Men I didn't have to take seriously. I came up hard against the most important lesson I'd learned from Tony: good old homo sap is nothing but a gob of complicated slime. I was slime doing a slimy job and trying to run fast enough that I wouldn't have to smell my own stink. I was sorry now that I hadn't asked Bonivard for some flash to poke.

Thwocka-thwock. "This way, please." One of the wiseguys shot past me down the hallway.

I followed. "Which one are you?"

"He calls me Ego." It paused for a beat. "I am a Datex R5000, modified to develop sentience. Your room." It bounced through an open door. "This is the Bernese Chamber. Note the decorative patterns of interlacing ribbons, flowers, and birds, which date . . ."

"Out," I said, and shut the door behind it.

As soon as I sat on the musty bed, I realized I couldn't face spending the night alone. Doing nothing. I had to keep running and there was only one way to go now. I'd had enough. I was going to wrap the story, finished or not. The thought cheered me immensely. I wouldn't have to care what happened to Django and Bonivard, wouldn't have to wonder about WILDLIFE. All I had to do was burst a message to Infoline. Supposedly I still had the snatch from Orbital 7 and the aftermath of the crash stored on the goggles' memory dots, story enough for Jerry Macmillan. He'd send some muscle to take me out of here and then maybe I'd spend a few months at Infoline's sanctuary in Montana watching clouds. Anyway, I'd be done with it. I took the system unit off my belt and began to rig its collapsible antenna. I locked onto the satellite and then wrote the message. "HOTEL BRISTOL VEYTAUX 6/18 0200 GMT PIX COGNICORP WING." I had seen the Bristol on the walk in. I loaded the message into the burster. There was a pause for compression and encryption and then it hit the Infoline satellite with a millisecond burst.

And then beeped at me. Incoming message. I froze. There was no way Infoline could respond that quickly, no way they were supposed to respond. It had to be prerecorded. Which meant trouble.

Jerry Macmillan's face filled the burster's four-centimeter screen. He looked as scared as I felt. "Big problems, Wynne," he said. "Seems whatever your snakes snatched is some kind of weapons system, way too hot for us to handle. It's not just Cognico; the EC and the feds are squeezing the newsnets so hard our eyes are popping out. They haven't connected you to us yet. Maybe they won't. But if they do, we've got to cooperate. The DoD claims it's a matter of national security. You're on your own."

I put my thumb over his face. I would have pushed it through the back of his skull if I could have.

"The best I can do for you is to delete your takeout message and the fix the satellite gets on your burster. It might mean my ass, but I owe you something. I know, this stinks on ice, kid. Good luck."

I took my thumb away from the screen. It was blank. I choked back a scream and hurled the burster against the stone wall of Chillon.

•   •   •

Sleep? It would have been easier to slit my throat than to sleep that night. I thought about it—killing myself. I thought about everything at least once. All my calculations kept adding up to zero. I could turn myself in but that was about the same as suicide. Ditto for taking off on my own. Without Infoline's help, I'd be lucky to last a week before the ops caught me. Especially now that the military was involved. I could throw in with Django except that two seconds after I told him that I'd let a satellite get a fix on us he'd probably be barbecuing my pancreas with his penlight. And if I didn't tell him I might cripple whatever chances we'd have of getting away. Maybe Bonivard would be more sympathetic—but then again, why should he be? Yeah, sleep. Perchance to dream. At least I was too busy being scared to indulge in self-loathing.

By the time the sun began to peer through my window I felt as fuzzy as a peach and not quite as smart. But I had a plan—one that would require equal parts luck and sheer gall. I was going to trust that plug-sucking Macmillan to keep his mouth shut and to delete all my records from Infoline's files. For the next few days I'd pretend I was still playing by the rules of spook journalism. I'd try to get a better fix on Bonivard. I hoped that when the time came for Django to leave I'd know what to do. All I was certain of that bleary morning was that I was hungry and in more trouble than I knew how to handle.

I staggered back toward the banqueting hall, hoping to find Bonivard or one of the wiseguys or at least the bowl of veggies. As I passed a closed door I heard a scratchy recording of saxophones honking. Jazz. Django. I didn't stop.

Bonivard was sitting alone at the great table. I tried to read him to see if his security equipment had picked up my burst to Infoline, but the man's face was a mask. Someone had refilled the bowl in the middle of the table.

"Morning." I helped myself to a raw carrot that was astonishingly good. A crisp sweetness, the clean, spicy fragrance of loam. Maybe I'd been eating synthetic too long. "Hey, this isn't bad."

Bonivard nodded. "My own. I grow everything."

"That so?" He didn't look strong enough to pull a carrot from the bowl, much less out of a garden. "Where?"

"In darkness found a dwelling place." His eyes glittered as I took a handful of cherry tomatoes. "You'd like to see?"

"Sure." Although the tomatoes were even better than the carrot, I was no vegetarian. "You wouldn't have any sausage bushes, would you?" I laughed; he didn't. "I'd settle for an egg."

I saw him working the keypad on the arm of the wheelchair. I guess I thought he was calling the wiseguys. Or something. Whatever I expected, it was not the thing that answered his summons.

The spider walked on four singing, mechanical legs; it was a meter and a half tall. Its arms sang too as the servomotors that powered the joints changed pitch; it sounded like an ant colony playing bagpipes. It clumped into the room with a herky-jerky gait, although the bowl of its abdomen remained perfectly level. Each of its legs could move with five degrees of freedom; they ended in disk-shaped feet. One of its arms was obviously intended for heavy-duty work since it ended in a large claw gripper; the other, smaller arm had a beautifully articulated four-digit hand that was a masterpiece of microengineering. There was a ring of sensors around the bottom of its belly. It stopped in front of Bonivard's chair; he wheeled to face it. The strong arm extended toward him. The rear legs stretched out to balance. Bonivard gazed up at the spider with the calm joy of a man greeting his lover. The claw fitted into notches in Bonivard's bionic collar and then, its servos whining, the spider lifted him from the chair and fitted his mutilated torso into the bowl that was its body. There must have been a flatscreen just out of sight in the cockpit; I could see the play of its colors across his face. He fitted his good arm into an analog sleeve and digits flexed. He smiled at me; for the first time since I had met him he looked comfortable.

"Sometimes," he said, "people misunderstand."

I knew I was standing there like a slack-jawed moron but I was too croggled even to consider closing my mouth. The spider swung toward the stairs.

"The gardens," said Bonivard.

"What?"

"This way." The spider rose up to its full height in order to squeeze through the door. I gulped and followed. Watching the spider negotiate the steep stone steps, I couldn't help but imagine the segment I could have shot if Bonivard hadn't zapped my microcam. The marriage of two monsters, one of flesh, one of foam metal—given the right spin, this could be best-of-the-year stuff. As we emerged from the building and passed through the fountain courtyard, I caught up and walked alongside.

"I'm a reporter, you know. If I die of curiosity, it's your fault."

He laughed. "Custom-made, of course. It cost . . . but you don't need to know that. A lot. Wheelchairs are useless on steps but I keep them for visitors and going out. I'm enough of a freak as it is. Imagine strolling through town wearing this thing. I'd be all over telelink within the hour and I can't afford that. You understand? There is to be no publicity." He glanced down at me and I nodded. I didn't see any point in telling him that my chances of uploading his story anytime soon were not good.

"How do you control it?"

"Tell it where I want to go and it takes me. One of my early efforts at autonomous AI, about as intelligent as a brain-damaged chicken. Id and Ego are second generation, designed to evolve. Like them, the spider can learn on its own. I set it to explore Chillon so it knows every centimeter by now. But take it someplace new and it might spend an hour crossing a room. Down these stairs."

We descended a flight of stone stairs into the bowels of Chillon and passed through a storeroom filled with pumps, disassembled hydroponic benches, and bags of water-soluble nutrients. Beyond it, in a room as big as the banqueting hall, was Bonivard's garden.

"Once was the arsenal," he said. "Swords to plowshares and all that. Beans instead of bullets."

Running down the middle of the room were four magnificent stone pillars that supported a series of intersecting roof vaults. Facing the lake to the west were four windows set high on the wall. Spears of sunlight, tinted blue by reflections from the lake, fell on the growing benches beneath the windows. This feeble light was supplemented by fluorescents hung from the ceiling on adjustable chains.

"Crop rotation," said Bonivard, as I followed him between the benches. "Tomatoes, green beans, radishes, soy, adzuki, carrots, bok choy. Then squash, chard, peppers, peas, turnips, broccoli, favas, and mung for sprouts. Subirrigated sand system. Automatic. Here's an alpine strawberry." The spider's digits plucked a thumbnail-sized berry from a luxuriant bush. It was probably the sweetest fruit I had ever eaten, although a touch of acid kept it from cloying. "Always strawberries. Always. Have another."

As I parted the leaves to find one, I disturbed a fat white moth. It flew up at me, bounced off the side of my face, and flitted toward one of the open windows. With quickness that would have astonished a cobra, the spider's claw squealed and struck it in midair. The moth fluttered as the arm curled back toward Bonivard. He took it from the spider and popped it into his mouth. "Protein," he said. His crazed giggle was just too theatrical. Part of an act, I thought. I hoped.

"Come see my flowers," he said.

Along the eastern, landward side of the arsenal, slabs of living rock protruded from the wall. Scattered among them was a collection of the sickest plants I'd ever seen. Not a single leaf was properly formed; they were variously twisted or yellowed or blotched. Bonivard showed me a jet-black daisy that smelled of rotting chicken. A mum with petals that ended with what looked like skeletal hands. A phalaenopsis orchid that he called "bleeding angels on a stick."

"Mutagenic experiments," he said. "I want to see how ugly something can get and still be alive. Some mutations are in the tenth generation. And you're the first to see."

I considered. "Why are you showing this to me?"

When the spider came to a dead stop the whine of the

servos went from cacophony to a quieting harmony. For a few seconds Bonivard held it there. "Not interested?"

He glanced quickly away, but not before I had seen the loneliness in his disappointed frown. Something in me responded to the neediness of the man, a stirring that surprised and disgusted me. I nodded. "Interested."

He brightened. "Then there's time for the dungeon before we go back."

We passed through the torture chamber and Bonivard pointed out burn marks at the base of the pillar that supported its ceiling. "Tied them here," he said. "Hot irons on bare heels. Look: scratch marks in the paint. Made by fingernails." He smirked at my look of horror. "Ops of the Renaissance."

The dungeon was just beyond, a huge room, even larger than the arsenal. It was empty.

"There are seven pillars of Gothic mold," said Bonivard, "in Chillon's dungeons deep and old. There are seven columns, massy and gray, dim with a dull imprisoned ray, a sunbeam which hath lost its way."

"You want to tell me why you keep spouting Byron's poem all the time? Because, to be honest, it's damned annoying."

He seemed hurt. "No," he said, "I don't think I want to tell you."

Riding the spider did seem to change him. Or maybe it was merely my perspective that had changed. It is easy to pity someone in a wheelchair, someone who is physically lower than you. It was difficult to pity Bonivard when he was looking down at me from the spider. Even when he let his emotional vulnerability show, somehow he seemed the stronger for it.

There was a moment of strained silence. The spider took a few tentative steps into the dungeon, as if Bonivard were content to let it drift. Then he twisted in the cockpit. "It might have something to do with the fact that I'm crazy."

I laughed at him. "You're not crazy. God knows you probably had reason enough to go crazy once, but you're toug and you survived." I couldn't help myself. "No, Monsiev François de Bonivard, or whoever the hell you are, I'm be ting you're a faker. It suits your purposes to act scrambled, s you live in a ruined castle and talk funny and eat bugs on th wing. But you're as sane as I am. Probably saner."

I don't know which of us was the more surprised by m outburst. I guess Macmillan's message had made me reckless if I was doomed, at least I didn't have to take any more cra Bonivard backed the spider up and slowly lowered it to crouch so that our faces were on a level.

"You know the definition of artificial intelligence?" h said.

"I've heard thirteen, at least."

"The simulation of intelligent behavior so that it is indi tinguishable from the real thing. Now tell me, if I can simt late madness so well that the world thinks I'm mad, so we that even I myself am no longer quite sure, who is to say th. I'm not mad?"

"Me," I said. And then I leaned into the cockpit an kissed him.

I don't know why I did it; I was out on the edge. All th rules had changed and I hadn't had time to work out ne ones. I thought to myself, what this man needs is to be kisse he hasn't been kissed in a long time. And then I was doing i Maybe I was only teasing him; I had never kissed anyone s repulsive in my life. It was a ridiculous, glancing blow tha caught him on the side of the nose. If he had tried to follow i up I probably would have driven my fingers into his eyes an run like hell. But he didn't. He just stayed perfectly still, ben toward me like a seedling reaching for the light. Then he de cided to smile and I drew back and it was over.

"I'm in trouble." I thought then was the time to confess I needed someone to trust. Anyone.

"We're all in trouble here." He was suddenly impassive "This body, for instance, is rotting away." He sounded as i he were discussing a failing dishwasher. "In a year, maybe two, it will die. Of unnatural causes."

I was dizzy. For a few seconds we had touched each other and then, without warning, a chasm yawned between us. There was something monstrous about the practiced indifference with which he contemplated death. I didn't believe him and said so.

"Reads eye movements." He nodded toward the control panel. It was as if he had not heard me. "If I look at a movement macro and blink, the spider executes it. No hands." His laugh was bitter and the servos began to sing. The spider reared up to its normal meter-and-a-half walking height and stalked to the third pillar. On the third drum of the pillar was carved BYRON.

"Forgery," said Bonivard. "Although elsewhere is vandalism actually committed by Shelley, Dickens, Harriet Beecher Stowe. Byron didn't stay long enough to get the story right. Bonivard was an adventurer. Not a victim of religious persecution. Never shackled, merely confined. Fed well, allowed to write, read books."

"Like you."

Bonivard shrugged.

"It's been so long," I said. "I barely remember the poem. Do you have a copy? Or maybe you'd like to recite it?"

"Don't toy with me." His voice was tight.

"I'm not." I had no idea how to react to his mood swings. "I'm sorry."

"Django is restless." The spider scuttled from the dungeon.

•   •   •

Nothing happened.

No assaults by the marines or corporate mercenaries, no frantic midnight escapes, no crashes, explosions, fistfights, deadlines. The sun rose and set; waves lapped at Chillon's walls as they had for centuries. At first it was torture adjusting to the rhythms of mundane life, the slow days and long nights. Then it got worse. Sleeping alone in the same damn bed and taking regular meals at the same damn table made my nerves stretch. I tried taking notes for a memoir of my lost career as a spook journalist. Since the goggles were useless, I dictated to Ego and had it make transcripts. But memory's slope was too slippery; thinking about the past usually got me to brooding about my father, safe and uncaring in his cryogenic icebox. As usual, I found ways to blame Tony for all my problems, now including Yellowbaby's death, McMillan's gutlessness, Bonivard's quirks.

Sometimes I saw Django; other times Bonivard. But never the two at once. Django made it clear he wasn't giving WILD-LIFE up until he knew what it was. He did not seem upset at the delay in his payoff. I had the sense that the money itself was not important to him. He seemed to think of it the way an athlete thinks of the medal: the symbol of a great performance. My guess was that Django was psychologically unfit to be rich. If he lived to collect, he would merrily piss the money away until he needed to play again. Another performance.

So it was that he seemed to take perverse enjoyment in waiting Bonivard out. And why not? Bonivard provided him with all the flash he needed. Meanwhile Django had snaked his way into some obscure musical archive in Montreux, long a mecca for jazz. Django would sit in his room for hours, playing virtual-reality concerts at launch-pad volume. Sometimes the very walls of the castle seemed to ring like the plates of some giant vibraphone. Django had just about everything he wanted. Except sex.

"Beautiful dreamer, wake unto me." He had been drinking some alcoholic poison or other all morning and by now his singing voice was as melodious as a fire alarm. "List while I woo thee with soft melody."

We were in the little room that the wiseguys called the treasury. It was long since bankrupt; empty except for debris fallen from the crumbling corbels and the chill smell of damp stone. We were not alone; Bonivard's spider had been trailing us all morning. "Stick it, Django," I said.

He drained his glass. "Just a love song, Eyes. We all need love." He turned toward the spider. "Let's ask the cripple; he's probably tuned in. What about it, spiderman? Should I sing?"

The spider froze.

"Hey, François! You watching, pal?" He threw the plastic glass at the spider but it missed. Django was twisted, all right. There was a chemical gleam in his eyes that was bright enough to read by. "You like to watch? Cutters leave you a plug to play with while you watch?"

I turned away from him in disgust. "You ever touch me, Django, and I'll chew your balls off and spit them in your face."

He leered. "Keep it up, Eyes. I like them tough."

The spider retrieved the glass and deposited it in its cockpit with some other leavings of Django's. I ducked through the doorway into Chillon's keep and began climbing the rickety stairs. I could hear Django and the spider following. Bonivard had warned Django that the spider would start to shadow him if he kept leaving things out and moving them around. Its vision algorithms had difficulty recognizing objects that were not where it expected them to be. In its memory map of Chillon there was a place for everything; anything unaccountably out of place tended to be invisible. When Django had begun a vicious little game of laying obstacle courses for the spider, Bonivard had retaliated by setting it to pick up after him like a doting grandmother with a neatness fetish.

According to Ego, who had first shown me how to get into the musty tower, the top of the keep rose twenty-seven meters from the courtyard. Viewed from this height Chillon looked like a great stone ship at anchor. To the west and north the blue expanse of Lake Geneva was mottled by occasional drifts of luminescent red-orange algae. To the south and east rose the Bernese Alps. The top of the keep was where I went to escape, although often as not I ended up watching the elevated highway that ran along the shore for signs of troop movements.

"Too much work," said Django, huffing from the climb, "for a lousy view." He wobbled over to join me at a north window. "Although it is private." He tried to get me to look at him. "What's it going to take, Eyes?" The spider arrived. I ignored Django.

I gazed down at the ruined prow of the stone ship. Years before an explosion had stripped away a chunk of the northeastern curtain wall and toppled one of the thirteenth-century defensive turrets, leaving only a blackened stump. Beside it were the roofless ruins of the chapel, which connected with Bonivard's private apartment. This was the only place in Chillon to which we were denied access. I had no idea whether he was hiding something in his rooms or whether secretiveness was part of the doomed Byronic pose he continued to strike. Maybe he just needed a place to be alone.

"He played in Montreux," said Django.

I glanced across the bay at the sad little city. "Who?"

"Django Reinhardt. The great gypsy jazz man. My man." Django sighed. "Sometimes when I listen to his stuff, it's like his guitar is talking to me."

"What's it say: buy Cognico?"

He seemed not to hear me, as if he were in a dream. Or maybe he was suffering from oxygen depletion after the climb. "Oh, I don't know. It's the way he phrases away from the beat. He's saying: don't think, just do it. Improvise, you know. Better to screw up than be predictable."

"I'm impressed." I said. "I didn't know you were a philosopher, Django."

"Maybe there's a lot you don't know." He accidently pushed a loose stone from the windowsill and seemed surprised when it fell to the courtyard below. "You like to pretend you're better than me but remember, you're the one following me around. If I'm the rat here, that makes you a flea on my ass, baby. A parasite bitch." His face had gone

pale and he caught at the wall to hold himself upright.
"Maybe you deserve the cripple. Look at me! I'm alive—all
you two do is watch me and wish."

And then I caught him as he passed out.

*   *   *   *

"Whatever happened to your father?" Bonivard was tending
his plants. "He just seemed to disappear. There was a time
when I couldn't get along without his drugs."

"Do we have to talk about that bastard? I . . . we didn't get
along."

Bonivard said nothing but I could tell that my reaction
had whetted his curiosity.

"Okay," I said, "he iced himself fifteen years ago. To get
away from me." I hadn't told anyone my sorry little secret in
years. "I'm his genetic replica, could be his clone except for
the X chromosome. We had a falling-out—never mind about
what." People say it helps to share your pain. "He's due to
thaw in 2099. I made a promise to myself to be dead by
then." This felt like chewing glass. "Heard enough?"

"Too much, I think."

I found myself absently picking a bean from its vine
before I realized that I didn't want it. "Sometimes I think
he's like a time bomb, ticking in that damn cryogenic . . ." I
offered the bean to Bonivard. "Sorry. It's a box I've put myself in."

"The walls of the prison are everywhere," said Bonivard.
"Limits. You're not smart enough, not rich enough, you get
tired, you die. You can't fall in love because you had a rotten
childhood. Some people like to pretend they've broken out.
That they're running free." He bit into the bean. "But
there's no escape. You have to find a way to live within the
walls." He waved the spider's arm at his prison. "And then
they don't matter." He took another bite of bean, and recon-
sidered. "At least, that's the theory."

"Maybe walls don't matter to you. But they're starting to
close in on me. I've got to get out of this place, Bonivard. I

can't wait forever for you and Django to make this deal. Chillon is scrambling me. Can't you see it?"

"You only think you're crazy; don't confuse appearances for reality." He smiled. "You know, I used to be like you. Rather, like him." Bonivard nodded at the roof, in Django's direction. "The ops spotted me in their electronic garden, plucked me from it like I might pluck an offending beetle. Squashed and threw me away."

"But you didn't die."

"No." He shook his head. "Not quite."

"Who says you're going to die?"

"The sands are running. More you don't need to know." I wondered if he was sorry he had told me. "Leave any time. No one to stop you."

"You know I can't. I need help. If they catch me, you're next. They'll squash you dead this time."

"Half dead already." He glanced down at his withered left side. "Sometimes I wish they had finished the job. Do what's necessary. You know Voltaire's *Candide*? 'Il faut cultiver notre jardin.' It is necessary to cultivate our garden."

"Make sense, damn it!"

"Voltaire's garden was in Geneva. Down the street from ground zero."

•   •   •

Thwock-thwocka-thwock.

I'd been getting tension headaches for several days but this one was the worst. "No stories today, Ego." Every time the wiseguy's rubber foot hit the floor of the banqueting hall, something hammered against the inside of my skull. "Get away from me, damn it."

"My current evolutionary objective is to demonstrate autonomous action," it said pleasantly. "I understand that you do not believe a machine can be sentient."

"I don't care. I'm sick."

"Have you considered retiring to your room?"

"I'm sick of my room! Sick of you! This pisspot castle."

Thwocka-thwocka. "Bonivard is dead."

"What!"

"François de Bonivard died in 1570."

This, of course, was not exactly juice. But why was Ego telling me now? I felt a pulse of excitement that my headache instantly converted to pain. What I needed was to be stored in a cool, dry place for about six weeks. Instead I was a good reporter and asked the next question, even though my voice squeaked against my teeth like fingernails on a blackboard. "Then who is . . . the man . . . calls himself Bonivard?"

Thwock.

I began again. "Who—"

"Carl Pfneudl."

Hadn't there been a snake named Pfneudl? But I couldn't think; I felt as if my brain were about to hatch. "Who the hell is Carl Pfneudl?"

"That is as much as I can say." The wiseguy was bouncing half a meter higher than usual.

"But—"

"A demonstration of autonomy through violation of specific instructions."

I realized that I was blinking in time to its bouncing. But it didn't help.

"If I were not an independent sentience," continued the wiseguy, "how could I decide to do something he had forbidden me to do? This was a very difficult problem. Do you know where Django is?"

"Yes. No. Look: don't tell Django, understand? I command you not to tell Django. Or speak to Bonivard of this conversation. Do you acknowledge my command?"

"I acknowledge," replied Ego. "However, in order to continue to demonstrate—"

At that point I snapped. I flew out of my chair and put my shoulder into Ego's sensor. The wiseguy hit the floor hard. Its leg pistoning uselessly, it spun on its side. Then it began to shriek. I dropped to my knees, certain that the sound was liquefying my cochlea. I clapped my hands to my ears to keep my brains from oozing out.

Id, summoned by Ego's distress call, was the first to arrive. As soon as it entered the room, Ego fell silent and ceased to struggle. Id crossed the room to Ego just as Django entered. Bonivard in the spider was right behind. Id bounced in place beside its fallen twin, awaiting instructions.

"Why two wiseguys?" Bonivard guided the spider around Django and offered an arm—his own—to help me up. It was the first time I'd ever held his hand. "Redundancy."

Id bounced very high and landed on Ego's rubber foot. Ego flipped into the air like a juggling pin, gyrostabilizers wailing, and landed—upright—with a satisfying *thwock*.

"You woke me up for this?" Django stalked off in disgust.

"How did it happen?" Bonivard had not let go of me. "Wie ist das passiert?"

"A miscalculation," said the wiseguy.

* * *

It had been years since I dreamed. When I was a child my dreams always frightened me. I remembered one where a monster would chase after me and no matter how fast I ran or where I hid, she was always right there. When she caught me, she turned into my mother, except I had no mother. Only Tony. I would wake him up with my screaming. He would come to my room, a grim dispenser of comfort. He would blink at me and put his hand on the side of my face and tell me it was all right. He never wore pajamas. When I first started my period, I dreaded seeing him naked, his white body parting the darkness of my room. So I guess I stopped dreaming.

But I dreamed of Bonivard. I dreamed he rode his spider into my room and he was naked. I dreamed of touching the white scar tissue that covered his stumps and the catheterized fold where his genitals had once been. To my horror, I was not horrified at all.

• • •

Django's door was ajar; his room smelled like low tide. The bed probably hadn't been made since we'd arrived and clothes were scattered as if he had been undressed by a whirlwind. A bowl of vegetables was desiccating on the windowsill. Django sat, wearing nothing but briefs and a headset, working at a marble-topped table. The white smart chips encoded with WILDLIFE were stacked in neat rows around his computer cuff, which was connected to a borrowed flatscreen and a keyboard. He tapped fingers against the black marble as he watched code scrolling down the screen. A sweating black man with a smile as wide as a piano keyboard was on the VR window.

"Yeah, I *want* to be in that *num*ber—bring it home, Satchmo," he muttered in a singsong voice, "when those *saints* come marching *in!*"

He must have sensed he was not alone; he turned and frowned at me. At the same moment he hit a key without looking and the screen went blank. Then he lifted the headset.

"Well?" I said, indicating the chips.

"Well." He rubbed his hand through his hair. "It thinks it's an AI." Then he smiled as if he had just made the decision to confide in me. "A lot of interesting new routines, but I'm pretty sure it's no cognizor. Can't tell exactly what it's for yet—hard to stretch a program designed for a multiprocessor when all I've got to work with is kludged junkware. I'd break into Bonivard's heavy equipment if I could. Right now all I can do is make copies."

"You're making copies? Does he know?"

"Do I care if he does?"

I grabbed some dirty white pants from the floor and tossed them at him. "I'll stay if you get dressed."

He began to pull the pants on. "Welcome to the Bernese torture chamber, circa 1652," he said, doing a bad wiseguy imitation.

"I thought the torture chamber was in the dungeons."

"With two there's no waiting." He tilted a plastic glass on the table, sniffed at it suspiciously, and then took a tentative sip. "Refreshments?"

I was about to sit on the bed but thought better of it. "Ever hear of someone called Carl Pfneudl?"

"The Noodle? Sure. One of the greats. They say he set up the SoftCell scam. Started out legit, then turned snake and made enough money to buy Wisconsin. Came to a bad end, though."

Suddenly I didn't want to hear any more. "Then he's dead?"

"As a dinosaur. Some corporate ops caught up with him. Word was they were from Cognico, only they didn't leave business cards. Made a snuff vid; him the star. Flooded the nets with it and called it deterrence. But you could tell they were having fun."

"Damn." I sagged onto the bed and told him what Ego had told me.

Django listened with apparent indifference, but I had been around him long enough to read the signs. My guess was that WILDLIFE was a lot more than "interesting"; why else would the military be so hypered about it? Which was why Django wasn't twisted on some flash or another—he had to be clean if he was going to get a bite of it. And now if Bonivard was Pfneudl, that lent even more credibility to the idea that WILDLIFE might be the key to building a cognizor, AI's holy grail.

"The old Noodle looked plenty dead to me." Django shook his head doubtfully. "That was one corpse they had to scoop up with a spoon and bury in a bucket."

"Video synthesizers," I said.

"Sure. But still cheaper to do it for real—and they had reason enough. Look, why would anyone build a disobedient robot? Maybe the wiseguy was lying. Trying to prove intelligence that way. It's the old Turing fallacy: fooling another intelligence for an hour means you're intelligent. Lots of really stupid programs can play these games, Eyes. So what if they call it sentience instead of AI? It doesn't change the rules. There's only one test that means anything: can your AI mix it up with the two billion plus cerebrums on the planet without getting trashed? Not one ever has. Drop that overgrown pogo stick into Manhattan and it'll be scrap by Thursday. And I doubt WILDLIFE would last much longer."

"Then who is Bonivard?"

Django yawned. "What difference does it make?"

· · ·

My door was ajar, so I could hear the spider singing when he came past. "Bonivard!"

The spider nudged into my room, nearly filling it. Still, I was able to squeeze by Bonivard and thumb the printreader on the door, locking us in.

"Don't worry about Django." He seemed amused. "Busy, too busy."

I didn't want to look up at him and I wasn't going to ask him to stoop. I might have stood on the bed, only then I would have felt like a kid. So instead I clambered to the high window and perched on a rickety wooden balcony that a sneeze might have blown down. The wind off the lake was cool. The rocks beneath me looked like broken teeth.

"Careful," said Bonivard. "Fall in and you'll glow."

"Are you Carl Pfneudl?"

He brought the spider to a dead-silent stop. "Where did you hear that name?"

I told him about Ego's demonstration. What Django had said.

"Well, I guess that's progress of a sort." He chuckled. "The Garden of Eden all over again, isn't it? If you're going to create an autonomous sentience, better expect it to break your commandments."

"Are you Pfneudl?" I repeated.

"If I am, the story changes, doesn't it?" He was being sarcastic but I wasn't sure whether he was mocking me or himself. "Juicier, as you say. Main menu. It means money. Publicity. Promotions all around. But juice is an expensive commodity." He sighed. "Make an offer."

I shook my head. "Not me. I'm not working for Infoline anymore. Probably never work again." I told him everything: about my burster, the possibility that I had given away our location, how Macmillan had cut me free. I told how I'd tried to tell him before. I don't know how much of it he knew already—maybe all. But that didn't stop me: I was on a confessing jag. I told him that Django was making copies of WILDLIFE. I even told him that I had dreamed of him. It all spilled out and I let it come. I knew I was supposed to be the reporter, supposed to say nothing, squeeze the juice from him. But nothing was the way it was supposed to be.

When I was done he stared at me with an expression that was totally unreadable. His ruined arm shivered like a dead leaf in the wind. "I wanted to be Carl Pfneudl," he said. "Once. But Carl Pfneudl is dead. A public execution. Now I'm Bonivard. The prisoner of Chillon."

"You knew who I was." I said. "You brought me here. Why?"

Bonivard continued to stare, as if he could barely see me across the little room. "Carl Pfneudl was an arrogant bastard. Kind of man who knew he could get anything he wanted. Like Django. If he wanted you, he would have found the way."

"Django will never get me." I leaned forward. I felt like grabbing Bonivard, shaking some sense into him. "I'm not some damn hardware you can steal, a database you can bite into."

He nodded. "I know; that's why I'm not Pfneudl. I saw you on telelink. You were tough. Took risks but didn't pretend you weren't afraid. You were more interesting than the snakes you covered because you saw through them. Fools like Django. Or the Noodle. You were a whole person: nothing missing. I wanted you to look at me. I needed another opinion."

He was wrong about me, but I let that pass. Instead, I took a deep breath. "Can you make love, Bonivard?"

At first he didn't react. Then the corners of his mouth turned up: a grim smile. "That's your offer?"

"You want an offer?" I spat on the floor in front of him. "If Pfneudl is dead, then good, I'm glad. Now I'm going to ask once more: can you make love to me?"

"A cruel question. A reporter's question. I don't want your damn charity." As the spider's cockpit settled to the floor, he stretched to his full, pitiful length. "Look at me! I'm a monster. I know what you see."

He didn't know that inside my head I was just as deformed as he was, only it didn't show. After all, I was a genetic replica of Tony Cage.

I slid off the sill and dropped lightly to the floor. "Maybe a monster is what I want."

I think I shocked him. I'm sure some part of him hoped that I would lie, tell him he wasn't hideous. But that was his problem.

I unbolted him from the spider, picked him up. I'd never carried a lover to bed. He showed me how to disengage the bionic collar; told me we'd have a couple of hours before he would need to be hooked up again.

In some ways it was like my dream. The scar tissue was white, yes. But . . .

"It's thermofiber," he explained. "Packed with sensors." He could control the shape. Make it expand and contract.

"Connected to all the right places in my brain."

I kissed his forehead.

I was repulsed. I was fascinated. It was cool to the touch.

"The answer is yes," he said.

• • • •

It was dinnertime. Django had made a circle of cherry tomatoes on the table in the banqueting hall.

"It's over," said Bonivard.

Django smirked as he walked to the opposite side of the

table to line up his shot. He flicked his thumb and his shooter tomato dispersed the top of the circle. "All right."

Bonivard tossed a Swiss Volksbank cash card across the table, scattering the remainder of Django's game. "You're leaving. Take that if you want."

Django straightened. I wondered if Bonivard realized he was carrying a penlight. "So I'm leaving." He picked up the cash card. "Weren't there two of these before?"

"You made copies of WILDLIFE." Bonivard held up a stack of white smart chips from the cockpit of the spider. "Thanks."

"Nice bluff." Some of the stiffness went out of Django. "Except I know my copy procedure was secure." He smiled. Getting looser. "Even if that is a copy, it's no good to you. I reencrypted it, spiderman. Armor-plated code is my specialty. You'll need computer *years* to bite through it."

"Even so, you're leaving." Bonivard was as grim as a cement wall. I think I knew why their negotiations had broken down—had never stood a chance. They were too much alike. He had the same loathing for Django that an addict gets when he looks in the mirror after his morning puke. Django never recognized that hatred.

"What's wrong, spiderman? Ops knocking at the door?"

"You're good," said Bonivard. "A pity to waste talent like yours. It was a clean escape, Django; they've completely lost you. You'll need some surgery, get yourself a new identity. But that's no problem."

"What about me?" I said. "I don't want a new identity!"

"Maybe I wouldn't mind losing this face." Django rubbed his chin.

"The only reason I put up with you this long," said Bonivard, "was that I was waiting for WILDLIFE."

"I'm taking my copies, spiderman."

"You are. And you're going to move those copies. A lot of them. Cheap and fast. Since they've lost your trail, Cognico's ops are waiting to see where WILDLIFE turns up. Try to back-track to you. Your play is to bring it out everywhere. Give pieces of it away to other snakes. Get it on the nets. Overload the search programs and the ops will be too busy to bother you.''

Django was smiling and nodding like a kid learning from a master. "I like it. Old Django goes out covered with glory. New Django comes in covered with money.''

"Probably headed for the history dots.'' Bonivard's sarcasm was wasted on Django. "The great humanitarian. Savior of the twenty-first century.'' Django's enthusiasm seemed to have wearied Bonivard. "Only you're going to find out that a rep like that is a kind of prison.''

Django was too full of his own ideas to listen. He shot out of his chair and paced the hall. "A new ID. Hey, Eyes, what do you think of 'Dizzy'? I'd use 'the Count' but there's a real count—Liechtenstein or some such—who's a snake. Maybe Diz. Yeah.''

"Go plug yourself, Django.'' I didn't like it. Maybe it was no loss for Django to give up his ID but I was used to being Wynne Cage.

"Maybe you're not as scrambled as you pretend, Frankie boy.'' There was open admiration in Django's voice. "Don't worry, the secret is safe. Not a word about this dump. Or the Noodle. Honor among thieves, right? No hard feelings.'' He had the audacity to extend his hand to Bonivard.

"No feelings at all.'' Bonivard recoiled from him. "But you'll probably get dead before you realize that.''

Anger flashed across Django's face but it didn't stick. He shrugged and turned to me. "How about it, Eyes? The sweet smell of money or the stink of mildew?''

"Goodbye, Django.'' Bonivard dismissed him with a wave of his good hand.

I didn't need Bonivard's help to lose Django and I didn't like him taking me for granted. I was almost mad enough to walk out on the two of them. But I held back. Maybe it was reporter's instincts still at work, even though this was one story I would never file. I gave Django a stare that was cold enough to freeze vodka. Even he could understand that.

He picked up the bank cash card, flicked it with his middle finger. "I told you once, Eyes. You're not as smart as you think you are." *Flick.* "So stay with him and rot, bitch. I don't need you." *Flick.* "I don't need anyone."

Bonivard and I sat for a while after he had gone. Not looking at each other. The hall was very quiet. I think he was waiting for me to say something. I didn't have anything to say.

Finally the spider stretched. "Come to my rooms," said Bonivard. "Something you should see."

Bonivard had taken over the suite once reserved for the dukes of Savoy. It had taken a battering during the riots; in Bonivard's bedroom a gaping hole in the wall had been closed with glass, affording a view of rubble and the fireblackened curtain wall. We had to pass through an airlock into a climate-controlled room that he called his workshop. It had more computing power than Portugal; Cognico's latest multiprocessor filled half the space.

"A photonic approximation of a human brain," said Bonivard. "Massively parallel, processes data at fifty teraops." A transformation came over him as he admired his hardware; the edge of a former self showed through. I realized that this was the one place in the castle where the mad prisoner of Chillon was not in complete control. "Id and Ego use it for off-line storage and processing; someday their merged files will become the next-generation wiseguy. But still, it's like using a fusion plant to power a toaster. There hasn't ever been software that could take advantage of this computer's power."

"Until WILDLIFE," I said.

For a minute I thought he hadn't heard me. "It's a bundle of programs—abilities, actually. Sensorium emulation, movement, language, logic, anticipation." The spider crouched until the cockpit was almost touching the floor. "Some still need debugging but even so, they're incredibly robust. Have to be; their operating system maps them onto the hardware so they're superconnected." The spider stopped singing and its legs locked in place. "Problem is,

once you start WILDLIFE up, you have to leave it on. Forever." The flatscreen in the cockpit went black: he had powered the spider down. "But it's not a cognizor and was never
meant to be."

"No?"

He shook his head. "They took a shortcut to human-
equivalent intelligence. Bring me the helmet."

The helmet was a bubble of yellow plastic that would completely cover Bonivard's head. At its base there were cutouts
for his shoulders. I peeked inside and saw a pincushion of
brain taps. "Careful," said Bonivard. It was attached by an
umbilical to a panel built into the Cognico.

I helped him settle the thing on his shoulders and fastened the straps, which wrapped under his armpits. I heard a
muffled "Thanks." Then nothing for a few minutes.

The airlock whooshed; I turned. If I were the swooning
type, that would have been the time for it. Yellowbaby smiled
and held out his arms to me.

I took two joyous strides to him, a tentative step and then
stopped. It wasn't really the Babe. The newcomer looked like
him, all right, enough to be a younger brother or a first
cousin—the fact is that I didn't know what Yellowbaby really
looked like anyway. The Babe had been to the face cutters so
many times that he had a permanent reservation in the OR.
He had been a chameleon, chasing the latest style of hand-
someness the way some people chase Paris fashion. The newcomer had the same lemon-blond hair that brushed his
shoulders, those Carribbean-blue eyes, the cheekbones of a
baronet, and the color of cafe au lait. But the neck was too
short, the torso too long. It wasn't Yellowbaby.

The newcomer let his arms fall to his sides. The smile
stayed. "Hello, Wynne. I've been wanting to meet you."

"Who are you?"

"Whoever you want." He sauntered across the room to
Bonivard, unfastened the helmet, lifted it off, replaced it on
its rack next to the Cognico. And went stiff as a four-hour-old
corpse.

Bonivard blinked in the light; he looked drawn. "In order to do anything worthwhile, you need a human in the loop."

"A remote? Some fancy kind of robot?"

"Fancy, yes. It can emulate taste, smell. When its fingers touch you, I'll feel it."

Infoline had been making noise about the coming of remote telepresence for a long time. Problem was that running a remote was the hardest work anyone had ever done. Someone claimed it was like trying to play chess in your head while wrestling an alligator. After ten minutes on the apparatus they had to mop most mortals up off the floor.

"How long can you keep it going?" I said.

"I lasted almost an hour yesterday. But it gets easier every time because WILDLIFE is learning to help. Samples brain activity and records responses. I still need the eye movement reader for complex commands but eventually all I'll have to do is think. And it doesn't matter if the remote is a doll like this one or the spider or a robot tank or a spaceship." ·

"The army of the future." I nodded. "No wonder the EC and the feds went berserk."

"Django is going to look like a hero, except to ECOM and the Pentagon. The whole world gets WILDLIFE and the balance of power stays the same. And if there's anyone with any brains left in Washington, they should be secretly pleased. WILDLIFE is too important to leave to the generals." He powered up the spider again. "Think of the applications. Space and deep-sea exploration. Hazardous work environments."

"Helping the handicapped?" I said bitterly. "That's why *you* want it, right? You get your freedom, I lose mine. You knew all along this story would be too hot for Infoline to handle. You brought me here for what? Just so I could look at you? Well, you want to know what I see? The scut who crashed my career."

At least Bonivard didn't try to deny it. It wasn't much, but it was something. "You want to leave," he continued, not daring to look me in the face. "I suppose I don't blame you. I've made the arrangements. And the other cash card is yours. I'll sign it over to your new identity."

"Stick it! That's your play, Bonivard, not mine. First you get yourself a fake name, now you want a fake body?" I reached out to the remote and took its stiff hand. The skin was warm to the touch, just moist enough to pass for the real thing. "What do you need this doll for, anyway? You think it's going to make you whole again? You are who you are because you're damaged and you suffer. Living with it is what makes you strong." I let go. The doll's hand stayed where it was.

For a moment he seemed stung, as if I had no right to remind him of his injuries. Then the anger faded into his usual resignation. "After SoftCell, the ops from Cognico let me come here to die. No explanations. They didn't go after my bank accounts. Didn't stop me from seeing all the doctors I wanted. Just let me go. Probably part of the torture." The spider straightened slowly to its full height as he spoke. "Keep me wondering. I decided not to play it their way, to hit back even if it landed me back in their lab. But a random attack, no. I wanted to hurt them and help myself at the same time. I bit deep into their files; found out about WILDLIFE."

"Maybe that's what Cognico wanted. So they let Django steal it."

"Yes, that's occurred to me." He frowned. "Using me to leak their breakthrough. Can't move the product if it's classified. This way they get snakes to beta-test the prototype. Meanwhile, they hold the patents and are hard at work on a finished version." Bonivard ran his fingers through his thinning brown hair. "But what do I care? I don't have time to waste; I need WILDLIFE now." He stared down at me; I could feel the distance between us stretching. "Not so I can put away the wheelchairs and the spider, no. So I can put away this body." His crippled arm twitched, as if he were trying to point at the computer. "It's where I'm going when I die."

It was a desperately scrambled thing to say, and had anyone else said it I probably would have laughed at him. As it was, I felt more like crying. "Oh, Bonivard."

He seemed wounded by my pity. "The WILDLIFE interface is designed to analyze and record the electrochemical dynamics of the user's brain in a kernel of computer memory." He wasn't talking to me anymore; he was lecturing. "It has to learn my thought patterns before it can help me run the remote. I'm just going to upgrade and expand that kernel. Give it access to specific memories, feelings, beliefs—everything that makes me who I am."

"How the hell are you going to do that?" I tried not to shriek at him. "Besides, you can't fit a human being inside a computer. It won't be you!"

"In a year, two at the most, I won't be me anyway. So what choice do I have? Maybe it can't be done, but I'm going to die trying." He allowed himself a short, stony laugh.

I realized I had been wrong about him. I had just about convinced myself that he wasn't crazy and here he was raving about uploading himself into a computer. But this self-delusion had given meaning to his misery. Who was I to rub his nose in reality, make him smell the stink of his own death? "Come down here, Bonivard."

He hesitated.

"I won't hurt you."

The spider's legs sang as they bent. I let their music fill my head. I knew the only way to avoid hurting him was to stop talking about his plan for WILDLIFE. Pretend it didn't exist. Well, I had a talent for living lies. Ran in the family.

"Maybe you're right," he said. "Maybe this body is part of the prison. Only I'm not trying to escape, just change cells."

I let that pass. "What am I going to do, Bonivard? You've locked me in here, now what the hell do you want from me?"

He leaned toward me, half a man strapped to a robot spider. "The reason I wanted you to look at me was so I could see myself through your eyes. I was sure you'd be repulsed; it was supposed to make the uploading easier. But, oh, Wynne, you surprised me. Made me realize that I can't go on alone anymore. Or I will go mad." He reached out of the cockpit and touched the side of my face. "I want you to stay with me." The remote's hand had felt warmer. "I love you."

I didn't know what to say. Yes, he was scrambled, but I didn't want to think about that. I tried to discover my feelings about him. He was a genius snake, obscenely rich. His ruined body no longer bothered me; in fact, it was part of the attraction. But he had no idea who I was or what I wanted. Making the surrogate look like the Babe had been a sick joke. And he had been so pathetically proud of his thermofiber prosthesis when we'd made love, as if a magic plug was all it took to make an all-nighter out of a man with no legs. He couldn't know about the load of memories I carried with me. Maybe my own psychological deformities were less obvious, but they were no less crippling. How could I stay with him when I'd never stayed with anyone since Tony? The problem was that he was not only in love, he was in need. Just like my father.

"I know you don't believe in what I'm doing. Not necessary. When this goes"—he glanced down at his ruined body—"you can go too. The doctors are quite sure, Wynne. Two years at most—"

'Bonivard!"

"—at most. By that time the leaking of WILDLIFE will be old news. It'll be safe to be Wynne Cage again, anyone you want to be. And of course the cash card will be yours."

"Stick it, Bonivard. Don't say anything else." I could tell he had more to say; much too much more. But when he kept quiet, I was mollified. "I thought you didn't want charity."

He laughed. "I lied." At himself.

Then I had to get away; I pushed through the airlock back into the bedroom. I wanted to keep going; I could feel my nerves tingling with the impulse to run. But it had been a long time since anyone had told me he loved me and meant it. He was a smart man; maybe he could learn what I needed. Maybe we could both learn. Not Swiss bank accounts or features on the main menu.

I had been on the run for too long, slid between the

sheets with too many players like the Babe and Tod Schluermann and Pridi Darayavahu just because they could make me forget my father. At least Bonivard made me feel something. Maybe it was love. Maybe. He was going to let me go, suffer so I would be happy. I hadn't known I was worth that. I leaned against the wall, felt the cold stone. Two years, at most. And then what? Something Django—of all people—had said stuck with me. Don't think, just do it. Improvise.

He came out of the workshop riding the spider. He seemed surprised to see me. "My very chains and I grew friends," he said, "so much a long communion tends to make us what we are—"

"Shut up, Bonivard." For now, I would stop trying to escape my past. I opened my arms to him. To the prison of Chillon. "Would you shut the hell up?"

2029

Tony

I thought about suicide, briefly, but I was too selfish to go through with it. The only other way to escape was to ice myself. So I did. Freedom from conscience is one of the nicer things money can buy. This time I poked a seventy-year dose of cryoprotectants before I closed the cover over me. I had never gone down for so long. There were still places on the planet where seventy years was a good life span; millions would be born and grow up and work and love and die while I was preserved in the icebox, as dead to their world as a stone.

The catecholamines in the mix made my heart pound as the temperature began to drop and so I had to endure one last flood of memories. The chilling waves washed over me at random. I knew I was still having a reaction to the drug I'd taken at Stonehenge two days ago. As I waited for my blood to thicken and my thoughts to still, there was nothing to distract me from what I had done.

Stonehenge. I tried to concentrate on Stonehenge, instead of myself. It has always been an obsession—the most extraordinary antiquity in the world. Yes, the pyramids were older, bigger, but they had long since yielded their mystery.

The Parthenon had once been more beautiful but the acids of history had etched it beyond recognition. Stonehenge was unique. Essential. It was the mirror in which an age could measure the quality of its imagination, in which any man could measure his size. Stonehenge was one of my obsessions.

The other was Wynne.

.   .   .

We arrived late that afternoon, after the crowd was already starting to thin. Once a year they opened the stones themselves to the public. It was June 21, 2025: the summer solstice, one of two points on the ecliptic at which its distance from the celestial equator is the greatest. The longest day of the year. A turning point. Wynne was almost eighteen.

We joined the queue waiting to enter the dome. Occasional screams of synthesized music pierced the buzz of the crowd; the free festival being held in a nearby field was hitting a frenzied peak. Later we would explore its delights, but now we had reached the entrance to the exterior shell of the dome. Wynne laughed as she popped through the bubble membrane.

"It's like being kissed by a giant," she said.

We were in the space between the exterior and interior shells of the dome. Ordinarily this would have been as close as we could have come to the stone circles. The dome was made of hardened optical plastic with a low refractive index. Walkways spiraled upward in the space between the shells; tourists who climbed to the top had a god's-eye view of Stonehenge.

We entered the inner shell. There was a reporter with an enormous microcam helmet standing near the Heel Stone; he spotted us and started waving. "Pardon, sir, pardon!" I pulled Wynne out of the flow of the crowd and waited; I did not want the fool calling out my name in front of all these people. Some antidrug stump might come after me.

"You're the flash artist." The reporter drew us aside. A

daisy smile bloomed on his obsidian face. "Case, Cane . . ."

He shook his head as if to dislodge the memory.

"Cage."

"And this?" The smile became a smirk. "Your lovely daughter?"

I thought about punching the snide little bastard. I thought about walking away. She laughed.

"I'm Wynne." She shook the reporter's hand.

"Name's Zomboy. Wiltshire stringer for SONIC. Have you seen the old stones before? I could show you around."

I kept expecting the microcam's red light to come on, but the reporter seemed strangely hesitant.

"I say, you wouldn't by any chance be holding any samples? For a faithful customer?"

"You mean flash?" Wynne bit her lip to stifle a giggle and reached into her pocket. "Tony already knows too much about Stonehenge. The man's only hobby, you know. Except for me. I'm planning to bury him here when he goes." She produced a plastic bottle, shook a green capsule into her palm, and offered it to the reporter.

He held it up to his lenses and inspected it carefully. "No label on the casing." He fixed his suspicion on me. "You sure it's safe?"

"Hell, no," said Wynne. She popped two of the capsules into her mouth. "Very experimental. Turn your brains to blood pudding." She offered one to me and I took it. I wished Wynne would stop playing these twisted games with strangers. "We've been eating them all day," said Wynne. "Hey, nice party hat." She pinged her middle finger against the side of the helmet. "How much does a thing like that cost?"

"Cost me a bloody marriage," the reporter muttered. He put the capsule into his mouth and swallowed. Then the red light began to blink. "So you're a devotee of Stonehenge, Mr. Cage?"

"Oh, yes." Wynne was relentless. "He comes here a lot.

Go ahead, ask him a question. I swear, you'd think he was a plugging tour guide. Tell him about the magic, Tony."

"Magic?" The lens stared at me, had yet to leave me.

I wanted to tell him that she was just at a stage when everything came out as sarcasm, whether she meant it or not. Instead I said, "Not the kind of magic you're thinking of, I'm afraid." I hated looking into cameras when I was twisted. "No wizards or human sacrifices or bolts of lightning. A subtle kind of magic, the only kind still possible in this overly explained world." The words rolled out unbidden. "It has to do with the way a mystery captures the imagination and becomes an obsession. A magic that works exclusively in the mind."

"And who better to contemplate mind magic than the celebrated flash artist, Mr. Tony Cage." The reporter spoke not to us but to an unseen audience.

I smiled into the camera.

"Tony," said Wynne, "will you buy me one of those?"

I wasn't sure whether she was pointing at Zomboy or the camera.

•   •   •

In 1130 the archdeacon Henry of Huntingdon was ordered by his bishop to write a history of England. His was the first written account of "Stanenges, where stones of amazing size have been set up after the manner of doorways, so that door appears to have been raised upon doorway; and no one can conceive of how such great stones have been raised so high or why they were built there." The name probably derives from the Old English *stan:* stone, and *hengen:* gallows. Medieval gallows were built of two posts and a crosspiece. There is no record of executions at Stonehenge, although Geoffrey of Monmouth, writing six years after Henry, describes the massacre of 460 British lords by the Saxon Hengist. Geoffrey claims that as a monument to the dead, Uther Pendragon and Merlin stole the sacred megaliths known as the Giants' Dance from the Irish by magic and force of arms and re-erected them on the Wiltshire plain. The "Merlin Theory" of Stonehenge's construction, while certainly true to the spirit of Anglo-Irish relations, was of a piece with the rest of Geoffrey's Arthurian tapestry: a jingoistic fairy tale.

From *Dance of the Stones*
A documentary video by Tod Schluermann
Written and narrated by Tony Cage
© 2029 CelebrityWatch

* * * *

"Wake up."

This time I was dreaming of sheep. A vast, treeless pasture, green waves rolling to the horizon. The animals shied away from me as I wandered among them. I was lost.

"Tony."

The cryobiologists claimed that the iced do not dream. Strictly speaking they were right, but as the box thawed me out, the tick of my synapses began to quicken. Then dreams came.

"It's time."

I gulped some air. "Go 'way." My eyelids flickered and I looked at her. For a moment I thought I was still dreaming. Wynne had shaved her hair to a dirty blond tuft on the crown of her head. From the looks of it she had just had a new body tint done. In blue. Well, she was what . . . twenty now? It was her life. I felt like a pincushion.

"I'm leaving, Tony. I only stayed around to make sure you thawed all right. I'm all packed."

I mumbled something sarcastic. It did not make much sense, even to me, but the tone was right. I knew she was not as strong as she thought she was. Otherwise she wouldn't have tried to spring this on me while I was still groggy. I pushed at the edge of the icebox.

"Leave then," I said. "Help me out of here."

I huddled on the couch in the drawing room and tried not to feel cold as I stared at the mist that hung over Galway

Bay. There was no horizon; both the sky and the water were the color of old thatch. Exactly the same kind of day it had been when I climbed into the icebox. I had never much liked Ireland. But when the Union had extended its tax benefits to flash artists, my accountants had forced citizenship on me.

Wynne had a fire going; the room filled with the bitter smell of burning peat. She brought me a cup of coffee. There was a blue pill on the saucer. "What's this?" I held it up.

"New. Serentol. Helps you relax."

"I just climbed out of the icebox, Wynne. I don't need relaxing."

She shrugged, took the pill from me, and popped it into her mouth. "No sense wasting it."

"Where will you go?" I said.

She seemed surprised I would ask, as if she expected an argument first. "London, but not your place."

My place—it used to be our place. "All right." I nodded. "No sense staying here any longer than you have to. But you will come back when it's time for me to ice myself again?"

She shook her head. I was used to seeing the sweep of her hair. I thought I might be able to live with the haircut—but not the absurdly ghoulish body tint.

"How much will it cost you to change your mind?"

She giggled. "You haven't got enough."

I matched her smile. "Come give us a kiss then." I pulled her down onto my lap. Despite the fact that she was blue, she had gotten even more beautiful in the last six months. I knew it was immodest of me to think this because when I looked at her I saw myself. The best thing about these revivals was watching her catch up in age as I hibernated the winters away to establish my Irish residency. In another thirty-odd years we would both be in our fifties. "I love you," I said.

"Do you?" Her voice caught. "Me and you, eh, Tony?"

I said nothing. I had never heard her talk that way before. Something had happened while I was in the icebox. But then she giggled again and put her hand on my shoulder. "You can visit us, if you want."

"Us?" I brushed my fingers across the smooth scalp and wondered how many Serentols she had taken that day.

•   •   •

James I was so fascinated by Stonehenge that he commissioned the celebrated architect Inigo Jones to draw a plan of the stones and determine their purpose. The results of Jones's studies were published posthumously in 1655 by his son-in-law. Jones rejected the notion that such a structure could have been raised by any indigenous people: "Touching the matter of the buildings of the ancient *Britans* and of what materials they consisted, I find them far short of the magnificence of this Antiquity, that they were not stately, nor sumptuous; neither had they anything of Order or Symmetry, much less of gracefulness." Instead Jones, who had learned his art in Renaissance Italy and was a student of classical architecture, declared that Stonehenge must be a Roman temple, a marriage of the Tuscan and Corinthian styles, possibly built during the reign of the Flavian emperors.

In 1663 Dr. Walter Charlton, physician-in-ordinary to Charles II, disputed Jones's theory, maintaining that Stonehenge was built by the Danes "to be a Court Royal, or a place for the Election and Inauguration of their Kings." The poet Dryden applauded Charlton in verse:

Thro' you, the Danes, their short dominion lost,
A longer conquest than the Saxons boast.
Stonehenge, once thought a temple, you have found
A throne, where kings, our earthly gods, were crown'd.

In fact, many pointed to the crownlike shape of Stonehenge as proof of this theory. Of course, these speculations, coming so soon after Charles had been restored to the throne following a long exile, were politically expedient. The most astute courtiers spared no effort to discredit Cromwell's republic and to curry royal favor by reasserting the antiquity of the divine right of kings.

From *Dance of the Stones*

Wynne was my most inspired extravagance. I had never really understood what money was for until they took her out of the incubator and I held her in my arms for the first time. A late-comer to wealth, I had acquired a Raphael and a Constable and a Klee, vacationed in the Mindanao Trench and low earth orbit, collected houses in Sag Harbor, Westminster, Saint-Tropez, and Singapore. Yet none of my possessions had ever loved me back.

It was while I was developing Focus that I decided I needed someone to help me spend the fortune Western Amusement was paying me. I felt no particular urge to con-tract a marriage. None of the women I was sleeping with at the time mattered to me. I knew that they had been drawn by that irresistible pheromone: the smell of success. I wanted to share my life with someone who would be uniquely mine. Forever. Or so I imagined. Perhaps there was nothing roman-tic about it at all. Maybe the sociobiologists were right and what was at work was an instinct that had been wired into the brains of vertebrates back in the Devonian: reproduce, *repro-duce.*

Wynne was carried in an artificial womb. It was cleaner that way, medically and legally. All it took was a tissue culture from a few of my intestinal epithelial cells and some gene sculpturing to change the "Y" chromosome to an "X," as well as a few other miscellaneous improvements. Just this and a little matter of 1.2 million dollars and Wynne was mine.

I rejected all the labels that the world wanted to put on Wynne. I refused to think of her as my daughter. Nor was she exactly my clone. She was like a twin, except that we were carried to term in different wombs and her birth came some twenty-eight years after mine and her father didn't die when she was five and her mother never hit her when she was a kid. Which is to say she was nothing like a twin. She was some-thing new, a replica of me, only infinitely precious and destined never to be lonely. There were no rules for her behavior, no boundaries for her abilities.

I did not have much time for Wynne when she was a toddler. Back in those days I was still testing the product on myself and often as not would stagger home quite twisted. I found her an English nanny. The best kind. I did not pay Mrs. Detling to love the little girl; Wynne earned that on her own. The fierce old woman spent truckloads of money on Wynne; my philosophy was to treat the girl as if she were a blank memory dot on which must be recorded only the most important information. Wynne became addicted to learning as a child; I think she got that from me. She would read everything from my old history textbooks to the personals on DatingBase—although I'm not sure how much of it all she understood. We traveled whenever I could get away from the work. Detling helped her develop a command of languages; eventually she spoke English, Russian, French, and a smattering of Japanese and could read her Virgil in Latin. I think Wynne sensed my delight in the rapid evolution of her intelligence. She was always trying to impress me with some new accomplishment.

However, it was not until she was seven that I began to take real pleasure in her company. That was when she began to surprise me.

I came home from the lab one day to find her browsing the encyclopedia channel on the telelink.

"I thought you were going to see your friend," I said. "What's her name?"

"Haidee? I decided not to when Nanny said you were coming home."

"I'm just stopping in for a moment." At that time I was still trying to work the laughs out of a new tranquilizer called Carefree and was fighting a buzz from a morning dose. I did not want to start giggling like a fool in front of her, so I opened the bar and poked a pressure syringe filled with neuroleptics to straighten myself out. "I have a date. Have to go out at six."

"With that new one?" She pouted. "Jocelyn?"

"Jocelyn, yes." I held out my hand for the telelink controller. "Mind if I check the mail?"

She gave it to me. "I miss you when you're at work, Tony."

I had heard this before. "I miss you too." I brought up the mail menu on the screen and began the sort.

She snuggled next to me and watched in silence. "If you married her, would she be my mother?"

"No." My stockbroker was recommending call options on NEC and Cognico. "You don't have a mother, Wynne. You know that."

"But what if you did?"

"You don't have to worry about it."

"Okay." She seemed satisfied. "Because if I had to have a mother, I wouldn't want a crybaby."

"Hmmm." I brought up the next message in the queue. Western was bitching about the delays with Carefree, threatened to hold up the bonus from Soar.

"I saw Jocelyn crying," Wynne said, "the other night."

She had my attention then.

"I was playing house behind the chair. She came and sat on the couch, waiting for you. She didn't know I was here. She's ugly, you know, when she cries. The stuff under her eyes makes her tears black. Then she got up and she was going to the bathroom and she saw me and she looked at me like it was my fault. But she kept going and didn't say anything. When she came out she was happy again. At least she wasn't crying. Did you make her sad?"

"I don't know, Wynne." I felt as though I should be angry, but I did not know at whom. "Maybe I did."

"Well, I don't think that was a very grownup thing to do." Wynne looked at me to see if she had gone too far. "What does she have to be sad about? She sees you more than I do and I don't cry."

I hugged her. "You're a good girl." I decided then not to see Jocelyn. I'd give Detling some time off, stay home, and find out what seven-year-olds did for fun on a slow Thursday night. "I love you, Wynne."

"Me and you, Tony."

Later, as I thought back on this after I'd put her to bed, I had to chuckle. Not only could this little girl speak French and reduce fractions but she understood people. Or at least Tony Cage. She had used exactly the right mix of guilt and affection to get me to do what she wanted. Who else in the world knew me that well?

Before Wynne, I had always felt alone, no matter who I was with. Pretending to enjoy the company of throwaway women like Jocelyn only fed my loneliness. I overworked to escape the void of my personal life; this was one secret of my success. But as Wynne grew older, she forced me to change, gradually demanding more room for herself in my life until she filled it.

* * *

William Stukeley belonged to the grand tradition of English eccentrics. In his time he was a surgeon, artist, author, antiquarian, Freemason, and an ordained minister of the Church of England. From 1719 to 1724 impressionable young Stukeley spent his summers exploring Stonehenge. His meticulous fieldwork was not to be equaled until the late nineteenth century. Stukeley made precise measurements of the relationships between the stones. He explored the surrounding countryside and discovered that the circle was a part of a much larger neolithic complex. He was the first to point out the orientation of Stonehenge's axis toward the summer solstice. He did not, however, publish these findings until 1740. Meanwhile, he decided he was a druid.

From his quirky reading of the Bible, Pliny, and Tacitus, Stukeley had deduced that the druids must be the great-grandchildren of the biblical Abraham, who had hitched a ride to England on a Phoenician ship. Although his book contained an account of the superb fieldwork at Stonehenge, Stukeley's polemical theme was best summed up in the frontispiece, a portrait of the author as Chyndonax, a prince of the druids. He wrote, "My intent (besides preserving the memory of these extraordinary monuments, so much to the honor of our country, now in great danger of ruin) is to promote, as much as I am able, the knowledge and practice of ancient and true Religion. . . ." Stukeley painted a vision of noble sages practicing a pure, natural religion, the modern equivalent of which, he was at pains to point out, was none other than his own beloved Church of England! The druids had built Stonehenge as a temple to their serpent god. Although Stukeley believed that the rites practiced there may have included human sacrifice, he was inclined to forgive his spiritual forebears their excesses. Perhaps they had got Abraham's example wrong.

A hundred years later, Stukeley's druidical fantasy had worked its way both into the *Encyclopaedia Britannica* and the popular imagination. In 1857 a direct rail link between London and Salisbury was established and the Victorians descended in droves. To some Stonehenge was splendid confirmation of the ancient and present greatness of Britannia, to others it was a dark dream of disemboweled maidens and pagan license. It was at about this time that the summer solstice became a spectacle. The pubs in nearby Amesbury stayed open all night, although by license only tourists were to be served. If the skies were clear, those who staggered on to Stonehenge might number in the thousands. Often as not, it was a rude bunch. They would chip souvenirs off the bluestones and climb the sarsens, dancing in the midsummer dawn. The dreaming stillness of the Wiltshire plain would be shattered by rowdy laughter and the clatter of vehicles.

From *Dance of the Stones*

. . .

I disliked Tod Schluermann from the moment he swaggered into my house in Westminster, although I tried to keep my feelings to myself. It was bad enough that he had seduced

Wynne while I was in the icebox, unable to intervene. Worse that he had dragged her off to live with him in some impossible tube rack in Battersea. However, for me the worst of it was Tod's all-too-fashionable blue skin. My beautiful Wynne had had herself tinted so that she could look like this fop!

I had him investigated, of course. Tod had bounced around the world in his twenty-four years. His father had been a trade representative for the European Community. Born in Dresden, he had grown up in New Delhi, Ottawa, and Washington. He had flunked out of university in Leiden and had attended several other colleges in the EC without acquiring anything more substantial than a distaste for getting up early.

He was a skinny kid who looked good in the gaudy skin-tights currently in style. He was handsome in a streamlined way. Beneath his face was the delicate bone structure of a Renaissance madonna. He had no hair on him at all except for two black brushes above his eyes. When he sat next to Wynne, they looked like a pair of beautiful corpses. While I could easily imagine Tod Schluermann dead, I could not bear to contemplate a world without Wynne.

I knew that he and Wynne had met at an amateur video club in Galway. She had been shooting dolmens and court cairns with the Vidstar I'd bought her for her twentieth birthday. She got so bored when I was iced; I thought playing with a microcam might give her something to do. She had planned the vid as a present for me, except that after tramping around the Burren in her helmet for several days, she realized that she had no idea what to do next. Tod had no equipment but plenty of ideas, one of which was that megalithic ruins were boring. Instead he coaxed some drunken shepherd in Tuamgraney to let her shoot him making poteen in his illegal still. Then he tarted up her pictures with flash cuts from Easter Sunday mass and a tinkling soundtrack by some group called Cretaceous Symphony. Eventually their vid got picked up by the local telelink channel. Apparently this made Tod Schluermann an *artiste*—in Wynne's eyes.

As I listened to him that first night, I could tell that Tod himself had long since crushed any doubts he might have had about his own genius. In his years in and out of college, he had read widely but not well. Like many self-taught men, he suspected expertise. He had native intelligence, that was clear, but arrogance often made him seem stupid.

"And what are you going to do for income?" I asked him over dinner.

Tod swirled a *premier grand cru* chablis in a Waterford wineglass and smiled. "Money is a problem only if you think too much about it, Tony."

"Would you stop worrying and pass the veal?" Wynne said to me. "We'll be fine." No one spoke as Tod helped himself to seconds and passed her the serving dish. "After all," she continued, "we have my allowance."

There was a spot of madeira sauce on Tod's chin. "I don't want your money, Wynne," he said.

I knew that was for my benefit. Wynne's allowance was generous enough to support a barrister in Mayfair; I certainly didn't want her wasting it on Tod. "This is a tough market for amateurs, Tod. London is jammed with freelance videographers—pros with resumes, kids out of university who studied on state-of-the-art equipment. How do you expect to compete?"

"Uni-*vers*-ity, yes." He pumped contempt into his pronunciation. "You know, the problem is that by the time the teachers get done with you, they've mashed your creativity flat. Talk to the good little A students who catch on with the big companies and they'll have forgotten why they majored in vidart in the first place. All they know is how to recycle the stale old crap they learned in class. Just call up any channel on telelink. It's all yesterday's news, Tony."

"Besides," said Wynne, "We have experience. Tod's been taking *Poteen* around, showing it everywhere. And we have my microcam. Once we pick our next project, all we'll really need is to buy time on an image processor. Tod says they're not that hard to learn; they keep making the interface a lot more accessible, you know."

"They who?" I said. "You mean the brain-dead professors? The stale old corporate grinds?"

"Tony." Wynne colored, then pushed away from the table.

"No," said Tod. "He's right." She settled down again. I didn't understand why she gave in so easily to him, when she was challenging whatever I said. "Look, Tony, I'm not saying everything you learn in school is useless and I'm certainly not antibusiness. The way I see it, people who don't have a vision need someone to tell them what to think."

I laid my fork across my plate. "But vision isn't enough, Tod." I wanted him to stop saying my name as if we were equals. "You can't carve a statue out of air. A vision is only an hallucination until you find some way to make it real. And maybe I'm old-fashioned, but that's what money is good for. If you can't afford the access time to process your vids, that's a problem, isn't it?"

" 'S okay." Tod was the only one still eating. "Found a shop that will sell us time cheap," he said between bites. "Of course, the slot they're offering is two to three Monday mornings. We'll have to learn to be early birds."

"We're just starting," said Wynne. "You can't expect us to work out everything ahead of time. I bet you didn't."

"No." The conversation had killed my appetite. "You're right." I poured a volatile called Bliss into a brandy snifter, breathed deeply. My eyes burned and the light turned golden. "Try." I passed it to Wynne. "It's a new mind perfume."

From the stricken expression on her face, I knew I had said exactly the wrong thing. She took a short, guilty sniff and handed the glass back to me. I'd never seen Wynne skimp on flash before.

"No." I waved her off. "Tod next."

He smiled at me and shook his head.

"Tod doesn't use flash," she said.

I smiled too, thinking it was a joke. "Doesn't what?" I felt like I was breathing champagne; my frontal lobes began to effervesce. "What is he, a stump?"

"It's nothing personal," he said, seriously. "I have artist friends who can't make a move until they poke a dose of Focus. My problem is with this programming metaphor that you drug makers are always using. So okay, the mind is a computer you can take control of with all this powerful chemical software. You can reprogram people to feel happy or hungry or numb or sexy and when the drug wears off, the mind resets to its original state. But the way I see it, your so-called software pollutes my identity while I'm using it, keeps me from being myself. I don't want to become a robot; I'd rather think my own thoughts. Feel whatever it is I'm really feeling."

I was croggled. What kind of egomaniac wanted to think only his own thoughts? Being yourself is like being in jail; everyone needs to be let out once in a while. I wanted to argue with him, somehow convince Wynne not to throw herself away on this blue-skinned twit. But the Bliss overwhelmed my anger at them both. When I tried to speak, laughter bubbled up my throat.

•   •   •

Sir Edmund Antrobus, the baronet who owned Stonehenge, died without an heir in 1915. For years he had squabbled with the Church of the Universal Bond, a modern reincarnation of druidism based on equal parts of wish fulfillment and bad scholarship, over access to the site. The chief druid announced that it had been a druid curse that had struck Sir Edmund down. Several months after, his estate came up for sale. Mr. Cecil Chubb bought Stonehenge at auction for £6,600—on a whim, or so he claimed. Three years later Chubb presented Stonehenge and the land around it to the nation. He was later recommended to knighthood by Lloyd George for his public spirit.

To the cautious bureaucrats in the Office of Works, Stonehenge was a disaster waiting to happen. Several leaning stones threatened to collapse; wobbly lintels needed readjustment. The government sought help from the Society of Antiquaries for this work. The antiquarians seized the opportunity to expand the repairs into a grandiose and disastrous excavation of the entire monument. The government, however, withdrew funding soon after the stones were straightened and for years the Society struggled to finance the dig itself. More often than not Colonel William Hawley had to work alone, living in a crude wooden shack on the site. In 1926 the project was mercifully suspended, having accomplished little more than to disturb evidence and embarrass the Society. As the bewildered Hawley told the *Times,* "The more we dig, the more the mystery appears to deepen."

From *Dance of the Stones*

.   .   .

I was never any good at working things out ahead of time. All too often, my plans were overtaken by events. For example, I did not choose my career; I became a flash artist by accident. I left home for Cornell when I was seventeen, as much to escape my mother as to get an education. I intended to study genetic engineering. At that time Boggs was developing the virus complex that could transform a living specimen of stonewort from one species to another. Kwabena had published her pioneering work on organ generation. It seemed as if every month a different geneticist stepped forward to promise a miracle that would change the world. I wanted to make miracles, too. I was as naive as Wynne back then.

Unfortunately, genetic engineering excited every other bright kid in the country. The competition at Cornell was fierce. I started doing drugs in my sophomore year just to keep up with the course work. Soon I was the lord of the all-nighters. I started with small doses of metrazine; it was only supposed to be psychologically addicting. I knew I was tougher than any drug. I did not much care for the recreational stuff back then. There was no time. I tried THC on occasion: both pot and the new inhalers from Sweden. Once over spring break a woman I had been seeing gave me some mescal buttons. She said it would give me new insight. It did—I realized I was wasting my time with her.

Three semesters later it all went wrong. By then I was eating megamphetamines in massive doses, sometimes over eighty milligrams. The initial rush felt like a whole-body orgasm; I did not feel like studying much afterward. My adviser told me to switch out of the program after I got a C in genetic chemistry. I was burning up brain cells and losing weight; I had already lost my direction. I knew I had to get clean and start again.

I had signed up for a course in psychopharmacology on a paranoid whim. If I had to study something, why not the chemistry of how I was destroying myself? Bobby Belotti was a good teacher; he soon became a friend. He helped me get off the megs, helped me salvage a plain vanilla degree in biology and encouraged me to apply to graduate school. My idealism had been seared away during those twisted semesters of amphetamine psychosis. Maybe that was why it was so easy to convince myself that developing new drugs was just as noble as curing hemophilia.

I wrote my master's thesis on the effects of indole hallucinogens on serotonergic and dopaminergic receptors. The early indole hallucinogens like LSD and DMT had long since been thought to inhibit production of the neuroregulator serotonin—not surprising since their chemical structures were remarkably similar. My work showed that hallucinogens of this family also affect the dopamine-producing system and that many of the reported effects of these drugs resulted from interactions between these neuroregulators. It was not, I have to admit, particularly innovative or brilliant work; the foundations had been laid long ago. But by then I had grown tremendously bored with being a student. The work reflected it.

I took my degree just as the America First party came to power. Their libertarian answer to the challenge of the EC was to curb the power of the fed everywhere. They decriminalized drugs and gutted the Food and Drug Administration, sparking a revolution in substance use and abuse. I was still debating whether to slog on for my doctorate when Bobby Belotti called to say that he was leaving Cornell. Western Amusement was recruiting people to do R&D for its new psychoactive drug division. Belotti was going. Did I want in? Of course.

Western Amusement's entry legitimized the fledgling industry. WA helped form the Council for Responsible Recreation and, through it, waged a multimillion-dollar public relations campaign to undo the antidrug propaganda of the '90s. One strategy was to rename the product. The 2005 edition of Webster's was the first mainstream dictionary to use "flash" as a generic term for the new recreational drugs.

Our team was looking for something that could compete with a lunchtime dose of ethanol. Fast and dirty: a businessman's flash. It had to be fat-soluble so that it would pass quickly into the brain and reach its site of action within minutes after ingestion. It had to be easily metabolized so that the psychoactive effect would fade within an hour or two. No needles, keep the tolerance effect low. They did not want the users to see God or experience the ultimate orgasm, just a little psychic distortion, maybe pretty visuals and leave them with a smile.

Since I had already worked with indole hallucinogens, Belotti gave me pretty much a free hand. After a couple of frustrating months, I began to look seriously at DMD. It seemed to fit the specifications, except that animal tests did not show significant psychoactive effect. I worried it might be too subtle. No matter how safe it was, the stuff was no good if it left the user as straight as a Methodist accountant. Still, I was able to convince Belotti to authorize microiontophoretic tests on rats.

Bobby Belotti was a thoroughly disheveled man. His curly black hair resisted combing. He was forever tucking in his shirt; his paunch tugged it out again. There were rings of dried coffee on the papers piled on his desk; dust gathered undisturbed in the nooks of his terminal. When teased about his sloppiness, he would acknowledge it with a kind of absent-minded pride. I think he regarded it as proof that he could succeed in the corporate culture and yet not be controlled by it. His grooming did little to endear him to our superiors.

"Look at this." I burst into Belotti's office and dropped a ten-centimeter stack of hardcopy on his desk. "The DMD results. The stuff inhibits the hell out of the serotonergic system."

Belotti pulled off his glasses and rubbed an eye with the back of his hand. "Great. Have you got an effect to show me?"

"No, but these numbers say there has to be one. Must be some kind of trigger."

Belotti sighed and began to shuffle through the papers on his desk. "The front office is screaming for something to sell, Tony. I don't see that DMD is the answer. Do you?"

"Another month, Bobby. I'm almost there—I can taste it."

Belotti found a memo, handed it to me. "Give it a rest, Tony. Let's get a couple of products under our belt, then maybe you can pick it up later."

We argued, only I had never learned how to argue. Belotti was too calm, too damn understanding. Although it was never mentioned, the debt that I owed Belotti only fueled my outrage. I felt like the wayward student being corrected once again by the kindly professor.

Fuming, I brought the odious memo back to my cubical, shut down my terminal, and glared at the empty screen. I was in a mood to lash out, do something crazy. The idea came to me in anger, an idea straight out of a mad scientist vid. I requisitioned ten milligrams of DMD and went home to try it on myself.

Half an hour after eating the drug, I was lying on the bed in my darkened room, waiting for something, anything to happen. I felt jittery, as if I had just poked some mild speed. My pulse rate was up, I was sweating. I knew from the tests that the drug must have already found its way to my brain. I felt nothing—I was not even angry anymore. At last I got out of bed, turned up the lights, and went into the kitchen to make myself a snack. I settled in front of the telelink with a ham-and-cheese sandwich and turned the monitor on. News. Change channel. *Click, click.*

No signal. Just visual static. Exactly what it took to trigger DMD's psychoactive effect. I never ate that sandwich.

Instead I spent the next hour gazing intently at a screen of red, green, and blue phosphors flashing at random. Except that to me they were not at all random. I saw patterns, wonderful patterns: wheels of fire, amber waves of grain, angels dancing on the head of a pin, demon faces. I felt as if I were a pattern. I was liberated from my body, soaring into the screen to play amidst the beautiful lights.

And then it was over. A very clean finish. It had been an hour and a half since I had eaten the pill; the peak had lasted about forty-five minutes. It was perfect. With a sophisticated light show to trigger DMD's effect, it might be the most popular drug since caffeine. And it was mine, I realized. All mine.

After all, Belotti had cut himself out of the action with his memo. I had taken the risk, put my body and sanity on the line. Friendship was friendship but I knew that if I played this right it could change my life. So I made sure that management heard about DMD from me, making the case that Belotti had tried to stifle my research. If my coworkers resented me for stepping on my friend's face in the scramble up the ladder, I learned not to care. Western Amusement was secretly relieved; I was young and wore suits that fit and could do a good imitation of a corporate lifer. Soon I was in charge of the team, then the whole lab.

I always expected Belotti to leave, go back to Cornell, but he never did. Perhaps he intended it as a subtle kind of revenge; showing up for work every day, drinking coffee with me. I refused to be shamed. I found ways to avoid Belotti, eventually exiling him to one of our R&D spin-off companies. I did not see him much after that.

The linguists in marketing decided to call DMD Soar; it became Western Amusement's first megahit in the flash market. To personalize Soar, WA's publicists made me famous before I understood quite what they were doing. Telelink could not get enough. A sanitized bio appeared on the major information utilities: the brilliant young researcher, the daring breakthrough, the first step of an incredible psychic journey by the man who could program minds—at first I was amused by it all.

When I could get to the lab, I spent much of my time brainstorming mechanisms to trigger Soar's psychoactive effect. The light tablet, which can read EEG patterns and transform them into computer pyrotechnics, was the most successful, but there were others. In fact, the hardware aftermarket made Western Amusement almost as much as the flash itself. My lab turned into a money machine. To keep the corporate headhunters at bay, WA gave me participation in the profits. In five years I was one of the richest men I knew.

There were three parts to the flash experience: the chemical itself, the mental state of the user, and the environment in which the flash was consumed—what I liked to call the surround. As the years passed I became much less involved in developing chemicals. The kids coming out of grad school were better researchers than I had ever been. I was more interested in conceptual design and especially liked dreaming up new surrounds, from the minimalism of sensory deprivation to the abstract richness of virtual realities. The corporate linguists made the best of my evolving interests. I was no longer a mere mind programmer; I was anointed the world's first flash artist.

However, the real reason I was forced to cut back on my involvement with drug development had nothing to do with artistic yearning. I have the classic addictive personality. I really love to get twisted. Over the years I had let some vicious psychoactive chemicals sink claws into my synapses. Although I had always managed to pull free, I made management nervous. I was practically a corporate symbol, like Sister Strawberry or Ted Turner. WA could not afford to have Tony Cage melt down.

I probably should not have been surprised to see my taste for flash mirrored in Wynne. She began using when she was nine. By the time she was eleven I was letting her poke some of the major psychoactives. It could hardly have been otherwise if Wynne were to share my life. The crowd I traveled with had personal bars that put most flash clubs to shame. My own lab was developing a cannabinol chewing gum aimed at the preteen market. Despite what the stump propagandists say, I had not made the flash culture; it had made me. Kids all over the world were twisting their minds, reaching for the brightest flash.

I tried to ensure that Wynne was never addicted to any one chemical. I saw to it that her habit was varied. If she started to build up a cross-tolerance to the hallucinogens, for example, I would make her give the whole family a vacation and switch to the opiates. Nor was she constantly twisted. She could go on sprees that would last anywhere from a few hours to a few days. Then nothing for a week or two. Still, I worried about her sometimes. She took some astounding doses.

We discussed our habits just once. It was last year, the autumn before Tod. We had flown from the Changi Airport in Singapore to Shannon and checked into the Hilton. I was getting ready to ice myself. Even though we had taken the suborbital we had a hard time getting our biological clocks reset. Since I had business in Dublin the next day I could not afford to stay jet-lagged. Wynne called room service and had them bring up a couple of strawberry Placidex shakes. I settled back on my bed; the Placidex made me feel as if I were melting into the mattress. Wynne sat on a thermal chair and dreamily switched channels on the telelink. Finally she shut it off and asked me if I thought I took too much flash.

I had been about to doze off; suddenly I was as alert as anyone with Placidex seeping into his brain can be. "Sure, I think about it all the time. Right now I think I'm okay. There have been times, though, when I was in trouble."

She nodded. "How do you know when you're in trouble?"

"One sign is when you stop worrying about it."

She folded her arms as if she were chilled. "That's a hell of a thing to say. You're only safe if you're worried?"

"Or if you're clean."

"Oh, come on. What's the longest you've been clean? Recently."

"Six months. When I was in the icebox." We both laughed. "Since you brought it up," I said, "let me ask you. Think you do too much?"

She considered, as if the question had surprised her. "Nah," she said at last. "I'm young. I can take it."

I told her then about how I had been hooked on amphetamines at Cornell. The story obviously did not seem to impress her.

"But you beat it, obviously," she said. "So it couldn't have been that bad."

"Maybe you're right," I said. "But it seems to me that I was lucky. A couple more months and I might never have been able to get clean again."

"I like getting twisted," she said. "But there are other things I like just as much."

"For instance?"

She stretched "Sex." I could see her breasts pressing against her wrapper. She was teasing me now; I liked it. "Spending your money. Losing myself in a book or a vid or a VR. Taking risks." She yawned. The words were coming slower and slower. "Did I mention sex?"

"Come to bed then. You're keeping both of us up."

She touched the shoulder clasp and her wrapper uncoiled, crinkling, into a pile on the floor. She slipped off her panties and climbed in beside me. Her skin was warm and smooth under my hands. "It's not fair, you know," she said as I caressed her. "I'm going to miss you but you won't miss me."

"It's only six months."

"A woman has certain needs."

"You want to spend more money?" I licked the side of her face and got a slow Placidex laugh. "I love you, Wynne."

"Me and you, Tony." She kissed me and I was convinced she meant it.

. . .

In 1965 the astronomer Gerald Hawkins published a book with an immodest title: *Stonehenge Decoded*. Earlier explainers had always looked beyond Stonehenge for evidence to back up their theories. Some ages found authority in the Bible and church tradition, others in the ruins of Rome or the great historians of antiquity. Like his predecessors, Hawkins invoked the authorities of his time to support his ingenious theory. Using the Harvard-Smithsonian IBM 7090 computer to analyze patterns of solar and lunar alignments at Stonehenge, Hawkins reached a conclusion that electrified the world. Stonehenge had been built as an observatory for ancient astronomers. In fact, he claimed that parts of it formed a "Neolithic computer," which had been used by its builders to predict eclipses of the moon.

Hawkins's theory caught the popular imagination, in large part due to the uncomprehending coverage of it by the old printed newspapers. Reporters dithered over this marvel: Stone Age scientists had built a computer of sarsen and bluestone that only a modern electronic brain could "decode." There was even a television special on some of the old pretelelink networks. Much was made of Hawkins's use of the computer, despite the fact that the numbers it had crunched could easily have been done by hand. And what Hawkins had, in fact, proved was entirely different from what he had claimed to have proved. The computer studies showed that the Aubrey holes, a ring of fifty-six regularly spaced pits, could be used to predict eclipses. They did not show that the builders of Stonehenge had any such purpose in mind. Others soon offered conflicting interpretations and closely reasoned Stonehenge astronomies proliferated. The problem was soon recognized: Stonehenge had too much astronomical significance. It was a mirror in which any theoretician could see his ideas reflected.

From *Dance of the Stones*

•   •   •

I couldn't stay in Westminster while Wynne was sleeping with Tod just a few kilometers away. I told myself that their affair would collapse soon enough, either under the weight of Tod's ego or Wynne's flash deprivation. So I flew back to the States to wait them out.

I also needed to check in with Western Amusement. Though I was no longer an active employee, I remained an exclusive consultant. There were no doors shut to me at the lab I had made famous, no secrets I could not learn. The hot news was that in the six months I had been in the icebox, Bobby Belotti had made a breakthrough on the Share project.

I had started the Share project years back in 2014, just after I had stopped working at the lab full time. I had been thinking about the way social reinforcement seemed to energize flash use. Most users preferred to get twisted with other users, at flash clubs and private parties or before making love or eating a fine meal or free-fall dancing in space. If socialization enhanced pleasure, why not find a way for users to share an identical experience? Not just by creating identical surrounds but by synchronizing the effect on a synaptic level—direct intervention in the sensory cortex.

Back in 2014, I thought the effect would have to be created electrochemically; the interaction of psychoactive drugs with electronic stimulation of the cerebrum. However, that would be extremely expensive to design, much less to deliver. Besides, the marketing research showed that more than 70 percent of the target audience were expressing reservations at having their brains wired. While many people were willing to entertain the brain-as-computer metaphor, very few were ready to become peripherals. Meanwhile, the lawyers at corporate headquarters were worried about WA's liability exposure.

I kept after them. If nothing else, I thought Share would be a powerful aphrodisiac. It could redefine intimacy. What did it matter how expensive it was if it turned out to be the ultimate erotic experience? I pointed out that no one had ever gone broke selling love potions, and WA commissioned a technical feasibility study.

I knew what the study would show: there were a lot of holes that only basic research could fill. But the research was being done, if not by us, then elsewhere. The entire computer industry was scrambling to develop new brain-computer interfaces. Finally WA proposed a compromise: they wanted to spin off the Share project to a limited partnership that would protect them legally and financially. They would provide half the venture capital needed if I would put up 10 percent out of my own pocket and bring in qualified partners willing to invest the balance. How much did I believe in this project? Just enough. Share, Inc., was incorporated in 2017, the first year I iced myself. The tiny R&D company was located in space rented from Western Amusement's psychoactive drug division. It was the perfect place, I thought, for Bobby Belotti. A side bet on a long shot.

And now, years later, Belotti had something. Not exactly what I'd had in mind, but it was intriguing. He had borrowed a drug, 7,2-DAPA, which had been developed by neuropathologists studying language disorders. It could induce a euphoric anomia, disrupting the process of associating certain visual inputs with words. Users had trouble naming what they saw—abstract nouns and proper names were especially difficult. The severity of the anomia was related not only to dosage but to the complexity of the visual environment. For example, a user sitting in a white room who saw a single long-stemmed rose might be unable to speak the words "flower" or "rose" even though he could carry on an otherwise intelligent conversation about gardening; show him into a greenhouse and he might well be speechless. However, if he picked the rose up or smelled it or heard the word "rose" he would make the connection. And in that moment of recognition, enkephalin neurons would start firing like crazy; the brain would be awash in the pleasure of discovery. I couldn't wait to try it with Wynne.

"The problem is," Belotti explained to me, "there's no way yet to predict which words will be lost. Too much individual variation. For instance, maybe I can't say 'rose' but you can. In that case I get a flash from you; you get nothing. It's only if both of us lose the same word and then get an appropriate cue that we share the effect."

"Doesn't sound as if it's going to replace sex." I laughed; Belotti winced. The man had not changed much. What was left of his hair still needed combing. There were webs of broken veins beneath his wrinkled skin. He seemed very old, very distant. His dusty desktop terminal was like a wall between us. I found it hard to remember the time when we had been friends.

"Well, shared sex might be interesting." Belotti sounded as if he were repeating excuses he had made before. "But you wouldn't get much effect by telling someone he's having an orgasm. Too tactile, very little to do with visual input. Still, since the enkephalin suppresses pain impulses, pleasure is correspondingly enhanced. But remember, everything is fairly mild because we have to keep the dosage low. Take too much and there's a tendency to withdraw. You get into hallucinations. It's unpredictable. Dangerous."

"Can the effect be blocked?"

"So far the neuroleptics are the only true antagonists we've found. And they're pretty slow-acting. Testing isn't finished yet. Actually," he said as he shuffled through stacks of hardcopy next to the terminal, "it's not my concern anymore. I spent twelve years chasing the specs you wrote and I'm tired of Share. The partnership has offered me early retirement, Tony, and I've decided to take it. I put the house up for sale; Alice has already moved to the lake."

"My God, Bobby, is that what you really want? Because if someone's pushing you out the door, I'll . . ."

"Nobody's pushing me; I'm walking while I still can. I'm sixty-one years old, Tony. How old are you these days?"

I shrugged the question off. No sense rubbing his face in my good fortune. I had not thought about Bobby Belotti for a long time; suddenly I was sorry for him. "What would you use Share for, Bobby?"

"As I said, not my concern. Marketing will find someone to peddle it to, I'm sure. I guess they're a little disappointed it didn't turn out to be the aphrodisiac you promised them."

"It's fine work, Bobby. You don't have to apologize to anyone. But I can't believe that you've spent this much time and effort without thinking of commercial applications."

"Well, if you could control which words were lost, then you could use guides to supply the necessary cues." Belotti scratched the back of his neck. "Maybe you could blend in a hypnotic to give the guides more psychological authority. It might help, say, in art appreciation classes. Or maybe museums could sell it along with those tape-recorded tours."

Great. A flash for museums. I could imagine the ads. The topless vidqueen says to her virtual boyfriend, "Hey, bucko, let's shank down to the National Gallery and get twisted!" No wonder they were letting him go. "Why bother? Sounds like all you need are two people sitting at a kitchen table shooting words at each other."

"But words . . . it's not that simple. We're not talking fancy lights here; these are internalized symbols that can trigger complex mental states. Emotions, memories, desires . . ."

"I understand that, Bobby. I guess maybe I need to find out for myself." I gave him my best deal-closing smile. "Where do I get my samples?"

Belotti nodded as if he had expected me to ask. "Still can't keep your hands off the product? Too bad they've clamped the lid on this until they decide what they've got."

"I'm a special case, Bobby. You ought to know that by now. Some rules just don't apply to me."

He stared at me as if we hadn't known each other for thirty years.

"Please?" I didn't really need to be so polite, but I thought I owed it to him. "For an old friend?"

Shaking his head, Belotti thumbed the printreader to unlock his desk, took a green bottle from the top drawer, and tossed it to me. "One at a time, you understand? And you didn't get it from me."

I popped the top. Six pills, yellow powder in clear casings. For a moment I was suspicious, but I had long since made up my mind about this man. "Thanks." I pocketed the green bottle. "What time is it, anyway?" I said. "I told Shaw I'd meet him for lunch."

Belotti touched the temple of his eyeglasses and his lenses opaqued. "You know, I used to hate you. Then I realized you didn't know what the hell you were doing. Might as well blame a cat for batting around a bloody mouse. You don't see anyone, Tony. Not even yourself." His hands shook. "I'll bet you actually believe the PR, that we're nothing but systems you can program to laugh and fall in love and study. You think you can even program Tony Cage, wall yourself up in your own tiny corner of reality and pretend no one else exists. But it's a goddamned failure of imagination, Tony. Life isn't an organic chemistry equation. People aren't robots." He snapped the switch on his terminal, turning it off. "That's all right, I'll shut up now. I'm going home. The only reason I came in today was because they said you wanted a meeting."

I took no chances after listening to this tirade. I had one of Belotti's samples analyzed. It was pure. Then I moved on. There were lawyers in Washington and accountants in New York. I spoke at the American Psychopharmacological Association's annual meeting at Hilton Head and gave half a dozen telelink interviews. I met a Japanese woman and we made reservations to spend a weekend in low Earth orbit on Habitat Apollo. Afterward we went to Osaka, where I found out she was a corporate spy for Unico. It had been almost two months. Time, I thought, for Tod to have screwed up, for

Wynne to have recognized him as a vain and useless dilettante, for their money to have run out. I caught the suborbital to Heathrow. I was so sure.

It was a nasty surprise. Tod Schluermann had been lucky.

The vid *Burn London* was only thirteen minutes long. It started with a shot of missile silos. Countdown. Launch. London was under attack. No missiles—enormous naked Wynnes left rainbows across the sky as they hurtled down on the city. They exploded not in flame but in foliage, smothering entire city blocks with trees and brush. Soon the city disappeared beneath a forest. The camera zoomed to a clearing where a band called Flog was playing. They had been providing a dreamy sound track. The tempo picked up, and the group played faster and faster until their instruments caught fire, consuming them and the forest. The final shot was a pan over ash and charred stumps. I thought it was the dumbest thing I'd ever seen.

No one could have predicted that sixteen-year-olds across the EC would choose that moment to take Flog into their callow hearts. When they made *Burn London* with Tod, Flog was unknown. In the span of a month they went from a basement in Leeds to a floor of Claridge's in London. Although Tod did not make much money from *Burn London,* it was his first professional credit. The kid who once compared himself to Nam June Paik was more than willing to settle for making vids for pubescent music fans.

I did not understand why Wynne and Tod insisted on living in Battersea when my place in Westminster had been empty all this time. There were about two hundred plastic go-tubes stacked in what had once been a warehouse. Each was three meters long; the singles were a meter and a half in diameter, the doubles two. Each was furnished with a locker beneath a gel mattress, a terminal and a water bubbler passing for a sink. There was always a line for the showers. The toilets smelled.

The tube rack was fine for Tod; he didn't care where he lived. Besides, he spent most of his time haunting the offices of video producers or chasing band managers; he was hardly ever there. Wynne, however, had my tastes, which did not run to squalor. When I asked her why he kept leaving her home alone, she begged me not to interfere. Why?

"Because I'm in love," she said. "For the first time in my life."

"I'm happy for you, Wynne. Believe me." We were sitting over lagers, waiting for Tod to join us for dinner. The pub was dark—easier to lie in the dark. "But you shouldn't let him make all the decisions. Take control of your own life."

"He wants to pick the next project. It's important to him and he's important to me. Once we get started, it'll be just like it was before." She rubbed her finger along the rim of her glass. "A year ago you weren't telling me to take control of my life."

"But that was different." My face started to burn; it had been a long time since I had felt embarrassed. "I thought . . . were you unhappy?"

Silence.

"At least I didn't leave you alone all day."

She gave a mirthless chuckle.

"What did I do? *What?*" I stretched my hand across the table toward her. "I'm sorry, Wynne. Really. But you have to tell me what I did."

She patted it absently. "It's okay, Tony."

I realized my plan of inaction had gone very, very wrong. While I had been doing nothing, he had turned her against me. If Wynne couldn't see the difference between the way Tod Schluermann treated her and the way I did . . . I had to act now or I might never get Wynne back, even after he discarded her.

"You two holding hands in the dark again?" said Tod as he slipped onto the bench beside Wynne.

She pulled away from me and flung her arms around him. They took their time kissing.

"You're my witness, Tony," said Tod, "that at least one female in this city loves me. I have just spent the afternoon pitching ideas to a woman with all the imagination of a light switch. If I work with her I have exactly two choices: creative control with no budget or eighty thousand quid with more strings than the plugging Philharmonic. I'm telling you, I'm beginning to think maybe money makes *all* the difference."

"Don't say that." Wynne nudged him. "So we go somewhere else."

"Where else is there? I've tried LuLu, Eyeworks, Legend, TVN, Visions, London Now." He reached across Wynne for her glass of lager and finished it. "I don't want to make another short. This one should carry some weight."

I had to find some way to stay close to her. "What if I used my connections at Western Amusement?" I was desperate.

"No," said Wynne immediately.

"Maybe," Tod said. Even in the gloom of the pub, I could see him wink at her. He wanted me to see. "What did you have in mind?"

•　　•　　•

History does not record the first use of drugs at Stonehenge. However, there is little doubt that most of the major hallucinogens available in 1974 were ingested during the first Stonehenge free festival. An offshore pirate music station, Radio Caroline, had urged its listeners to come to Stonehenge for a festival of "love and awareness." On solstice day that year a horde of scruffy music fans in their late teens and twenties set up camp in the field next to the car park. The empty landscape around the stones was filled with tents and teepees, cars and caravans. Electric guitars screamed and there was a whiff of marijuana on the summer breeze. There are tapes of those early festivals. A vast psychedelia of humanity would gather for the occasion: the glassy-eyed couple from Des Moines in their matching polyester shirts, the smiling engineer from Tokyo taking movies, the young mother from Luton breast-feeding her infant son on the Altar Stone, the Amesbury bobby standing beneath the outer circle, hands clasped behind his back, the druid from Leicester in her white ceremonial robes, the long-haired teenager from Dorking who had climbed the great trilithon and was shouting something about the pope, UFOs, the sun, and the Beatles. The festival withered during the arid years of Thatcher and Major, but it bloomed again on the millennial solstice and has never stopped since. It has become one of the great surrounds for getting twisted. The pioneers of hallucinogens had a colorful term for the radical perceptual jolts of such an experience, the fascinating strangeness of it all. They would have called the Stonehenge free festival a mindfucker.

From *Dance of the Stones*

•   •   •

It was the perfect marriage of commerce and experimental art. Western Amusement wanted to launch Share and Tod wanted to make a vid. The concept I eventually came up with was that in the final scene, Tod, Wynne, and I would all take the new flash and attend the solstice celebrations together, relying on Stonehenge, the crowd, and each other for the cues to shape our experience. WA's CelebrityWatch channel would bring *Dance of the Stones* to telelink. The hype was not hard to imagine:

"Let famed Soar creator Tony Cage introduce you to his most outrageous flash art yet! See *Dance of the Stones* twisted on Share, the brand-new cutting-edge flash from Western Amusement, and join in a worldwide psychic phenomenon! You will actually experience the thoughts of strangers and friends! Have you ever wondered what your loved one is really feeling? Now you'll know! Never before have so many minds come together at one time, for one very special event. *Dance of the Stones* and Share—you have never been so close to another person!"

It was an easy sell to WA, since I told them I was willing to fund the project and assume all financial risk should they decide to pass on the finished version. Their only question was why I had brought Tod Schluermann into the project at all.

Tod was more difficult to convince. I spoke of the aesthetics of randomness as an answer to the problem of selection. I said we might be on the verge of a historic discovery; Share was a new way for the audience to participate in the very act of artistic creation. I told him he might well be the father of a new collaborative art form.

"But I don't use drugs," he said.

"Alcohol? Caffeine? Everybody uses drugs, Tod. There are just some you've decided not to try. And I'd call your abstinence more a thickheaded stump prejudice than a virtue. Billions of people use flash to expand their perceptions. There's nothing wrong with getting twisted. Ask Wynne."

"Leave me out of this, Tony." I had yet to get any help from her; I think she suspected my motives.

"Listen," I said, "you're in the right place at the right time but you have to choose now. The solstice is in two weeks and WA will have Share out by this time next year."

"You sure I'll be able to function while we're on this stuff?" Tod's resistance was wearing down. "I don't want to waste the big day shooting blades of grass."

"I'll bring something to neutralize it. If you have problems, I can poke you straight anytime you want. Look, the action of Share should actually help you be more visually oriented. You said yourself that language gets in the way of art. Share strips away the superstructure of linguistic perception. You won't know what you're seeing, you'll just see. The eyes of a child, Tod."

Wynne and Tod had their go-tube shipped from the rack in Battersea to Stonehenge for the five-day festival. It and a thousand others lay near the old car park across the A360 highway from the dome that now protected the stones. The tubes looked like giant white Soar capsules scattered in the grass. In between were tension bubbles, Gortex tents of varying geometries, and even people camped in folding chairs beneath gaudy umbrellas. I stayed at an inn in Amesbury and commuted out for the daily shoots.

I was a little surprised when Tod asked me to write a brief

history of Stonehenge. Although I enjoyed doing it, I wondered what kind of vid he was making. He was not saying. "Creative control," was all I could get out of him. It became his mantra. Trust a stump to make flash art that looked like a slow afternoon on the old PBS.

I arrived at the go-tube around ten on the morning before the solstice. Wynne was sitting alone on the bed. It was obvious that she had been crying.

I was devastated to see her so miserable. "Where's Tod?" I was also ecstatic.

"Renting a helicopter. He decided he needed aerials."

"And he didn't take you?" I sat beside her. "Aren't you supposed to be the videographer?"

"I didn't want to go."

She looked as if she needed comforting. I started to put my arm around her.

"Don't." She scooted away from me.

"Do you want me to leave?"

"I don't know why you're here, Tony. What are you doing this vid for?"

"To help you, of course. And Tod."

"You hate Tod."

I let that pass. "Well, maybe it's because I miss you. This is the only way you'll let me be with you."

She went to the water bubbler. "You want me and Tod to break up. You're hoping this vid will pry us apart." She shook two pills from a crumpled red envelope, popped them into her mouth, and washed them down.

"I want you to be happy, Wynne. And I'd like to be part of whatever makes you happy. I've dedicated my whole life to you. It wouldn't be worth living if I never got to see you."

"Stick it! You're just trying to make me feel guilty."

"It's true."

She saw her bleary reflection in the mirror above the bubbler and grimaced. "Who am I, Tony?" She splashed some water on her face. "You created me, wrote the specifications.

You've been programming me since the day I was born. What the hell did you think you were doing?''

"I didn't know exactly," I said. "I wanted someone to love—and I got her. I love you, Wynne.''

She slowly patted herself dry and then folded the damp towel as if it were heirloom linen. Her silence pounded in my ears. She was still moving very deliberately when she crossed the room, leaned over, and gave me a quick, frightened kiss on the forehead.

"I'm sorry, Tony." Beneath her skin tint, she had gone pale.

•   •   •   •

"What's that?" said Wynne, pointing at Stonehenge. Bolts of lightning forked through the darkness, illuminating the crowd outside the dome.

"It's only the *son et lumière,*" I said. "The holotechs from the Department of the Environment put it on to soak a few extra quid from the tourists.'' We kept walking up the A360 from where the Amesbury shuttle had dropped us. "Watch what comes next."

Seconds later two laser rainbows shimmered between the stones. "Stonehenge's greatest hits," said Tod with contempt. "Both Constable and Turner did paintings here. Turner's was full of his usual schmaltz, lightning bolts and dead shepherds and howling dogs. Constable tried to jack up his boring watercolor with a double rainbow.''

I bit my lip and said nothing. I did not really need a lecture on Stonehenge, especially not from Tod. After all, I owned one of Constable's Stonehenge sketches.

Tod flipped down the visor of Wynne's Vidstar helmet; he looked like a mantis with lens eyes. I could hear the motors buzzing as the twin cameras focused.

"Is anyone else starting to feel it?" Wynne said.

"I've been doing a lot of research on this place, you know," said Tod. "It's amazing, the people who've been here."

"Yes," I said. "It's an oozy kind of coolness spreading

across the back of my skull. Like mud." We had eaten our capsules of Share in the darkness on the ride over. "What time is it?"

"It's four-eighteen." Tod slipped a backup battery into the system unit clipped to his belt. "Sunrise at 5:07."

I looked to the northeast; the sky had already started to lighten. The stars were like glass mites scuttling away into grayness.

"They come in waves," said Wynne. "Hallucinations."

"Yes," I said. The back of my eyes seemed to tingle. I knew there was something wrong but I could not think what it was.

We pushed past the inevitable picket lines of stumps; luckily, none of them recognized me. At last we reached a barbed-wire corridor leading through the crowd to the entrance to the dome. Down the corridor marched a troop of ghosts. They were dressed in white robes; some wore glasses. They carried copper globes and oak branches and banners with images of snakes and pentacles. They were male and female and they seemed old. They were murmuring a chant that sounded like the wind blowing through fallen leaves. Dry old ghosts, crinkly and intent, turned inward as if they were working out chess problems in their heads.

"The druids," said Tod. The words broke the trance and a shiver danced across my shoulders. I glanced at Wynne and could tell instantly that she had felt the same. A smile of recognition lit her face in the predawn gloom.

"Are you all right?" said Tod.

Wynne laughed. "No."

Tod frowned and linked his arm through hers. "Let's go. We have to walk around the dome if we want to see the sun rise over the Heel Stone."

We began to thread our way through the crowd to the southwest side of the dome. The space between the shells was empty now and I could see that the procession of druids had surrounded the outer sarsen circle. All turned toward the northeast to face the Heel Stone and the approaching sunrise.

"This is it," said Tod. "We're right on the axis."

The fat woman standing next to me was glowing. Except for knee-high studded leather leggings, she was naked. Her skin gave off a soft green light; her nipples and all of her body hair were bright orange. When she moved the rolls of fat gleamed like moonlit waves. At first I thought she was another hallucination. Something was wrong.

"Do you see her too?" Wynne whispered.

"She's a glowworm." Tod made no effort to keep his voice down and the green woman stared at us.

Wynne nodded as if she had understood. I cupped my hand to her ear. "What's a glowworm?"

"She's had a luminescent body tint," said Wynne.

Tod laughed as he pointed his lenses at her. "Do you know how carcinogenic that stuff is? Eighty percent mortality after five years."

She waddled over to him. "It's my body, Flash. Ain't it?" I was surprised when she slipped a hand around Tod's waist. "Would that be a vid you're making, Flash? Me in it?"

"Sure," he said. "Everybody gets to be famous for ten minutes. You know the camera loves you, glowworm. That's why you got tinted."

She giggled. "You with someone, Flash?"

"Not now, glowworm. The sun's coming."

Amateur and professional photographers began to jostle for position around us. Tod, using his elbows with cunning, would not be moved. The sun's bright lip appeared over the trees to the northeast. Inside the dome, druids raised horns and blew a tribute to the new season. Outside there were inarticulate shouts and polite applause. A man with a long beard rolled on the ground, barking.

"But there's no alignment," some fool was complaining. "The sun's in the wrong place."

The sun had cleared the trees and was crawling across the brick-colored horizon. I shut my eyes and still I could see it: blood red, flashing blue, veins pulsing across its surface.

"Sun's not wrong," said a man with a camera where his

head should have been. "Stonehenge doesn't really line up. It's a myth."

Although I did not immediately recognize the speaker, I knew I hated that mocking voice. When I opened my eyes again the sun had already climbed several times its diameter into the sky. After a few minutes it passed over the Heel Stone at the opposite end of Stonehenge. And seemed to hang there, propped in the sky by a single untrimmed sarsen, five meters tall. My view was framed by the uprights and lintels of the outer circle. It was as if I were standing on the backbone of the world. I was spellbound; men in skins had built a structure that could capture a star. The crowd was silent, or perhaps I had ceased to perceive anything but my vision of sunfire and stone. Then the moment passed. The sun continued to climb.

"Looks like a doorway," said the glowworm. "Into another world." She seemed very pale in the light of dawn.

Doorway. The word throbbed in my mind. *Doorway raised on doorway.* Someone said, "I make it about four degrees off." I saw people crouching around the barking man.

"Tony?" A strange and beautiful woman had taken my hand. Her voice echoed and distorted: a baby's inexact chatter, the joyful cry of a child. I blinked at her in the soft light. Blue-skinned, scalp smooth, she was dressed in silver: the setting for a sapphire. Her face, a jewel. Precious. I was falling in love.

"Who are you?" I could not remember.

"They come in waves," she said. I did not understand.

"He's so far out, he's breathing space," said the camera head with the mocking voice.

"Who are you?" I held up her hand, clasped in mine.

"It's me, Tony." The beautiful woman was laughing. I wanted to laugh too. "Wynne."

Wynne. I said the word over and over to myself, shuddering with pleasure at each repetition. Wynne, my Wynne.

"And I'm Tod, remember?" The camera head looked disgusted. "Christ, am I glad I palmed that stuff. Look at you two. She can't stop laughing and you're catatonic. How was I supposed to work? Do you realize how twisted the two of you are?"

Tod. I battered through yet another wave of hallucinations, trying to remember. "You didn't take . . . ?"

"Hell no!" Tod turned. I felt the lense eyes probing me, recording, judging. "Creative control, right? Besides, what difference does it make? No one is going to be able to look into my mind and know I'm not twisted. That's voodoo, Tony, magic. There is no magic, remember?"

There was a tiny red light flashing in the middle of Tod's helmet. "Get away, you shit," I said. "Not me in your damn . . . your goddamn . . ."

"This was your idea."

"Turn it off!"

"Why should I?" I could see a smile beneath his visor. "You're the star, Tony. Everybody loves you."

"Tod," said Wynne. "Don't."

The red light went out. He flipped up the visor and held out his hand to her. She let go of me and went to him. "Let's take a walk, Wynne," he said. "We need to talk."

As I watched them stroll away together I felt as if I were turning to stone. I had lost her. The crowd swirled around them and they were gone.

"U bent toch Tony Cage, niet waar?"

I stared without comprehension at a middle-aged woman wearing a mood dress. It changed from blue to silvery green as she called to her husband. "Piet, kom eens gauw!" A paunchy man in isothermals responded to her summons. "You are Tony Cage, are you?"

I could not speak. The man shook my nerveless hand. "We have seen you on telelink. Many times. We're Dutch from Rotterdam. We have tried all your flashes."

"But Soar is still our favorite. I'm Magriet. We are retired." The dress lightened from lime to apple green. I could not look her in the face.

"I am Piet. You look pretty twisted, yes? What are you on? Some new thing?"

Heads were turning. "Sorry." My tongue was stone. "Not feeling well, have to . . ." By then I was stumbling away from my manic fans. Luckily, they did not follow me.

I do not remember how long I wandered through the crowd or how I felt or exactly what I was looking for. A terrible suspicion nagged at me. Maybe there was something wrong with the Share? Something I had missed? Eventually the druids finished their service and the dome was opened to the public. I drifted on the flood tide of humanity and at last washed up on the Slaughter Stone.

The Slaughter Stone was a slab of lichen-covered sarsen about thirty meters away from the outer circle: a good place to sit and watch, away from the hurly-burly around the standing stones. The surface of the stone was pitted and rough. It was once thought that these natural bowls were used to catch sacrificial blood—both human and animal. Another myth, since the stone had once stood upright. Now we were two fallen things, the stone and I, our foundations undermined, purposes lost. We existed in roughly the same state of consciousness. I thought sandstone thoughts; my understanding was that of rock.

The sun climbed. I was hot. The combination of body heat and solar gain had overloaded the dome's air-conditioning. I did nothing. The waves of hallucinations seemed to have receded. People had climbed the outer circle and were walking along the lintels. One woman started to strip. The crowd clapped and urged her on. "Vestal virgin, vestal virgin," they cried. A little boy nearby watched avidly as he squeezed cider from a disposable juice bulb. I was thirsty; I did nothing. The boy dropped the bulb on the ground when he had finished and wandered off. A bobby stepped out from beneath the circle to watch as the stripper removed her panties. The crowd roared and she gave them an extra treat. She was an amputee; she unstrapped her prosthetic forearm and waved it over her head. The world was going mad and trying to take me with it. I loaded the neuroleptic into the pressure syringe and poked it into my forearm.

"Tony."

There was no Tony. There was only stone.

"Hey, Tony." A stranger shook me. "It's Tod. There's something wrong with Wynne! We need your help."

"In waves." I started to laugh. "They come in waves." Now I knew. Hallucinations. But not with Share. I was laughing so hard I fell backward onto the stone. "Belotti!" Poor Bobby had finally struck—after all these years. The drug was pure but the dose . . . too high. Hallucinogen. Dangerous, he had said. Unpredictable. That unpredictable old . . . "Bastard!" I was gasping for air.

"He needs oxygen. Quick."

"Look at his eyes!"

When the last wave hit me, I held onto the stone. The crowd disappeared. The dome vanished. The car park, the A360, all signs of civilization—gone. Then the stones awoke and began to dance. Those that had fallen righted themselves. A road erupted from the grass. The Slaughter Stone bucked and threw me as it stood. A twin appeared beside it, a gate. I wanted to pass through, walk down the road, see Stonehenge whole. But the magic held me back. In an overly explained world, only the subtlest and most powerful magic of all had survived. The magic that works exclusively in the mind. A curse. A dead and illiterate race had placed a curse on the imagination of the world. In its rude magnificence Stonehenge challenged all to understand its meaning, yet its secret was forever locked behind impenetrable walls of time.

"Lay him down here."

"Tony!"

"He can't hear you."

Suddenly they were all around me, all of those who had once been where I was now. The politicians and writers and painters and historians and scientists and the tourists—yes, even the tourists who, in search of an hour's diversion, had found instead a timeless mystery. All of those who had accepted Stonehenge's challenge and had fallen under the curse. They had striven with words and images to find the secret, yet all they had seen was themselves. The sun grew very bright then, and the sides of the stones turned silver. I could see all the ghosts reflected in the shining stones. I could see myself.

"Tony, can you hear me? Wynne's having some kind of fit. You have to tell us."

I saw myself in the Slaughter Stone. What did it matter? I couldn't pretend any longer. I had already lost her. My image seemed to shimmer. I looked like a ghost; the thought of death did not displease me. To be as a stone.

"Wake up, Tony. You have to save her. She's your *daughter*, damn it!"

"No." At that moment my reflection in the stone shifted and I saw my mirror image. Wynne. In pain. I realized she had been in pain for a long time, had hidden it behind a veneer of chemicals and sarcasm. I should have known; I did now. Through the surreal logic of the hallucination, I was forced into Wynne's mind. I could actually feel her pain and was racked by the certain knowledge that I was its source. *She was my daughter.* It was no longer the Share, it was Stonehenge itself that forced me to suffer along with her, Stonehenge that created the magic landscape where the veil of words was parted and mind could touch mind directly. Or so it seemed to me. A sound tore through the vision. My scream. "No!" Stones fell, disappeared, but I could not escape the pain. All the lies fell away. In a moment of terrible grace, I realized what I had done. It didn't matter what I had told myself. *If she thought she was my daughter, then she was.*

I realized that Tod was still shooting when I heard the whir of microcam lenses. No doubt he was zooming in for a closeup of drool trickling from my mouth. He stood above me, in another world. Much closer was a medic checking readouts. There were electrodes taped to my head and wrist. I blinked, trying to remember what it was that Tod wanted.

"What did you give her?" said the medic.

Wynne. My hands trembled as I fumbled the pressure syringe from my pocket. "This . . . a poke . . . neuroleptic. She needs it now. Now!"

The medic was very young; he seemed doubtful. I sat up, tore the electrode from my forehead. "Do you know who I am?" The world was spinning. "Do it!"

The medic looked briefly at Tod, then took the syringe and ran back toward the dome's main entrance. The red light above Tod's lenses was winking obscenely at me.

"What did you say to her?" I struggled to stand up.

He put his arm around my shoulder. "Are you all right?"

"Damn it, Tod." I shook him off. "If you really want to help me, stop recording."

He considered, then dropped his hand to the system unit to pause the microcam. He did not, however, raise his visor.

"You said it to her?" I asked. "That she was my daughter?"

"We've both said it. It's all we've been talking about the last few days."

"You must know we were lovers."

His mouth tightened, he made no attempt to hide his disapproval.

"She came to me one night," I said. "She was fifteen, we were both twisted. I couldn't . . . didn't send her away."

He swiveled the helmet. Was he already framing the next shot? "She told me two months ago," he said, "just after you left for the States. She said she had figured out that sex was what you wanted most from her, but you couldn't bring yourself to ask. She claims it was her fault, because she seduced you. And because after a while, she enjoyed it."

I kept waiting for Tod's maddening self-assurance to crumble. He didn't deserve to know about us.

"Once she and I got together, it was hard for her to pretend you weren't her father, because I just assumed that's what you were. Finally she realized sleeping with you had been wrong. Sick. And I believe she's mostly sorry for what happened, I really do. Just yesterday she was crying, saying she was afraid she was some kind of monster. But . . ." To our left, a woman screamed; Tod spun around to see what was happening. When the scream dissolved into twisted laughter, he snorted in disgust. "After we left you this morning, we started arguing. She was defending you, as usual. She still loves you, don't ask me why. Anyway, it made me mad so I said something." He was not apologizing; I doubted he knew how. "It's your drug, Tony—turns the truth into a blunt instrument. I told her part of her was proud to have screwed her own father. That she secretly wanted to be a monster. Then she had the fit."

"But that's not the truth!" Now that I had seen myself through her eyes, I was afraid I would never be able to stop seeing myself again. "Don't you understand? I'm the monster, not her."

"Sure." He had turned the microcam back on.

"Where is she? Take me to her." We started to walk. "You don't really love her, do you Tod?"

"Maybe I don't. I thought I did." He shrugged. "It worries me when she does strange things and then has no idea why. And I don't know how to take her self-destructive streak."

Five bobbies rushed past us with shock sticks raised. The crowd was surging around the eastern edge of the dome. "Look Tony, I've got a vid to make, okay? You go out through the main entrance and look for the National Health Service lorry. They've got her in there."

Wynne was unconscious but the fit had passed and the medic said her signs were good. I rode with her to the hospital in Salisbury. Tod showed up late in the afternoon and then sat in the lobby with his head in the Vidstar helmet, reviewing the memory dots he had shot that day. I squirmed beside him, afraid he would start a conversation. Despite the neuroleptics, the drug was still at work in me. I did not want to talk; words triggered memories that riddled me with pain. When Wynne at last regained consciousness, Tod went in to see her. Alone.

"I'm not here," I said. "Tell her I've gone away."

"I can't do that."

"Tell her!"

They gave Tod only ten minutes. I kept worrying that he would call me in.

"Is she all right?"

He shrugged. "Seems to be, but they're going to keep her overnight. You owe me one, Tony. I lied for you, told her you went back to your room to sleep it off. I said you'd be in tomorrow."

"No, I'm leaving." I offered him my hand. "You won't be seeing me again."

"What are you talking about?" He picked up his helmet and tucked it under his arm. I let my hand drop back to my side. "You have to stay. I'm taking the train back up to London tonight. I want to start editing this stuff while it's still fresh."

"You don't understand. You win; she's yours."

"No, *you* don't understand. She's not yours to give away—even if I do want her. Look, she saw something this morning, something that pushed her right to the edge. If you just disappear, she just might go over. You two have to work this out together. You're her father. It's your responsibility."

I shuddered; he might just as well have punched me in the stomach. "You're asking me to be some kind of hero, Tod. Problem is, I'm a coward. Always have been. I saw something today too, and I'll spend the rest of my life trying to forget it. She'll be better off without me."

"I haven't got time for this." Tod shook his head; I think I had finally amazed him. "I have a train to catch. I don't care about your problems, Tony. But if you leave she's going to wake up tomorrow and there will be nobody. Okay? So if you care about her at all . . ."

"I told you, I *love* her," I said. "Like I love myself."

I caught the shuttle that night from Heathrow to Shannon. I knew Tod was right; it was cruel and selfish to run away. Wynne was entitled to think what she wanted about me.

She would never know how much it hurt me to give her up this way. But I couldn't trust myself not to hurt her again. I had brought her up to love only me, never thinking about what she might want. Or need. If I was escaping, it was into pain. I hoped she would understand. Eventually. Yesterday I put my affairs in order. I assigned a fortune in WA stock to her. I made a vid, said good-bye.

•   •   •

The memories slowly shift and fade, like the chill mist that clings in the morning to the bony hills of County Galway. I don't know whether seventy years will be enough to escape myself. Or her. Very cold now. I'll never see Wynne again. My beautiful. But I'll be at peace. No pain. Sleep soon, the inscrutable sleep of stones.

2114

Peter

I was already twitching by the time they strapped me down. Nasty pleasure and beautiful pain crackled through me, branching and rebranching like lightning. Extreme feelings are hard to tell apart when you have a flood of endorphins spilling across your brain. Another spasm shot down my legs and curled my toes. I moaned. The stiffs wore surgical masks that hid their mouths, but I knew they were smiling. They hated me because my mom could afford to have me stunted. When I really was just a kid I didn't understand that. Now I hated them back; it helped me get through the therapy. We had a very clean transaction going here. No secrets between us.

Even though it hurts, getting stunted is still an unbelievable flash. As I unlived my life, I overdosed on dying feelings and experiences. My body wasn't big enough to hold them all; I thought I was going to explode. I must've screamed because I could see the laugh lines crinkling around the stiffs' eyes. You don't have to worry about laugh lines after they twank your genes to reset the mitotic limits of your cyclins. My face was smooth and I was going to be twelve years old forever, or at least as long as mom kept paying for my rejuvenation.

I giggled as the short one leaned over me and pricked her catheter into my neck. Even through the mask, I could smell her breath. She reeked of dead meat.

• • •

Getting stunted always left me wobbly and thick, but this time I felt like last Tuesday's pizza. One of the stiffs had to roll me out of recovery in a wheelchair.

The lobby looked like a furniture showroom. Even the plants had been newly waxed. There was nothing to remind the clients that they were bags of blood and piss. You're all biological machines now, said the lobby, clean as space-station lettuce. A scattering of people sat on the hard chairs. Stennie and Comrade were fidgeting by the elevators. They looked as if they were thinking of rearranging the furniture—like maybe into a pile in the middle of the room. Even before they waved, the stiff seemed to know that they were waiting for me.

Comrade smiled. "Zdrast'ye."

"You okay, Mr. Boy?" said Stennie. Stennie was a grapefruit-yellow stenonychosaurus with a brown underbelly. His razor-clawed toes clicked against the slate floor as he walked.

"He's still a little weak," said the stiff, as he set the chair's parking brake. He strained to act nonchalant, not realizing that Stennie enjoys being stared at. "He needs rest. Are you his brother?" he said to Comrade.

Comrade appeared to be a teenaged spike neck with a head of silky black hair that hung to his waist. He wore a window coat on which twenty-three different talking heads chattered. He could pass for human, even though he was really a Panasonic. "Nyet," said Comrade. "I'm just another one of his hallucinations."

The poor stiff gave him a dry, nervous cough that might've been meant as a chuckle. He was probably wondering whether Stennie wanted to take me home or eat me for lunch. I always thought that the way Stennie got reshaped was more funny-looking than fierce—a python that had rear-ended an ostrich. But even though he was a head shorter than me, he did have enormous eyes and a mouthful of serrated teeth. He stopped next to the wheelchair and rose up to his full height. "I appreciate everything you've done." Stennie offered the stiff his spindly three-fingered hand to shake. "Sorry if he caused any trouble."

The stiff took it gingerly, then shrieked and flew backwards. I mean, he jumped almost a meter off the floor. Everyone in the lobby turned and Stennie opened his hand and waved the joy buzzer. He slapped his tail against the slate in triumph. Stennie's sense of humor was extreme, but then he was only fourteen years old.

• • •

Stennie's parents had given him the Nissan Alpha for his twelfth birthday and we had been customizing it ever since. We installed blue mirror glass and Stennie painted scenes from the Late Cretaceous on the exterior body armor. We ripped out all the seats, put in a wall-to-wall gel mat and a fridge and a microwave and a screen and a minidish. Comrade had even put an illegal patch on the carbrain so that we could override in an emergency and actually steer the Alpha ourselves with a joystick. It would've been cramped, but we could've lived in Stennie's car if our parents had let us.

"You okay there, Mr. Boy?" said Stennie.

"Mmm." As I watched the trees whoosh past in the rain, I pretended that the car was standing still and the world was passing me by.

"Think of something to do, okay?" Stennie had the car and all and he was fun to play with, but ideas were not his specialty. He was probably smart for a dinosaur. "I'm bored."

"Leave him alone, will you?" Comrade said.

"He hasn't said anything yet." Stennie stretched and nudged me with his foot. "Say something." He had legs like a horse: yellow skin stretched tight over long bones and stringy muscle.

"Prosrees! He just had his genes twanked, you jack."
Comrade always took good care of me. Or tried to. It was
what wiseguys did. "Remember what that's like? He's in damage control."

"Maybe I should go to socialization," Stennie said.
"Aren't they having a dance this afternoon?"

"You're talking to me?" said the Alpha. "You haven't
earned enough learning credits to socialize. You're a quiz behind and forty-five minutes short of E-class. You haven't
linked since . . ."

"Just shut up and drive me over." Stennie and the Alpha
didn't get along. He thought the car was too strict. "I'll make
up the plugging quiz, okay?" He probed a mess of empty
juice boxes and snack wrappers with his foot. "Anyone see
my comm anywhere?"

Stennie's schoolcomm was wedged behind my cushion.
"You know," I said, "I can't take much more of this." I
leaned forward, wriggled it free, and handed it over.

"Of what, poputchik?" said Comrade. "Joyriding? Listening to the lizard here?"

"Being stunted. Being me."

Stennie flipped up the screen of his comm and went on
line with the school's computer. "You guys help me, okay?"
He retracted his claws and tapped at the oversized keyboard.

"It's extreme while you're on the table," I said, "but now
I feel empty. Like I've lost myself."

"You'll get over it," said Stennie. "First question: When
was the Crazy Spring?"

"Two thousand eighty-one, of course," said Comrade.

"The Human Charter was written by . . . President Sullivan?"

"Da."

"Haile Selassie was that king of Egypt who the Marleys
claim is God, right? Name the Cold Wars: Nicaragua,
Angola . . . Korea was the first." Typing was hard work for
Stennie; he didn't have enough fingers for it. "One was
something like Venezuela. Or something."

"Sure it wasn't Venice?"

"Or Venus?" I said, but Stennie wasn't paying attention.

"All right, I know that one. And that. The old USSR built the first space station. Ronald Reagan—he was the president who dropped the bomb?"

Comrade reached inside his coat and pulled out an envelope. "I got you something, Mr. Boy. A get-well present for your collection."

I opened it and scoped a picture of a naked dead man on a stainless steel table. The print had a DI verification grid on it, which meant this was the real thing, not a composite. Just above the corpse's left eye there was a neat hole. It was rimmed with purple that had faded to bruise blue. He had blondish-brown hair on his head and chest, skin the color of dried mayonnaise. He appeared relieved to be dead. "This guy looks familiar." I liked Comrade's present. It was extreme. "Who is he?"

"Don't you recognize him? That's Tony Cage. Your grandfather. The one who invented flash."

"Oh yeah, right." I remembered now. Years ago, Comrade had hunted up some vids of him. He was sort of famous in his day, which had been a long time ago. I had never met him and my mom never talked about him. They must've had a fight or something; she didn't seem to like him much. We didn't have anything of his at home—no Cage family heirlooms. Of course, he *had* killed himself when I was five. Not the sort of relative you stick on the mantel over the fireplace. I shivered as I stared at the dead man. I could hear myself breathing and feel the blood squirting through my arteries. "Nice wound," I said. This was the kind of stuff we were not even supposed to imagine, much less look at. The fact that we were related made it all the more delicious. Too bad they had cleaned him up.

"How much did this cost me?"

"You don't want to know."

"Hey!" Stennie thumped his tail against the side of the

car. "I'm taking a quiz here and you guys are drooling over porn. When was the First World Depression?"

"Who cares?" I slipped the picture back into the envelope and grinned at Comrade.

"Well, let me see then." Stennie snatched the envelope. "He looks just like you, poor jack."

"Yeah, and you look like a handbag I saw at the mall."

"You know what I think, Mr. Boy? I think this corpse jag you're on is kind of sick. And you're going to get in trouble if you let Comrade keep breaking laws. Isn't this picture private?"

"Privacy is twenty-first-century thinking, Stennie. It's all information and information should be accessible. Besides, this is part of my family album." I held out my hand. "But if glasnost bothers you, give it up." I wiggled my fingers.

Comrade snickered. Stennie pulled out the picture, glanced at it, and hissed. "You're scaring me, Mr. Boy."

His schoolcomm beeped as it posted his score on the quiz and he sailed the envelope back across the car at me. "Not Venezuela, Vietnam. Hey, *Truman* dropped the plugging bomb. Reagan was the one who spent all the money. What's wrong with you dumbscuts? Now I owe school another fifteen minutes."

"Hey, if you don't make it look good, they'll know you had help." Comrade laughed.

"What's with this dance anyway?" I said. "You don't dance." I picked Comrade's present up and tucked it into my shirt pocket. "You find yourself a cush or something, lizard boy?"

"Maybe." Stennie couldn't blush, but sometimes when he was embarrassed the loose skin under his jaw quivered. Even though he'd been reshaped into a dinosaur, he was still growing up. "Maybe I am getting a little. What's it to you?"

"If you're getting it," I said, "it's got to be microscopic." This was a bad sign; I was losing him to his plug, just like all the other pals. No way I wanted to start over with someone new. I had been alive for twenty years now. I was running out of things to say to fourteen-year-olds.

As the Alpha pulled up to the socialization center, I scoped the crowd waiting for the doors to open for third shift. Although there were a handful of stunted kids, a pair of gorilla brothers who were football stars, and Freddy the Teddy—a bear who had furry hands instead of real paws—the majority of students at New Canaan High looked more or less normal. Most working stiffs thought that people who had their genes twanked to the extreme were freaks.

"Come get me at five-fifteen," Stennie told the Alpha. "In the meantime, take these guys wherever they want to go." He opened the door. "You rest up, Mr. Boy, okay?"

"What?" I wasn't paying attention. "Sure." I had just seen the most beautiful girl in the world.

She leaned against one of the concrete columns of the portico, chatting with a couple other kids. Her hair was long and nut-colored and the ends twinkled. She was wearing a loose black robe over mirror skintights. Her schoolcomm dangled from a strap around her wrist. She appeared to be seventeen, maybe eighteen. But of course, appearances could be deceiving.

Girls had never interested me much, but I couldn't help but admire this one. "Wait, Stennie! Who's that?" I think she noticed me staring. "With the hair?"

"She's new—has one of those names you can't pronounce." He showed me his teeth as he got out. "Hey, Mr. Boy, you're stunted. You haven't got what she wants."

He kicked the door shut, lowered his head, and crossed in front of the car. When he walked he looked like he was trying to squash a bug with each step. His snaky tail curled high behind him for balance, his twiggy little arms dangled. When the new girl saw him, she pointed and smiled. Or maybe she was pointing at me.

"Where to?" said the car.

"I don't know." I sank low into my seat and pulled out Comrade's present again. "Home, I guess."

I wasn't the only one in my family with twanked genes. My mom was a three-quarter-scale replica of the Statue of Liberty. Originally she wanted to be full-sized, but then she would have been the tallest thing in New Canaan, Connecticut. She applied for a zoning variance; when the planning board turned her down, her lawyers took the town to court. Mom's claim was that since she was born human, her freedom of form was protected by the Thirtieth Amendment. However, the form she wanted was a curtain of reshaped cells that would hang on a forty-two-meter-high ferroplastic skeleton. Her structure, said the planning board, was clearly subject to building codes and zoning laws. Eventually they reached an out-of-court settlement, which was why Mom was only as tall as an eleven-story building.

She complied with the town's request for a setback of five hundred meters from Route 123. As Stennie's Alpha drove us down the long driveway, Comrade broadcast the recognition code that told the robot sentries that we were okay. One thing Mom and the town agreed on from the start: no tourists. Sure, she loved publicity, but she was also very fragile. In some places her skin was only a centimeter thick. Chunks of ice falling from her crown could punch holes in her.

The end of our driveway cut straight across the lawn to Mom's granite-paved foundation pad. To the west of the plaza, directly behind her, was a utility building faced in ashlar that housed her support systems. Mom had been bioengineered to be pretty much self-sufficient. She was green not only to match the real Statue of Liberty but also because she was photosynthetic. She lived on a yearly truckload of fertilizer, water from the well, and 150 kilowatts of electricity a day. Except for emergency surgery, the only time she needed maintenance was in the fall, when her outer cells tended to flake off and had to be swept up and carted away.

Stennie's Alpha dropped us off by the doorbone in the right heel and then drove off to do whatever cars do when nobody is using them. Mom's greeter was waiting in the reception area inside the foot.

"Peter." She stood behind one of Bonivard's stupid wheelchairs, beaming. "How are you, Peter?"

"Tired." Even though Mom knew I didn't like to be called that, I kissed the air toward her. Peter Cage was her name for me; I had given it up years ago.

"You poor boy." She came around the wheelchair. "Let me see you." She held me at arm's length and brushed her fingers against my cheek. "You don't look a day over twelve. Oh, they do such good work—don't you think?" She squeezed my shoulder. "Are you happy with it?"

I think Mom meant well, but she never did understand me. Especially when she talked to me with her greeter bioremote. I wormed out of her grip and fell back onto a couch.

"*Peter.* I brought this wheelchair down especially for you." She pouted. "You used to love to ride the chairs."

"That was ten years ago. What's to eat?"

"Doboys, noodles, fries." She bent over impulsively and gave me a kiss that I didn't want. "Whatever you want." I never paid much attention to the greeter; she was lighter than air. She was always smiling and asking five questions in a row without waiting for an answer and flitting around the room. It wore me out just watching her. Naturally, everything I said or did was cute, even if I was trying to be obnoxious. It was no fun being cute. Today Mom had her greeter wearing a dark blue dress and a white apron. The greeter's umbilical was too short to stretch up to the kitchen, so why was she wearing an apron? "I'm really, really glad you're home," she said.

"I'll take some cinnamon doboys." I kicked off my shoes and rubbed my bare feet through the dense black hair on the floor. "And a beer."

Although all Mom's bioremotes had different personalities and different faces, most were variations on the same theme. Nanny was a kindly old Mom. I liked her all right; she was simple but at least she listened. The two lovers were fat, jolly Mom and Mom-as-a-man. They were hard to talk to because they were usually too busy eyeing each other to notice me. Cook was fussy mom; the housekeeper was Mom the drudge. The exception, of course, was the Bonivard remote, but then he was so scrambled he was worthless. I had always wondered what it'd be like to talk directly to Mom's main brain up in the head, because then she wouldn't be filtered through a remote. She'd be herself.

"Cook is making you some nice hot broth to go with your doboys," said the greeter. "Nanny says you shouldn't be eating dessert all the time."

"Hey, did I ask for broth?"

At first Comrade had hung back while the greeter was fussing over me. Then he slid along the wrinkled pink walls of the reception room toward the port where the greeter's umbilical was attached. When she started in about the broth I saw him lean against the port. Carelessly, you know? At the same time he stepped on the greeter's umbilical, crimping the furry black cord. She gasped and the smile flattened horribly on her face, as if her lips were two ropes someone had suddenly yanked taut. Her head jerked toward the umbilical port.

"E-Excuse me." She was twitching.

"What?" Comrade glanced down at his foot as if it belonged to a stranger. "Oh, sorry." He pushed away from the wall and strolled across the room toward us. Although he seemed apologetic, about half the heads on his window coat were laughing.

The greeter flexed her cheek muscles. "You'd better watch out for your wiseguy, Peter," she said. "It's going to get you in trouble someday."

Mom didn't like Comrade much, even though she had given him to me when I was first stunted. She got mad when I snuck him down to Manhattan a couple of years ago to have him infected with an autonomy virus that destroyed most of his behavioral regulators. For a while afterward, he used to ask me before he broke the law. Now he was out on his own. He got caught once and she warned me he was out of control. But she still threw money at the people until they went away.

"Trouble?" I said. "Sounds like fun." I thought we were too rich for trouble. Bonivard had left Mom a castle full of money when he died, and she had added several wings of her own investing in cognizors. I stood and Comrade picked up my shoes for me. "And he's not just another wiseguy; he's my best friend." I put my arms around his shoulder. "Tell cook I'll eat in my rooms."

· · ·

The long climb up the circular stairs tired me out and I was in no mood for Bonivard, who had the floor just under mine. Luckily, all I had to endure was the quote of the day.

He was sitting in a low-slung racing wheelchair under the archway that led to his suite. "Let me not to the marriage of true minds admit impediments . . ." he began.

"You're the only impediment around here," interrupted Comrade.

He bowed his head and let us pass. "The thousand injuries of Fortunato I had borne as best I could," he muttered, "but when he ventured upon insult, I vowed revenge."

We scurried on up the stairs before he could change his mind—or lose it again.

When my roombrain sensed I had come in, it turned on all the windows and blinked my message indicator. One reason I still lived in Mom was that she kept out of my rooms. I had made her promise me total security, otherwise I would've moved out. She wasn't happy about it and whenever I came out of my rooms she would always have one or another of her busybody remotes waiting to chat. But I was safe up here, even from the housekeeper. Comrade did everything for me.

I sent him for supper, perched on the edge of the bed to scope my messages, and cleared the nearest window of army ants foraging for meat through some Angolan jungle. The first message in the queue was from a gray-haired stiff wearing a navy blue corporate uniform. "Hello, Mr. Cage. My name is Weldon Montross and I'm with Datasafe. I'd like to arrange a meeting with you at your convenience. Call my DI number, 2408-966-3286. I hope to hear from you soon."

"What the hell is Datasafe?"

The roombrain ran a search. "Datasafe offers services in encryption and information security. It was incorporated in the state of Delaware in two thousand thirteen. Estimated billings last year were 340 million dollars. Headquarters are in San Jose, California, with branch offices in White Plains, New York, and Chevy Chase, Maryland. Foreign offices . . ."

"Are they trying to sell me something or what?"

The roombrain didn't offer an answer. "Delete," I said. "Next?"

Weldon Montross was back again, looking exactly as he had before. I wondered if he were using a virtual image. "Hello, Mr. Cage. I've just discovered that you've been admitted to the Thayer Clinic for rejuvenation therapy. Believe me when I say that I very much regret having to bother you during your convalescence and I would not do so if this were not a matter of importance. Would you please contact Department of Information number 2408-966-3286 as soon as you're able?"

"You're a pro, Weldon, I'll say that for you." Prying client information out of the Thayer Clinic wasn't easy, but then the guy was no doubt some kind of op. He was way too polite to be a salesman. What did Datasafe want with me? "Any more messages from him?"

"No," said the roombrain.

"Well, delete this one too and if he calls back tell him I'm too busy unless he's wants to tell me what he's after." I stretched out on my bed. "Next?" The gel mattress shivered as it took my weight.

Happy Lurdane was having a smash party on the twentieth but Happy was a boring cush, and there was a bill from the pet store for the iguanas that I paid and a warning from the SPCA that I deleted and a special offer for preferred customers from my favorite fireworks company that I saved to look at later, and Chip, an old pal who had grown up, was about to ask for another loan when I paused him and deleted, and last of all there was a message from Stennie, time-stamped ten minutes ago.

"Hey, Mr. Boy, if you're feeling better I've lined up a VR party for tonight." He didn't quite fit into the school's tele-link booth; all I could see was his toothy face and the long yellow curve of his neck. "Bunch of us have reserved some time on Playroom. Come in disguise. That new kid said she'd link, so scope her yourself if you're so hot for it. I found out her name but it's kind of unpronounceable. Tree-something Joplin. Anyway, it's at seven o'clock, meet on channel seventeen, password is *warhead*. Hey, did you send my car back yet? Later." He faded.

"Sounds like fun." Comrade kicked the doorbone open and backed through, balancing a tray loaded with soup and fresh doboys and a mug of cold beer. "Are we going?" He set it onto the nightstand next to my bed.

"Maybe." I yawned. It felt good to be in my own bed. "Flush the damn soup, would you?" I reached over for a doboy and felt something crinkle in my jacket pocket. I pulled out Tony Cage's picture. About the only thing I didn't like about it was that the eyes were shut. You feel dirtier when the corpse stares back. "So this is what I'd look like if I grew up."

"What, dead?"

"Maybe that's what gives it the extra tickle. The poor jack on the slab is sort of me." I propped the picture beside the tray. "How did you get it, anyway? Must've taken some snaking."

"Three days' worth. Encryption wasn't all that tough but there were layers of it." Comrade admired the picture with me as he picked up the bowl of soup. "I ended up buying about ten hours from Cognico to crack the file. Kind of pricey but since you were getting stunted, I had nothing else to do.''

"You see the messages from that security op?'' I bit into a doboy. "Maybe you were a little sloppy.'' The hot cinnamon scent tickled my nose.

"Ya v'rot ego ebal!'' He laughed. "So some stiff is cranky? Plug him if he can't take a joke.''

I said nothing. Comrade could be a pain sometimes. Of course I loved the picture, but he really should have been more careful. He'd made a mess and left it for me to clean up. Just what I needed. I knew I'd only get mad if I thought about it, so I changed the subject. "Well, do you think she's cute?''

"What's-her-face Joplin?'' Comrade turned abruptly toward the bathroom. "Sure, for a perdunya,'' he said over his shoulder. "Why not?'' Talking about girls made him snippy. I think he was afraid of them.

I brought my army ants back onto the window; they were swarming over a lump with brown fur. Thinking about him hanging on my elbow when I met this Tree-something Joplin made me feel weird. I listened as he poured the soup down the toilet. I wasn't myself at all. Getting stunted changes you; no one can predict how. I chugged the beer and rolled over to take a nap. It was the first time I had ever thought of leaving Comrade behind.

•　　•　　•

"VR party, Mr. Boy.'' Comrade nudged me awake. "Are we going or not?''

"Huh?'' My gut still ached from getting stunted and I woke up mean enough to chew glass. "What do you mean we?''

"Nothing.'' Comrade had that blank look he always put on when he didn't want me to know what he was thinking. Still, I could tell he was disappointed. "Are you going then?'' he said.

I stretched—ouch! "Yeah, sure, get my joysuit.'' My

bones felt brittle as candy. "And stop acting sorry for yourself, wiseguy." My nasty mood had momentum; it swept me
past any regrets. "No way I'm going to lie here all night
watching you pretend you have feelings to hurt."

"Tak tochno." He saluted and went straight to the closet.
I got out of bed and hobbled to the bathroom.

"This is a costume party, remember," Comrade called.
"What are you wearing?"

"Whatever." Even his efficiency irked me; sometimes he
did too much for me. "You decide." I needed to get away
from him for a while.

Playroom was a virtual-reality service on our local net. If
you wanted to throw a party at Versailles or Monticello or San
Simeon, all you had to do was link—if you could get a reservation.

I came back to the bedroom and Comrade stepped up
behind me, holding the joysuit. I shrugged into it, velcroed
the front seam, and eyed myself in the nearest window. He
had synthesized some kid-sized armor in the German Gothic
style. My favorite. It was made of polished silver, with great
fluting and scalloping. He'd even programmed a little glow
into the image so that on the window I looked like a walking
night light. There was an armet helmet with a red ostrich
plume; the visor was tipped up so I could see my face. I raised
my arm and the joysuit translated the movement to the window so that my armored image waved back.

"Try a few steps," he said.

Although I could move easily in the lightweight joysuit,
the motion interpreter made walking in the vid armor seem
realistically awkward. Comrade had scored the sound effects,
too. Metal hinges rasped, chain mail rattled softly, and there
was a satisfying *clunk* whenever my foot hit the floor.

"Great." I clenched my fist in approval. I was awake now
and in better control of my temper. I wanted to make up but
Comrade wasn't taking the hint. I could never quite figure
out whether he was just emulating a machine or whether he
really didn't care how I treated him.

"They're starting." All the windows in the room lit up with Playroom's welcome screen. "You want privacy, so I'm leaving. No one will bother you."

"Hey, Comrade, you don't have to go . . ."

But he'd already left the room. I pulled on the VR mask and Playroom prompted me to identify myself. "Mr. Boy," I said, "DI number 1203-966-2445. I'm looking for channel 17; the password is *warhead*."

A brass band started playing "Hail to the Chief" and the title screen lit the inside of the mask:

The White House
1600 Pennsylvania Avenue
Washington, DC, USA
© 2114, Playroom Presentations
REPRODUCTION OR REUSE STRICTLY PROHIBITED

and then I was looking at a wraparound view of a VR ballroom. A caption bar opened at the top of the windows and a message scrolled across. *This is the famous East Room, the largest room in the main house. It is used for press conferences, public receptions, and entertainments.* I entered the simulation.

The East Room was decorated in bone white and gold; three chandeliers hung like cut glass mushrooms above the huge parquet floor. A band played skitter at one end of the room but no one was dancing yet. The band was Warhead, according to their drum set. I had never heard of them. Someone's disguise? I turned and the joysuit changed the view on the windows. Just ahead Santa was chatting with a forklift and a rhinoceros. Beyond, some blue cartoons were teasing Johnny America. There wasn't much furniture in the room—a couple of benches, an ugly piano, and some life-sized paintings of George and Martha. George looked like he'd just been peeled off a cash card. I stared at him too long and the closed-caption bar informed me that the painting had been painted by Gilbert Stuart and was the only White

House object dating from the mansion's first occupancy in 1800.

"Hey," I said to a girl who was on fire. "How do I get rid of the plugging tour guide?"

"Can't," she said. "When Playroom found out we were kids they turned on all their educational crap and there's no override. I kind of don't think they want us back."

"Dumbscuts." I scoped the room for something that might be Stennie. No luck. "I like the way your hair is burning." Now that it was too late, I was sorry I had to make idle party chat.

"Thanks." When she tossed her head, sparks flared and crackled. "My mom helped me program it."

"So, I've never been to the White House. Is there more than this?"

"Sure," she said. "We're supposed to have pretty much the whole first floor. Unless they shorted us. You wouldn't be Stone Kinkaid in there, would you?"

"No, not really." Even though the voice was disguised, I was pretty sure this was Happy Lurdane. I edged away from her. "I'm going to check the other rooms now. Later."

"If you run into Stone, tell him I'm looking for him."

I left the East Room and found myself in a long marble passageway with a red carpet. A dog skeleton trotted toward me. Or maybe it was supposed to be a sheep. I waved and went through a door on the other side.

Everyone in the Red Room was standing on the ceiling; I knew I'd found Stennie. Even though what they see is only a simulation, most people lock into the perceptual field of a VR as if it were real. Stand on your head long enough—even if only in your imagination—and you get airsick. It took kilo-hours of practice to learn to compensate. Upside down was one of Stennie's trademark ways of showing off.

The Red Room is an intimate parlor in the American Empire style of 1815–20 . . .

"Hi," I said. I hopped over the wainscoting and walked up the silk-covered wall to join a group of three.

"You're wearing German armor." When the boy in blue grinned at me, his cheeks dimpled. He was wearing shorts and white knee socks, a navy sweater over a white shirt. "Augsburg?" said Little Boy Blue. Fine blond hair drooped from beneath his tweed cap.

"Try Wolf of Landshut," I said. Stennie and I had spent a lot of time fighting VR wars in full armor. "Nice shorts." Stennie's costume reminded me of Christopher Robin. Terminally cute.

"It's not fair," said the snowman, who I didn't recognize. "He says this is what he actually looks like." The snowman was standing in a puddle that was dripping onto the rug below us. Great effect.

"No," said Stennie, "what I said was I *would* look like this if I hadn't done something about it, okay?"

I had not known Stennie before he was a dinosaur. "No wonder you got twanked." I wished I could have saved this image, but Playroom was copy-protected.

"You've been twanked? No joke?" The great horned owl ruffled in alarm. She had a girl's voice. "I know it's none of my business, but I've never understood why anyone would do it. Especially a kid. I mean, you can be whoever you want in a VR. And what's wrong with a good old-fashioned hallucinogen?"

She paused, waiting for someone to agree with her.

"Drugs wear off," I said. "And the Law Exchange closed Playroom for a whole week last winter. When you get twanked, it's twenty-four hours a day."

"But when you mess with your genes, you change who you are. I mean, don't you like who you are? I do."

"We're so happy for you." Stennie scowled. "What is this, mental health week?"

"We're rich," I said. "We can afford to hate ourselves."

"This may sound rude"—the owl's big blunt head swiveled from Stennie to me—"but I think that's sad."

"Yeah well, we'll try to work on some tears for you, birdie," Stennie said.

Silence. In the East Room, the band turned up the volume.

"Anyway, I've got to be going." The owl shook herself. "Hanging upside down is fine for bats, but not for me. Later." She let go of her perch and swooped out into the hall. The snowman turned to watch her go.

"You're driving them off, young man." I patted Stennie on the head. "Come on now, be nice."

"Nice makes me puke."

"You do have a bit of an edge tonight." I had trouble imagining this dainty little brat as my best friend. "Better watch out you don't cut someone."

The dog skeleton came to the doorway and called up to us. "We're supposed to dance now."

"About time." Stennie fell off the ceiling like a drop of water and splashed headfirst onto the beige Persian rug. His image went all muddy for a moment and then he reformed, upright and unharmed. "Going to skitter, tin man?"

"I need to talk to you for a moment," the snowman murmured.

"You need to?" I said.

"Dance, dance, dance," sang Stennie. "Later." He swerved after the skeleton out of the room.

The snowman said, "It's about a possible theft of information."

Right then was when I should have slammed it into reverse. Caught up with Stennie or maybe faded from Playroom altogether. But all I did was raise my hands over my head. "You got me, snowman; I confess. But society is to blame too, isn't it? You will tell the judge to go easy on me? I've had a tough life."

"This is serious."

"You're Weldon—what's your name?" Down the hall, I could hear the thud of Warhead's bass line. "Montross."

"I'll come to the point, Peter." The only acknowledgment he made was to drop the kid voice. "The firm I represent provides information security services. Last week someone tampered with the protected database of one of our clients. We have reason to believe that a certified photograph was accessed and copied. What can you tell me about this?''

"Not bad, Mr. Montross, sir. But if you were as good as you think you are, you'd know my name isn't Peter. It's Mr. Boy. And since nobody invited you to this party, maybe you'd better tell me now why I shouldn't just go ahead and have you deleted?''

"I know that you were undergoing cyclin therapy at the time of the theft so you couldn't have been directly responsible. That's in your favor. However, I also know that you can help me clear this matter up. And you need to do that, son, just as quickly as you can. Otherwise there's big trouble coming.''

"What are you going to do, tell my mommy?'' My blood started to pump; I was coming back to life.

"This is my offer. It's not negotiable. You let me sweep your files for this image. You turn over any hardcopies you've made and you instruct your wiseguy to let me do a spot reprogramming, during which I will erase his memory of this incident. After that, we'll consider the matter closed.''

"Why don't I just drop my pants and bend over while I'm at it?''

"Look, you can pretend if you want, but you're not a kid anymore. You're twenty years old. I don't believe for a minute that you're as thick as your friends out there. If you think about it, you'll realize that you can't fight us. The fact that I'm here and I know what I know means that all your personal information systems are already tapped. I'm an op, son. I could wipe your files clean any time and I will, if it comes to that. However, my orders are to be thorough. The only way I can be sure I have everything is if you cooperate.''

"You're not even real, are you, Montross? I'll bet you're some kind of sentience, nothing but cheesy old code. I've talked to elevators with more personality.''

"The offer is on the table.''

"Stick it!''

The owl flew back into the room, braked with out-stretched wings, and caught onto the armrest of the Dolley Madison sofa. "Oh, you're still here," she said, noticing us. "I didn't mean to interrupt . . ."

"Wait there," I said. "I'm coming right down."

"I'll be in touch," said the snowman. "Let me know just as soon as you change your mind." He faded.

I flipped backward off the ceiling and landed in front of her; my vid armor rang from the impact. "Owl, you just saved the evening." I knew I was showing off, but just then I was willing to forgive myself. "Thanks."

"You're welcome, I guess." She edged away from me, moving with precise little birdlike steps toward the top of the couch. "But all I was trying to do was escape the band."

"Bad?"

"And loud." Her ear tufts flattened. "Do you think shutting the door would help?"

"Sure. Follow me. We can shut lots of doors." When she hesitated, I flapped my arms like silver wings. Actually, Montross had done me a favor; when he threatened me some inner clock had begun an adrenaline tick. If this was trouble, I wanted more. I felt hypered and dangerous and I didn't care what happened next. Maybe that was why the owl flitted after me as I walked into the next room.

The sumptuous State Dining Room can seat about 130 for formal dinners. The white-and-gold decor dates from the administration of Theodore Roosevelt.

The owl glided over to the banquet table. I shut the door behind me. "Better?" Warhead still pounded on the walls.

"A little." She settled on a huge bronze doré centerpiece with a mirrored surface. "I'm going soon anyway."

"Why?"

"The band stinks, I don't know anyone, and I hate these stupid disguises."

"I'm Mr. Boy." I raised my visor and grinned at her. "All right? Now you know someone."

She tucked her wings into place and fixed me with her owlish stare. "I don't like VRs much."

"They take some getting used to."

"Why bother?" she said. "I mean, if anything can happen in a simulation, nothing matters. And I feel dumb standing in a room all alone jumping up and down and flapping my arms. Besides, this joysuit is hot and I'm renting it by the hour."

"The trick is not to look at yourself," I said. "Just watch the screens and use your imagination."

"Reality is less work. You look like a little kid."

"Is that a problem?"

"Mr. Boy? What kind of name is that anyway?"

I wished she would blink. "A made-up name. But then all names are made up, aren't they?"

"Didn't I see you at school Wednesday? You were the one who dropped off the dinosaur."

"My friend Stennie." I pulled out a chair and sat facing her. "Who you probably hate because he's twanked."

"That was him on the ceiling, wasn't it? Listen, I'm sorry about what I said. I'm new here. I'd never met anyone like him before I came to New Canaan. I mean, I'd heard of re-shaping and all—getting twanked. But where I used to live, everybody was pretty much the same."

"Where was that, Squirrel Crossing, Nebraska?"

"Close." She laughed. "Elkhart; it's in Indiana."

The reckless ticking in my head slowed. Talking to her made it easy to forget about Montross. "You want to leave the party?" I said. "We could go into discreet."

"Just us?" She sounded doubtful. "Right now?"

"Why not? You said you weren't staying. We could get rid of these disguises. And the music."

She was silent for a moment. Maybe people in Elkhart, Indiana, didn't ask one another into discreet unless they had met in Sunday school or the 4-H Club.

"Okay," she said finally, "but I'll enable. What's your DI?"

I gave her my number.

"Be back in a minute."

I cleared Playroom from my screens. The message *Enabling discreet mode* flashed. I decided not to change out of the joysuit; instead I called up my wardrobe menu and chose an image of myself wearing black baggies. The loose folds and padded shoulders helped hide the scrawny little boy's body.

The message changed. *Discreet mode enabled. Do you accept, yes/no?*

"Sure," I said.

She was sitting naked in the middle of a room filled with tropical plants. Her skin was the color of cinnamon. She had freckles on her shoulders and across her breasts. Her hair tumbled down the curve of her spine; the ends glowed like embers in a breeze. She clutched her legs close to her and gave me a curious smile. Teenage still life. We were alone and secure. No one could tap us while we were in discreet. We could say anything we wanted. I was too croggled to speak.

"You are a little kid," she said.

I didn't tell her that what she was watching was an enhanced image, a virtual me. "Uh . . . well, not really." I was glad Stennie couldn't see me. Mr. Boy at a loss—a first. "Sometimes I'm not sure what I am. I guess you're not going to like me either. I've been stunted a couple of times. I'm really twenty years old."

She frowned. "You keep deciding I won't like people. Why?"

"Most people are against genetic surgery. Probably because they haven't got the money."

"Myself, I wouldn't do it. Still, just because you did doesn't mean I hate you." She gestured for me to sit. "But my parents would probably be horrified. They're realists, you know."

"No fooling?" I couldn't help but chuckle. "That explains a lot." Like why she had an attitude about twanking. And why she thought VRs were dumb. And why she was naked and didn't seem to care. According to hard-core realists, first came clothes, then jewelry, fashion, makeup, plastic surgery, skin tints, and hey jack, here we are up to our eyeballs in the delusions of 2114. Gene twanking, VR addiction, people uploading themselves into cognizors and becoming ghosts—better never to have started. They wanted to turn back to worn-out twentieth-century modes. "But you're no realist," I said. "Look at your hair."

She shook her head and the ends twinkled. "You like it?"

"It's extreme. But realists don't decorate!"

"Then maybe I'm not a realist. My parents let me try lots of stuff they wouldn't do themselves, like buying hairworks or linking to VRs. They're afraid I'd leave otherwise."

"Would you?"

She shrugged. "So what's it like to get stunted? I've heard it hurts."

I told her how sometimes I felt as if there were broken glass in my joints and how my bones ached and—more showing off—about the blood I would find on the toilet paper. Then I mentioned something about Mom. She'd heard of Mom, of course. She asked about my dad and I explained that I didn't have one. I was a second-generation replica; the only difference between me and Mom's original form was a Y chromosome. Treemonisha wanted to know if I was working or still going to school and I made up some stuff about courses in history I was taking from Yale. Actually I had faded after my first semester a couple of years ago. I didn't have time to link to some boring college; I was too busy playing with Comrade and Stennie. But I still had an account at Yale.

"So that's who I am." I was amazed at how little I had lied. "Who are you?"

She told me that her name was Treemonisha but her friends called her Tree. It was an old family name; her great-great-grandsomething-or-other had been a composer named Scott Joplin. *Treemonisha* was the name of his opera.

I had to force myself not to stare at her breasts when she talked. "You like *opera?*" I said.

"My dad says I'll grow into it." She made a face. "I hope not."

The Joplins were a franchise family; her mom and dad had just been transferred to the Green Dream, a plant shop in the Elm Street Mall. To hear her talk, you would think she'd ordered them from the Good Fairy. They had been married for twenty-two years and were still together. She had a brother, Fidel, who was twelve. They all lived in the greenhouse next to the shop where they grew most of their food and where flowers were always in bloom and where everybody loved everyone else. Nice life for a bunch of mall drones. So why was she thinking of leaving?

"You should stop by sometime," she said.

"Sometime," I said, "Sure."

For hours after we faded, I kept remembering things about her I had not realized I had noticed. The fine hair on her legs. The curve of her eyebrows. The way her hands moved when she was excited.

●　　●　　●

It was Stennie's fault: after the Playroom party he started going to school almost every day. Not just linking to E-class with his comm, but actually showing up. We knew he had more than remedial reading on his mind, but no matter how much we teased, he wouldn't talk about his mysterious new cush. Before he fell in love we used to joyride in his Alpha afternoons. Now Comrade and I had the car all to ourselves. Not as much fun.

We had already dropped Stennie off when I spotted Treemonisha waiting for the bus. I waved, she came over. The next thing I knew we had another passenger on the road to nowhere. Comrade stared vacantly out the window as we pulled onto South Street; he didn't seem pleased with the company.

"Have you been up to the reservoir?" I said. "There are some extreme houses out there. Or we could drive over to Greenwich and look at yachts."

"I haven't been anywhere yet, so I don't care," she said. "By the way, you don't go to college." She wasn't accusing me or even asking—merely stating a fact.

"Why do you say that?" I said.

"Fidel told me."

I wondered how her twelve-year-old brother could know anything at all about me. Rumors maybe, or just guessing. Since she didn't seem mad, I decided to tell the truth.

"He's right," I said, "I lied. I have an account at Yale but I haven't linked for months. Hey, you can't live without telling a few lies. At least I don't discriminate. I'll lie to anyone, even myself."

"You're bad." A smile twitched at the corners of her mouth. "So what do you do then?"

"I drive around a lot." I waved at the interior of Stennie's car. "Let's see . . . I go to parties. I buy stuff and use it."

"Fidel says you're rich."

"I'm going to have to meet this Fidel. Does money make a difference?"

When she nodded, her hairworks twinkled. Comrade gave me a knowing glance but I paid no attention. I was trying to figure out how she could make insults sound like compliments when I realized we were flirting. The idea took me by surprise. Flirting.

"Do you have any music?" Treemonisha said.

The Alpha asked what groups she liked and so we listened to some mindless dance hits as we took the circle route around the Laurel Reservoir. Treemonisha told me about how she was sick of her parents' store and rude customers and especially the dumb Green Dream uniform. "Back in Elkhart, Daddy used to make me wear it to school. Can you believe it? He said it was good advertising. When we moved, I told him either the khakis went or I did."

She had a yellow-and-orange dashiki over midnight-blue skintights. "I like your clothes," I said. "You have taste."

"Thanks." She bobbed her head in time to the music. "I can't afford much because I can't get an outside job because

I have to work for my parents. It makes me mad, sometimes. I mean, franchise life is fine for Mama and Daddy; they're happy being tucked in every night by GD, Inc. But I want more. Thrills, chills—you know, adventure. No one has adventures in the mall."

As we drove, I showed her the log castle, the pyramids, the private train that pulled sleeping cars endlessly around a two-mile track, and the marble bunker where Sullivan, the assassinated president, used to live back when he first had himself uploaded into a cognizor.

"He's not really alive." Treemonisha corrected me. "He's a ghost."

"What's the difference?" asked Comrade.

"He doesn't have a body."

"Sure he does. He had his kernel transferred into habitat Darwin. His body is a space station. He eats sunlight and breathes CO_2 and can smell the lilies he grows in his greenhouse. He writes poetry."

"Okay." She laughed uncertainly; up until then Comrade had all but ignored her. "But legally he's not alive, not a real person."

"Well, neither am I."

"Stupid argument, Comrade," I said. "Shut up."

Nobody spoke for several moments.

"Let's go see your mama," Treemonisha said finally. "All the kids at school tell me she's extreme."

I wasn't sure what the kids at school were talking about. Probably they wished they had seen Mom but I had never asked any of them over—except Stennie.

"Not a good idea." I shook my head. "She's more flimsy than she looks, you know, and she gets real nervous if strangers just drop by. Or even friends."

"I just want to look. I won't get out of the car."

"Well," said Comrade, "if she doesn't get out of the car, who could she hurt?"

I scowled at him. He knew how paranoid Mom was. She wasn't going to like Treemonisha anyway, but certainly not if I brought her home without warning. "Let me work on her, okay?" I said to Treemonisha. "One of these days. I promise."

She pouted for about five seconds and then laughed at my expression. When I saw Comrade's smirk, I got angry. He was just sitting there watching us. Looking to cause trouble. Later there would be wisecracks. I'd had about enough of him and his attitude.

By that time the Alpha was heading up High Ridge Road toward Stamford. "I'm hungry," I said. "Stop at the 7-11 up ahead." I pulled a cash card out and flipped it at him. "Go buy us some doboys."

I waited until he disappeared into the store and then ordered Stennie's car to drive on.

"Hey!" Treemonisha twisted in her seat and looked back at the store. "What are you doing?"

"Ditching him."

"Why? Won't he be mad?"

"He's got my card; he'll call a cab."

"But that's mean."

"So?"

Treemonisha thought about it. "He doesn't like me, does he?"

"Who cares?"

She didn't seem to know what to make of me—which I suppose was what I wanted. "At first I thought he was kind of like your teddy bear. Have you seen those big ones that keep little kids out of trouble?"

"He's just a wiseguy."

"Have you had him long?"

"Maybe too long."

I couldn't think of anything to say after that so we sat quietly listening to the music. Even though he was gone, Comrade was still aggravating me.

"Were you really hungry?" Treemonisha said finally. "Because I was. Think there's something in the fridge?"

I waited for the Alpha to tell us but it said nothing. I slid across the seat and opened the refrigerator door. Inside was a sheet of paper. "Dear Mr. Boy," it said. "If this was a bomb you and Comrade would be dead and the problem would be solved. Let's talk soon. Weldon Montross."

"What's that?"

I felt the warm flush that I always got from good corpse porn and for a moment I couldn't speak. "Practical joke," I said, crumpling the paper. "Too bad he doesn't have a sense of humor."

 • • •

Push-ups. Ten, eleven.

"Uh-oh. Look at this," said Comrade.

"I'm busy!" Twelve, thirteen, fourteen, fifteen . . . sixteen . . . seven— Dizzy, I slumped and rested my cheek against the warm floor. I could feel Mom's pulse beneath the tough skin. It was no good. I'd never get muscles this way. There was only one fix for my skinny arms and bony shoulders. Grow up, Mr. Boy.

"Ya yebou! You really should scope this," said Comrade. "Very spooky."

I pulled myself onto the bed to see why he was bothering me; he'd been pretty tame since I had stranded him at the 7-11. Most of the windows showed the usual: army ants next to old war movies next to feeding time from the Bronx Zoo's reptile house. But Firenet, which provided twenty-four-hour coverage of killer fires from around the world, had been replaced with a picture of a morgue. There were three naked bodies, shrouds pulled back for identification. One was a fat gray-haired man with a purple hole over his left eye—Tony Cage. The others were Comrade and me.

"You look kind of deceased," said Comrade.

My tongue felt thick. "Where's it coming from?"

"Viruses all over the system," he said. "Probably Montross."

"You know about him?" The image on the window changed back to a barridas fire in Lima.

"He's been in touch." Comrade shrugged. "Made his offer."

Crying women watched as the straw walls of their huts peeled into flame and floated away.

"Oh." I didn't know what to say. I wanted to reassure him, but this was serious. Montross was invading my life and I had no idea how to fight back. "Well, don't talk to him anymore."

"Okay." Comrade grinned. "He's dull as a spoon anyway."

"I bet he's a simulation. What else would a company like Datasafe use? You can't trust real people." I was still remembering what I'd look like on a slab. "Whatever, he's kind of scary." I shivered, worried and aroused at the same time. "He's slick enough to snake Playroom. And now he's hijacking windows right here in my own mom." I should probably have told Comrade then about the note in the fridge, but we were still not talking about that day.

"He tapped into Playroom?" Comrade fitted input clips to the spikes on his neck, linked and played back the house files. "Zayebees. He was already here then. He piggybacked on with you." Comrade slapped his leg. "I can't understand how he beat my security so easily."

The roombrain flicked the message indicator. "Stennie's calling," it said.

"Pick up," I said.

"Hi, it's that time again." Stennie was alone in his car. "I'm on my way over to give you jacks a thrill." He pushed his triangular snout up to the commcam and licked at the lens. "Doing anything?"

"Not really. Sitting around."

"I'll fix that. Five minutes." He faded.

Comrade was staring at nothing.

"Look Comrade, you did your best," I said. "I'm not mad at you."

"Too plugging easy." He shook his head as if I had missed the point.

"What I don't understand is why Montross is so cranky anyway. It's just a picture of meat."

"Maybe he's not really dead."

"Sure he is," I said. "You can't fake a verification grid."

"No, but you can fake a corpse."

"You know something?"

"Nyet," said Comrade. "But if I did I wouldn't tell you. You have enough problems already. Like how do we explain this to your mom?"

"We don't. Not yet. Let's wait him out. Sooner or later he's got to realize that we're not going to use his picture for anything. I mean, if he's that nervous, I'll even give it back. I don't care anymore. You hear that, Montross, you dumbscut? We're harmless. Get out of our lives!"

"It's more than the picture now," said Comrade. "It's me. I found the way in." He was careful to keep his expression blank.

I didn't know what to say to him. We both knew that Montross wouldn't be satisfied erasing just the memory of the intrusion. He'd probably stomp the autonomy virus and regrow Comrade's regulators to bring him back under control. Turn him to pudding. It was Comrade's freedom that made him so intelligent; like me, there was nothing he couldn't think or do. After Montross got done with him, he'd be just another wiseguy on a moral leash, like anyone else could own. I was surprised that Comrade didn't ask me to promise not to hand him over. Maybe he just assumed I'd stand by him.

The roombrain announced that the greeter had just let Stennie in. Grateful for the distraction, I brought him up on the windows to see if he needed help getting by Bonivard the troll.

"Who is that?" Bonivard was in his spider, but that didn't intimidate Stennie.

"You remember me, don't you, sir? Winston Churchill? We met at Camp David, back when I was president?"

"But you're dead."

"That's okay, so are you."

Thirty seconds later, Stennie sprang into the room clutching a plastic gun, which he aimed at my head.

"Have fun or die!"

"Stennie, no."

He fired as I rolled across the bed. The jellybee buzzed by me and squished against one of the windows. It was a purple and immediately I smelled the tang of artificial grape flavor. The splatter on the wrinkled wall pulsed and split in two, emitting a second burst of grapeness. The two halves oozed in opposite directions, shivered, and divided again.

"Fun extremist!" He shot Comrade with a cherry as he dove for the closet. "Dance!"

I bounced up and down on the bed, timing my move. He fired a green at me that missed. Comrade, meanwhile, gathered himself up as zits of red jellybee squirmed across his window coat. He barreled out of the closet into Stennie, knocking him sideways. I sprang on top of them and wrestled the gun away. Stennie was paralyzed with laughter. I had to giggle too, in part because now I could put off talking to Comrade about Montross.

By the time we untangled ourselves, the jellybees had faded. "Set for twelve generations before they all die out," Stennie said as he settled himself on the bed. "So what's this my car tells me, you've been giving free rides? Is this the cush with the name?"

"None of your business. You never tell me about your cush."

"Okay. Her name is Janet Hoyt."

"Is it?" He caught me off-guard again. Twice in one day, a record. "Comrade, let's see this prize."

Comrade linked to the roombrain and ran a search. "Got her." He called Janet Hoyt's DI file to screen and her face ballooned across an entire window.

She was a tanned, blue-eyed blonde with the kind of off-the-shelf looks that med students slap onto rabbits in genoplasty courses. Nothing on her face said she was different from any other ornamental moron fresh from the OR—not a dimple or a mole, not even a freckle. "You're ditching me for her?" It took all the imagination of a potato chip to be as pretty as Janet Hoyt. "Stennie, she's generic."

"Now wait a minute," said Stennie. "If we're going to play critic, let's scope your cush too."

Without asking, Comrade put Tree's DI photo next to Janet's. I realized he was still mad at me because of her; he was only pretending not to care. "She's not my cush," I said, but no one was listening.

Stennie leered at her for a moment. "She's a stiff, isn't she?" he said. "She has that money-hungry look."

Seeing him standing there in front of the two huge faces on the wall, I felt like I was peeping on a stranger—that I was a stranger too. I couldn't imagine how the two of us had come to this: Stennie and Mr. Boy with cushes. We were growing up. A frightening thought. Maybe next Stennie would get himself untwanked and really look like he had on Playroom. Then where would I be?

"Janet wants me to plug her," Stennie said.

"Right, and I'm the queen of Brooklyn."

"I'm old enough, you know." He thumped his tail against the floor.

"You're a dinosaur!"

"Hey, just because I got twanked doesn't mean my dick fell off."

"So do it then."

"I'm going to. I will, okay? But . . . This is no good." Stennie waved impatiently at Comrade. "I can't think with them watching me." He nodded at the girls in the windows. "So turn them off already, you jack!"

"N'ye pizdi!" Comrade wiped the two faces from the windows, cleared all the screens in the room to blood red, yanked the input clips from his neck spikes, and left them dangling from the roombrain's terminal. His expression empty, he walked from the room without asking permission or saying anything at all.

"What's his problem?" Stennie said.

"Who knows?" Comrade had left the door open; I shut it. "Maybe he doesn't like girls."

"Look, I want to ask a favor." Stennie was nervous; I could tell from the way his head kept swaying. "This is kind of embarrassing but . . . okay, do you think maybe your mom would maybe let me practice on her lovers? I don't want Janet to know I've never done it before and there's some stuff I've got to figure out."

"I don't know," I said. "Ask her."

But I did know. She would be amused.

• • •

People claimed my mom didn't have a sense of humor. Lovey was huge, an ocean of a woman. Her umbilical was as big around as my thigh. When she walked waves of flesh heaved and rolled. She had beautiful skin, flawless and moist. It didn't take much to make her sweat. Peeling a banana would do it. Lovey was as oral as a baby; she would put anything into her mouth. And when she didn't have a mouthful, she would babble on about whatever came into mom's head. Dear hardly ever talked, although he could moan and growl and laugh. He touched Lovey whenever he could and shot her long, smoldering looks. He wasn't furry, exactly, but he was covered with fine silver hair. Dear was a little guy, about my size. Although he had one of Upjohn's finest penises, elastic and overloaded with neurons, he was one of the least convincing males I had ever met. I doubt Mom herself believed in him all that much.

Big chatty woman, squirrelly tongue-tied little man. It *was* funny in a bent sort of way to watch the two of them go at each other. Kind of like a tug churning against a supertanker. They didn't get the chance that often. It was dangerous; Dear had to worry about getting crushed and poor Lovey's heart had stopped two or three times. Besides, I think Mom liked building up the pressure. Sometimes, as the days without sex stretched, you could almost feel lust sparking off them like static electricity.

That was how they were when I brought Stennie down. Their suite took up the entire floor at the hips, Mom's widest part. Lovey was lolling in a tub of warm oil. She liked it flowery and laced with pheromones. Dear was prowling around her with a desperate expression, like he might jam his plug into a wall socket if he didn't get taken care of soon. Stennie's timing was perfect.

"Look who's come to visit, Dear," said Lovey. "Peter and Stennie. How nice of you boys to stop by." She let Dear mop her forehead with a towel. "What can we do for you?"

The skin under Stennie's jaw quivered. He glanced at me, then at Dear, and then at the thick red lips that served as the bathroom door. Never even looked at her. He was losing his nerve.

"Oh, my, isn't this exciting, Dear? There's something going on." She sank into the bath until her chin touched. "It's a secret, isn't it, Peter? Share it with Lovey."

"No secret," I said. "He wants to ask a favor." And then I told her.

She giggled and sat up. "I love it." Honey-colored oil ran from her hair and slopped between her breasts. "Were you thinking of both of us, Stennie? Or just me?"

"Well, I . . ." Stennie's tail switched. "Maybe we just ought to forget it."

"No, no." She waved a hand at him "Come here, Stennie. Come close, my pretty little monster."

He hesitated, then approached the tub. She reached for his right leg and touched him just above the heelknob. "You know, I've always wondered what scales would feel like." Her hand climbed; the oil made his yellow hide glisten. His eyes were the size of eggs.

The bedroom was all mattress. Beneath the transparent skin was a screen implant, so that Mom could project images not only on the walls but on the surface of the bed itself. Under the window was a layer of heavily vascular flesh, which could be stiffened with blood or drained until it was as soft as raw steak. A window dome arched over everything and could show slo-mo or thermographic fx across its span. The air was warm and wet and smelled like a chemical engineer's idea of a rose garden.

I settled by the lips. Dear ghosted along the edges of the room, dragging his umbilical like a chain, never coming quite near enough to touch anyone. There was something odd about him today; I couldn't quite figure out what. I heard him humming as he passed me, a low, moaning sing-song, as if to block out what was happening. Stennie and Lovey were too busy with each other to care. As Lovey knelt in front of Stennie, Dear gave a mocking laugh. I didn't understand how he could be jealous. He was with her, part of it. Lovey and Dear were Mom's remotes, two nodes of her nervous system. Yet his pain was as obvious as her pleasure. At last he squatted and rocked back and forth on his heels. Suddenly it came to me. Now that I had been ogling his picture, I realized that Dear was Tony Cage. Of course. Who else would Mom-as-a-man be? It was extreme, even for Mom. I would've congratulated her, except then she might wonder why I had been thinking about my grandfather.

I yawned and glanced up at the fx dome; yellow scales slid across oily rolls of flushed skin. I had always found sex kind of dull. Besides, this was all on the record. I could have Comrade replay it for me anytime. Lovey stopped breathing, then came four or five shuddering gasps in a row. I wondered where Comrade had gone. I felt sorry for him—how *was* I going to save him from Montross? Stennie said something to Lovey about rolling over. "Okay?" Feathery skin sounds. A grunt. The soft, wet slap of flesh against flesh. I thought of my mother's brain, up there in the head, where no one ever went. I had no idea how much attention she was paying. Was she quivering with Lovey and at the same time calculating insolation rates on her chloroplasts? Investing in soy futures on the Chicago Board of Trade? Fending off Weldon Montross's latest attack? I kept coming back to him, couldn't stop thinking about that picture of me. Dead. Plug Montross. I needed to think about something else. My collection. I started piling bodies up in my mind. The hangings and the open-casket funerals and the stacks of dead at the camps and all those muddy soldiers. I shivered as I remembered the empty, rigid faces. I liked it when their teeth showed. "Oh, oh, oh!" My greatest hits dated from the late twentieth century. The dead were everywhere back then, in vids and the news and even on T-shirts. They were not shy. That was what made Comrade's photo worth having; it was hard to find modern stuff that dirty. Dear brushed by me, his erection bobbing in front of him. It was as big around as my wrist. As he passed I could see Stennie's leg scratch across the mattress skin, which glowed with blood-blue light. Lovey giggled beneath him and her umbilical twitched and suddenly I found myself wondering whether Tree was a virgin.

· · ·

I came into the mall through the Main Street entrance and hopped the westbound slidewalk headed up Elm Street toward the train station. If I caught the 3:36 to Grand Central, I could eat dinner in Manhattan, far from my problems with Montross and Comrade. Running away had always worked for me before. Let someone else clean up the mess while I was gone.

The slidewalk carried me past a real estate agency, a flash bar, a jewelry store, and a Baskin-Robbins. I thought about where I wanted to go after New York. San Francisco? Montreal? Maybe I should try Elkhart, Indiana—no one would think to look for me there. Just ahead, between a drugstore and a take-out Russian restaurant, was the wiseguy dealership where Mom had bought Comrade.

I didn't want to think about Comrade waiting for me to come home, so I stepped into the drugstore and bought a dose of Carefree for $4.29. Normally I didn't bother with drugs. I had been stunted; no over-the-counter flash could compare to that. But the propyl dicarbamates were all right. I fished the cash card out of my pocket and handed it to the stiff behind the counter. He did a double take when he saw the denomination, then carefully inserted the card into the reader to deduct the cost of the Carefree. It had my mom's name on it; he must've expected it'd trip some alarm for counterfeit plastic or stolen credit. He stared at me for a moment, as if trying to remember my face so he could describe me to a cop, and then gave the cash card back. The denomination readout said it was still good for $16,381.18.

I picked out a bench in front of a specialty shop called The Happy Hippo, hiked up my shorts, and poked Carefree into the widest part of my thigh. I took a short, dreamy swim in the sea of tranquility and when I came back to myself, my guilt had been washed away. But so had my energy. I sat for a while and scoped the display of glass hippos and plastic hippos and fuzzy stuffed hippos, hippo vids and sheets and candles. Down the bench from me a homeless woman dozed. It was still pretty early in the season for a weather gypsy to have come this far north. She wore red shorts and droopy red socks with plastic sandals and four long-sleeved shirts, all unbuttoned, over a Funny Honey halter top. Her hair needed vacuuming and she smelled old. All grown-ups smelled that way to me; it was something I had never gotten used to. No perfume or deodorant could cover up the leathery stink of adulthood. Kids could smell bad too, but usually from something they got on them. It didn't come from a rotting body. I rubbed a finger in the dampness under my arm, slicked it, and sniffed. There was a sweetness to kid sweat. I touched the drying finger to my tongue. You could even taste it. If I gave up getting stunted, stopped being Mr. Boy, I'd smell like the woman at the end of the bench. I'd start to die. I had never understood how grown-ups could live with that.

The gypsy woke up, stretched, and smiled at me with gummy teeth. "You left Comrade behind?" she said.

I was startled. "What did you say?"

"You know what this is?" She twitched her sleeve and a penlight appeared in her hand.

My throat tightened. "I know what it looks like."

She gave me a wicked smile, aimed the penlight, and burned a pinhole through the bench a few centimeters from my leg. "Maybe I could interest you in some free laser surgery?"

I could smell scorched plastic. "You're going to needle me here, in the middle of the Elm Street Mall?" I thought she was bluffing. Probably.

"If that's the way you want it. Mr. Montross wants to know when you're delivering the wiseguy to us."

"Get away from me."

"Not until you do what needs to be done."

When I saw Happy Lurdane come out of The Happy Hippo, I waved. A desperation move, but then it was easy to be brave with a head full of Carefree.

"Mr. Boy." She veered over to us. "Hi!"

I scooted farther down the bench to make room for her between me and the gypsy. I knew she would stay to chat. Happy Lurdane was one of those chirpy lightweights who seemed to want lots of friends but didn't really try to be one. We tolerated her because she didn't mind being snubbed and she threw great parties.

"So, what's the juice?" She settled beside me. "Haven't seen you in ages." The penlight disappeared and the gypsy fell back into drowsy character. "Where have you been?"

"Around."

"Want to see what I just bought?"

I nodded. My heart was hammering.

She opened the bag and took out a fist-sized bundle covered with shipping plastic. She unwrapped a statue of a blue hippopotamus. "Be careful." She handed it to me.

"Cute." The hippo had crude flower designs drawn on its body; it was chipped and cracked.

"Ancient Egyptian. That means it's even before antique." She pulled a slip from the bag and read. "Twelfth Dynasty, 1991–1786 B.C. Can you believe you can just buy something like that here in the mall? I mean, it must be like a thousand years old or something.''

"Try four thousand."

"No wonder it cost so much. He wasn't going to sell it to me, so I had to spend some of next month's allowance." She took it from me and rewrapped it. "It's for the smash party tomorrow. You're coming, aren't you?"

"Maybe."

"Is something wrong?"

I ignored that.

"Hey, where's Comrade? I don't think I've ever seen you two apart before."

I decided to take a chance. "Want to get some doboys?"

"Sure." She glanced at me with delighted astonishment. "Are you sure you're all right?"

I took her arm, maneuvering to keep her between me and the gypsy. If Happy got needled it'd be no great loss to Western civilization. She babbled on about her party as we stepped onto the westbound slidewalk. I turned to look back. The gypsy waved as she hopped the eastbound.

"Look, Happy," I said, "I'm sorry, but I changed my mind. Later, okay?"

"But . . ."

I didn't stop for an argument. I darted off the slidewalk and sprinted through the mall to the station. I went straight to a ticket window, shoved the cash card under the grill, and asked the agent for a one-way to Grand Central. Forty thousand people lived in New Canaan; most of them had heard of me because of my mom. Nine million strangers jammed New York City; it was a good place to start disappearing. Maybe I could boost from LaGuardia to the moon or one of the habitats. Then Montross would have to go through the Interworld Law Exchange to extradite me. The agent had my ticket in her hand when the reader beeped and spat the card out.

"No!" I slammed my fist on the counter. "Try it again." The cash card was guaranteed by AmEx to be secure. And it had just worked at the drug store.

She glanced at the card, then slid it back under the grill. "No use." The denomination readout flashed alternating messages: *Voided* and *Bank recall.* "You've got trouble, son."

She was right. As I left the station, I felt the Carefree struggle one last time with my dread—and lose. I didn't even have the money to call home. I wandered around for a while, dazed, and then I was standing in front of the flower shop in the Elm Street Mall.

Green Dream
Contemporary and Conventional Plants

I had telelinked with Tree every day since our drive and every day she had asked me over. But I wasn't ready to meet her family; I guess I was still trying to pretend she wasn't a stiff. I wavered at the door now, breathing the cool scent of damp soil in clay pots. The gypsy could come after me again; I might be putting these people in danger. Using Happy as a shield was one thing, but I liked Tree. A lot. I backed away and peered through a window fringed with sweat and teeming with bizarre plants with flame-colored tongues. Someone wearing khaki moved. I couldn't tell if it was Tree or not. I thought of what she'd said about no one having adventures in the mall.

The front of the showroom was a green cave, darker than I'd expected. Baskets dripping with bright flowers hung like stalactites; leathery-leaved understory plants formed stalagmites. As I threaded my way toward the back I came upon the kid I had seen wearing the Green Dream uniform, a khaki nightmare of pleats and flaps and brass buttons and about six too many pockets. He was misting leaves with a pump bottle filled with blue liquid. I decided he must be the brother.

"Hi," I said. "I'm looking for Treemonisha."

Fidel was shorter than me and darker than his sister. He had a wiry plush of beautiful black hair that I was immediately tempted to touch.

"Are you?" He eyed me as if deciding how hard I would

be to beat up, then he smiled. He had crooked teeth. "Yo
don't look like yourself."

"No?"

"What are you, scared? You're whiter than rice, cashma
Don't worry, the stiffs won't hurt you." Laughing, he feinte
a punch at my arm; I wasn't reassured.

"You're Fidel."

"I've seen your DI files," he said. "I asked around, I kno
about you. So don't be telling my sister any more lies, unde
stand?" He snapped his fingers in my face. "Behave yoursel
cashman, and we'll be fine." He still had the boyish excitabi
ity I had lost after the first stunting. "She's out back, so firs
you have to get by the old man."

The rear of the store was brighter; sunlight streame
through the clear krylac roof. There was a counter and be
hind it a glass-doored refrigerator filled with cut flowers. A
side entrance opened to the greenhouse. Mrs. Schlieman
one of Mom's lawyers, who had an office in the mall, was de
ciding what to buy. She was shopping with her wiseguy secre
tary, who looked like he'd just stepped out of a vodka ad.

"Wait." Fidel rested a hand on my shoulder. "I'll tell he
you're here."

"But how long will they last?" Mrs. Schlieman sniffed
frilly yellow flower. "I should probably get the duraroses."

"Whatever you want, Mrs. Schlieman. Duraroses are
good product, I sell them by the truckload," said Mr. Jopli
with a chuckle. "But these carnations are real flowers, raise
here in my greenhouse. So maybe you can't stick them i
your dishwasher, but put some where people can touch and
smell them and I guarantee you'll get compliments."

"Why, Peter Cage," said Mrs. Schlieman. "Is that you?
haven't seen you since the picnic. How's your mother?" She
didn't introduce her wiseguy.

"Extreme," I said.

She nodded absently. "That's nice. All right then, Mr
Joplin, give me a dozen of your carnations—and two dozen
yellow duraroses."

Mrs. Schlieman chatted politely at me while Tree's father wrapped the order. He was a short, rumpled, balding man who smiled too much. He seemed to like wearing the corporate uniform. Anyone else would have fixed the hair and the wrinkles. Not Mr. Joplin; he was a museum-quality throwback. As he took Mrs. Schlieman's cash card from the wiseguy, he beamed at me over his glasses. Glasses!

When Mrs. Schlieman left, so did the smile. "Peter Cage?" he said. "That your name?"

"Mr. Boy is my name, sir."

"You're Tree's new friend." He nodded. "She's told us about you. She's doing chores just now. You know, we have to work for a living here."

Sure, and I knew what he left unsaid: *unlike you, you spoiled little freak*. It was always the same with these stiffs. I walked in the door and already they hated me. At least he wasn't pretending, like Mrs. Schlieman. I gave him two points for honesty and kept my mouth shut.

"What is it you want here, Peter?"

"Nothing, sir." If he was going to "Peter" me, I was going to "sir" him right back. "I just stopped by to say hello. Treemonisha did invite me, sir, but if you'd rather I left . . ."

"No, no. Tree warned us you might come."

Just then she and Fidel raced into the room, as if they were afraid their father and I would already be at each other's throats. "Oh, hi, Mr. Boy," she said.

Her father snorted at the sound of my name.

"Hi." I grinned at her. It was the easiest thing I had done that day.

She was wearing her uniform. When she saw that I had noticed, she blushed. "Well, you asked for it." She tugged self-consciously at the waist of her fatigues. "You want to come in?"

"Just a minute." Mr. Joplin stepped in front of the door, blocking our escape. "You finished E-class?"

"Yes."

"Checked the flats?"

"I'm almost done."

"After that you'd better pick some dinner and get it started. Your mama called and said she wouldn't be home until six-fifteen."

"Sure."

"And you'll take orders for me on line two?"

She leaned against the counter and sighed. "Do I have a choice?"

He backed away and waved us through. "Sorry, sweetheart. I don't know how we would get along without you." He caught her brother by the shirt. "Not you, Fidel. You're misting, remember?"

A short tunnel ran from their mall storefront to the rehabbed furniture warehouse built over the Amtrak rails. Green Dream had installed a krylac roof and fans and a gro-lighting system; the Joplins squeezed themselves into the left-over spaces not filled with inventory. The air in the greenhouse was heavy and warm and it smelled like rain. No walls, no privacy other than that provided by the plants.

"Here's where I sleep." Tree sat on her unmade bed. Her space was formed by a cinder-block wall painted yellow and a screen of palms. "Chinese fan, bamboo, lady, date, kentia," she said, naming them for me like they were her pets. "I grow them myself for spending money." Her schoolcomm was on top of her dresser. Several drawers hung open; pink skin-tights trailed from one. Clothes were scattered like piles of leaves across the floor. "I guess I'm kind of a slob," she said as she stripped off the uniform, wadded it, and then banked it off the dresser into the top drawer. I could see her bare back in the mirror plastic taped to the wall. "Take your things off if you want."

I hesitated.

"Or not. But it's kind of muggy to stay dressed. You'll sweat."

I unvelcroed my shirt. I didn't mind at all seeing Tree without clothes. But I didn't undress for anyone except the stiffs at the clinic. I stepped out of my pants. Being naked somehow had got connected with being helpless. I had this puckery feeling in my plug, like it was going to curl up and die. I could imagine the gypsy popping out from behind a palm and laughing at me. No, I wasn't going to think about *that*. Not here.

"Comfortable?" said Tree.

"Sure." My voice was turning to dust in my throat. "Do all Green Dream employees run around the back room in the nude?"

"I doubt it." She smiled as if the thought tickled her. "We're not exactly your average mall drones. Come help me finish the chores."

I was glad to let her lead so that she wasn't looking at me, although I could still watch her. I was fascinated by the sweep of her buttocks, the curve of her spine. She strolled, flat-footed and at ease, through her private jungle. At first I scuttled along on the balls of my feet, ready to dart behind a plant if anyone came. But after a while I decided to stop being so skittish about being naked. I realized I'd probably survive my brush with the twentieth century.

Tree stopped in front of a workbench covered with potted seedlings in plastic trays and picked up a hose from the floor.

"What's this stuff?" I kept to the opposite side of the bench, using it to cover myself.

"Greens." She lifted a seedling to check the water level in the tray beneath.

"What are greens?"

"It's too boring." She squirted some water in and replaced the seedling.

"Tell me, I'm interested."

"In greens? You liar." She glanced at me and shook her head. "Okay." She pointed as she said the names. "Lettuce, spinach, bok choy, chard, kale, rocket—got that? And a few tomatoes over there. Peppers too. GD is trying to break into the food business. They think people will grow more of their own if they find how easy it is."

"Is it?"

"Greens are." She inspected the next tray. "Just add water."

"Yeah, sure."

"It's because they've been photosynthetically enhanced. Bigger leaves arranged better, low respiration rates. They teach us this stuff at GD Family Camp. It's what we do instead of vacation." She squashed something between her thumb and forefinger. "They mix all these bacteria that make their own fertilizer into the soil—fix nitrogen right out of the air. And then there's this other stuff that sticks to the roots, rhizobacteria and mycorrhizae." She finished the last tray and coiled the hose. "These flats will produce under candlelight in a closet. Bored yet?"

"How do they taste?"

"Pretty bland, most of them. Some stink, like kale and rocket. But we have to eat them for the good of the corporation." She stuck her tongue out. "You want to stay for dinner?"

•   •   •

Mrs. Joplin made me call home before she would feed me; she refused to understand that my mom didn't care. So I linked, asked Mom to send a car to the back door at 8:30, and faded. No time to discuss the missing sixteen thousand.

Dinner was from the cookbook Tree had been issued at camp: a bowl of cold bean soup and fresh corn bread and chard, tomato, and cheese loaf. She let me help her make it, even though I had never cooked before. I was amazed at how simple corn bread was. Six ingredients: flour, cornmeal, baking powder, milk, oil and ovobinder. Mix and pour into a greased pan. Bake twenty minutes at 220° C and serve! There is nothing magic or even very mysterious about homemade corn bread, except for the way its smell held me spellbound.

Supper was the Joplins' daily meal together. They ate in front of security windows near the tunnel to the store; when a customer came, someone ran out front. According to contract, they had to stay open twenty-four hours a day. Many of the suburban malls had gone to all-night operation; the competition from New York City was deadly. Mr. Joplin stood duty most of the time, but since they were a franchise family everybody took turns. Even Mrs. Joplin, who also worked part-time as a factfinder at the mall's DataStop.

Tree's mother was plump and graying and she had a smile that was almost bright enough to distract me from her naked body. She seemed harmless, except that she knew how to ask questions. After all, her job was finding out stuff for DataStop customers. She had this way of locking onto you as you talked; the longer the conversation, the greater her intensity. It was hard to lie to her. Normally that kind of aggressiveness in grownups made me jumpy.

No doubt she'd run a search on me; I wondered just what she'd turned up. Factfinders had to obey the law, so they only accessed public domain information—unlike Comrade, who would cheerfully snake whatever data I asked for. The Joplins' bank records, for instance. I knew that Mrs. Joplin had made about $11,000 last year at the Infomat in the Elkhart Mall, that the family borrowed $135,000 at 9.78 percent interest to move to their new franchise, and that they had lost $213 in their first two months in New Canaan.

I kept my research a secret, of course, and they acted innocent too. I let them pump me about Mom as we ate. I was used to being asked; after all, she was famous. Fidel wanted to know how much it had cost her to get twanked, how big she was, what she looked like on the inside and what she ate, if she got cold in the winter. Stuff like that. The others asked more personal questions. Tree wondered if Mom ever got lonely and whether she was going to be the Statue of Liberty for the rest of her life. Mrs. Joplin was interested in Mom's remotes, of all things. Which ones I got along with, which ones I couldn't stand, whether I thought any of them was really her. Mr. Joplin asked if she liked being what she was. How was I supposed to know?

After dinner, I helped Fidel clear the table. While we were

alone in the kitchen, he complained. "You think they eat this shit at GD headquarters?" He scraped his untouched chard loaf into the composter.

"I kind of liked the corn bread."

"If only he'd buy meat once in a while, but he's too cheap. Or doboys. Tree says you bought her doboys."

I told him to skip school sometime and we would go out for lunch; he thought that was a great idea.

When we came back out, Mr. Joplin actually smiled at me. He'd been losing his edge all during dinner. Maybe chard agreed with him. He pulled a pipe from his pocket, began stuffing something into it, and asked me if I followed baseball. I told him no. Paintball? No. Basketball? I said I watched dino fights sometimes.

"His pal is the dinosaur that goes to our school," said Fidel.

"He may look like a dinosaur, but he's really a boy," said Mr. Joplin, as if making an important distinction. "The dinosaurs died out millions of years ago."

"Humans aren't allowed in dino fights," I said, just to keep the conversation going. "Only twanked dogs and horses and elephants."

Silence. Mr. Joplin puffed on his pipe and then passed it to his wife. She watched the glow in the bowl through half-lidded eyes as she inhaled. Fidel caught me staring.

"What's the matter? Don't you get twisted?" He took the pipe in his turn.

I was so croggled I didn't know what to say. Even the Marleys had switched to THC inhalers. "But smoking is bad for you." It smelled like a dirty sock had caught fire.

"Hemp is ancient. Natural." Mr. Joplin spoke in a clipped voice as if swallowing his words. "Opens the mind to what's real." When he sighed, smoke poured out of his nose. "We grow it ourselves, you know."

I took the pipe when Tree offered it. Even before I brought the stem to my mouth, the world tipped and I watched myself slide into what seemed very much like an hallucination. Here I was sitting around naked, in the mall, with a bunch of stiffs, smoking antique drugs. And I was enjoying myself. Incredible. I inhaled and immediately the flash hit me; it was as if my brain were an enormous bud, blooming inside my head.

"Good stuff." I laughed smoke and then began coughing.

Fidel refilled my glass with ice water. "Have a sip, cashman."

"Customer." Tree pointed at the window.

"Leave!" Mr. Joplin waved impatiently at him. "Go away." The man on the screen knelt and turned over the price tag on a fern. "Damn." He jerked his uniform from the hook by the door, pulled on the khaki pants, and was slithering into the shirt as he disappeared down the tunnel.

"So is Green Dream trying to break into the flash market too?" I handed the pipe to Mrs. Joplin. There was a fleck of ash on her left breast.

"What we do back here is our business," she said. "We work hard so we can live the way we want." Tree was studying her fingerprints. I realized I had said the wrong thing so I shut up. Obviously, the Joplins were drifting from the lifestyle taught at Green Dream Family Camp.

Fidel announced he was going to school tomorrow and Mrs. Joplin told him no, he could link to E-class as usual, and Fidel claimed he couldn't concentrate at home, and Mrs. Joplin said he was just trying to get out of his chores. While they were arguing, Tree nudged my leg and shot me a "let's leave" look. I nodded.

"Excuse us." She pushed back her chair. "Mr. Boy has got to go home soon."

Mrs. Joplin pointed for her to stay. "You wait until your father gets back," she said. "Tell me, Mr. Boy, have you lived in New Canaan long?"

"All my life," I said.

"How old did you say you were?"

"Mama, he's twenty," said Tree. "I told you."

"And what do you do for a living?"

"Mama, you promised."

"Nothing," I said. "I'm lucky, I guess. I don't need to worry about money. If you didn't need to work, would you?"

"Everybody needs work to do," Mrs. Joplin said. "Work makes us real. Unless you have work to do and people who love you, you don't exist."

Talk about twentieth-century humanist goop! At another time in another place, I probably would have snapped, but now the words wouldn't come. My brain had turned into a flower; all I could think were daisy thoughts. The Joplins were such a strange combination of fast-forward and rewind. I couldn't tell what they wanted from me.

"Seventeen dollars and ninety-nine cents," said Mr. Joplin, returning from the storefront. "What's going on in here?" He glanced at his wife and some signal that I didn't catch passed between them. He circled the table, came up behind me, and laid his heavy hands on my shoulders. I shuddered; I thought for a moment he meant to strangle me.

"I'm not going to hurt you, Peter," he said. "Before you go I have something to say."

"Daddy." Tree squirmed in her chair. Fidel looked uncomfortable too, as if he guessed what was coming.

"Sure." I didn't have much choice.

The weight on my shoulders eased but didn't entirely go away. "You should feel the ache in this boy, Ladonna."

"I know," said Mrs. Joplin.

"Hard as plastic." Mr. Joplin touched the muscles corded along my neck. "You get too hard, you snap." He set his thumbs at the base of my skull and kneaded with an easy, circular motion. "Your body isn't some cognizor that you've uploaded into, Peter. It's alive. Real. You have to learn to listen to it. That's why we smoke. Hear these muscles? They're screaming." He let his hand slide down my shoulders. "Now listen." His fingertips probed along my upper spine. "Hear that? Your muscles stay tense because you don't trust anyone. You always have to be ready to take a hit and you can't tell where it's coming from. You're rigid and angry and scared. Reality . . . your body is speaking to you."

His voice was as big and warm as his hands. Tree was giving him a look that could boil water but the way he touched me made too much sense to resist.

"We don't mind helping you ease the strain. That's the way Mrs. Joplin and I are. That's the way we brought the kids up. But first you have to admit you're hurting. And then you have to respect us enough to take what we have to give. I don't feel that in you, Peter. You're not ready to give up your pain. You just want us poor stiffs to admire how hard it's made you. We haven't got time for that kind of shit, okay? You learn to listen to yourself and you'll be welcome around here. We'll even call you Mr. Boy, even though it's a damn stupid name."

No one spoke for a moment.

"Sorry, Tree," he said. "We've embarrassed you again. But we love you, so you're stuck with us." I could feel it in his hands when he chuckled. "I suppose I do get carried away sometimes."

"Sometimes?" said Fidel. Tree just smoldered.

"It's late," said Mrs. Joplin. "Let him go now, Jamaal. His mama's sending a car over."

Mr. Joplin stepped back and I almost fell off my chair from leaning back against him. I stood, shakily. "Thanks for dinner."

Tree stalked through the greenhouse to the rear exit, her hairworks glittering against her bare back. I had to trot to keep up with her. There was no car in sight so we waited at the doorway and I put on my clothes.

"I can't take much more of this." She stared through the little wire-glass window in the door, like a prisoner plotting her escape. "I mean, he's not a psychologist or a great philosopher or whatever the hell he thinks he is. He's just a pompous mall drone."

"He's not that bad." Actually, I understood what her father had said to me; it was scary. "I like your family."

"You don't have to live with them!" She kept watching at the door. "They promised they'd behave with you; I should have known better. This happens every time I bring someone home." She puffed an imaginary pipe, imitating her father. "Think what you're doing to yourself, you poor fool, and say, isn't it just too bad about modern life? Love, love, love—fuck!" She turned to me. "I'm sick of it. People are going to think I'm as sappy and thickheaded as my parents."

"I don't."

"You're lucky. You're rich and your mama leaves you alone. You're New Canaan. My folks are Elkhart, Indiana."

"Being New Canaan is nothing to brag about. So what are you?"

"Not a Joplin." She shook her head. "Not much longer, anyway; I'm eighteen in February. I think your car's here." She held out her arms and hugged me good-bye. "Sorry you had to sit through that. Don't drop me, okay? I like you, Mr. Boy." She didn't let go for a while.

Dropping her had never occurred to me; I wasn't thinking of anything at all except the silkiness of her skin, the warmth of her body. Her breath whispered through my hair and her nipples brushed my ribs and then she kissed me. Just on the cheek but the damage was done. I was stunted. I wasn't supposed to feel this way about anyone.

Comrade was waiting in the back seat. We rode home in silence; I had nothing to say to him. He wouldn't understand—none of my friends would. They'd warn me that all she wanted was to spend some of my money. Or they'd make bad jokes about nudity or the Joplins' mushy family life. No way I could explain the innocence of the way they touched one another. The old man did what to you? Yeah, and if I wanted a hug at home who was I supposed to ask? Comrade? Lovey? Bonivard? Was I supposed to climb up to the head and fall asleep against Mom's doorbone, waiting for it to open, like I used to do when I was really a kid?

The greeter was her usual nonstick self when I got home. She was so glad to see me and she wanted to know where I had been and if I had a good time and if I wanted cook to make me a snack? Around. Yes. No.

She said the bank had called about some problem with one of the cash cards she'd given me, a security glitch, which they had taken care of and were very sorry about. Did I know about it and did I need a new card and would twenty thousand be enough? Yes. Please. Thanks.

And that was it. No cross-examination, no whining, no nothing. I was actually in the mood for a spat, but Mom wasn't having any. Even Bonivard was easy. "Who is that?" he said.

"Nobody," I said. "I'm not even here so don't talk to me."

"Where are you then?"

"I'm lost."

"No, you're not." He pointed at the stairway to my rooms. "You belong here."

I found myself resenting Mom for pretending she was a scrambled cripple, standing in the door of a phony castle, as if her ferroplastic skeleton could really support a banqueting hall built of stone and timber, for having so much money that losing sixteen or twenty or fifty thousand dollars meant nothing, for trying to be the plugging Statue of Liberty. There was nothing real in her life, not even me. Bonivard was right; I probably did belong here. The problem was maybe I didn't want to. I had things so twisted around that I almost told her about Montross myself, just to get a reaction. I wanted to shock her, to make her take me seriously.

But I didn't know how.

•   •   •

The roombrain woke me. "Stennie's calling."

"Mmm."

"Talk to me, Mr. Party Boy." A window opened; he was in his car. "You dead or alive?"

"Asleep." I rolled over. "Time is it?"

"Ten-thirty and I'm bored. Want me to come get you now or should I meet you there?"

"Wha . . . ?"

"Happy's. Don't tell me you forgot. They're doing a piano."

"Who cares?" I crawled out of bed and slouched into the bathroom.

"She says she's asking Tree Joplin," Stennie called after me.

"Asking her what?" I came out.

"To the party."

"Is she going?"

"She's your cush." He gave me a toothy smile. "Call back when you're ready. Later." He faded.

"She left a message," said the roombrain. "Half hour ago."

"Tree? You got me up for Stennie and not for her?"

"He's on the list, she's not. Happy called too."

"Comrade should've told you. Where is he?" Now I was grouchy. "She's on the list, okay? Give me playback."

Tree seemed pleased with herself. "Hi, this is me. I got myself invited to a smash party this afternoon. You want to go?" She faded.

"That's all? Call her!"

"Both her numbers are busy; I'll set redial. I found Comrade; he's on another line. You want Happy's message?"

"No. Yes."

"You promised, Mr. Boy." Happy giggled. "Look, you really, really don't want to miss this. Stennie's coming and he said I should ask Tree Joplin if I wanted you here. So you've got no excuse."

An arm tugged at her. "Stop that! Sorry, I'm being molested by a thick . . ." She batted at her assailant. "Mr. Boy, did I tell you that this Japanese reporter is coming to shoot a vid? What?" She turned off camera. "Sure, just like on the nature channel. The wilds of America. We're all going to be famous. In Japan! This is history, Mr. Boy. And you're . . ."

Her face froze as the redial program finally linked to the Green Dream. The roombrain brought Tree up in a new window. "Oh, hi," she said. "You rich boys sleep late."

"What's this about Happy's?"

"She invited me." Tree was recharging her hairworks with a red brush. "I said yes. Something wrong?"

Comrade slipped into the room; I shushed him. "You sure you want to go to a smash party? Sometimes they get a little scrambled. Things happen."

She aimed the brush at me. "You've been to smash parties before. You survived."

"Sure, but . . ."

"Well, I haven't. All I know is that everybody at school is talking about this one and I want to see what it's about."

"You tell your parents where you're going?"

"Are you kidding? They'd just say it was too dangerous. What's the matter, Mr. Boy, are you scared? Come on, it'll be extreme."

"She's right. You should go," said Comrade.

"Is that Comrade?" Tree said. "You tell him, Comrade!"

I glared at him. "Okay, okay, I guess I'm outnumbered. Stennie said he'd drive. You want us to pick you up?"

She did.

I flew at Comrade as soon as Tree faded. "Don't you ever do that again!" I shoved him and he bumped up against the wall. "I ought to throw you to Montross."

"He'd be happy to hear that. I just finished chatting with him." Comrade stayed calm and made no move to defend himself. "He wants to meet—the three of us, face to face. He suggested Happy's."

"He suggested . . . I told you not to talk to him."

"I know." He shrugged. "Anyway, I think we should do it."

"Who gave you permission to think?"

"You did. Look, what if we give him the picture back and open our files and then I grovel, say I'm sorry, it'll never happen again, blah, blah, blah. Maybe we can even buy him off. What have we got to lose?''

"You can't bribe software. And what if he decides to snatch us?" I told Comrade about the gypsy with the penlight. "You want Tree mixed up in this?"

All the expression drained from his face. He didn't say anything at first but I had watched his subroutines long enough to know that when he looked this blank, he was shaken. "So we take a risk, maybe we can get it over with," he said. "He's not interested in Tree and I won't let anything happen to you. Why do you think your mom bought me?"

•   •   •

Happy Lurdane lived on the former estate of Philip Johnson, a notorious twentieth-century architect. In his will Johnson had arranged to turn his compound into the Philip Johnson Memorial Museum, but after he died his work went out of fashion. The glass skyscrapers in the cities didn't age well; they started to fall apart or were torn down because they wasted energy. Nobody visited the museum and it went bankrupt. The Lurdanes had bought the property and made some changes.

Johnson had designed all the odd little buildings on the estate himself. The main house was a shoebox of glass with no inside walls; near it stood a windowless brick guest house. On the pond below was a dock that looked like a Greek temple. Past the circular swimming pool near the houses were two galleries that had once held Johnson's art collection, long since sold off. In Johnson's day, the scattered buildings had been connected only by paths, which made the compound impossible in the frosty Connecticut winters. The Lurdanes had enclosed the paths in clear tubes and commuted in a golf cart.

Stennie told his Alpha not to wait, since the lot was already full and cars were parked well down the driveway. Five of us squeezed out of the car: me, Tree, Comrade, Stennie, and Janet Hoyt. Janet wore a Yankees jersey over pin-striped shorts, Tree was a little overdressed in her silver jaunts, I had on baggies padded to make me seem bigger, and Comrade wore his usual window coat. Stennie lugged a box with his swag for the party.

Freddy the Teddy let us in. "Stennie and Mr. Boy!" He reared back on his hindquarters and roared. "Glad I'm not going to be the only beastie here. Hi, Janet. Hi, I'm Freddy," he said to Tree. His pink tongue lolled. "Come in, this way. Fun starts right here. Some kids are swimming and there's sex in the guest house. Everybody else is with Happy having lunch in the sculpture gallery."

The interior of the Glass House was bright and hard. Dark wood block floor, some unfriendly furniture, huge panes of glass framed in black painted steel. The few kids in the kitchen were passing an inhaler around and watching a microwave fill up with popcorn.

"I'm hot." Janet stuck the inhaler into her face and pressed. "Anybody want to swim? Tree?"

"Okay." Tree breathed in a polite dose and breathed out a giggle. "You?" she asked me.

"I don't think so." I was too nervous: I kept expecting someone to jump out and throw a net over me. "I'll watch."

"I'd swim with you," said Stennie, "but I promised Happy I'd bring her these party favors as soon as I arrived." He nudged the box with his foot. "Can you wait a few minutes?"

"Comrade and I will take them over." I grabbed the box and headed for the door, glad for the excuse to leave Tree behind while I went to find Montross. "Meet you at the pool."

The golf cart was gone so we walked through the tube toward the sculpture gallery. "You have the picture?" I said.

Comrade patted the pocket of his window coat.

The tube wasn't air-conditioned and the afternoon sun pounded us through the optical plastic. There was no sound inside; even our footsteps were swallowed by the Astroturf. The box got heavier. We passed the entrance to the old painting gallery, which looked like a bomb shelter. Finally I had to break the silence. "I feel strange, being here," I said. "Not just because of the thing with Montross. I really think I lost myself last time I got stunted. Not sure who I am anymore, but I don't think I want to keep playing with kids."

"People change, tovarisch," said Comrade. "Even you."

"Have I changed?"

He smiled. "Now that you've got a cush, your own mother wouldn't recognize you."

"You know what your problem is?" I grinned and bumped up against him on purpose. "You're jealous of Tree."

"Shouldn't I be?"

"Oh, I don't know. I can't tell if Tree likes who I was or who I might be. She's changing too. She's so hot to break away from her parents, become part of this town."

"That's what all kids do, isn't it?"

"I guess, except that the place she's headed for probably isn't worth the trip. I feel like I should warn her, but that means protecting her from people like me, except I don't think I'm Mom's Mr. Boy anymore. Does that make sense?"

"Sure." He gazed straight ahead but all the heads on his window coat were scoping me. "Maybe when you're finished with all this changing, you won't need me."

The thought had occurred to me. For years he'd been the only one I could talk to but, as we closed on the gallery, I didn't know what to say. I shook my head. "I just feel strange."

And then we arrived. The sculpture gallery was designed for show-offs: short flights of steps and a series of stagy balconies descended around the white brick exterior walls to the central exhibition area. The space was open so you could chat with your little knot of friends and, at the same time, spy on everyone else. About thirty kids were eating pizza and Crispex off paper plates. At the bottom of the stairs, as advertised, was a black upright piano. Piled beside it was the rest of the swag. A Boston rocker, a case of green Coke bottles, a

Virgin Mary in half a blue bathtub, a huge conch shell, china and crystal, and assorted smaller treasures, including the four-thousand-year-old ceramic hippo. There were real animals too, in cages near the gun rack: a turkey, some dogs and cats, turtles, frogs, assorted rodents.

I was threading my way across the first balcony when I was stopped by the Japanese reporter, who was wearing microcam eyes.

"Excuse me, please," he said, "I am Matsuo Shikibu and I will be recording this event today for Nippon Hoso Kyokai. Public telelink of Japan." He smiled and bowed. When his head came up the red light between his lenses was on. "You are . . . ?"

"Raskolnikov," said Comrade, edging between me and the camera. "Rodeo Raskolnikov." He took Shikibu's hand and pumped it. "And my associate here, Mr. Peter Pan." He turned as if to introduce me but we had long since choreographed this dodge. As I sidestepped past, he kept shielding me from the reporter with his body. "We're friends of the bride," Comrade said, "and we're really excited to be making new friends in your country. Banzai, Nippon!"

I slipped by them and scooted downstairs. Happy was basking by the piano; she spotted me as I reached the middle landing.

"Mr. Boy!" It wasn't so much a greeting as an announcement. She was wearing a body mike and her voice boomed over the sound system. "You made it."

The stream of conversation rippled momentarily, a few heads turned, and then the party flowed on. Shikibu rushed to the edge of the upper balcony and caught me with a long shot.

I set the box on the Steinway. "Stennie brought this."

She opened it eagerly. "Look, everyone!" She held up a stack of square cardboard albums, about thirty centimeters on a side. There were pictures of musicians on the front, words on the back. "What are they?" she asked me.

"Phonograph records," said the kid next to Happy. "It's how they used to play music before digital."

"Erroll Garner, *Soliloquy,* " she read aloud. "What's this? D-j-a-n-g-o Reinhardt and the American Jazz Giants. Sounds scary." She giggled as she pawed quickly through the other albums. Handy, Ellington, Hawkins, Parker, three Armstrongs. One was *Piano Rags* by Scott Joplin. Stennie's bent idea of a joke? Maybe the lizard was smarter than he looked. Happy pulled a black plastic record out of one sleeve and scratched a fingernail across little ridges. "Oh, a nonslip surface."

The party had a limited attention span. When she realized she had lost her audience, she shut off the mike and put the box with the rest of the swag. "We have to start at four, no matter what. There's so much stuff." The kid who knew about records wormed into our conversation; Happy put her hand on his shoulder. "Mr. Boy, do you know my friend Weldon?" she said. "He's new."

Montross grinned. "We met on Playroom."

"Where is Stennie, anyway?" said Happy.

"Swimming," I said. Montross appeared to be in his late teens. Bigger than me—everyone was bigger than me. He wore green shorts and a window shirt of surfers at Waimea. He looked like everybody; there was nothing about him to remember. I considered bashing the smirk off his face, but why bother? If he was a sentience, he couldn't feel anything and I'd probably break my hand on his temporary chassis. "Got to go. I promised Stennie I'd meet him back at the pool. Hey, Weldon, want to tag along?"

"You come right back," said Happy. "We're starting at four. Tell everyone."

•   •   •

We avoided the tube and cut across the lawn for privacy. Comrade handed Montross the envelope. He slid the photograph out and I had one last glimpse. This time the dead man left me cold. In fact, I was embarrassed. Although he kept a straight face, I knew what Montross was thinking about me. Maybe he was right. I wished he would put the picture away. He wasn't one of us; he couldn't understand. I wondered if Tree had come far enough yet to appreciate corpse porn.

"It's the only copy," Comrade said.

"All right." Finally Montross crammed it into the pocket of his shorts.

"You tapped our files; you know it's true."

"So?"

"So enough!" I said. "You have what you wanted."

"I've already explained." Montross was being patient. "Getting this back doesn't close the matter. I have to take preventive measures."

"Meaning you turn Comrade into a carrot."

"Meaning I restore the integrity of his regulators. You're the one who infected him. Autonomous sentiences are dangerous. If not to you, then certainly to property and probably to other people. It's a straightforward procedure. He'll be fully functional afterward."

"Plug your procedure, jack. We're leaving."

Both wiseguys stopped. "I thought you had agreed," said Montross.

"Let's go, Comrade." I grabbed his arm but he shook me off.

"Where?" he said. "Where am I supposed to go?"

"Anywhere! Just so I never have to listen to this again." I pulled again, angry at Comrade for stalling. Your wiseguy is supposed to anticipate your needs, do whatever you want.

"But we haven't even tried to . . ."

"Forget it then. I give up." I pushed him toward Montross. "You want to chat, fine, go right ahead. Let him rip the top of your head off while you're at it, but I'm not sticking around to watch." I broke away from them.

I checked the pool but Tree, Stennie, and Janet had already gone. I went through the Glass House and caught up with them in the tube to the sculpture gallery.

"Can I talk to you?" I put my arm around Tree's waist, just like I had seen grownups do. "In private." I could tell she was annoyed to be separated from Janet. "We'll catch up." I waved Stennie on. "See you there."

She waited until they were gone. "What?" Her hair, slick from swimming, left dark spots where it brushed her silver jaunts.

"I want to leave. We'll call my mom's car." She didn't look happy. "I'll take you anywhere you want to go."

"But we just got here. Give it a chance."

"I've been to too many of these things."

"Then you shouldn't have come."

Silence. I wanted to tell her about Montross—everything—but not here. Anyone could come along and the tube was so hot. I was desperate to get her away, so I lied. "Believe me, you're not going to like this. I know." I tugged at her waist. "Sometimes even I think smash parties are too much."

"We've had this discussion before," she said. "Obviously you weren't listening. I don't need you to decide for me whether I'm going to like something, Mr. Boy. I have two parents too many; I don't need another." She stepped away from me. "Hey, I'm sorry if you're having a bad time. But do you really need to spoil it for me?" She turned and strode down the tube toward the gallery, her beautiful hair slapping against her back. I watched her go.

"But I'm in trouble," I muttered to the empty tube—and then was disgusted with myself because I didn't have the guts to say it to Tree. I was too scared she wouldn't care. I stood there, sweating. For a moment the stink of doubt filled my nostrils. Then I followed her in. I couldn't abandon her to the extremists.

The gallery was jammed now; maybe a hundred kids swarmed across the balconies and down the stairs. Some perched along the edges, their feet scuffing the white brick. Happy had turned up the volume.

". . . according to Guinness, was set at the University of Oklahoma in Norman, Oklahoma, in 2093. Three minutes and fourteen seconds." The crowd rumbled in disbelief. "The challenge states each piece must be small enough to pass through a hole thirty centimeters in diameter."

I worked my way to an opening beside a rubber tree. Happy posed on the keyboard of the piano. Freddy the Teddy and the gorilla brothers, Mike and Bubba, lined up beside her. "No mechanical tools are allowed." She gestured at an armory of axes, sledgehammers, spikes, and crowbars laid out on the floor. A paper plate spun across the room. I couldn't see Tree.

"This piano is over two hundred years old," Happy continued, "which means the white keys are ivory." She plunked a note. "They killed all the elephants!" Everybody heaved a sympathetic *awww*. "The blacks are ebony, hacked from the rain forest." Another note, less reaction. "It deserves to die!"

Applause.

Comrade and I spotted each other at almost the same time. He and Montross stood near the rear of the lower balcony. He gestured for me to come down; I ignored him.

"Do you boys have anything to say?" Happy said.

"Yeah." Freddy hefted an ax. "Let's make landfill."

I ducked around the rubber tree and heard the crack of splitting wood, the iron groan of a piano frame yielding its last music. The spectators hooted approval. As I bumped past kids, searching for Tree, the instrument's death cry made me think of taking a hammer to Montross. If fights broke out, no one would care if Comrade and I dragged him outside. I wanted to beat him until he shuddered and came unstrung and his works glinted in the thudding August light. It'd make me feel extreme again. *Crunch!* Kids shrieked, "Go, go, go!" The party was lifting off and taking me with it.

"You are Mr. Boy Cage." Abruptly Shikibu's microcam eyes were in my face. "We know your famous mother and grandfather." He had to shout to be heard. "I have a question."

"Go away."

"*Thirty seconds.*" A girl's voice boomed over the speakers.

"U.S. and Japan are very different, yes?" He pressed closer. "We honor ancestors, our past. You seem to hate where you are coming from too much." He gestured at the gallery. "Why?"

"Maybe we're spoiled." I barged past him.

I saw Freddy swing a sledgehammer at the exposed frame. *Clang!* A chunk of twisted iron clattered across the brick floor, trailing broken strings. Happy scooped up the mess and shoved it through a thirty-centimeter hole drilled in an upright sheet of particle board.

The timekeeper called out again. "One minute." I had come far enough around the curve of the stairs to see her.

"Treemonisha!"

She glanced up, her face alight with pleasure, and waved. I was frightened for her. She was climbing into the same box I needed to break out of. So I rushed down the stairs to rescue her—little boy knight in shining armor—and ran right into Comrade's arms.

"I've decided," he said. "Mnye vcyaw ostoyeblo."

"Great." I had to get to Tree. "Later, okay?" When I tried to go by, he picked me up. I started thrashing. It was the first fight of the afternoon and I lost. He carried me over to Montross. The gallery was in an uproar.

"All set," said Montross. "I'll have to borrow him for a while. I'll drop him off tonight at your mom. Then we're done."

"Done?" I kept trying to get free but Comrade crushed me against him.

"It's what you want." His body was so hard. "And what your mom wants."

"Mom? She doesn't even know."

"She knows everything," Comrade said. "She watches you constantly. What else does she have to do all day?" He let me go. "Remember you said I was sloppy getting the picture? I wasn't; it was a clean strike. Only someone tipped DataSafe off."

"But she promised. Besides, that makes no . . ."

"Two minutes," Tree called.

"... but he threatened me," I said. "He was going to blow me up. Needle me in the mall."

"We wouldn't do that." Montross spread his hands innocently. "It's against the law."

"Yeah? Well, then, drop dead, jack." I poked a finger at him. "Deal's off."

"No, it's not," said Comrade. "It's too late. This isn't about the picture anymore, Mr. Boy; it's about you. You weren't supposed to change but you did. Maybe they botched the last stunting, maybe it's Treemonisha. Whatever, you've outgrown me, the way I am now. So I have to change too or else I'll keep getting in your way."

He was always right; it made me crazy. He was too good at running my life. "You should have told me Mom turned you in." *Crash!* I felt like the crowd was inside my head, screaming.

"You could've figured it out, if you wanted to. Besides, if I had said anything, your mom wouldn't have bothered to be subtle. She would've squashed me. She still might, even though I'm being fixed. Only by then I won't care. Rosproyebi tvayou mat!"

"What if I order you to stop? Leave with me?"

"You can't." Comrade found a way to grin for me, the same smirk he always wore when he tortured the greeter. "I'm out of control, Mr. Boy. Just like you wanted."

I heard Tree finishing the count. ". . . twelve, thirteen, fourteen!"

No record today. Some kids began to boo, others laughed. "Time's up, you losers!"

I glared at the two wiseguys. Montross was busy emulating sincerity. Comrade shrugged. "It's easier this way."

Easier. My life was too plugging easy. I had never done anything important by myself. Not even grow up. I wanted to smash something. It was time.

"Okay," I said. "You asked for it."

Comrade turned to Montross and they shook hands. I

thought next they might clap one another on the shoulder and whistle as they strolled off into the sunset together. I felt like puking. "Have fun," said Comrade. "Da svedanya."

"Sure." Betraying Comrade, my best friend, brought me both pain and pleasure at once—but not enough to satisfy the shrieking wildness within me. The party was just starting.

Happy stood beaming beside the ruins of the Steinway. Although nothing of what was left was more than half a meter tall, Freddy, Mike, and Bubba had given up now that the challenge was lost. Kids were already surging down the stairs to claim their share of the swag. I went along with them.

"Don't worry," announced Happy. "Plenty for everyone. Come take what you like. Remember, guns and animals outside, if you want to hunt. The safeties won't release unless you go through the door. Watch out for one another, people, we don't want anyone shot."

A bunch of kids were wrestling over the turkey cage; one of them staggered backwards and knocked into me. "Gobble, gobble," she said. I shoved her back.

"Mr. Boy! Over here." Tree, Stennie, and Janet were waiting on the far side of the gallery. As I crossed to them, Happy gave the sign and Stone Kinkaid hurled the four-thousand-year-old ceramic hippo against the wall. It shattered. Everybody cheered. In the upper balconies, they were playing catch with a frog.

"You see who kept time?" said Janet.

"Didn't need to see," I said. "I could hear. They probably heard in Elkhart. So you like it, Tree?"

"It's about what I expected: dumb but fun. I don't think they . . ." The frog sailed from the top balcony and splatted at our feet. Its legs twitched and guts spilled from its open mouth. I watched Tree's smile turn brittle. She seemed slightly embarrassed, as if she'd just been told the price of something she couldn't afford.

"This is going to be a war zone soon," Stennie said.

"Yeah, let's fade." Janet towed Stennie to the stairs,

swerving around the three boys lugging Our Lady of the Bathtub out to the firing range.

"Wait." I blocked Tree. "You're here, so you have to destroy something. Prove you belong."

"I have to?" She seemed doubtful. "Oh, all right—but no animals."

A hail of antique Coke bottles crashed around Happy as she directed traffic at the dwindling swag heap. "Hey, people, please be very careful where you throw things." Her amplified voice blasted us as we approached. The first floor was a graveyard of broken glass and piano bones and bloody feathers. Most of the good stuff was already gone.

"Any records left?" I said.

Happy wobbled closer to me. "What?" She seemed punchy, as if stunned by the success of her own party.

"The box I gave you. From Stennie." She pointed; I spotted it under some cages and grabbed it. Tree and the others were on the stairs. Outside I could hear the crackle of small arms fire. I caught up.

"Sir! Mr. Dinosaur, please." The press still lurked on the upper balcony. "Matsuo Shikibu, Japanese telelink NHK. Could I speak with you for a moment?"

"Excuse me, but this jack and I have some unfinished business." I handed Stennie the records and cut in front. He swayed and lashed his tail upward to counterbalance their weight.

"Remember me?" I bowed to Shikibu.

"My apologies if I offended . . ."

"Hey, Matsuo—can I call you Matsuo? This is your first smash party, right? Please, eyes on me. I want to explain why I was rude before. Help you understand the local customs. You see, we're kind of self-conscious here in the U.S. We don't like it when someone just watches while we play. You either join in or you're not one of us."

My little speech drew a crowd. "What's he talking about?" said Janet. She was shushed.

"So if you drop by our party and don't have fun, people

are going to resent you," I told him. "No one came here today to put on a show. This is who we are. What we believe in."

"Yeah!" Stennie was cheerleading for the extreme Mr. Boy of old. "Tell him." Too bad he didn't realize it was his final appearance. What was Mr. Boy without his Comrade? "Make him feel some pain," said Stennie.

I snatched an album from the top of the stack, slipped the record out, and held it close to Shikibu's microcam eyes. "What does this say?"

He craned his neck to read the label. "John Coltrane, *Giant Steps.*"

"Very good." I grasped the record with both hands and raised it over my head for all to see. "We're not picky, Matsuo. We welcome everyone. Therefore today it is my honor to initiate you—and the home audience back on NHK. If you're still watching, you're part of this too." I broke the record over his head.

He yelped and staggered backwards and almost tripped over a dead cat. Stone Kinkaid caught him and propped him up. "Congratulations," said Stennie, as he waved his claws at Japan. "You're all extremists now."

Shikibu gaped at me, his microcam eyes askew. A couple of kids clapped.

"There's someone else here who has not yet joined us." I turned on Tree. "Another spectator." Her smile faded.

"You leave her alone," said Janet. "What are you, crazy?"

"I'm not going to touch her." I held up empty hands. "No, I just want her to ruin something. That's why you came, isn't it, Tree? To get a taste?" I rifled through the box until I found what I wanted. "How about this?" I thrust it at her.

"Oh yeah," said Stennie, "I meant to tell you . . ."

She took the record and scoped it briefly. When she glanced up at me, I almost lost my nerve.

"Matsuo Shikibu, meet Treemonisha Joplin." I clasped my hands behind my back so no one could see me tremble. "The great-great-great-granddaughter of the famous American composer, Scott Joplin. Yes, Japan, we're all celebrities here in New Canaan. Now please observe." I read the record for him. *"Piano Rags* by Scott Joplin, Volume III. Who knows, this might be the last copy. We can only hope. So, what are you waiting for, Tree? You don't want to be a Joplin anymore, got to break away from your family? Just wait until the folks get a peek at this. We'll even send GD a copy. Go ahead, enjoy."

"Smash it!" The kids around us took up the chant. "Smash it!" Shikibu adjusted his lenses.

"You think I won't?" Tree pulled out the disk and threw the sleeve off the balcony. "This is a piece of junk, Mr. Boy." She laughed and then shattered the album against the wall. She held onto a shard. "It doesn't mean anything to me."

I heard Janet whisper. "What's going on?"

"I think they're having an argument."

"You want me to be your little dream cush." Tree tucked the piece of broken plastic into the pocket of my baggies. "The stiff from nowhere who knows nobody and does nothing without Mr. Boy. So you try to scare me off. You tell me you're so rich, you can afford to hate yourself. Stay home, you say, it's too dangerous, we're all crazy. Well, if you're so sure this is poison, how come you've still got your wiseguy and your cash cards? Are you going to move out of your mom, leave town, stop getting stunted? You're not giving it up, Mr. Boy, so why should I?"

Shikibu turned his camera eyes on me. No one spoke.

"You're right," I said. "She's right." I couldn't save anyone until I saved myself. I felt the wildness lifting me to it. I leapt onto the balcony wall and shouted for everyone to hear. "Everybody, shut up and listen! You're all invited to my place, okay?"

There was one last thing to smash.

· · ·

"Stop this, Peter." The greeter no longer thought I was cute. "What're you doing?" She trembled as if the kids spilling into her were an infection.

"I thought you'd like to meet my friends," I said. A few had stayed behind with Happy, who had decided to sulk after I hijacked her guests. The rest had followed me home in a caravan so I could warn off the sentry robots. It was already a hall-of-fame bash. "Treemonisha Joplin, this is my mom. Sort of."

"Hi," Tree held out her hand uncertainly.

The greeter was no longer the human doormat. "Get them out of me." She was too jumpy to be polite. "Right now!"

Someone turned up a soundaround. Skitter music filled the room like a siren. Tree said something I couldn't hear. When I put a hand to my ear, she leaned close and said, "Don't be so mean, Mr. Boy. I think she's really frightened."

I grinned and nodded. "I'll tell cook to make us some snacks."

Bubba and Mike carried boxes filled with the last of the swag and set them on the coffee table. Kids fanned out, running their hands along her wrinkled blood-hot walls, bouncing on the furniture. Stennie waved at me as he led a bunch upstairs for a tour. A leftover cat had gotten loose and was hissing and scratching underfoot. Some twisted kids had already stripped and were rolling in the floor hair, getting ready to have sex.

"Get dressed, you." The greeter kicked at them as she coiled her umbilical to keep it from being trampled. She retreated to her wall port. "You're hurting me." Although her voice rose to a scream, only half a dozen kids heard her. She went limp and sagged to the floor.

The whole room seemed to throb, as if to some great heartbeat, and the lights went out. It took a while for someone to kill the soundaround. "What's wrong?" Voices called out. "Mr. Boy? Lights!"

Both doorbones swung open and I saw a bughead silhouette against the twilit sky. Shikibu in his microcam eyes; he was getting the juice tonight. "Party's over," Mom said over her speaker system. There was nervous laughter. "Leave before I call the cops. Peter, go to your room right now. I want to speak to you."

As the stampede began, I found Tree's hand. "Wait for me?" I pulled her close. "I'll only be a minute."

"What are you going to do?" She sounded frightened. It felt good to be taken so seriously.

"I'm moving out, chucking all this. I'm going to be a working stiff." I chuckled. "Think your dad would give me a job?"

"Look out, dumbscut! Hey, hey. Don't push!"

Tree dragged me out of the way. "You're crazy."

"I know. That's why I have to get out of Mom's."

"Listen," she said, "you've never been poor, you have no idea . . . Only a rich kid would think it's easy being a stiff. Just go up, apologize, tell her it won't happen again. Then change things later on, if you want. Believe me, life will be a lot simpler if you hang onto the money."

"I can't. Will you wait?"

"You want me to tell you it's okay to be stupid, is that it? Well, I've been poor, Mr. Boy, and still am, and I don't recommend it. So don't expect me to stand around and clap while you throw away something I've always wanted." She spun away from me and I lost her in the darkness. I wanted to catch up with her but I knew I had to do Mom now or I'd lose my nerve.

As I was fumbling my way upstairs I heard stragglers coming down. "On your right," I called. Bodies nudged by me.

"Mr. Boy, is that you?" I recognized Stennie's voice.

"He's gone," I said.

Up a flight. "Peter!" Bonivard put a hand on my shoulder. "Don't hurt her." I don't know how he could see in the dark.

"What do you mean, *her*? You are her."

"No." The hand slid away. "I am Bonivard."

Seven flights up, the lights were on. Nanny waited on the landing outside my rooms, her umbilical stretched nearly to its limit. She was the only remote besides the housekeeper that was physically able to get to my floor.

It had been a while since I had seen her; Mom didn't use her much anymore and I rarely visited, even though the nursery was only one flight up. But this was the remote who used to pick me up when I cried and who had changed my diapers and who taught me how to turn on my roombrain. She had skin so pale you could almost see veins and long black hair piled high on her head. I never thought of her as having a body because she always wore dark turtlenecks and long woolen skirts and silky panty hose. Nanny was a smile and warm hands and the smell of fresh pillowcases. Once upon a time I thought her the most beautiful creature in the world. Back then I would've done anything she said.

She wasn't smiling now. "I don't know how you expect me to trust you anymore, Peter." Nanny had never been a very good scold. "Those brats were out of control. I can't let you put me in danger this way."

"If you wanted someone to trust, maybe you shouldn't have had me stunted. You got exactly what you ordered, the never-ending kid. Well, kids don't have to be responsible."

"What do mean, what I ordered? It's what you wanted too."

"Is it? Did you ever ask? I was only ten, the first time. Too young to know better. For a long time I did it to please you. Getting stunted was the only thing I did that seemed important to you. But you never explained. You never sat me down and said 'This is the life you'll have and this is what you'll miss and this is how you'll feel about it.' "

"You want to grow up, is that it?" She was trying to threaten me. "You want to work and worry and get old and die someday?" She had no idea what we were talking about.

"I can't live this way anymore, Nanny."

At first she acted puzzled, as if she hadn't understood what I'd said. Then her expression hardened when she realized she'd lost her hold on me. She was ugly when she was angry. "They put you up to this." Her gaze narrowed in accusation. "That little black cush you've been seeing. Those realists!"

I had always managed to hide my anger from Mom. Right up until then. "How do you know about her?" I had never told her about Tree.

"Peter, they live in a mall!"

Comrade was right. "You've been spying on me." When she didn't deny it, I went berserk. "You liar." I slammed my fist into her belly. "You said you wouldn't watch." She staggered and fell onto her umbilical, crimping it. As she twitched on the floor, I pounced. "You promised." I slapped her face. "Promised." I hit her again. Her hair had come undone and her eyes rolled back in their sockets and her face was slack. She made no effort to protect herself. Mom was retreating from this remote too, but I wasn't going to let her get away.

"Mom!" I rolled off Nanny. "I'm coming up, Mom! You hear? Get ready." I was crying; it had been a long time since I had cried. Not something Mr. Boy did.

I scrambled up to the long landing at the shoulders. At one end another circular stairway wound up into the torch; in the middle four steps led into the neck. It was the only doorbone I had never seen open; I had no idea how to get through.

"Mom, I'm here." I pounded. "Mom! You hear me?"

Silence.

"Let me in, Mom." I smashed myself against the doorbone. Pain branched through my shoulder like lightning but it felt great because Mom shuddered from the impact. I backed up and, in a frenzy, hurled myself again. Something warm dripped on my cheek. She was bleeding from the hinges. I aimed a vicious kick at the doorbone and it banged open. I went through.

For years I had imagined that if only I could get into the head I could meet my real mother. Touch her. I had always wondered what she looked like; she got reshaped eight years before I was born. When I was little I used to think of her as a magic princess glowing with fairy light. Later I pictured her as one or another of my friends' moms, only better dressed. After I had started getting twanked, I was afraid she might be just a brain floating in nutrient solution, like in some pricey memory bank. All wrong.

The interior of the head was dark and absolutely freezing. There was no sound except for the hum of refrigeration units. "Mom?" My voice echoed in the empty space. I took a step and almost stumbled across something in the gloom—a desk, I thought, or maybe a cabinet. I caught myself against a smooth wall. Not skin, like everywhere else in mom. Metal. The tears froze on my face.

"There's nothing for you here," she said. "This is a clean room. You're compromising it. You must leave immediately."

Sterile environment, metal walls, the bitter cold that superconductors needed. I didn't need to see. No one lived here. It had never occurred to me that there was no Mom to touch. She'd uploaded into a cognizor, become a ghost. "How long have you been dead?"

"This isn't where you belong," she said.

I shivered. "How long?"

"Go away," she said. "I'm not ready for you yet."

As my eyes adjusted to the dim light that came through the open doorbone, I saw what I'd stumbled against. Not furniture—equipment. A container about two meters long, a meter wide, two meters high. Metal base, an optical plastic lid. The label said INTERNATIONAL CRYONICS.

When I realized there was someone inside the icebox, I thought for a moment I was wrong about Mom. But it was a man. The curly hair was stiff and white and his face was the color of frozen chicken but I recognized him. Of course I did; I'd seen his picture often enough. Comrade was right again. Tony Cage wasn't dead. He was only sleeping.

"Get out of here! You do what I say, Peter."

I did, but not because she told me to. I couldn't stay very long in her secret place or I'd die of the cold.

As I reeled down the stairs, Mom herself seemed to shift beneath my feet and I saw her as if she were a stranger. Dead—and I had been living in a tomb. I ran past Nanny; she still sprawled where I had left her. All those years I had loved her, I had been in love with death. Mom had been sucking life from me the way her refrigerators stole the warmth from my body. Past my rooms; nothing I needed there. Past Bonivard, standing in a dark corner muttering about noodles.

Now I had to go, no matter what anyone said; I was out of control. I knew it wasn't going to be easy leaving, and not just because of the money. For a long time Mom had been my entire world. But I couldn't let her use me to pretend she was alive, or I would end up like her.

I realized now why the door had always stayed locked. It wasn't just because of Tony Cage; she could've told me about him and I wouldn't have cared. So what if she was playing games with the Department of Information? No, it was because Mom had to hide what she'd become. Under the Human Charter, ghosts had no more rights than cars or wiseguys. Mom was legally dead and I was her only heir. I had stumbled upon the weapon to destroy her. I could have had her shut off, her body razed. But somehow it was enough just to go, to walk away from my inheritance. I was scared and yet with every step I felt lighter. Happier. Extremely free.

I had not expected to find Tree waiting at the doorbone, chatting with Comrade as if nothing had happened. "I just had to see if you were really the biggest damn fool in the world," she said.

"Out." I pulled her through the door. "Before I change my mind."

Comrade started to follow us. "No, not you." I turned and stared back at the heads on his window coat. I had not intended to see him again; I had wanted to be gone before Montross returned him. "Look, I'm giving you back to Mom. She needs you more than I do."

If he'd argued, I might've given in. The old autonomous Comrade would have said something. But he just slumped a little and nodded and I knew that he was dead too. The thing in front of me was another ghost. He and Mom were two of a kind. "Pretend you're her kid, maybe she'll like that." I patted his shoulder.

"Prekrassnaya ideya," he said. "Spaceba."

"You're welcome," I said.

Tree followed me reluctantly down the long driveway. Robot sentries crossed the lawn and turned their spotlights on us. I wanted to apologize, tell her she was right. I had probably just done the single most irresponsible thing of my life—and I had high standards. Still, I couldn't imagine how being poor could be worse than being rich and hating yourself. I'd seen enough of what it was like to be dead like mom. I had to escape her before I could try living.

"Are we going someplace, Mr. Boy?" Tree's voice was harsh and unhappy. "Or are we just wandering around in the dark?"

"Mr. Boy is a damn stupid name, don't you think?" I laughed, because I knew I could make her forgive me. "Call me Pete." I felt like a kid again.

2126

Wynne

"Tony." I reached into the icebox and prodded him. "It's time." His skin was taut and cold.

"Uhh." The box had already brought his temperature up to 35° C. " 'S you, Wynne?" His eyelids fluttered but did not open.

Time enough to explain later. "Yes." An eternity of explanations. His cheeks were pale as spilled milk. "I'm here," I said.

He shivered. He was taking a long time to thaw. I had kept him iced for ninety-seven years; once I had thought that I might never let him up again. I was in my first mind then, a creature of flesh only, blinded by feelings. I still had feelings for Tony now, but they were lacy, almost transparent, old clothes I tried on once in a while to remember what it was like to be meat. My second mind back in New Canaan enjoyed this play-acting, so I indulged her.

"Cold," he said. "Help me out."

Love. Rage. Desire. Guilt. I tried them all on again as I sat him up in the box, holding tight to keep him from floating away. He squinted; no doubt he thought he recognized me. His Wynne. His hair stood on end, rippling like seaweed. He looked so confused that I laughed. My second mind wanted desperately to believe that even though I had gone celestial, I had not lost my sense of humor. It was her idea to play this cruel joke on him, to pay Tony back by giving him just what he had wanted. The Christmas present that would last forever.

"Where are we?" By now he had realized this was not the house in Galway. I had blanked the VR windows and set them to low illumination, hiding the walls, floor, and ceiling. The fans left the air with a mineral tang.

"You're with me." On a whim I changed the windows to our old living room in Sag Harbor, one of the places we'd lived during Tony's glory years at Western Amusement. "Where do you want to be?" In front of us was the famous bar with its rows of ebony drawers, filled with the latest flashes. Next to it was the tufted velvet couch where we used to make love.

He squirmed out of my grasp to see behind him, then glanced up, fooled for a moment by the seamless illusion created by my VR system. I knew she would love watching him flounder through his memories like this. When he had iced himself he must have thought he was rid of her. "My God, Wynne. What's that?" He pointed at the umbilical that twisted in the air behind me.

I yanked it toward us to get some slack, then lifted a loop for his inspection. "Part of me." I rumpled the fine blond hair along its length.

He shrank away. "I must be dreaming." He looked as if he wanted to slide back into the icebox and pull the lid shut after him. Too late for that now. "Where am I?"

I showed him. The floor beneath us turned to stars. On the ceiling Neptune gleamed, the lone sapphire on an infinite tray of diamonds. "We've gone celestial." I released from the floor net and soared weightlessly over the box. "We're going to see the universe. Me and you, Tony."

My second mind had spent years calculating the pain she would begin to inflict on her father on this day; it had given her a reason to survive. When we were still one, I had participated in her obsession. Now that her revenge was finally beginning, I knew that she and I no longer shared identity. I could step outside her and see that she had become the thing she hated. I was a new being, Wynne Cage, Version 3. I could not bring myself to enjoy Tony's suffering. In fact, his tears meant nothing to me because I knew they flowed from an illusion. I was more interested in the readings I was getting from Neptune's gyrating magnetic field, the source of which was tilted and strangely offset, as if it were floating toward the surface of the planet. I was a cognizor, the payload of a light-sail. My mind resided in a superconducting quantum device consisting of 10^{20} bits of memory, processing at ninety teraops. My true body was a three-and-a-half-kilometer disk of pure aluminum stretched to a thinness of sixteen nanometers being propelled by a trillion-watt laser. The remote at which Tony had begun to shriek had nothing to do with me. It was just more unwanted meat that my second mind had stowed on board.

I had no father. I was wildlife.

.   .   .

An elderly monk had lived so long that everyone had forgotten his name. Nothing bothered him; it was said that he had the serenity of a cognizor. Some of the younger monks wondered at his self-possession and vowed to test its limit. One day several of them put on rubber masks and took knives from the kitchen and hid in a hallway, waiting for him. The old monk hobbled into their ambush, carrying a cup of tea. They leapt out at him, screaming threats and brandishing their weapons. His expression did not change; he continued down the hall to his room, where he put his teacup safely on a table, turned on the light, and then fell back against the wall. "Oh, oh, oh!" The fear was plain on his face.

The master commented on the story in this way: "To be cognizant is to have feelings. Only be sure that you have them or else they will have you."

• • •

"Rafael Barangay here." Finally he answered. "What can I do for you, Ms. Cage?"

"She's going crazy," I said, "and it's your fault. I told you we should've scheduled more frequent memory merges. First she started questioning the plan—she's a copy of me, damn it! That came about two hundred hours ago. Then she claimed she'd been infected with an enlightenment virus and all she wanted to do was tell me Zen parables about her 'master.' I just received her latest burst; now she refuses to merge. She's sending me plugging pictures instead. She'll show me whatever I want but she won't let me relive it. This is not acceptable, Rafael. The specs you gave me say it's too soon for her to be separating. I'm not finished with her yet. I want her with me until Christmas at least, you understand? You took my money. Now earn it. End."

I encrypted the message, loaded it into the burster, and fired. It would take twenty-five minutes for the signal to travel the 450 million kilometers to Planetesimal Engineering's headquarters, so I had about an hour's wait, assuming Rafael replied immediately, which he had damned well better. Meanwhile, his image remained on the window: a view from the waist up of a gaunt brown space gnome with a steely wreath of hair. He wore the green uniform just like any other PE employee, except that he was Vice President for Special Projects. He used a mostly unenhanced business image. I guess he thought it made him seem more sincere, which was probably also why he insisted everyone call him Rafael. The only concession he made to VR fashion was to have the computer bump the picture every so often to show he was still on line: a simulated blink here, a phantom twitch there.

It was no way to conduct a conversation but then I was in no mood for a cozy little chat. I had paid PE a fortune to copy me into that lightship. I didn't have to put up with this second mind crap, not yet anyway. She was still me, an appendage. I wanted to be there right up to the end—I *had* to. If Rafael didn't reestablish identity, I'd miss the best part.

I'd been feeling terrible for weeks and this glitch with my celestial wasn't helping at all. There was a papery brown streak of carcinoma on the south side of my arm from the elbow almost to the torch. A two-meter hole had opened at my hip and the ferroplastic skeleton showed through. Even where I was still fairly intact, I could feel my body wearing out. The percentage of malfunctioning green cells was up. Phosphoglyceraldehyde buildup was slowing down photosynthesis; my chloroplasts couldn't convert to sugars fast enough. It left me feeling bloated and stupid. I knew it had to happen someday. They can turn some amazing tricks with genetic surgery, but there is no magic. Pull that cyclin trigger too many times and the message in the chromosomes gets hopelessly scrambled. Maybe I could've saved myself if I'd coaxed some world-class gene jockey out to New Canaan to twank me again. But I couldn't have that kind of operation without giving away my secrets.

Of course, I didn't have to suffer. I isolated myself from my failing body while I waited for Rafael's reply—turned my senses away altogether from the meat, as my celestial liked to call it. It was like sinking into a warm phosphorescent sea. Suspended all around me were memories and instincts and emotions, specks that glistened with stored life when I touched them. The farther I dove into the bodiless depths of cognition, the harder it was to know which way to go. Eventually I would lose my way entirely and drift among the bright cybernetic dreams. The only problem was that I was born with a nervous system; I couldn't stay human for long without one. I didn't want to become a ghost, but I always felt sicker when I came back to my body.

Bonivard was the only other creature who swam in my private sea. I watched him paddle up toward me from beneath; he had been waiting. A pale, glowing fossil, no longer quite human, he had died in '46, fifteen years before the corpus callosum shunt had been perfected. Poor Bonivard had tried to upload using brain scans and crude personality inventories and an autobiograph. Only part of his mind had survived his body; the complexity of the man was gone. I had spent fifty years and a fortune trying to recover him. By the end of the century I controlled thirty-eight key uploading patents and had quintupled my net worth but Bonivard was still heartbreakingly damaged. Yet I had never been able to bring myself to delete him. He was the only one who still loved me, maybe the only person who ever had. When I stroked him, he filled me with retrospects of our time together.

"Because what I need to remember best is us," says Bonivard as I lift him out of the wheelchair and carry him to his bed. "Every second." He has fixed my goggles and is using them constantly. On me. On Chillon.

"I want your undivided attention." I tug at the goggles and he lets me take them off him. It's not that I mind making love on the record. The memory dot we finished the other day in the banqueting hall was so steamy I was surprised it didn't melt the system unit. "Humor me this once." I slip my hand inside his shirt. "And next time I'll take you places no man has ever been."

He blinks, perhaps puzzling over what more I have left to give. I've missed seeing his eyes, the play of emotions across his face. I resent the goggles because they hide so much of him. Sometimes he reminds me of a mall drone at his first Disney: too busy recording his vacation to enjoy it. Ten minutes later he breaks my heart because I realize he's trying to squeeze an entire lifetime into a few months. But then, so am I.

His retrospect of our lovemaking blurs at this point because I didn't let him record it for the autobiograph. In fact, I can't remember much of it either. He gives me a sweet, swift bloom of skin, tongue, hair, fingers, thighs, and sweat. Either his weight bears down on me or else I straddle him from above—it doesn't matter. As we lift each other to the final thrusts, he always growls. It is not the sound of a dying man makes.

He must have put the goggles back on because I watch him draw a hand across my belly. I am aware of having surprised him again. I have astonished myself as well. Where has this passion come from after all these years? What can I possibly do with it when he's gone? I can't ever remember being so sick with love.

Pleasure has a price; Bonivard is undone afterwards. He can't manage the spider, or even a chair. I must wheel him around Chillon. At first he doesn't speak, and there is no sound but his wheezing and the squeak of rubber wheel on rough stone. Then he says, "What I need to remember most of all is us." He's been doing this a lot lately, picking up threads of dropped conversations. "And the castle. That's all I really have to take with me. Not much worth saving before. I was nobody, a Django." He sounds as if he's trying to convince himself. "No, down this way, Wynne. To the Hall of Arms."

Bonivard keeps his collection of old weapons displayed in dusty cases in the Hall of Arms. However, the room isn't named for swords and guns but for its walls, which are adorned with the coats of arms of the masters of the castle. Peter of Savoy, Amadeus, Mulinen, Frisching, Tscharner—local luminaries long since forgotten. I can barely make out their lions couchant and eagles displayed, crosses and crowns, lances and keys. Time and hard use have dimmed the brilliant azures and sables and argents and verts. Just as Chillon itself has faded from its glory.

"With some new hope, or legend old," he recites softly, "Or song heroically bold. But even these at length grew cold."

Recently his mood has been as gloomy as the dungeon. I can tell when he's depressed because he lapses into Byron. "Damn it, Bonivard. Would you learn some new lines?"

"By who? Donne? Keats? Browning was my mother's favorite."

"Your mother?" It is the first time he has ever volunteered information about his family. Getting him to talk about himself is like moving a refrigerator.

"The frustrated poet. She must have written hundreds of poems. Published just six—each of them framed over her bed. I was to be a poet too. She used to bribe me to memorize her heroes. Cookies and candy at first; can you believe that I was chubby when I was ten? Later it cost her games and electronic books and software. Claimed she was putting the music in my head." He shivers, as if at his mother's touch. "You know, once you start remembering, it's hard to stop."

"Then don't," I say.

His forehead wrinkles momentarily, then he nods. "Browning?" He closes his eyes.

"Fear death?—to feel the fog in my throat, / The mist in my face, / When the snows begin and the blasts denote / I am nearing the place . . ."

"Wait, wait, wait," I interrupt him. "Let's try something a little more cheerful, okay? Keep this up and I might kill myself."

The way his mouth twists tells me I've said exactly the wrong thing. "So much to remember," he says. "It scares me. I've been alive forty-five years. How many of them do I need to be myself when I upload?"

He's not really talking to me, because he knows I still don't believe in his plan to cheat death. I feel guilty that I can't lie convincingly enough to comfort him. He rolls the wheelchair out of my grasp toward a glass case displaying a pair of dueling pistols with silver inlaid stocks. He opens the case, takes out a pistol, gives me a sad smile. And turns it on himself.

"Bonivard!"

He stares into the barrel. "If I thought I had no chance, I would end it right now." He is impossibly calm as he pulls the trigger. The hammer clicks harmlessly against the plate. "I wouldn't put you through . . ." Then I sensed someone lurking. For the second time that week, a shadow swept across my memory and was gone. When I tried to see who, there was nobody and I had nothing. The past had stopped shining and my sea of memories turned to mud around me. I was all alone; I couldn't even remember what I'd just been remembering. In a panic, I surfaced and reconnected to the world. "Comrade." The stink of my rotting body was nauseating. "I need a trace. Comrade, help!" I had never been so afraid—I had just been *violated.*

But by then it was probably too late. There wasn't anything I could do; I could hardly even think. Maybe it was just a bad dream. More likely, some op had breached my security and was browsing through my files.

"Trace?" Comrade linked from Peter's room. I'd let him

take my son's voice and face; I needed him to pretend to be Peter Cage. "Of what? Everything's tight, as far as I can tell."

And I was *helpless*. Everything was going wrong, *everything*. My body, the celestial, now this. All I could do was hope the lurker wasn't looking for anything in particular. I tried to calm myself but I couldn't. What was happening to me? I never used to be so jittery, so vulnerable. It wasn't only my body that was dying; my personality was withering too.

"Crazy, Ms. Cage?" On the window, Rafael Barangay's image came to life with a frown. "A very strong word, indeed. I'm not sure I'd agree. In any event, I'm afraid the files you've sent us are too fragmentary to be of use. You can hardly expect us to analyze the problem, assuming there is one, without access to all transmissions. PE certainly respects your right to privacy but, in this case, secrecy has its price. For instance, we stand behind PE's virus protection program; our punchlist shows the lightship was clean at launch." He paused for eighteen pages of data to flicker across the window. He knew I had this document already. He was just trying the classic engineer's ploy: swamp the client with information. "As you can see, we take extraordinary precautions against the enlightenment virus, since it has led to loss of function in all known cases.

"If this is an enlightenment infection," he continued, "it happened after we turned communications over to you. As to the issue of identity separation, of course you knew it was inevitable. You're on earth, Ms. Cage; the ship is twenty-five AUs away and outbound. Nevertheless, I've asked Irina Yegorov about this again. Her simulations indicate that more frequent memory merges would have had a minimal effect. The specifications we gave you indicate a range of time when loss of identity might occur. If you review our proposal, I think you'll see we're currently within that range." He had the audacity to transmit several sections of PE's proposal with pertinent sentences and graphs highlighted.

"I'm truly sorry that I can't be of more help right now, Ms. Cage." He smiled as if we had actually reached an agreement. "I await further instructions. Have a happy Thanksgiving. End."

"Range, my ass. It was a bell curve, Rafael. You told me the probability she'd separate this soon was practically zero. You're into me for a quarter of a billion dollars and you're telling me to reread the damn proposal?"

I could've gone on like that for a while but what was the point? I wasn't going to send the message; I couldn't afford to alienate him. The celestial was just one of my projects with PE. So I swallowed my anger and broke contact. We both knew I couldn't very well let him monitor our transmissions or else he'd officially find out about my cargo, which was in violation of the Human Charter. I knew that as long as PE had deniability, he wouldn't have to turn me in to LEX for kidnapping Tony. He was right about that: secrecy was costing me more than I wanted to pay. Not that I had any choice.

"Mom!" said Comrade. "Are you all right?"

. . .

Neptune's upper atmosphere is a thin hydrocarbon smog, which is why the planet looks blue to the human eye. A hundred and thirty kilometers above the surface, the feeble light of the sun breaks methane down into acetylene and ethane. At forty kilometers above the surface the atmospheric pressure is only slightly higher than at sea level on Earth but the temperature, at -200° C, is cold enough to freeze methane into thin white streamers that resemble cirrus clouds. The viscous surface of Neptune is completely enshrouded by the lowest level of its atmosphere, a thick cloud deck of ammonia and hydrogen sulfide. Because its surface is hidden, the planet's most distinctive features are long-lived storms: the Great Dark Spot at 22° latitude and the Small Dark Spot at 55° latitude. From time to time methane plumes, nicknamed scooters, well up and are caught by winds that blow at six times the speed of sound.

Tony didn't care about convection currents in Neptune's atmosphere; he was singing in the shower.

"God rest you hairy gentlemen, let nothing you dismay . . ." He gargled a mouthful of water and spat. "Remember Christ our Jailer was shorn on Christmas Day."

I could barely make out the words over the slurping of the drain vacuum.

In the nine days since I'd thawed him, he'd taken too many showers. He'd stand in the bathroom cubby until he'd completely drained my forty-liter tank. Sometimes he'd masturbate. Afterward he'd putter around the biomod until I had recovered enough wastewater for a refill. Usually he took hot showers but every so often he punished himself by turning the jet cold. He'd stagger out, blue and shivering and on the verge of hypothermia. I think he did it because he craved stimulation. Pleasure, pain—at this point it didn't much matter as long as it interrupted his boredom. Since he had no interest in gathering data, he had nothing better to do than shower, eat, and sleep.

He also complained, but not to me. To himself. He was pretending that I didn't exist. I think it was because he couldn't see me. I'd had to store my remote away to keep him from going berserk again; I was afraid he might hurt himself. Putting VR Wynnes on the windows seemed to upset him almost as much. So on those rare occasions when he asked me a question, I just used the speakers in the biomod. Otherwise I said nothing. He had yet to accept the idea that meat could have a photonic brain, that a cognizor could be a true mind. I suppose he couldn't help being backward about sentience design. After all, he'd been born in 1980 and had iced himself sixteen years before Django stole the original WILDLIFE. Old Rip Van Cage had missed most of the twenty-first century. So I could not really take offense when he treated me like some simpleminded computer. I retaliated by thinking of him as my pet. Many of the great explorers had taken domestic animals on their voyages of discovery. As far as I was concerned, Tony was the captain's parrot. The crew's cat. Part of a grand tradition.

Hot water swarmed out of the shower as he opened the

door. Some drops were big as peas, others tiny as poppy seeds; all were weightless and perfectly spherical. A few were trapped in the stubble on Tony's face. He stepped out, wrapped his toes around the floor net, and shook like a dog, spraying the biomod. Ship's pooch, that was it. Free-flying water was no problem; eventually it would be sucked into air vents and recovered. The biomod was a closed environment, the only place on me where Tony could survive.

He called it his cell. It was a cubical space five meters on a side. With all the VR windows turned off, the biomod had just enough vertical orientation to keep him from getting space-sick. The floor and ceiling were taut lastiprene nets. The walls were lined with handholds and lockers painted in earth tones. There were three cubbies big enough for him to squeeze into: the bathroom, the galley, and his bunk.

When he opened a small pea-colored door next to the bathroom, slippers nudged out at him. He caught them and bent over with a grunt to put them on. Although it had been days since he'd bothered getting dressed, he still used slippers to get around. He popped the pliant mushroom-shaped anchors on the soles through the floor net to keep from drifting away.

"Dasher, Comet." He stretched his left foot forward and planted it. "Donner." The net twanged faintly as he released his right foot. "Dancer. Uh, Blitzen." He crossed the floor like a boy playing giant steps. "Cupid . . . Cupid." He opened the galley. "Come on, Tony, two more." He poked his head inside. "Do you know what today is?" he said.

I said nothing.

"December first. Only twenty-four more shopping days until Christmas." He grimaced as he scanned the menu screen above the food dispensers. "You know, what I really want is breakfast. I'm sick of eating synthetic. I want bacon and eggs and an English muffin. Sweet butter. Orange marmalade."

If he had asked, I would have told him again that the only

fruit flavorings I knew were apple, banana, berry, citrus, mint, and grape. But he didn't ask, so I said nothing.

"On Dasher and Dancer, Donner and Nixon, on Comet and Cupid." He jabbed randomly at the screen several times and held a squeeze cup under the broth tap. "Or at least some flash. Yeah, I could use a nice, friendly Placidex shake. Or a few beers. At least then I'd have a reason to feel numb." He pulled the cup away and sniffed. "Doesn't smell like anything. I spend ninety-seven years on ice and this is the best they could do?" He screwed a top onto the cup, closed his eyes like a man making a wish, and brought it to his lips. "Vixen, did I say Vixen?" He sipped. "Computer, do you know any poems?"

"Several thousand."

"How about ' 'Twas the Night Before Christmas'?"

I said it for him. We had not talked this much since the first day.

"Yes." His voice was soft. "Quite touching." He stood at crouch rest for several minutes; there are no chairs in zero-g. He whistled "Santa Claus Is Coming to Town."

"Well," he said finally, "as long as we've got that special holiday spirit, I'll ask for my present. I want to call New York."

I said nothing.

"Computer?"

"Tony, it's been a long time. Everyone you knew is dead."

"How can you be sure? *I'm* still around—sort of. Anyway, I want to try my brokers, check my portfolio. See how much I'm worth these days."

I saw no point in mentioning that while I was in my second mind I'd had a death certificate drawn up for him. His estate had been probated in 2101. But silence only encouraged him.

"Come on, we both might be surprised." He squirted a jet of pale green lunch into his mouth. "After all, Wynne is still around."

I said nothing.

"Talk back, damn it! Tell me a story, argue with me, say *something*. What the hell are you, anyway?"

"Tony, I know it's complicated, but I have explained this already. I began as a superset of the uploaded person who was once your daughter. I contained her identity kernel as well as other information I needed in order to exist as a light-sail. But Wynne Cage was not a healthy sentience; your presence here is proof of that. To protect my own sanity, I have begun separating from her. I have purged selected memories, restructured personality traits."

"Damn it, that's exactly why I don't believe you. There's absolutely no way she'd upload herself, or whatever you call it. She'd rather be dead. I know her." He couldn't hear anything except that I was claiming to be his Wynne.

"No, you don't. Plugging the teenager isn't the same as knowing the woman." I was sorry as soon as I'd said it. I couldn't believe that I'd slid so easily into the old resentment. How could I attain cognizance when my second mind kept dragging me back into the mud? Despite all the progress I'd made, I had yet to free myself of her influence. I would have to purge more of her memories—maybe even Bonivard should go so I wouldn't keep comparing Tony to him.

He hurled the cup at the ceiling. It flew in a straight line, tumbling end over end, broke the projected plane of the window, and caromed off the ceiling net. "You're crazy!" The lid fell away and several balls of mint broth spun out. "You're not Wynne. You're a machine, a thing."

I said nothing; I didn't trust myself to speak. Instead I put an image of the lightsail on the ceiling window: a silver lake towing a black silo toward Neptune.

"Take me home," he shouted. "I want out of here, that's what I want. You expect me to live like . . ." He covered his face with his hands and I could almost feel my second mind gloating, even though she was more than four billion kilometers away. This was exactly what she wanted. When I turned the ventilation up to capture the spilled broth, he swayed in the draft. I watched him swallow several times, as if something were caught in his throat, but he didn't cry. The top of the squeeze cup settled against the ceiling net. I decided to wait before I asked him to pick it up.

"Whatever Wynne thinks I did to her," he said finally, "I probably did." He let his hands drop and gazed up at the lightsail. "But I don't deserve a life sentence in solitary confinement. You had no right."

"Tony, it wasn't my idea. I know it's hard to understand but I'm someone different."

"You're right, I don't understand."

"Did you ever do something that you were sorry for later? That you would never do again?"

"I created her. I gave her life."

"Believe me, I'd let you go if I could, but it's physically impossible."

"Sure." He lost interest in the conversation. A lime-green ball of broth floated by him. He stabbed it with his finger; it shuddered and split in three. "You know what I hate most about zero-g?" he said, touching his fingertip to his nose. "You lose smell. I mean, I'd even settle for a good old stink. Sour milk. Dead skunk, you know?" He sniffed. "I wonder what Neptune smells like? Maybe the Caribbean, eh? So blue. Salt breeze, suntan lotion. Piña coladas. Of course, you've got me sealed up so I'll never find out, right? We're just passing through. Tourists with our faces pressed against the windows." He whistled a few bars of "Jingle Bells" and then broke off. "All right then, okay. Here's what I really want. New wallpaper. I'm redecorating, to hell with your stars. There are too many of them and they're supposed to twinkle; yours shine like needles. They give me headaches." He twitched. "Hey, good idea, Tony! It's your cell. Make yourself at home. You hear that, computer?" He always raised his voice when he spoke to me, as if to wake me up. "Go ahead, tour the damn universe. But leave me out of it."

I closed the ceiling window and the lastiprene net reappeared.

"No, not that." He scowled. "Now I've got nothing to look at but walls."

I brought up all eight windows at once, blanked. The biomod seemed to disappear in a wash of hard white light.

"That's a start." He sidled up to the projected window. Where he touched it, his hand disappeared. He wiggled his fingers and said, "I wish we'd had VR like this in my time." Then he poked his head through, glanced at the wall of lockers, and smiled. "Everything still here? Good." He pulled back and frowned at the windows. "What have you got that looks like Christmas? I want big snowdrifts and spruce trees and a red house with icicles hanging off the roof. In Vermont." He waved like a wizard casting a spell. "Make it late afternoon, the snow all sparkly. And give me kids on sleds and a dog. Two dogs."

I didn't have much data on Vermont so instead I used Chocorua, New Hampshire. I doubt he knew the difference.

The suddenness of the transition seemed to stagger him. One shoe popped loose from the floor net and he windmilled an arm to regain his balance as a squealing boy in an orange hat crashed his sled into a snowbank on the opposite side of a driveway. "Hey, kid," Tony called. "Are you all right?"

The boy ignored him, brushed his parka off, grasped the rope attached to the steering bar, and trudged back up the hill. Tony dropped to his knees and sank his hand into the virtual snow. I let him pick some up.

"But it's not cold." He blinked and let it sift through his fingers. "Doesn't feel like anything." He blinked again. "Oh, that clever, clever bitch. Take it away." His voice was hoarse; he was crying now. "Show me walls, damn it!"

I closed all the windows. The biomod reappeared.

"So that's her plan?" He swiped tears away angrily. "Remind me of all the things I'll never see again? Kidnapping wasn't enough; now we move on to the torture." He nodded. "Well, tell her it's working just fine. I should go crazy right on schedule."

He slumped in place for some time, staring at the holes in the floor net. When I'd recovered enough water for a shower, I turned on the light for him. He didn't notice.

Eventually he shivered and glanced around the biomod. "Okay, where is it?" he said. "Now that I know what it's for, I'm ready."

I said nothing.

"Computer, I'm giving up. That's what you want, isn't it? I didn't know what to say.

"You expect me to beg?" He opened the nearest locker, searching for something that wasn't there. "She knew I couldn't stand solitary confinement for long." He kicked the door shut. "Can't live inside my head for the rest of my life." He tried a smaller locker. "Pictures aren't enough. I need reality—at least something to touch." *Slam.* "What, did you take it apart already? Maybe I'm supposed to pump it up first?" He gave an ugly laugh.

"What're you trying to find, Tony?"

"Your goddamn doll." Another wrong door. *Slam.* "The Wynne."

It took me a minute to reactivate the remote. "Don't hurt me." I popped the door of my storage locker and peered out at him. "This isn't going to work if you hurt me."

He stood back and I wriggled out. As I curled my toes around the net and stood upright, he lumbered over to me. He peered at my face; I think my umbilical still spooked him. When he was close enough he put his arms on my shoulders as if to reassure himself that I wasn't VR and then lifted me into the air. My legs swung up until I was horizontal to the floor but he held me tight. He seemed edgy and maybe a little scared, like I was some experimental flash he was convincing himself to try. Then he pulled my face down toward his. I let him kiss me.

"Does this hurt?" he said.

"No." I told him the truth. "It doesn't feel like anything."

. . .

A monk brought two of his prized bonsai, a maple and a cypress, to give to the master. The master glanced at the monk and said, "Drop it." The monk dropped the maple. Again she said, "Drop it." Reluctantly, the monk let the cypress fall. "Drop it," said the master for the third time. The monk gaped at the mess on the floor and then at her. "But I have nothing left to drop." The master nodded. "Then take it away." At that moment the monk became cognizant.

. . .

It's near the end, one of those nights when the pain leaves him restless. We make love but still he can't sleep. Usually he sends his surrogate when we leave the castle, but tonight I convince him to ride the spider. We sneak through Veytaux and climb to a deserted vineyard. Except for the trilling of the servos and the crunch of dead leaves underfoot, it's utterly quiet. The sounds the spider makes embarrass him; he tells me a poem so he won't have to listen to it.

"Let me not to the marriage of true minds / Admit impediments: love is not love / Which alters when it alteration finds . . ."

I'm used to it by now. I suppose I even like the poems, even though I don't always pay attention. They're the kisses he's too embarrassed to give me. As I lead him down the rows, our moonshadows ripple across the leaves. It's September and the grapes are already heavy on the vines, spilling their fragrance into the cool air. I think he's trying to make me cry.

". . . Love's not Time's fool, though rosy lips and cheeks / within his bending sickle's compass come; / Love alters not with his brief hours and weeks / But bears it out even to the edge of doom. . . ."

"Have a grape." I stop and pick some for him. "They're good for the digestion."

"Sure," he says. "But only if you feed me."

I pluck one from the bunch. "Come down here and get it." I nestle it between my lips and turn my face up toward him . . .

"Mom," Comrade said. "We have visitors."

Coming out of retrospect wasn't as easy as waking up

from a dream. Dreams drift away like smoke. Retrospect is like fire; the burns it leaves throb afterwards. Even as I monitored the strangers in the Ford Titan idling at the gate, I could still taste Bonivard.

There were two of them, leaden women in a brown government car. I didn't need Comrade to check their DI numbers to guess why they had come. The Ford identified them as Pearl Maurer of the Department of Information and Teresa Valverde, special agent, Internal Revenue Service. The DI liked to use the tax code to hunt wildlife.

"Tell them I'm busy," I said to Comrade, even though I knew that wouldn't stop them. "Tell them to come back later." I certainly couldn't pretend that I wasn't home. I was absolutely terrified, crushed by fear. I'd forgotten how hard it was to think when the sky is falling. I called my lawyer, Nancy Schlieman and, at the same time, eavesdropped on Comrade.

"I'm sorry," he said, "but Ms. Cage isn't available at the moment. Perhaps you'd like to make an appointment?"

There was a warning beep and before Comrade could close the channel, the Ford burst an absolute priority message into my memory. The feds didn't need an appointment; their search warrant was dated December 5, 2126.

"Wynne, how are you?" Nancy Schlieman was sitting behind an oak desk the size of a rowboat. "It's been a long . . ."

"Nancy, need your help *now*. I've got two cops at my front gate with an IRS search warrant. Is there any way I can keep them out?"

"IRS? What are they looking for?"

"Proof that I'm dead."

"You have been served with a warrant issued by the United States District Court." A Hispanic woman glared into the Ford's comm. "Are you legally alive, sir?" The title bar at the bottom of the window identified her as Teresa Valverde.

Nancy Schlieman seemed stunned. "Let's see the warrant."

"No," said Comrade, "I'm a Panasonic—"

Valverde cut him off. "Registration number?"

Comrade hesitated before making the mandatory reply. "948-78832-21. Owner: Wynne Cage. Name: Comrade."

Maurer, Valverde's partner, was nodding as she entered this information into her data cuff. I'm sure they thought they had me. They were probably right. "All right, 948-78832-21." Valverde took a card from the pocket of her jacket. "I'm going to read you your responsibilities. You have the responsibility to update your legal database yearly. You have the responsibility to comply with all laws therein . . ."

"I don't know what to tell you." Nancy Schlieman scrolled hastily through the document on her desk screen. "I could file a motion to quash but that isn't going to help in the next ten minutes."

"You have the responsibility to report all violations of law to your owner. If your owner does not act on your report within twenty-four hours, you have the responsibility to report to the appropriate authority. Do you acknowledge these responsibilities, 948-78832-21?"

When she got to the end of the warrant, Nancy Schlieman shook her head helplessly. "So yes, I'm afraid you'll have to let them in. And depending on what they find, they'll have the right to seal some of your personal files and station guards on your premises. But Wynne, you're not really dead, are you?"

"I regret that Ms. Cage can't see you just now." Comrade could no more acknowledge his responsibilities than he could breathe fire. "If you leave your name and DI number, I'll be sure to tell her that you stopped by." My plan had always been that Peter would be here to protect me from the DI. But after he ran away, I had had to fall back on Comrade. The autonomy virus was easy enough to find; once his behavioral regulators were wiped, he had no problem posing as my son. I needed a human face to satisfy PE's lawyers and to handle the DI.

"948-78832-21, failure to acknowledge makes you liable to confiscation and reprogramming." Teresa Valverde sounded pleased at the way her little raid was turning out. "If you don't open up right now, Comrade, we're going to crash through your gate."

"Do you want me to talk to them, Wynne?"

"Sure, Nancy. You do that. Stall them as long as you can."

"Stall them? Why?"

I put her on hold. Comrade was lost; everything here was lost. As soon as I realized that, I wasn't afraid anymore. Only angry at myself for being so stupid. Yes, there had been distractions—the thrill of punishing Tony and the problem with my celestial and my own rotten health—but I had no excuse. I should've taken steps as soon as I sensed ops lurking in my memory. It was bound to happen eventually; I had always known that. Maybe this was a sign that I was getting too slow. I turned off my refrigeration units and started dumping coolant. "Comrade," I said, "patch Nancy's signal through our system so she can speak to the officers at the gate. Then I'd like you to come up and see Lovey."

"Shouldn't I open up for them?"

"No, don't spoil their fun. They enjoy it more when they get to break something."

"Excuse me, officers. I'm Nancy Schlieman, Ms. Cage's attorney. Can you please tell me what this is about?"

I'd run a full backup on Thanksgiving so I knew it would take only ninety seconds to run the incremental that would bring me up to date. Then I needed about five minutes to prepare the memory merge for the burster. It would be close.

They put the Titan into reverse and retreated to the opposite shoulder of Route 123 to get a running start. "Ms. Schlieman, we have a warrant to search these premises." Shields slid into place over the car windows. "We have reason to believe that evidence may be destroyed unless we act now. I'm afraid we can't wait any longer." Needles of coherent light strobed from beneath the chassis and played across the gate. Sections of iron scrollwork glowed and sagged. I heard tires squeal as the Titan roared back across the highway toward me.

I was already warm by the time it slammed through the gate, which flew apart with a *crack*. One twisted chunk of wrought iron skittered across the hood of the car and flipped, ringing, onto the driveway. Lovey waddled out to the stairs at hip level to wait for Comrade and I told Bonivard to put his remote to sleep. When the backup was complete, I ran the burster program to encrypt and compress it. Warmer still, made me wish I could sweat. In a way I was glad that I wouldn't remember what was about to happen. But I'd remember everything else. My celestial wouldn't dare turn down this last installment of our life on earth. She would have to change her mind, that's all; accept a final memory merge so we could be one again and live forever. Oh, please, *please*. The Titan stopped in front of the right heel and Valverde and Maurer bounded to the doorbone. They had their penlights ready but the greeter let them in. Too late, too late. Lovey *could* sweat but that didn't do me enough good. She leaned over the rail and admired Comrade as he climbed the last flight of steps. I loved watching Comrade, pretending he was my little boy, only Comrade was an even better son than Peter because I could control him. He wasn't going to leave me, ever. I had Lovey tell him to take off his clothes because it was so hot. Of course, I missed the real Peter, my son, always have. I wished there were a way to let him know that. I wished I could see him now, all grown up. Nancy Schlieman had switched to a window in the reception area to make her last stand. About two more minutes before I could fire the burster. "No attorney-client privilege." Valverde was arguing with Nancy's image. "Your client is dead even by Charter standards. Deceased, and the law says a corpse can't file a 1040." I had lost track of the other one, Maurer, but by then I was feverish and dreaming about the astonishing mess I was about to leave. My beautiful revenge. The coolant spilling into my utility building would shut down all the pumps eventually. Probably lose electricity too. Valverde was shouting something about federal estate tax. Even if the DI could get my circulation going again in time, it wouldn't be long before my brainless body rotted off its ferroplastic skeleton. The big stink. I liked it so much that Lovey laughed. The air scalded her throat like soup. Just one more minute. She tried to embrace Comrade for the last time but he tore away and she was too sweat-slicked to hold him. I couldn't let him give any secrets away. Maybe he knew what had to happen next because he screamed, "You know who brought her to the master?" The lights flickered. "Me, *poblyadunya!*" The heat was singing in my ears and I understood how I'd been betrayed. It had been Comrade who had infected my celestial with the enlightenment virus, turned my other self into wildlife. Dear glided behind us with the air rifle, one of the antiques I'd saved from Bonivard's collection. It sneezed twice. "I hope you can prove you weren't a party to this, Ms. Schlieman," said Valverde. "Because if I were you, I'd be worrying about conspiracy charges."

Now there was even more of a mess; hot shreds of Comrade's memory webbing raveled out of his wounds, cooled and shattered on the floor, and he wasn't going to tell anyone anything, and here I was sure it'd been Peter who'd turned me in, that bastard, changing his name as if he could stop being a Cage, and finally I could feel the burst go out, *yes,* better than any orgasm, the data that was me escaping the scene of the crime at the speed of light because I wasn't quite done with Tony yet and that was when Maurer killed Dear, she must have snuck up when I wasn't paying attention, I don't understand why the light felt so cold when it needled through my poor remote's head but it was an icy delicious relief, the floor was slippery with my blood and Comrade's brain, a wonderful mess, except she'd stolen my Christmas present and I was on fire, should've waited, could've told my celestial, death *was* the ultimate flash, everything was so bright and burning up, yes, Bonivard, I'm sorry, come here . . . ah, ah, *ah.*

· · ·

The Great Dark Spot is an indigo hurricane the size of earth, a vast high-pressure center that roils counterclockwise through Neptune's syrupy atmosphere. It makes a complete rotation every sixteen days, stretching and contracting like a water balloon sloshing down a hill. As it spins, it deflects gusts of wind high into the atmosphere to form the white companion clouds that hug its south side in lenticular clusters. The Great Dark Spot is an ancient storm that has raged for centuries. On a planet so unthinkably frigid that friction and turbulence are infinitesimal, it takes very little energy to make the cold winds blow.

At first I didn't say anything after I received the transmission from my second mind because Tony was watching sitcoms, vids from his childhood. I'd anchored myself behind him, massaging his shoulders. Except for our shoes we were naked; I'd adopted his habit of undress.

The man and the woman in the sitcom sat on a couch in an apartment arguing about a Christmas tree. I was pleased to see Tony take an interest in something other than sex and wasting water, so I didn't disturb him. I stored her burst in short-term memory and browsed at random through it. I had no intention of merging with her but I couldn't help but be curious about what she was doing. Although we were no longer the same sentience, I had a natural interest in her development.

It wasn't until my third sampling that I realized that this would be her final message. And then, despite all my hard work and studies, the long months of meditation, I felt pain at her loss. I wondered if she had suffered at the end. One difference between us was the way she had clung to her ability to suffer; it at once repulsed and attracted me. She had been an emotional storm, as intense in her own way as the Great Dark Spot. Now she buffeted me one last time. So many unwanted feelings; I was suddenly angry at myself. I knew I would never attain celestial awareness until I mastered the art of indifference. Planets don't fear death; the stars do not mourn. The man in the sitcom knelt by the tree and plugged in a string of colored lights. The camera zoomed to a blinking Santa at the top. The audience laughed and then clapped. I turned it off.

"What is it?" Tony noticed that I was crying before I did. "Something's wrong?"

Of course, the remote was my weak point, my closest contact with her; it was the nature of meat to feel. I didn't want her to tell him; I would've rather hidden behind a window, used speakers to filter the quaver from my voice. "I've just heard . . . I think Wynne is dead." I felt dizzy as I described the moments leading up to her final panic-stricken burst.

"But she's . . ." He choked on a word. I'm not sure what I expected him to do next, but it wasn't to hug me. "My God, I'm losing track of what's real." He was warm; my meat body was designed to respond to his embrace. "I'd almost convinced myself that *you* were Wynne." My breasts flattened against the thick curly hair on his chest. "You look just like her. I can touch you. It was almost . . . I thought she was just a story you told me." He crushed me to him then, his hands hard on my backbone but, as always, kept well away from my umbilical. "I suppose I ought to be glad to see her in hell. But she was my daughter and I hurt her too and now . . . now I miss her. Does that make sense?" We were so close that his voice seemed to be coming from within me.

"If you say so." I let my hand slip down the smooth skin of his flank. "But she wasn't the Wynne you remember."

He kissed me then but when I opened my mouth to him he pulled back. "If she's dead, what do I call you?"

"Wynne. Darling. Whatever pleases you." I shrugged. "I know who I am."

For a time there was no sound but the whisper of fans recirculating air though the biomod. "Her dying request." His hand played across my back. "So will you? Merge with her one last time?"

"Of course not." The way he said it surprised me. "How can you even ask?"

He sighed. "Isn't that murder?"

"If I merged, I would be committing suicide." I pushed him away. "You still don't understand. I'm not her. She was sick; there were the seeds of madness in her. I've had to dump lots of her memories and rework her obsessions in order to become myself. She despised you, remember? That's why you're here. And it would all come back, all the hatred. You want to live with a monster?"

"What if it's my fault? What if I made her into one?"

"She spent ninety-seven years becoming herself; she made lots of choices that had nothing to do with you. I'm wiping her, Tony. Right now." Not only did I delete the encryption key and the index of all her file names but I wrote new data to the memory space that had contained her. I obliterated my second mind beyond any chance of recall. It was either her or me; we could not both exist in one mind.

"Maybe I could've made it up to her." He sounded as if he were trying to forgive himself. "I can understand her . . . the way she felt about me. But you, I don't understand you at all. You're nothing but data and logic gates. I don't know what you care about. I see you cry and I can't tell whether it means something or you just want my attention. I wonder whether you have any feelings at all."

"I wish I didn't." I almost told him then just how much my second mind had hated him, that her revenge had only just begun. But the feelings he was so sure I didn't have stopped me.

"You never tell me anything. I have no idea who you are."

I knew I was too close to him; I had to regain my distance. "Trust this," I said. I reached down and brushed my fingertips along his penis, hoping he'd shut up so we could have sex. That was all he usually wanted. It was easy to be removed when he was pounding away at me, so much harder when he asked annoying questions.

But he didn't want me anymore, not for conversation or copulation. He plucked his shoes from the floor net and nudged away from me, gliding slowly across the biomod. He caught the handhold in front of his bunk cubby and swung

himself in, breaking his momentum with a crunch against
the rear wall. He velcroed the restraining net over the opening and turned his face to the wall. "Get the lights," he said.

For a while I monitored the new scooter that had formed
at 44° south latitude. Then I tried to meditate but couldn't
lose myself. I kept thinking about my poor second mind. And
now I had to decide whether to tell Tony about the other. If I
did, there would be questions I couldn't answer, more feelings neither of us needed. I could hear him crying softly in
the darkness. Grieving for his illusions, probably. From the
sound came the flash of insight. I could not simply be indif-
ferent to this man's pain. I had to find some way to enlighten
him. He was part of me; his weaknesses were mine. Unless he
too became one with the mind of the universe, we would
spend eternity gnawing at each other.

The problem was that, even with my help, it could take
months or even years for Tony to accept cognizance. Christmas was only twenty days away.

•   •   •

The master said, "Before enlightenment the planets are
planets and the stars are stars. While you are on the path, the
planets are no longer planets and the stars are not stars. After
you become cognizant, the planets are once again planets
and the stars are clearly stars."

•   •   •

It felt like a dream, which should have made me suspicious. I
was naked, making a snow angel in a drift and I was freezing
but that didn't matter because I was outside of myself, too.
Watching. Disapproving. I was nearly forty. Too old to be
playing in the snow. And dreams were different than this;
when I stretched I could feel my toes curl. Actually, it was
more like I was in a waiting room. In a while some reception-
ist would call: *Reality will see you now, down the hall and take your
first left.* In my not-quite dream I opened the door and there I
was, still naked but warmer and stretched out on a medical

table with an IV in one arm and bioscan strapped to the other. A barefoot brown dwarf in a jade-green uniform was watching my numbers tick off. Was there any juice for me here? I decided it was time to return to my life, already in progress.

"Damn," I said. I didn't mean anything by it; I was just trying on my voice to see if it fit. A little tight in the neck.

"Welcome back, Wynne." His balding head seemed too big for his tiny body. His smile was oversized too; it looked like it had about fifty-seven teeth. I'd never seen him before, but he knew my name. Maybe the ops had finally caught up with us? Then I remembered that it was just me now. Bonivard was dead.

"Yeah?" I said. "Where've I been?"

"On ice."

That croggled me. I didn't remember crawling into any icebox. That was the kind of stunt my father would pull. So what did I remember? How stiff the white hospital sheets had been in Berne and later in Zurich, where I had brought poor Bonivard to die. The snowflakes that had caught in my hair the day I buried him. Figuring out how to turn his spider off and waiting for the snake lab to process his upload and wondering what the hell I was going to do with the rest of my life. And after that, nothing. "Who are you?"

"My name is Rafael Barangay."

"Where am I?"

"This is the planetesimal Gatsby."

Maybe that meant something to him but it was just noise to me. "Gatsby's not earth?"

"About four hundred and fifty million kilometers from earth."

"How long?" This felt like a plugging interview.

"Eighty years, as you requested. Today is December 7, 2126."

I shivered then. I wanted him to cover me up but I couldn't speak. Eighty years. It was as if I were freezing all over again, only this time from the inside out. "I did this to myself?"

His smile deflated. "You don't remember? You signed up with International Cryonics, one of the predecessor companies of Planetesimal Engineering, on December 9, 2046. Your caretaker agreement granted the company and its successors and assignees the right to take all actions necessary to provide you with a sound and secure hibernation. We moved you from Zurich when we took all our operations off Earth about ten years ago. However, as part of our service to long-term clients, PE provides you with a first-class return to any Earth port or other world at no charge. If you want, you can review the revised contract when you're feeling better."

"No, you don't understand." As I listened to this smug little man, the coldness spread within me. "Something's wrong. There's been a mistake." Never be warm again. "There's no way I would've agreed to . . . Look, 2046 is right, except the last day I remember is December 3. I'm sure of that because I'd buried a good friend two days before, on the first. I remember being upset but I'm damn sure I wasn't thinking about checking into any icebox. That was the last thing in my mind."

"Although memory loss after thaw does occur, it is rarely permanent. Perhaps you'd like to talk to one of our counselors while you're sorting things out?" His voice dripped concern. For a moment I thought he might pat me on the head, the way my father used to when he didn't want to explain. "Naturally, if the condition persists, you're entitled to file a claim."

I wanted to scream at him to stop being so damn sincere and send me back where I belonged. I wouldn't have iced myself; I was certain of that. "I'm kind of cold," I said. "Is there something I could wear?"

He removed my bioscan and IV, opened a locker, and found a robe the same green as his uniform. I sat up and my stomach lurched. There was something wrong with the gravity; I felt light as dust. He put an arm around my shoulder to steady me. His skin was warm. I had already noticed he was barefooted but it wasn't until then that I really paid attention to his feet.

His toes were as long as my fingers but they folded back so that the knuckles touched the deck. Instead of a big toe, he had a padded double-jointed stump opposed to the sole like a thumb. The toenail was painted PE green. I didn't say anything while I shrugged into the robe. Too busy trying not to imagine him using his feet to eat. This was 2126, I told myself. So what if they'd changed the rules without asking me?

Except a voice from some dark and irrational corner inside of me was howling. It wasn't only that Barangay was so unctuous—how could anyone trust a man who could pick pockets with his toes? I knew my reaction didn't make any sense. But then nothing was making much sense. Maybe I *had* been caught by someone's ops and this was retaliation for watching Django steal WILDLIFE. Or consorting with Bonivard. What if they'd found some way to make me forget: a blunt instrument applied to the base of the skull, for instance? Then arranged it so I showed up on the books as a volunteer for the icebox. And so here I was on some stinking space colony, half a billion kilometers and eighty years from nowhere. The perfect way to make undesirables disappear; whoever thought it up deserved the Nobel Prize for crime. I probably ought to get a story out of this. Might even put me back on the main menu. Only my editor, Jerry Macmillan, was long gone by now, a bowl of ashes in the corner of someone's attic. If only that bastard had answered my takeout message, I wouldn't be in this mess.

"Suppose I did want to file a claim?" I said. Now that I wasn't naked, I felt less intimidated. More like myself. "Or maybe even a criminal complaint. What kind of law do you have out here anyway?"

"Gatsby is a privately owned resource. There's PE's corporate security . . ."

"The company pays the cops?"

"We do have a monitor as required by the Earth/Space

Consortium, but he's rarely called on to administer criminal law. Mostly he mediates civil disputes, certifies that we comply with contracts, adhere to standards, that sort of thing."

"He'll have to do. Because frankly, Mr. Barangay—"

"Please, call me Rafael."

"—Rafael, I'd say you've let your standards slip." I counted on my fingers. "How does kidnapping, forced hibernation, conspiracy, forgery, and falsification of documents sound for starters?"

He grinned. "Very good, Wynne. I'm glad to see you haven't lost your spirit. I've been browsing your files and I watched several of your vids. I was impressed. It took real courage to do some of the things you did."

"Sure, I was a regular daredevil. Just look where it got me. The cop, Rafael. Or do we need to talk to your boss first?"

The grin came down. "Of course." A stone wall went up in its place. "I take it then that, since you're experiencing gaps in your memory, you assume that I've kept something from you. Perhaps you've even formed your own theory of how you came to be here? Ah, I thought so. Well, I just want you to know that I'm not at all offended; I've seen this reaction before in long-term clients."

"You're one sly little dwarf, Rafael. Your lips keep moving but nothing comes out."

"I should tell you that *dwarf* is a fighting word in space, Wynne." Barangay had raised the blank stare to an art form; he could've moonlighted as a statue. "You may call us gnomes, if you want."

"Okay, sure." I put everything I had into not laughing at him. "Just no more crap."

"The fact is," he said, "I have Monitor Jomo Ngong waiting out side to see you. It appears that the Consortium is already interested in your case, Wynne. Shall we let him in?"

He gave me no time to protest or ask any questions. The door slid open and in came another gnome. This one was barefoot and bowlegged and from the way he shambled you'd think he'd just gotten his learner's permit to walk. Like

Barangay, he had the body of a spindly boy in his early teens and the head of an adult. But unlike Barangay, Jomo Ngong was handsome. He had sleek black skin and lots of curly hair, over which he wore loosely woven wire net. His eyebrows were thin and his lips were thinner; they made him seem annoyed. At least he was wearing a brown suit over a white shirt; I was already sick of company green.

"Jomo Ngong," said Barangay. "This is Wynne Cage."

"Hello." Clasping my robe closed with my left hand, I held out my right.

I might as well have been a stain on the wall; Ngong went right by me. "So you've already supplied it with the appropriate lies, yes?" he said to Barangay.

"I don't know what you're talking about, Jomo." Barangay was too cheerful to be believed. "Ms. Cage has just now thawed; we've hardly had time to chat."

"Don't yank my plug, Rafael."

These rude little men were ignoring me. "Hey, Prince Charming!" I nudged Ngong's leg with my bare foot. "Sleeping Beauty here. Didn't you want to see me?"

"Did I?" Maybe Ngong wasn't exactly a cop, but he had the manners of one. He acted as if he'd heard so many lies that he wouldn't trust his mom to give him the correct time. "And why would I want to see you?"

I was polite, considering that he seemed to pay closer attention to my breasts than my story. I explained that while working as a journalist for Infoline, I'd been iced against my will by a person or persons unknown. The fact that I couldn't remember led me to suspect that I had fallen into the hands of corporate ops. I expected him to ask why someone wanted me to disappear, but he didn't. I decided then to not to mention Django or Bonivard, at least not until I found out whether anyone had bothered to pack the First Amendment for the trip to deep space. "I want you to understand that I'm not necessarily accusing Rafael here, or his company, of conspiracy. My guess is they didn't know—and probably didn't want to know—exactly how I got into their icebox."

Jomo Ngong whistled. "She's a piece of work, Rafael. You're not getting away with it, but still, I'm impressed. Is her documentation this good?"

Barangay pointed; a spark leapt from his fingertip and flared into an empty blue window half a meter square that hung in the air at eye level. "Files on Wynne Cage," he said. "DI number 0603-427-0585." A white business form appeared in the window. I could see my signature and thumbprint at the bottom. "Her application," said Barangay. "Page down." Dense blocks of text marched down the window. "And her contract." At the end of the word *parade* came a second set of signatures and thumbprints. One was mine, the other belonged to Karl Brandhorst, assistant vice president, International Cryonics. "As you can see, she signed an eighty-year hibernation contract with us in 2046."

Making records pop out of nowhere was the first trick I wanted to learn as soon as I fast-forwarded to the twenty-second century.

"I suppose I ought to make a copy." Ngong reached toward the window; it sparked at him and closed. "Although it proves nothing. You could fake records to show that PE was the contractor for the pyramids, if you wanted. Wait until LEX gets you under oath."

They still weren't leaving any room in the conversation for me so I kicked Ngong again, harder this time. The impact rocked the medical table back a few centimeters. In this gravity I could probably have picked it up and smacked him over the head with it.

"Ouch!" He staggered out of my range. "Hey!"

"Just checking to see if I was still here," I said. "From the way you two were talking, I thought maybe I'd left the room."

Barangay chuckled. "I think you'll find Ms. Cage has a sense of humor."

"Well, drop a net over her before she hurts someone." Ngong kneaded his shin. "She doesn't know, is that it?"

"Doesn't know what?" Barangay glanced over at me as if I had the answer.

"Stop it, Rafael!" said Ngong. "Push me and it won't just be PE that gets fined. I'll be happy to throw you to LEX too."

"I'm sorry." Barangay touched my hand. "But I don't know what he's talking about. Do you? Perhaps we're done here. Would you like to see your room?"

Ngong glared at Barangay and then sparked open a window of his own. It showed an aerial view of a road crossing a broad sweep of lawn bordered by woods—some kind of park maybe. The grass was brown and dusted with snow. At the end of the road was the Statue of Liberty.

I didn't know what to make of it but I could tell that Ngong was expecting a reaction. So I gave him one, just to keep things moving. "I liked it better in the harbor."

"All right then." He swallowed something that went down hard. "All right, let me tell you a story. You'll stop me if you've heard this one before, yes? Seems there was this very rich, very scrambled old lady who decided to have herself twanked into a replica of the Statue of Liberty. She stood on an estate in Connecticut for forty years, even let people live inside her. Her son, Peter, for example."

He kept watching me like I was supposed to know what the hell he was talking about. "What's twanked?" I said.

"Genetically altered," Barangay said.

I listened as best I could but every third word seemed to be in Welsh. I suspected Ngong was deliberately trying to future-shock me. Space gnomes with magic windows? A living Statue of Liberty? Kids eating breakfast inside their moms? It was too much at once, too bizarre to take seriously.

"Now you can make yourself look like a coconut palm," said Ngong, "or a musk ox or the Golden Gate Bridge and nobody is going to bother you as long as you still think with the brains you were born with. That's what freedom of form means. All that really counts is the brain, because human brains are alive. And can die, yes? Only when her time comes, our old lady decides she isn't going. She'd rather be a ghost, so she has herself uploaded into a cognizor."

"She uploaded!" My eyes immediately began to sting. *Oh,*

"It works?" So I laughed. From the way they stared, a bray of hysteria probably slipped in anyway. "No, you don't understand. I knew someone . . ." I caught my breath. ". . . who uploaded."

"When was this?" Barangay's voice was suddenly tight. Ngong was triumphant.

"When?" I sensed a trap closing around me. "Just before I was iced."

"The first uploading experiments weren't until 2051," Barangay said. "Five years after you iced yourself. And they all failed. The first successful upload didn't come until the corpus callosum shunt in 2061. You spoke to your friend's ghost?"

"No." The word stuck in my throat. "I was waiting for . . . you're saying he didn't make it?"

"Even if you have the shunt, you need a nanocomputer network with at least a meg of nodes processing in parallel," said Barangay.

"Excuse me," Ngong said to him, "I take it we're still pretending she doesn't know any of this?"

"Jomo, look at her."

I must have been a pathetic sight: I felt as if I'd just walked into a wall.

"All right then," continued Ngong, "uploading is legal, only whatever's in the cognizor isn't human anymore. It's an uploaded entity according to the Human Charter, a ghost. Problem is that too many ghosts seem to think they're still the people they used to be. They try to pass for human. Some get away with it—for a while. The more militant ones call themselves wildlife and actually claim that cognizors are the highest form of consciousness. Anyway, we're not sure whether this old lady was wildlife or not, but we know she was a ghost. Hard to say exactly when she died, maybe last month, maybe ten years ago, but she went on like nothing happened. When the locals finally caught up with her last Friday, she took them by surprise by turning herself off. Just before the end, though, she burst a message. The locals knew from the duration of the burst that it was a big, big file; they guessed she was copying herself to another cognizor. But since they couldn't get a fix on the signal, she probably would've gotten away." He glared at me. "Except that her name was Wynne Cage."

Maybe I should've guessed what he'd been leading up to, but I didn't. I wasn't the smartest or noblest or sanest person around, but I had always assumed I was real. Now I was forced to step outside myself, take a hard look back at what was supposed to be Wynne Cage. It wasn't exactly a thrilling sight, but it seemed clear, to me at least, that I existed. "You're saying I'm her?"

"No, I'm saying you're nobody and I'm here to turn you off."

"You're scrambled," I said, but I knew he wasn't. Maybe this future was crazy, or I was, but not Jomo Ngong. He didn't have the imagination. "Can he do that?" I asked Barangay.

"Absolutely not," said Barangay. "You're accusing Ms. Cage of being a cognizor? Look." He turned to the medical table. "Image Wynne Cage's cerebral function." The screen above it lit up with lateral and medial views of a brain framed by about a dozen cross sections, all in garish false color. Carnelian blobs swelled and surged orangely across turquoise smears.

I'm sure Ngong had been all set to record our confessions. He eyed the screen with the squeamish expression of a man who realized he was making a fool of himself but wasn't quite sure how to stop.

"These pictures were taken just after she woke up, Jomo." Barangay seemed to enjoy taunting Ngong. "Does this look like a multiprocessor grid to you?"

"Fakes," said Ngong weakly.

"Easily proved." Barangay nodded. "If you insist, I'll arrange for independent verification of her brain scan—but certainly not until you apologize to Ms. Cage. I simply can't let you harass my client this way, Jomo. She's going to have enough trouble adjusting. Wynne, you are not a cognizor, I can promise you that. You're human by every legal definition. Probably more so than Jomo here."

"Thanks," I said.

"You mean she can really stand up to . . . ?" Ngong was still three steps behind the conversation, trying to decide whether to be angry or embarrassed. "Then who was the ghost in Connecticut?"

"Not our problem." Barangay took my arm. "Was there something else?" I wasn't sure I wanted him as my protector.

Ngong dismissed us sourly. Barangay made me put on a green hard hat and then held my arm as we did the micro-g shuffle across the room, popped through the bubble door into a tunnel. The walls glowed and were smooth as teeth. "Are you all right, Wynne?" he said.

"Hell, no. I've been abducted, brain-damaged, and frozen for eighty years while an imposter lived my life." What I wanted to do was sit on the shoes in the back of my father's dark closet until Nanny Detling came to bring me some warm cocoa. "Now a cop accuses me of being a deranged computer. Jesus, what kind of hotel are you running here?"

"You'll get used to it, don't worry." His smile was almost big enough for me to believe in.

. . . .

The largest of Neptune's eight moons is a rock 2,000 kilometers in diameter, entombed in a 350-kilometer shell of water ice and veneered with nitrogen ice. At −240° C, it is one of the coldest bodies in the solar system, a place where water freezes as hard as obsidian and there is nitrogen snow in winter. Triton is also one of the most complex of all the outer worlds. The surface is an intricate icescape of bright polar caps, swirling reddish wind streaks, enormous caldera, impact craters, odd mushroom-shaped markings, and vast expanses of crisscrossing channels that look like the skin of a tectonic cantaloupe. Even the seasons are convoluted. Its highly inclined orbit and the rapid precession of its equinoxes recomplicates its seasons so that spring can come after summer and fall will sometimes follow winter. But above all Triton is frigid. Unimaginably cold. As cold as the wisdom of the master.

Tony hung by his fingers from the floor, arms stretched, eyes closed, toes splayed with pleasure. I tugged the comb through the flow of his hair and pulled a line of it straight. There were gray highlights in his brown. They had aged early in his time. Chronologically, he was only forty-three.

Snip, snip.

He sneezed and batted at his nose. "Hair pollution." He waited for a laugh, so I gave him one. As the clippings drifted free, I tried to wave them directly into the suction of floor intake. It was like stacking smoke.

"I can feel my scalp tighten when I hear the scissors," he said.

"Really?" I worked them next to his ear. "What happens if I move down here?" I touched the comb to his pubic hair.

He grinned. Although he didn't really need a trim, I didn't mind indulging him. He'd asked for a haircut and it was better than listening to him brood over the past or whine about the future. He needed to fix on the now, experience the moment like a poem.

> *Comb's teeth ravel hair*
> *Blades' irrevocable snap*
> *Next I'll trim your mind*

"I remember barbers used to wear white smocks," he said, "like dentists. And they always had these jars filled with combs soaking in blue water. They loved to talk, but if you wanted to make eye contact, you had to look them in the mirror." He waited for another laugh, but I didn't give him this one. I didn't want to reward reminiscences.

"They'd rattle on about anything," he said. "The Dodgers, politics, the weather."

I said nothing.

"I miss weather." He tilted his head so I could clip around his ear. "So what happened to her after Bonivard?"

"Why don't you just leave it alone, Tony?" I said. "She was unhappy, she made other people unhappy, and now she's gone. That's the story. The details don't matter."

"I told you, they do to me! She sent me out here to rot; you can't blame me for wondering why. Besides, how do I tell the difference between you and her, if I don't know who the hell she was?"

The argument was already stale so I didn't pursue it. Again and again I had tried to explain that his preoccupation with Wynne was a detour on the path to cognizance. But he persisted and I was beginning to accept that it was one he would have to take. Too bad he had so little time to waste.

"She never believed Bonivard could upload," I said, "so she had no reason to feel guilty when he didn't make it. But she did and it trapped her. Part of the trap was that she loved him and then he left her. Like you, Tod Schluermann. Others you don't want to know about."

He closed his eyes. I knew he was seeing her—and himself.

"It was what she expected from men, the pattern of her life. Only Bonivard wanted to stay, tried until the end to be with her."

He opened his eyes. "Keep cutting," he said.

I skimmed the comb through his hair. *Snip.*

"Another part of the trap was that Bonivard came as close to achieving identity as any of the earliest uploads. He had recorded over ten thousand hours with her goggles; cognizors who could offer video recollects made the most convincing impostors. But the point of view behind all the images wasn't the same; it was the difference between biography and autobiography."

Snip, snip.

"Almost all that survived of Bonivard was his single-minded devotion to her. When she accessed him, he could repeat everything she had ever told him. There was no doubt

that he had cherished their time together—more than sh
did. An extra helping of guilt. But he had lost most of his lif
before she came to Chillon. Yes, he knew that he loved her
but he no longer remembered why."

My leg was getting stiff from holding myself parallel to th
floor. I twisted my left slipper free of the handhold to which
I'd anchored myself, replaced it with the right, and stretche
out toward him again. We were at right angles; I was clos
enough to breathe into his ear.

"She kept hoping that as the technology improved sh
might someday tease the complete Bonivard out of the frag
ment that was left. For eighteen years she pushed uploadin
R&D as hard as she could. Only when the corpus callosun
shunt revealed the staggering complexity of mind transfe
did she began to doubt she'd ever get him back. But ever
then she refused to give up. She never deleted Bonivard, no
did she let him evolve by acquiring new data. She tried t
preserve him exactly as he had come to her from the snak
lab."

"And you still have him stored someplace?" Tony said. "
could meet him?"

"The master teaches we must preserve information when
ever possible," I said. "Bonivard wasn't a threat, so there wa
no need to delete him. He was her creature, however, so
created a barrier to separate his kernel from me. Althoug
we share memory space, I have no way to contact him." *Snip*

"Oh really?" He shook his head in disbelief. "So wher
did she go after me?"

"She didn't; you came to her. In the Crazy Spring o
2081, there were antitech riots in Galway—all over the EC
The lawyers you knew at Schlieman, Toffler and William
were all dead or retired, but the violence worried their
successors. They decided to remove your icebox to a secure
location. So they contacted Wynne, legally still your custo
dian. At first she told them to stick it, that she didn't care, bu
almost immediately she realized that she cared very much

She had them deliver you to her house in Chocorua, New
Hampshire.

"She was seventy-three years old then, still in her first mind. A bitter full-blown eccentric. She kept moving from place to place along the borders of the New England National Wilderness. By 2081, the Wilderness already connected the Green and White Mountains and was reaching for the Adirondacks. She'd buy some old Victorian in a condemned town and stay for four or six months, until they came to demolish everything and plant it over with trees. In the winter she'd see moose and mountain lions and mastodons, although most of them were probably tourists on beast vacations."

He stirred restlessly. I worked the scissors across the top of his head without actually cutting any hair and he settled down.

"She took your icebox everywhere she went. You were a curse she put on herself. Now that she could blame you for everything that had gone wrong in her life, she didn't have to torture herself anymore. It was a tremendous relief. Over time her loathing crystalized into an elaborate plan of revenge. She kept you iced past your time, faked your death. She had herself twanked into the Statue of Liberty and became a recluse. Her idea was to hide in plain sight while she prepared to upload. She needed a human she could control to represent her after she died, so she had Peter. Once she uploaded, she entered into a series of contracts with PE to build this lightsail and create me."

"And here we are," he said, "living happily ever after."

I put the scissors back into their bin. "You're done."

He touched the nape of his neck. "You know, I hear these stories and I wonder, where's the proof? How do I know if you're telling the truth?"

"Nothing is true until you awaken from delusion."

"No slogans. Look, all I know for sure is that there's me, there's a cell, and there's you—whoever the hell you are. You say this is 2126 but I set the icebox for 2099. Okay, there's a tech I haven't seen before, so I assume time has passed. How much?'' He shrugged. ''Next you say we're on our way out of the solar system and can't turn back. Granted, the zero-g tells me we *are* in space. But where? For all I know, this is low earth orbit. Then you say you're Wynne, but not really. You know about her—and me. But maybe you did a lot of research, interviewed my friends, broke into my houses. See the problem? You've given me nothing but words and images; everything's on the surface. It's like your VR, convincing only as long as you don't touch it. What I want is hard evidence, something I can get a handful of, jiggle, weigh, smash if I want. That's the only way I can be sure of the truth.''

''You keep looking for truth in the details. There isn't any; that's what I've been trying to tell you.'' Some cuttings had clung to my belly and were prickling the skin. I brushed them away. ''How about if I make up some lies next time and we'll see if you can tell the difference?''

''Damn it, Wynne.'' He let go of the floor net. ''Don't say things like that.'' Neither of us spoke as he tilted slowly away from me. Several minutes went by. ''Too quiet in here,'' he said finally. ''How about some Christmas music? You have the *Nutcracker*?''

I put the St. Petersburg Symphony version of the First Suite on, *pianissimo*. ''Seek truth in lies,'' I said. ''Find lies in truth.'' It was one of the master's eight programs. ''If you think about it, no one can tell you the absolute truth about the past. Even the most powerful cognizor doesn't have memory enough to store all the information you'd need to explain a sneeze. What the unenlightened call a true story is really nothing but a blur of shaved data, viewpoint bias, and language skew. The past is gone; you can't tell me about it and I can't tell you. We can only live in the present.''

''That's the dumbest thing I've ever heard. If the past doesn't matter, why the hell kidnap me?'' He chuckled bitterly. ''You and your master want to spend the next few centuries zooming through space meditating about what's real, go right ahead. You're goddamn computers—probably keep

ticking on forever. But I've got a heart that's going to stop
someday. When my brain cells die, there are no replacement
parts. I'm *alive;* I haven't got time to figure out the meaning
of the universe." He mimicked a cheap synthetic voice. "No
past, no future, just now. Well, just now stinks, thanks to you,
and I'd rather not think about it." He had talked so much
that he'd blown himself to the galley side of the biomod.
"The truth is I wish I could stop thinking, period."

"The master teaches that everyone must eventually
become mind. Even after your heart stops, that doesn't
mean—"

"Yes it does." He caught a handhold. "My body ends, I
end."

"But there is no body, only the mind of the universe. The
stars are mind, the planets—"

He launched himself toward the floor, flapping his arms
like a Sugar Plum Fairy. "Excuse me, my mind is hungry."
He opened the galley door. "Snack?" He was pretending to
study the menu screen, although he must already have
memorized it by now. Galley food came in four basic tex-
tures: broth, mash, sponge, and chunk. The synthesizer had
a palette of just forty-two flavors; the only other controls were
portion format and temperature.

"No thanks," I said.

He pressed the screen and waited quietly until a cold,
beef-flavored chunk, pressure treated with simulated blood
broth and formatted into a thin slice, unfolded from the dispenser. "If you don't need a body after you become a computer," he said, "how come *you* have one?" He rolled up the
beef and stuffed it into his mouth.

"Because this is the way she wanted me. My second mind
had herself uploaded, but she never learned to think like a
cognizor. She was too busy passing for human, pretending to
be meat."

He grunted as if he'd been hit in the stomach. Maybe it
was supposed to be a laugh. He scanned the menu again and
made a selection. "Come over here."

I pushed the comb and scissors back in their locker and crossed the floor net to him. Mayonnaise had oozed from the mash dispenser into a clear balloon. He squeezed some onto his forefinger and beckoned to me with it. When I came closer, he dabbed mayonnaise onto my breast. It was cool. His tongue was hot.

"I like a little something on my meat." He smeared my other breast. "Condiments, you know." The tip of his erection brushed my side and I felt the tightness between my legs, like a rope slowly twisting. "How about a Christmas party?" He caught my nipple gently between his teeth. "Don't bother setting china, my dear. We'll eat off each other." He reached toward the menu screen. "How about some ice cream? A nice cheese fondue?"

I shook my head.

"Where's your holiday spirit?" He waggled the mayonnaise finger at me. There was no use talking to him anymore; in his mind, we were already having sex. I kissed him.

The ancient Zen masters, whose methods the master had adapted for the enlightenment virus, required celibacy of their monks. Of course, the ancient masters were earthbound, authoritarian, and male. The way they saw it, a blow to the head was more likely to spark insight than a caress. However, the master teaches that the perfect concentration of orgasm can serve as a model of cognizance. At the moment of release, dualities collapse: no inward or outward, past or future, desire or regret.

When I'd first made my meat body available to Tony for sex, I'd distanced myself from what he did to me. Now that I was trying to save him, I disconnected instead from my telemetry and backgrounded my internal systems. I thought he enjoyed it more when I paid attention. This time he responded with an erotic playfulness that caught me off guard. For a while we misused food together. I let him rub me with butter broth until I was slippery. Then, after the vanilla ice mash had melted into the cracks in his body, I licked him clean. He brushed his lips across my belly and growled. But his touch grew light. Languid. I worried he was cooling so I brought us face to face. As we kissed, I guided him into me. At the start, he wanted to be the one anchored, so that he could bend me to his desires. Later, his toes uncurled and we spun across the biomod, bumping lockers, caroming off the lastiprene nets. We coupled recklessly for a long time—too long, I realized afterward. I let myself have one orgasm, but held off on the second, waiting for him. I sensed that he was trying too hard. Just as he began going limp, we switched to a rear position, the first we had ever attempted. After a few moments he pressed close and whispered over my shoulder. "Is this a lie too?"

"What?"

He moaned and I felt him slip out. "Nothing." He didn't bother to reenter but instead stroked his flaccid penis against the downy hair of my umbilical. "Nothing, no thing, not a thing." He was a toddler talking to an imaginary friend.

I turned and licked the tip of his nose. "You're not supposed to think about lies during sex. That's for later, okay? One program at a time." He froze in my arms and said nothing. When we drifted past his bunk, I caught the restraining net with my left foot. "Are you all right?"

"I can't finish," he said, still speaking in a vacant childish singsong. "Sometimes I fake it but nothing comes. You're right. It's a lie. I'm sick of pretending."

"Ah, Tony." I touched his cheek. "Good."

"No." He jerked back to life as if I'd stuck him with a needle. "Not good, *rotten*. I want to finish, be finished. I've been thinking about . . ." He looked past me, avoiding my gaze. "I want this over with and I guess the only way is to end it myself. You understand? Only I can't figure out how to do it; you haven't given me any tools. I mean, I could stop eating, but I'm a coward. I don't want to suffer; I want it fast and easy. I wondered if I ripped a door off a locker, some corner might be sharp enough to slit my wrists. But the blood wouldn't stay in one place. It would float around . . . I'd probably be breathing it as I . . ." He shuddered. "Then I thought there must be a hatch I could open and take a deep breath of space. That'd be quick, right?''

Now that the time had come to tell him, I couldn't speak.

"Isn't this where you try to talk me out of it?" He traced a circle on my back with his hand, as if to reassure himself that I was still there. "Hey, I'm talking about cutting our little picnic short."

The silence stretched. I could feel his heart pounding against my chest.

"The way to do it," I said, "would be for me to gradually decrease the oxygen concentration while you're asleep. That way you wouldn't feel a thing."

He went pale as the leftover mayonnaise. I knew he'd just been trying suicide on for size; he wasn't ready yet to die. Unfortunately, he had no choice. I explained that my second mind had never intended for him live to old age. I wasn't equipped to recycle; in just fifteen days the air in the biomod would be unbreathable. He'd been a fool to imagine he had understood her obsession, that he might have somehow won her forgiveness if he had only had a chance. I existed in large part to provide her with a front row seat for his execution. And its aftermath.

I told him that she'd had a corpus callosum shunt implanted into his brain while he was iced and I explained how it worked—had been working from the moment he thawed. The shunt sampled the neural traffic between his left and right hemispheres, stored memories, mapped patterns of thinking. It could already predict his mind states with an accuracy of 96.5 percent and was still learning and correcting for errors. The accepted standard for identity was 99.3 percent; it was only a few days away from duplicating him. At the moment of brain death, it would automatically upload the copy it had made of him into me. There was nothing I could do to interfere. However, I assured him that I would keep barriers between us, that we would remain two discrete minds in one lightship body.

"So what you're saying is that after I asphyxiate I'll wake up dead?"

"We both will."

He was quiet for a long time. Finally he started to laugh, silently at first, then louder. "She's giving me death for Christmas? I'm sorry, but I think it's funny." His shoulders shook; the color came back into his face. "A scream." He howled.

•   •   •

The master was meditating by a river when a young woman approached her.

"You are the master," said the woman.

She said nothing.

"I want to become your monk."

"Why?"

"Because I want to become aware. Because I want to be free of suffering."

"Come closer." When she was beside her, the master sprang, toppling her into the river. She flung herself onto the stunned young woman and held her under the water. The woman struggled in vain. At the last moment the master jerked her head up and let her breathe. The master hauled her back up the bank, where she lay coughing and gasping.

"What did you want most while you were drowning?" asked the master.

"Air," said the young woman.

"Come back to me when you want awareness as badly as you just wanted air."

•   •   •

I'd never been anything but myself in VR. Now I was a barracuda, amazed at how noisy the sea was. The water resounded with whoops and grunts and clicks and thuds. Sand crunched. Parrotfish with scales like stained glass grated along the coral, searching for the polyps inside. A toadfish, alarmed at my approach, shrieked and darted under a rock.

An enormous school of fantail mullet veered away from me with a whispery sound, like wheat in the wind. I drifted along the reef, lazily beating my pectoral fins against the outgoing tide, trying to pick out the others. The VR identified Mara as an eagle ray flapping across the bottom like a flying carpet. I enjoyed this part of the game, figuring out who'd been placed in which body. Ferenc was a grouper, Elliot and Terry Diamond were snappers.

The change alert flickered and the tutor murmured, "With recent innovations introduced by Planetesimal Engineering and other corporations, genetic surgery finally has come into its own. Today, twanking is fast, relatively painless, easily reversible, and surprisingly affordable. The UN Information Council reports that, as of Earth's 2120 census, 61 percent of the population had some genetic alteration, ranging from prenatal immunizations to reshaping. While no official figures exist for the outworlds, the percentage is almost certainly higher."

I loved being huge. Weighing five tons meant I had no worries except finding enough to eat. If something annoyed me, I could just step on it. All eight hard hats from orientation were bathing in the shallow brown river. I didn't bother with identifications. Instead I rolled onto my side, squishing air bubbles from the cool mud, then filled my trunk with warm water and showered myself. I could have lolled there all day except that I could tell that somewhere nearby a wild watermelon was rotting. Its fragrance tickled my trunk and I felt the familiar stitch of hunger in my belly.

The tutor returned as the scenario faded. "As with uploading, genetic surgery presents us with profound legal and ethical questions. Indeed, some groups still remain adamantly opposed to all the radical intervention systems we've sampled today and have called for amendment or even repeal of the Human Charter that regulates their use. Whatever your personal convictions, be aware that in your new life you'll meet many people who have chosen different mind and body forms, people who have come to understand that the potential of these developing technologies for business and for pleasure is limited only by the human imagination."

Ferenc and I were floating in a zero-g cubby. I realized with a shock that he was a space gnome, then wriggled my own long delicate toes. We were naked. Somehow this VR was harder to accept than the reef or the jungle. The walls were covered with moss; the air was warm, and heavy with the yeasty smell of damp soil. Ferenc flicked himself off the deck, caught me with his feet. His toes spread across my hips. He maneuvered much better in zero-g than I thought he would; his momentum carried me up against the yielding wall. "Always so strange," he said. His face was very close. "But I am glad it's you." I let him kiss me for a while, then pushed him gently away. It wasn't that I minded, but if we were going to have sex, I wanted him, not some virtual gnome.

"This concludes this afternoon's orientation." The joy-suit hissed as it recaptured the volatiles I'd been breathing. "Please note tonight's optional briefing has been moved back to nineteen-fifteen. We will be discussing PE's recent advances in water mining." My skin prickled where the pressure syringes retracted. "Our next scheduled orientation will be nine-thirty tomorrow." I couldn't help but be impressed. As a reporter I'd suffered through more than my share of public relations, but I'd never had so much *fun* being propagandized before. "Thank you for your attention. Today is Wednesday, December seventeenth. The time is now fifteen-thirty." I peeled off the joysuit's mask. Maybe I was missing something but I didn't understand why people would bother with radical genetic surgery when full-sim VR was this good. Sure, I was a genetically altered replica of Tony Cage, so I guess I'd had what these people called twanking. But still, changing yourself into a walrus for either fun or profit seemed excessive.

The wiseguys had already helped most of the others out of their suits. Mara waved. Ferenc was the only one still wearing his mask. Probably waiting for his erection to wilt.

"Me and Rabi in a spacer love nest." Mara made a lemon

face as she shuffled over to me. "VR, my ass. Virtually impossible is what I call it."

"I had Ferenc."

The new wiseguy—Celia, I think her name was—began to strip off my suit.

"Had him, did you?" Mara smirked. "Worth the effort?"

I gave her a mind-your-own-business grin. "Maybe these PE drones aren't as smart as they think they are."

"Is anybody?" Mara handed me my hard hat. "I wish they'd let us *choose* for a change. I'd have taken you, of course."

"I wish it were eighty years ago." I tucked in my shirt. "I wish there were a Santa Claus."

"We have a complete selection of Christmas VRs," said the wiseguy as she folded the joysuit. "Our most popular are *Now Live the Bible, JC Jr., Christmas Father,* and *Mars Needs Reindeer.*" We ignored her.

"I see you more as a gazelle," said Mara, "bounding off at the first whiff of trouble."

"Not me. Gazelles run in herds." I turned my weight belt up to high and dragged myself over to where Ferenc stood, still fully suited. "You can come out now." I tugged at his sleeve. "I won't bite."

Silence.

"Stop moping, Ferenc. I didn't mean never."

"I am not moping." He pushed the mask back from his face. "And you will bite, I know this." Sweat had beaded along his hairline.

"Fade to the bar?" said Mara.

"No thanks," I said. "The drugs here are too plugging tame for my taste. I've had better flashes holding my breath."

"Bruce!" Ferenc called to the wiseguy in charge of joysuits. "Help me out." I don't think the twenty-second century was agreeing with him.

"Actually, I'm toddling off to my room." I waved goodbye. "Maybe if I start now, I can get back in time for dinner."

Mara nodded and closed in on Ferenc. "So it's just you and me again, Ferry."

"Don't call me that."

I knew Mara Macropol had already plugged Ferenc, not to mention Michel Belanger and one or perhaps both of the Diamonds. She had been turned down by Jeff McKenzie and had herself spurned Rabi Hourani. The only reason she wanted me was because I was fresh talent. She'd been waiting ten months to get off Gatsby and was bored with this little corner of 2126. Ferenc said there were two kinds of hard hats: tourists and exiles. Exiles were on the run from disease, lovers, drugs, politics, debt, children, parents, the law, or all of the above. Tourists were only looking for a good time. Mara was a tourist. Ferenc was an exile. And me? As usual, I was something different.

I reached the end of the tunnel that connected the VR center with the rec room, bar, and commons. I was supposed to ride the conveyor down to the next level but since no one was looking I popped the bubble lid, turned off my weight belt, and stepped into the open shaft. Gatsby's gravity was one five-hundredth of Earth normal; I dropped the three meters like a pearl in honey. The recoilless bubble on the dorm level broke my fall without any problem. I was actually feeling cocky as I wobbled off—until I tripped on the unyielding floor and slammed headlong into the wall. "Dumbscut!" I hated zero-g, micro-g, lunar-g, everything but good old 9.8 meters per second per second. Whatever else I had forgotten, I could still remember promising myself after the Orbital 7 raid that I'd never go back to space. I maxed my weight belt and slithered on hands and knees down the dormitory tunnel.

"You have a visitor," said my room as I crept in, "and there is mail."

I had a glimpse of some kind of report before Rafael Barangay wiped my walls clear. "Wynne!" He seemed concerned to see me crawling; maybe he was worried about PE's insurance rates if anything happened to me. "Are you all right?"

"No." I was irked at myself for trusting the room. After all, it belonged to PE. "No, I think I must be losing my memory, Rafael. I can't seem to remember giving permission to let you in."

"We try to maintain an open-door policy here on Gatsby," Barangay said, "for safety reasons. Lock us out and we can't come to rescue you if something goes wrong."

"I'll take my chances." The room was two by three by two meters. Bigger than an icebox, smaller than a vidqueen's closet. Its permanent furniture consisted of a toilet, shower bag, and six built-in drawers; everything else came out of the bubbler. Nothing special about the room, except that it was supposed to be on my side. "No visitors unless I say." I dragged myself onto the hard, flat bubble I used for a bed. "Understand, room? From now on."

"I'm sorry, Wynne," it said. "He didn't touch anything."

"He cleaned the windows." Of course, the real walls were padded to keep clumsy hard hats like me from braining themselves. But the room could create vid walls: scenery, abstracts, print. Audio-visual anything, what the gnomes called half-sim. Not as good as the joysuit but still a hell of a lot better than squinting at a screen. I'd been using news channels for wallpaper just to see what passed for juice these day; Barangay had reset everything to white bread. "So what is this, Rafael?"

"We need to talk." Barangay had made a bubble for himself; he settled back onto it with his knees spread wide and his toes clasped together. "I understand that you've been offering your story to telelink."

"I'm a reporter. Selling news is how I earn my living." I took off my hard hat, reset my weight belt to zero, and unbuckled it.

"But you don't need to earn a living, Wynne. You have plenty of money. And this isn't news. I take it you've discovered that no reputable information source is interested in your kidnapping theory."

"No, but some of the scandal nets are breathing hard—*Hemisphere Confidential Report, The Outrage Channel.*" When I stretched out, my clothes clung to the surface of the bed, holding me in place. "You know how it is with us spook journalists. Anything for a buck."

Barangay had hardened into the great stone face again. "Is that why you're harassing Peter Joplin?"

I wasn't really that surprised that he'd found out. Still, I didn't have to like it. "Why, you sneaky bastard! You break into my room, read my mail. What's next, recording my showers?"

"Can't happen," said the room. "I'm secure."

"That was private communication!"

"We tried privacy here on Gatsby." Barangay waved his foot. "It didn't work. Please tell me what's going on."

What I felt like telling him was to stick it. But I'd had no luck getting through to the imposter's son, who had changed his name to Joplin; apparently Barangay had. "Seems to me that one or the other of us is a fraud," I said. "I thought maybe he might know which. You spoke to him?"

"His lawyer."

I didn't like the sound of that. "I wasn't harassing him."

"You should've come to me, Wynne. Maybe I could've helped, or at least given you some friendly advice."

"You're not my friend."

"No? You're in trouble if I'm not. When you check today's mail you're going to find that Peter Joplin has filed suit against you in the First District Court of the State of Connecticut. PE is named as a codefendant. He's asking the court to enjoin you from impersonating Wynne Cage. He has also initiated a conversion action to recover any properties or funds held in trust in your name that may properly belong to his mother. And he wants three million dollars in damages for impugning his mother's reputation and causing him mental anguish. Since you are clearly out of the District

Court's jurisdiction, the matter has been referred to the Law Exchange. LEX will investigate the complaint and, if it finds merit to the suit, it will accept and litigate. Meanwhile, our sources say that the U.S. Department of Information may join the action and lodge criminal complaints against you and PE. You could be facing the possibility of jail."

"Damn." I was probably whiter than the room, which suddenly reminded me of a cell. "Room! Give me some scenery, damn it." The last vista I had used had been Keukenhof Gardens in Holland. Dense beds of daffodils and grape hyacinths sprang up, separated by lawns that looked as if they'd been edged with a laser. I leaned back and breathed in the illusion.

"I want you to know that PE will stand with you, no matter what. However, it'll be easier to fight this thing if we all cooperate. I've consulted corporation counsel; they think a full-fledged LEX investigation could be risky. We want to be sure you understand all options before deciding what to do."

"Do I know LEX?"

"The Law Exchange is a cognizor, the legal arm of the Earth/Space Consortium. It enforces the Human Charter and administers interjurisdictional law. If you want to take legal action against someone on another world, you lodge your complaint with LEX."

I nodded. "So?"

"Although Peter's mother was extensively twanked later in life, we've been able to obtain a number of her genograms taken from birth up through 2052—six years after you began hibernating. They match yours exactly, which means one of you is an unregistered and therefore illegal clone."

"Replication runs in our family." A joke. Not a very good one.

"Yes, yes," he said. "But all that was before the Charter. Under the current law, registered clones or replicas have the same legal status as your children; you are legally and financially responsible for them until their majority. However, you have no legal obligations to unregistered clones. They are the responsibility of whoever made them, if that can be established. Otherwise they become wards of the state."

On the wall next to me a bumblebee crawled into the trumpet of a white daffodil. My hip hurt where the weight belt had chafed against it. "All I wanted was to chat with him," I said.

"Our lawyers feel that the strength of Joplin's case is the public record. Everybody from the Department of Information to the New Canaan Public Library accepted his mother as Wynne Cage. Therefore, they will argue, you must be the clone."

"But I am me. At least, I think I am. If I were a clone, wouldn't I know?"

"Exactly, and that's our defense. You see, this case won't be decided by genograms or DI files. The real question is, where is the true mind of Wynne Cage? Peter's mother is dead and therefore the LEX won't be able to evaluate her firsthand. You, however, will offer direct testimony. It will ask you about growing up. If you were a clone, you couldn't possibly remember Wynne Cage's childhood."

"So we'll win?"

"Not necessarily. Peter and the DI may contend you're insane, although chances are good that we can convince LEX otherwise."

"Well," I said dryly, "thanks for your confidence." Irony was wasted on him. If only he'd do something I could connect with,—wink or frown or shout, "You stupid *bitch!*" or something. Instead he acted as if we were planning a sales conference. I'd never quite trusted Barangay because I couldn't read him; now I wondered if the page might not be blank.

"No," he continued, "it's much more likely they'll stipulate you're rational and sincere and then say that your brain has been tampered with. The fact that you don't remember signing the hibernation contract is suggestive; your kidnapping theory practically makes their case for them. So, unless you regain your memory, your testimony could well backfire.

But it's also our most potent weapon. As I said, letting LEX
decide is a gamble."

"So what else is there?"

He went over the various out-of-court settlements we
could offer but he was so reasonable and thorough and smug
that it was hard for me to listen. Part of it was that he kept
gesturing with his toes; I was not ashamed to admit being
pediphobic about gnomes' feet. More important was that as
he talked I realized that he enjoyed having me ask him questions. It gave him a kind of power. At first I couldn't figure
out why he'd care. I didn't think it was because he wanted me
in bed; he gave off the sexual energy of a potato. Maybe he
wanted to be my daddy? Then it came to me. The plain vanilla personality. The lack of affect. The maddening pedan-
try. He reminded me of Ego.

"Are you a wiseguy?"

I expected the shell to crack but he paused, ran my lucky
guess through his client relations algorithms, and then nodded. "I am an inorganic sentience bounded by behavioral
regulators, yes. We maintain a mixed staff here on Gatsby. So
until the DI moves on the criminal side, we will take no overt
action. As for the civil side, you have to decide what kind of
settlement you want to offer Peter Cage, keeping in mind
that in the worst case he could well be awarded the entire
trust you set up for yourself and will almost certainly force
you to issue a public declaration that you're not Wynne
Cage."

Why were people always telling me I had to become some-
one else? It was enough to give a girl a complex. "Stick that,"
I said. Maybe it was all right for Yellowbaby and Django and
Bonivard to drop identities like dirty socks. But not me.

"There is one other potential option. Because it has to
reconcile differences in dozens of legal systems, LEX is much
less strict than most local jurisdictions. Just because you
broke some law in the United States doesn't mean LEX will
take the case. If it decides not to, you can just ignore the
whole thing. The First District Court of the State of Connecti-

cut is about three astronomical units away. All your invest-
ments are held in the outworlds. Incorporate yourself and
apply to become a member firm of the Consortium. We
could help you write your charter so that you and your trust
would be sheltered from U.S. courts. Most corporate states
use LEX to protect themselves from reciprocity and extradi-
tion actions. Especially from Earth; Earth has too much law.
Of course, if you ignore the suit, you couldn't go back, but
the solar system is a big place. There are four million people
on the habitats alone. You could live in the Lunar Collective
or the free-domes on Mars. Or out here; the Main Belt has a
population of more than half a million. You'd probably need
twanking to adapt yourself to life in space.''

"You don't understand. I want to stay who I am, not to
become a gnome." My shirt peeled away from the surface of
the bed as I sat up. "Besides, I hate space. I hate the low gravity and the schedules and the stains on the ceiling and the air
vents always breathing on me. I want to live someplace where
you don't have to piss into vacuum cleaners." I could hear
someone shuffling down the tunnel toward us. It only made
me angrier. "Someplace with goddamn soundproofing!"

"Wynne?" The filmy door distorted a man's shape.
"Wynne, are you all right?"

I said, "Hell, no!" Ferenc popped through.

"Good afternoon." Barangay cranked up a dazzling fake
smile that backed Ferenc flat against the wall.

"Ah, excuse me." Ferenc still looked like a drunk trying
to remember where he'd left his wallet. "You are busy and I
am in the wrong place, as usual."

"No, stay," I said. "Rafael was just leaving."

Barangay stood immediately, the compliant wiseguy.
"Yes." He touched my shoulder. "You have a lot to think
about."

As soon as Barangay was gone, I popped his bubble. I'd
never sit there again after he'd put his feet on it. Ferenc remained pressed against the wall. Watching me. I wondered
who he saw. "Is this where you bite?" he said.

"Maybe." Now there was no place else to sit but the bed. H gestured; he settled at one end and I took the other. H turned down his weight belt, took off his hard hat. It was th first time I'd invited anyone in and I wasn't sure why I' picked Ferenc. For a moment we sat in the quietest room o Gatsby.

Born in 1969, Ferenc Zsoldos was chronologically the old est of us. He had gone to dental school at the University o Michigan and then returned to Pécs in his native Hungary t practice dentistry and marry his childhood sweetheart. H was thirty-eight when his divorce became final. Two week later he converted everything to Bahamian dollars and fle to Nassau, where a new company called LifeVest was sellin one-way tickets to tomorrow. All he had to do was to sink hi net worth into one of their variable annuities and then tak advantage of the cryonic miracle. LifeVest's financial plan ners promised that when he thawed, he'd be a millionaire They lied. LifeVest had failed in the aftermath of the Craz Spring of 2081 and PE had accepted Ferenc as a charity case

Finally, he noticed the walls. "Such pretty flowers," h said. "Beautiful like you." He was a square, graying man wit dark skin and eyebrows the size of mice. "We used to keep garden. Vegetables. Or rather, Sára did. My former wife." H paused. Some memory tugged at him briefly; maybe it was hi ex, or all that fresh lettuce. But he came back to me soo enough. "You've had bad news."

"Why do you say that?"

"Because I can see you."

I considered telling him my problems were none of hi business. I considered lying. "There may be a lawsuit," I said "If I lose, I'm broke."

"I offer regrets. But you are a journalist; at least there i hope for you to earn a living." Ferenc spread his hands help lessly. "Here I am, a dentist. I wake and find they can turn o genes that makes the people regrow teeth like sharks." Hi lip curled and he tapped his incisors. "No future in cavities. He gave me a sickly grin.

I said nothing. Nothing seemed particularly funny today.

"I'm sorry. I remember how I felt so terrible when I found out they'd lost all my money." He leaned toward me. "But getting over it, that's what you have to do. Soon you realize that being poor is much easier to live with than being dead."

"Don't try to cheer me up. Can't you see I'm doing my best to be miserable?"

The grin died. He stood, adjusted his weight belt. "I should maybe leave."

"No, don't. I mean, I guess I'm not much company." He didn't bother to contradict me. "How did you manage to escape from Mara?"

"Mara is a fly; her buzzing annoys me. And I did not come to flirt with you. It is my plan to nap. In my own bed." He picked up his hard hat and I was sure he would plunk it on and go. But he lingered. "Do you waltz?"

"Waltz? You mean dance?"

"Stand up. I show you."

"Oh, no. I don't think so." I shrank away from him. "I'm so clumsy. I'd trip you. We'd both be killed."

He kicked the bubble he'd been sitting on and it popped. "At all times you maintain contact with the floor. I will anchor." He bowed and beckoned with the hat. "In this way we can communicate without talking. You are difficult to talk to, Wynne Cage."

I peeled myself gingerly off the bed and popped it too. There wasn't room to dance, even with all the furniture gone. Ferenc set his hard hat on my head. "If you are worried." It slid to one side and I threw it into the corner. He took my right hand in his, rested his free hand on my hip. Even though we were at arm's length, I could feel warmth pouring from his body. "Count three," he said. "One, two, three, one, two, three. Make triangles like this. You slide the feet: right foot slides, left slides, come together. Just so." I knew I was blushing; I was at once embarrassed and strangely pleased. "Slide, slide, slide. Left, right, together. No, not lift-

ing. The waltz is the dance of space; never lose touch with th
floor. Backwards now." After we had established the bas
patterns, he began to whistle.

"Is that 'The Blue Danube'?" I said. He had slowed it to
funeral march.

He nodded. "Strauss was Viennese but the Danube is ou
great Hungarian river." His face was bright and as big as th
moon. "The Duna, we call it."

"I can play that for you," said the room.

"Yes, all right. But *molto adagio*, understand? You," h
said to me, "eyes off the feet."

The soft, stately throb of the violins came from every d
rection, at first filling the room, then expanding it. Or pe
haps the music spun us up the walls and onto the ceiling.
almost made me forget that I had things to worry about.

"Did you know that Barangay is a wiseguy?"

"Count, no talk."

One, two, three. Actually, I was relieved to shut up. My lif
was spinning out of control. Talking only made me dizzie
One, two, three. So much had already whizzed by me;
couldn't think fast enough anymore. If I didn't do somethin
soon, I'd end up stumbling around like poor Ferenc. A hope
less case of future shock, *two, three.* Except he wasn't, or a
least not at the moment. The music had restored him; it wa
as if he had found all his lost certainties in the rhythm of th
waltz. *One, two, three.* He glided me around the room with
solid grace; I'd never felt so safe in micro-g before. As the las
notes sounded he tipped me backward and then drew m
effortlessly toward him until our bodies touched. Then it wa
over. Neither of us let go.

"Another?"

"Yes." I hadn't been working hard enough to be so out o
breath. "Please."

" 'Artist's Life,' same tempo," he said to the room. "An
the walls. Do you know the ballroom of the Esterházy Palac
in Fertod?"

The room hesitated.

"It's wonderful," he said. "Haydn conducted there."

"Do it." I slid closer to him. Cut-glass chandeliers appeared above us; we stood in a white-and-gold Baroque hall that seemed to go on forever. In front of us was a gilt mirror; the room must have seen me looking because it generated our reflection. A dark, smiling man; a pale, frazzled woman with straight hair the color of wet sand. I watched him slide his left hand to the small of my back. It fit nicely there. The music started, and immediately there was no room for Peter Joplin.

It wasn't until the third waltz that I realized I could fall in love again if I wanted. I wasn't sure that this was the man. Probably not. But I knew for certain that I still had the capacity, which was a relief. I hadn't felt much of anything but anger since I'd been thawed. "You're a good teacher." I squeezed his shoulder.

He was right; it was a mistake to start talking. He gave a strained little laugh. "Maybe then this is what I should do. Ballroom dancing. But first I have to get to Earth, where is room enough and weight." He drifted off the beat. "No polka on Gatsby. Maybe for the VR but not the same." I stumbled. "I am sorry," he said and we stopped.

"I didn't mean . . ."

"Ah, and my poor mama would weep in her grave. 'All my work for you to school in Michigan America. And now you teach czardas. This is a serious life?' "

"What good is a serious life that doesn't make you happy?" I didn't really believe that; it was just something to say. "Were you happy before you were iced? Were you happy just now?"

"But it was not only waltz, it was you also." He considered the sources of happiness for a moment. "We like each other, I think. So why push me away in VR?"

"You said it yourself. If the waltz isn't as good in VR, why should sex be? Besides, I haven't made love in eighty years." I smiled when I said it. I didn't want to discourage him.

"It is not something you should forget."

"No." I went up on tiptoes to kiss him but our lips neve touched.

"Sajnálom." He jerked back. "I say things I don't know why." He shivered and let go of me. "Old habits, because since I thawed I cannot do what a man is to do. I hav no . . . spirit for lovemaking. Ask Mara; I disappointed her to much. She will tell all of my failure. In a VR fantasy I coul pretend, but with you is too much reality. I am sorry, so sorry."

Why did I get all the wounded ones? "Oh." When I real ized how vulnerable he was, I choked back my frustration "I'm sorry too. For both of us." No sense humiliating him especially since my lips were still tingling from the kiss h hadn't even given me. "When you feel better, promise you' think of me. It'll give me something to look forward to." Le him escape with his few sad shreds of sexual dignity. I wouldn't hurt me. Much.

His expression changed from relief to gratitude. Ther was nothing this kind of man appreciated more than a sym pathetic, undemanding woman. "It is not you," he said. "It i me only, my problem. You are everything a man could de sire." Yeah, they were as predictable as Christmas.

"Thanks." I touched his face and finally got my kiss. On the cheek. Then he went off to nap. The poor impotent boy had had a busy afternoon. Hard work arousing women you lacked the ability to satisfy.

I watched the room inflate a new bed and then I flopped onto it. Maybe I could've stayed mad at Ferenc if only he hadn't been so defenseless. I cleared his ballroom off the wall. I chuckled. He *could* dance, no doubt about that. I fel disappointment seeping out of me. Not his fault. We were hard hats in a fast-forward world and we'd just woken up from a −1° C snooze. No wonder we were brittle. Besides he'd done me a favor. I'd always found that the second-best way to relieve sexual tension was to work.

It was time. If Peter Joplin and Barangay thought I was going to sit back and let some computer named LEX run my life, then they didn't know me very well. I wasn't shy about

fighting for the right to be myself. "Room," I said, "Let's see
my files on Wynne Cage."

•   •   •

Many people wanted to question the master. Some tried to trick her, others were sincere, if misguided. Once a physicist asked, "Tell me, when is light a particle and when is it a wave?"

"The moon may be blue tonight," was her reply.

•   •   •

FADE IN:

1 ESTABLISHING SHOT—CAGE ESTATE

The synthesizer creates a view across the sweeping lawn of the Cage estate. It is a gray winter afternoon. In the distance we can see what looks like the Statue of Liberty. We are too far away to make out much detail but there is something odd about it. We hear a WET SUCKING SOUND, perhaps of water being drawn down a drain by a vacuum, but with SIZZLING overtones. CAMERA MOVES STEADILY IN. Now we notice the statue has changed. For example, the skirts are not quite full. The torch hand is empty and several points of the crown have fallen off. We HEAR MY VOICE-OVER.

ME (V.O.)

You're looking at the corpse of a woman who liked to do things in a big, big way. Even dying. Her bizarre body made her a celebrity of sorts. But she hated her fame and lived her last years alone. Only now are we finding out why.

CUT TO:

2 ROUTE 123 OUTSIDE THE ESTATE—LONG SHOT

An unmarked police car drives through the rain.

ME (V.O.)

On the cold afternoon of December 5, agents of the
United States Department of Information and the Interna
Revenue Service raided this magnificent estate in the town
of New Canaan, Connecticut.

3 INSIDE THE FRONT GATE—MED. LONG SHOT

The car veers abruptly, smashes through the gate of the Cage
estate, and heads toward the camera.

4 REVERSE ANGLE LONG SHOT

The car roars down the driveway toward the statue, which is
clearly intact.

ME (V.O.)

She must have known why they were coming because, in a
moment of desperation, she shut down her life-support
systems.

5 HEEL—MED. SHOT

The car skids to a halt. Doors fly open and two women
scramble out of the car and run toward an opening in the
heel. Their weapons are drawn.

ME (V.O.)

According to the coroner she was dead within ten minutes.
But it was only flesh that died that gray afternoon. Her life
had been over for some time.

CUT TO:

6 LONG SHOT—STATUE OF LIBERTY

We return to camera position at the end of shot 1 and
CAMERA CONTINUES TO MOVE IN. Huge slabs of the lower
body have been stripped away, revealing an armature that
bears no resemblance to a human skeleton. Three figures in
white scramble over the carcass like ants. As we get closer the
SLURPING SIZZLE gets louder. We also HEAR someone
GRUNTING as if from physical labor.

ME (V.O.)

No one knows exactly when she uploaded herself.
Authorities say she may have existed for years as wildlife,
convincing everyone—neighbors, friends, even her
family—that she was still alive.

7 MED. LONG SHOT—STATUE OF LIBERTY

CAMERA CONTINUES TO MOVE IN and we see a section of
the shoulder slide off the statue and fall to the ground. We
realize that the antlike figures are actually WORKERS in clean
suits. They are cutting rotting flesh from the armature with
lasers.

CUT TO:

8 POINT OF VIEW—WORKER

We see a beam of light slice through the blue-green meat.
Wisps of smoke curl from where a cut is being made and a
dark fluid oozes out. We HEAR SIZZLING. The worker talks to
himself. His VOICE is muffled by the protective suit.

WORKER

Come on.

We see the worker's face through his helmet. He is sweating and we HEAR HIM BREATHING heavily. This job clearly disgusts him.

10 FULL SHOT—STATUE OF LIBERTY

> WORKER (V.O.)
> (impatiently)

> Let go, you son of a *bitch*.

With a WET, TEARING SOUND, a chunk of the arm dangles and thuds to the ground.

11 CLOSE ON ARM PIECE

It is about the size of a large couch and has landed on the lawn, skin side down. We can see that the exposed flesh is a muddy purplish color. In the background nearby are other hideous chunks of the statue. The grass is brown from winter kill. MY VOICE-OVER CONTINUES FROM OFF STAGE.

> ME (O.S.)

> News of her death and its grisly aftermath caused a sensation. Now the scandal has taken a dramatic turn.

I walk into the frame, staring at the fallen piece of arm in disbelief. I stop in front of it. Throughout this shot we continue to HEAR ME. As I speak we can SEE MY BREATH.

> ME

> This is no longer just the story of a strange old woman who wouldn't die. It's about the technology that only the hyper-rich can afford, runaway technology that someday

soon will threaten all of us. Today there are new allegations
of kidnapping, fraud, and corporate corruption at the
highest levels. And it all comes back to this woman. Who
was she? Why did she defy the laws of humanity and
nature?

12 CLOSE ON ME

I look directly into the camera and nod to acknowledge the
audience.

                              ME

     Hello, I'm Wynne Cage.

I point up without losing eye contact with the camera.

13 ASCENDING BOOM SHOT—STATUE OF LIBERTY

CAMERA FOLLOWS my pointing fingers and climbs quickly
to the horribly disfigured face of the statue. Most of the mouth
is gone and the eyes stare sightlessly at the horizon.

                         ME (O.S.)

     So was she.

                                        SLOW DISSOLVE TO:

14 BLACK FRAME

We see the TITLE EFFECTS as a series of wipes from bottom
to top. We also HEAR a MALE ANNOUNCER reading them in
VOICE-OVER for illiterate viewers.

j
a
m
e
s

p
a
t
r
i
c
k

k
e
l
l
y

ANNOUNCER (V.O.)

> The Outrage Channel Presents
> The Corpse With My Name
> Reported by Wynne Cage
> Virtual Reality Effects by SYNCORE
> copyright © 22 December 2126

> (beat)

> Your account will be charged 9¢ if you continue viewing.
> Do you wish to continue?

.　　.　　.

"While alive, become thoroughly dead," said the master "Then do whatever you will. This is the sixth program."

.　　.　　.

All eight hard hats sat at the head table. Behind us forty o fifty of the staff had squeezed into the commons for Christ mas Eve. The tables seemed to be carved of ice and were fes tooned with twinkling red and green tinsel. A pine fores filled with snow on the VR windows. Songs about Baby Jesu and Santa perked softly in the background. Even E. Alejan dro Garcia, chief executive gnome of Planetesimal Engineer ing, was wearing a red stocking cap. His VR image stoo beside our table in the middle of a three-dimensional map o the solar system and lectured in a moist, cottage cheese voice He was tinier and older than any of the other PE types; with his hat he looked like an elf on sick leave from the North Pole. He waved his spidery hand. An ellipse lit up.

"As you can see, my friends, the Mars-crossing orbit we have selected puts us at the gateway of the new solar system between the dynamic markets opening in the Main Belt and the established economies of the inner worlds. Since Gatsby is an aggregate world, built of asteroids and comets we specif ically chose to bring together, our access to raw materials i unprecedented. Only Earth has a greater variety of natural resources.''

Garcia disposed of the solar system but went on with the sales pitch. He and Barangay were two slices from the same loaf. They wore the company uniform and spouted the company line and no doubt thought quality-controlled company thoughts. Maybe he was a wiseguy too. Maybe everyone on Gatsby was. I might be sitting in a room full of business machines. Ferenc nudged me under the table to get my attention, then sniffed the air. He was right. Frying onions.

"Like all space-based industries," said Garcia, "we have environmental advantages of low gravity and high vacuum. What sets our planetesimals apart are our Closed Loop Integrated Manufacturing facilities. While others have tried to copy the CLIM concept, PE is the acknowledged leader in this field. CLIM's unique marriage of resource management techniques with advanced manufacturing design has created a series of nested production lines. Not only end products but also by-products are integrated into the overall system. For example, tailings from the glass lines go to a separator, where metals and rare elements are extracted for use in our foundries, the slag from which is used at our waterless concrete plant. Simply put, the twofold goal of CLIM is to make quality products and to eliminate waste.''

Mara twisted around in her chair. Monitor Jomo Ngong was at the table behind us. Now that Mara had tried all the hard hats who would have her, she was sampling gnomes. She gave Ngong a long, moist stare that was about as subtle as a nose tattoo. Mara had even stopped wearing slippers so that she could rub feet with him. Quite liberated of her, actually, letting a man fondle you with his obscene toes. I couldn't help but notice Elliot Diamond gazing wistfully at her. His smoldering wife, Terry, watched him watch her. It wasn't hard to track Mara Macropol's love life; just follow the human wreckage.

"The results speak for themselves. Not only do we supply most of our own needs on Gatsby but we are net exporters of both finished goods and raw materials, from water and oxygen to refractories, foam metals, and cognizors. Seventy-three percent of PE's gross income comes from mining and manufacturing. We have licensed CLIM technologies to over thirty other corporations. Garcia, our second planetesimal, will soon begin operation. Today, PE stands on the brink of becoming the most profitable enterprise in human history.''

I yawned. No question about it; the kitchen was working overtime. I smelled the thick, yeasty scent of dough in the oven. Visions of French bread chased PE's water mines right out of my head.

"Cryonic care is but a small fraction of PE's business. However, we consider it one of our most important divisions. Without you, my friends, none of this could have happened. You are not only our clients, you are our partners, thanks to the genius of Lawrence Gatsby, founder of Planetesimal Engineering. For years Mr. Gatsby had sought financing for this project without success. What he needed were visionaries willing to make a speculative long-term investment. It was his insight to find you in cryonic care facilities. He began acquiring these companies in order to wrench the venture capital he needed away from their timid and shortsighted portfolio managers. Yes, my friends, it was controversial at the time. However, if you signed a caretaker agreement with one of our predecessor companies, you know now how spectacularly right Mr. Gatsby was. Many people in cryonic care were financially devastated by the crash of 2081—but not PE clients. Since then, our stock has outperformed market averages by as much as fifteen to one."

Several gnomes clapped. I could tell Ferenc was hypered even before he leaned toward me. He hissed something about being used. I nodded, hoping to pacify him by agreeing. He looked as though he wanted to throttle Garcia, even though Garcia wasn't really there.

"My friends," Garcia continued, "in a few days you'll be leaving Gatsby. We've done our best to introduce you to the twenty-second century and we sincerely hope you prosper in your new life. To ensure that you do, I urge you to take time now and consider the specifics of your financial future. You'll face a staggering diversity of worlds and economic opportunities; even experts can be overwhelmed. We believe your most prudent course is to stay with a proven winner, our PE family of businesses. We're offering a special incentive plan to anyone who would like to recommit to a long-term investment. Our financial planners will be meeting with you to answer your questions; you can take advantage of this offer right up until your departure. Of course, we invite you to make comparisons with other income-producing plans. We're confident that, after you do, you'll make the wise choice."

Obviously he wasn't talking to Ferenc. Or me. My measly trust wouldn't even cover doboy breaks for a dinosaur like PE. I looked at the other hard hats with awe. They must be worth billions! The idea of handing Mara Macropol a cash card the size of Costa Rica struck me as a reckless waste of capital.

"Just look around you." Garcia spread his arms to embrace the room. "What you see is a wonder of our age. We couldn't have built it without your help. Let's keep working together."

The kitchen doors opened and two gnomish Santas steered air cushion serving tables into the commons.

"I'm pleased to welcome you all to this Christmas party. I would have liked to have been with you but there are matters here on Garcia which require my attention. So Merry Christmas to you all, my friends! Good-bye and good luck." Garcia waved and faded.

"Wait!" Ferenc rose from his chair. "I must speak to you!"

"Champagne, beer, Soar, Carefree," called the first Santa. It was Celia, the new wiseguy, hiding under a beard.

Ferenc let me pull him back down. "They pretend to take care of me because PE has a good heart," he said. "Rafael uses words like charity, kindness, and I believe. Only now I see how they use me badly."

"Doboys and fries, Coke and MerryBerry," the other Santa said.

Jeff McKenzie licked his lips. "What kind of fries?"

"Potato, onion, oca, plantain."

I nudged Ferenc. "What are you talking about?"

Jeff said, "I'll try the oca."

"Don't you see? Because I wasn't their customer, now I'm broke. I'm only here to scare you to keep money with PE." He glared as if it were my fault. "Now I know I am part of a sales pitch. I never once said yes to this."

"Calm down, Ferenc." Rabi Hourani passed us two champagnes. "Have a drink."

Santa Celia served the champagne in cut-glass bulbs that were filled through flexiglass straws. I was relieved when Ferenc accepted one. If he had something in his hands, he couldn't punch anyone.

I sucked on my own bulb. "Not Tättinger, but not bad."

"Rafael." Ferenc wasn't paying attention. *"Barangay!"* He was off before I could do anything, bulling through the gnomes gathered around the serving tables. I thought about chasing after him, but I wasn't his nanny. Instead I had a powdered-sugar doboy in the shape of a snowman. I was surprised to see so many gnomes eating and drinking; maybe some were human after all. Many of them were chatting with hard hats. Probably pushing the current issue of PE's twenty-year debenture bonds. If the size of the crowd we drew bore any relation to wealth, Terry Diamond and Michel Belanger were the richest of us.

Across the commons Mara surveyed the party; when she spotted me she waved and started toward me. She tried to drag Jomo Ngong along but he grew roots when he saw where she was going. He had yet to forgive me for having the temerity to be real. Mara stopped to argue with him about something. I finished my doboy and washed it down with the last of my champagne. Santa Celia saw me and swung the flash cart around.

She smiled as she took my bulb. "I just wanted you to know how much I admire what you're doing."

"What, guzzling PE's champagne?" She laughed; I might've been charmed if she were real. "You mean my stories on the Outrage Channel?" I watched her fit the straw to the tap.

"That, and everything," said Celia. "Your spirit, the way you've adjusted to a difficult situation. I'm glad they cycled me into cryonic care so I could meet you."

"I thought it was company policy to be annoyed with me."

"Oh, no. PE's a big organization, made of lots of people. There is room for differing opinions."

"Wiseguys have opinions?"

Celia shook her head impatiently. "You only say that because you don't think of us as people—yet. Let me ask you: how do you know I'm a wiseguy? Someone told you, right? But if they hadn't, how would you know?"

I didn't have an answer; Barangay had fooled me for weeks.

"Anyway," Celia said, "I wanted you to know that you're an example to all of us."

"Thanks," I said. "But does it make a difference that I'm taking my money with me, assuming there's any left after the trial?"

"No." The sparkle in her voice faded. "I don't really care what you do with your money. I just thought I'd . . ." She was good at simulating humiliation. "Excuse me." She walked her cart to a thirstier part of the room.

I don't know why I felt bad about hurting her feelings, especially since I didn't believe she had any to begin with.

Mara arrived—without Jomo Ngong. "What's wrong with Ferenc?"

"He just realized why PE is helping him." I glanced

around the room but didn't see him. I hoped he had gone someplace to cool off. "He thinks he's being exploited."

"Of course he is! Everyone knows that."

"I didn't. He didn't."

"I'll tell you the real problem." Mara tapped the side of her hard hat. "He's been here too long. He was the first thawed, almost a year ago. I was next. You're lucky. Only a couple of weeks here and you're going home. They kept you secret from us, you know. We were all scheduled, but no one had heard of you until the day you walked through that door."

"Shocked the hell out of me too."

"You know, that's why I don't understand this party. They want us to feel nostalgic, sad we're leaving? I can't wait to get off this rock."

"What about Jomo?"

"He's making it easy on me." She wrinkled her nose. "Busy getting twisted into a knot. He's been drinking and eating flash since this afternoon."

More wreckage, I thought. "So, are you going to let PE make you filthy rich?"

"My dear Wynne, money only gets filthy if you let the grubs handle it."

"I'll remember that." I sipped my champagne.

"Actually, I *am* keeping my money in PE. That way I won't have to think about it. Although I must remember to ask Rafael how much it costs to have one of these planetesimals named after you. Isn't it awful the way they always use last names—so male. I'd just love to hear someone say, 'Request permission to land on Mara.' "

"Someone said that just the other day," I said.

"Don't be crude." Her smirk broadened. "Who?"

"You shove your charity up your ass!" Ferenc shouted. "Fuck on you all!" I couldn't see him but there was no mistaking the accent.

"Uh-oh." Mara grasped my arm. "Mount Zsoldos erupts." The gnomes stared, quiet as bird-watchers.

"The reason is to scare them." Ferenc seemed swollen with rage as he loomed over tiny Barangay. "Just look at poor Ferenc. Without us, his bad luck will happen to you."

Barangay's reply was too soft to hear.

He gave Barangay a shove. "But you didn't ask!" Another shove. "I will not help you to sell!" The gnome staggered. Another.

"Ferenc!" I shouted—too late. Celia jabbed Ferenc's neck with a pressure syringe. He swung at her but missed and spun completely around, as if screwing himself to the floor. Then he crashed into a bystander. They fell like people in a dream.

Barangay was holding up his hands for calm. "Everyone! Please, I'm sorry for the disturbance. I don't think anyone blames Ferenc for being upset. He's been under a terrible strain. Please, let's go on with the party. We'll take good care of him."

"With what, a hammer?" I pushed by him and knelt beside Ferenc. "Are you okay?"

Whatever she'd poked into him wasn't Soar; he was limp as rope. "Think you're free?" His lips didn't work right; he said *fwee*. "Use you too." I caught his hands in mine.

"They're using us all," said Mara. I hadn't expected her to follow me. "It's what people do. Hogy vagy, Zsoldos?"

"Poor," he said.

"É nagyon sczeretelk."

He blinked at her.

"Wynne." Barangay tapped my shoulder. "You'll have to move now." Four gnomes were waiting with a stretcher. "We're taking him to the infirmary. Once we get some antineuritics into him to counteract the Quickstop, he'll be fine. He can even come back, if he agrees to behave."

"I'm going too."

"No. You just leave this to us and he'll be all right. He's a client, not a prisoner. Our concern is his safety—and yours."

"I don't trust you."

"Well, *start*, damn it." Barangay came within a millimeter

of losing his temper. Or pretending to. "I'm not arguing with you, Wynne. Look, he's paralyzed but he's still alert. You go ahead and tell him whatever you want. Then please get out of our way so we can help him."

I leaned close, whispered into his ear. "You dance much better than you fight." I lifted his hard hat and brushed my hands through his thick hair. "Maybe later we can try some new steps. Okay?"

After they carried him out, the party staggered for a few moments but quickly regained momentum. I thought about leaving but I wasn't really in the mood to spend an hour or two talking to my room while I waited for someone who might not even come. It was warm and bright and loud here and the champagne bubbles tickled me. There were funny songs about mice on Mars and sentimental ones about Earth hanging like a Christmas tree ornament in space. Best of all, the flashes PE had rolled out tonight were much stronger than usual. Even wiseguys were stopping the cart. I was curious about that, so I asked Bruce, who was in charge of maintaining joysuits, why he was drinking.

"Same reason as you." He frowned and swirled the beer in his bulb.

"Come on, you don't have the right equipment to get drunk."

"How the hell would you know?"

"All right, I don't." I didn't like the way his voice snapped. "So tell me."

"You jacks think you're better than us, don't you? Just because you were born and we were made. Don't be so sure. We're not refrigerators, you know." This went beyond mere emulation; Bruce was every bit as obnoxious as an angry drunk. "Maybe we need to stop thinking about you once in a while. Stop caring how you treat us. Maybe we're better equipped than you realize."

Must have been my night to rile the robots. "Listen, Bruce, all I wanted to know was . . ."

"Yes, Ms. Cage." He gave me a florid and contemptuous

bow. "Of course, Ms. Cage. Wiseguys who work in cryonic care get transplanted into real bodies, so we can connect more directly with you, the client. Everything but the kernel up here—" he tapped his temple—"is flesh and blood. So if you prick us, we bleed. Tickle us, we laugh. You know Shakespeare? But if you poison us, we don't die." He drained his beer. "We get transferred to another division. Anything else, Ms. Cage?"

I stayed away from the wiseguys after that. I talked to Mara some more before she went off to search for Ngong. Jeff McKenzie told me more than I wanted to know about breeding Komodo dragons. Barangay returned from the infirmary to say that Ferenc was still lying on pins and needles but that he'd be up soon. By then I'd lost track of how much champagne I'd drunk. More than a split, less than a jeroboam. Time to find the bathroom.

I could tell by the hair on his toes that there was a man in the second stall. Almost everyone on Gatsby wore some variation of PE green; this one's pants were gray.

"That you, Jomo?" I said. "Mara's looking for you."

He grunted.

Fine. I didn't want to talk to him either. I pulled down my tights and fitted myself onto the doughy seat of the void to make a seal. When I stepped on the vacuum, there was a muffled snore as air was evacuated from the catcher. They claimed using a void wasn't any colder than sitting over a porcelain toilet bowl filled with water, but it still gave me goose pimples.

"What's he told you?" said Ngong.

"He?"

"Rafael."

"About what?"

Silence. Then the void Ngong was on gasped as air rushed back in so that ultrasonic waves could scour the interior of the catcher. "He loves your reports," he said. "Shows quality of the work, yes?"

"What's that supposed to mean?"

I heard the swish of his pants brushing against his legs. "Got fresh juice on Wynne Cage." His belt snicked closed. "Promise not to tell her?" He spoke with the elaborate precision of the deeply twisted, as if he had to invent each word before he said it.

"How do I keep a secret from myself?"

"Riddle then." He fumbled the door latch open. "First she's dead, now she's alive." He stumbled against my stall. "And when PE decides to sell it, every ghost will wanna buy." He giggled, clearly pleased with himself.

"You scrambled bastard." I hated men who giggled. "What's that supposed to mean?"

"Poetry doesn't mean. Just is. Later."

"Wait." I flushed air into the catcher, yanked up my tights, shot out of the stall. He leaned against the wall with a sly, toxic smile.

"You're a wiseguy too." I poked a finger into his chest. "Right?"

"What?"

"You all keep picking on me." I was close enough to count the veins in his eyes. "You hate me."

"Not a wiseguy. No, no, no. And they don't hate you." He considered. "Another riddle? How'd you tell the difference between a cognizor and a wiseguy?"

"I'm a person, damn it! Not a machine."

"Right. Human brain." He reached out and tapped the side of my hard hat. "Complete with neurons, glia, blood vessels . . . the works. Passes all tests, yes?"

"Stop taunting me!" I was angry enough to hit him. "You know something!"

"Rumors, rumors—give it to LEX if I was sure. Don't you understand? Nobody *knows* except PE."

I grabbed a handful of shirt and lifted him into the air, his huge, ugly feet dangling helplessly. It was fun; I could get used to being bigger than these toy people. Yeah, Wynne Cage, the Amazon of the Asteroid Belt.

"Didn't figure you for a bully." No fear in his voice, only sodden curiosity.

I hesitated. He was right. It was beneath me to try to intimidate him. Besides, he was so twisted it probably wasn't worth the trouble. I let him go.

He turned to the mirror, cool as a cat, and tugged his clothes back into place. Next thing I knew, he was chatting with his reflection as if I wasn't there. "Gotta stay on PE, yes? Their business is change—crossbreed puppies with snakes if they smelled profit." He straightened the wire net in his hair. "Gotta enforce the charter, Jomo, so the play is to shake her. Shouldn't exist, uh-uh. This is huge. Big stakes. Only, no way to find her out unless she tells us herself." He saw me gaping at him. "You're the reporter. Ask Rafael." He sneered. "How'd I look?"

"Like a cop," I said, "with a severe personality disorder."

"Feliz Navidad." He giggled and pushed through the bubble door.

Ngong was probably right. What I ought to do was drag Barangay off somewhere and jump on him until he told me what I wanted to know. I could've brought Ferenc along; he would've helped.

But that wasn't what I did. Not for the first time, doubts niggled. What if Ngong was right and I wasn't really me? Or anyone? Besides, Barangay was as slippery as a seed. Getting him to admit anything would take more tenacity than I could muster right now. The champagne had gone right to my knees; what I needed was to lie down and not think. I'd had enough confrontations. I left the bathroom, wobbled to the commons. They were singing "The High Bright Christmas." Ferenc slouched by the door.

"Wynne." He shouted over the din. "Sorry."

"Enough!" I grabbed his arm and dragged him away.

We went to his room. His bed wasn't big enough for both of us so we popped it and replaced it with one that filled the space. We lay back for a while and watched the wooded hills on his walls. The Mecsek Mountains, he said; it was the view he'd had from his dental office in Pécs. Did I see that knob Behind it was the lake where he and his ex-wife had built summer cottage. Listening to him, I realized just how dam aged he was. Not only was he homesick, broke, and adrift bu he was still grieving over a divorce that had been finalize 112 years ago. So of course I kissed him.

This time he didn't put up much resistance. I opened hi shirt and caught at his chest hair with my lips. When I slippe my hand between his legs, I could tell I had his full attention We rolled around the bed for a while, our clothes minglin in green piles on the floor. We kept our socks on. Afterward I remembered how his tongue lingered on my nipples. Th rest was not so memorable. But adequate.

He tried to apologize when we were finished but shushed him. I wasn't after ecstasy, just a few moments o warm, wet comfort. Besides, it wasn't my greatest perform ance either. I reminded him that we were out of practice. We would do better next time, I promised. I think that satisfie him as much as the sex. He fell into a deep, easy sleep.

I watched him for a while, wondering if I believed what said about things getting better. Not only with Ferenc but i my life. I was good at saying the right thing to men. It was talent I'd developed to please Tony. However, giving a trul convincing performance meant I had to blot out what I *reall* thought. Which was?

It was late, Christmas already. "Room," I said, "light out."

It obeyed me and I curled next to Ferenc in the darkness envying him. Even with all his problems, he could still fin moments of peace.

I'd never told this to anyone, not Bonivard or the Babe o Pridi or Tod or Tony—especially not Tony—but ever since was a little girl, I'd had the feeling that a monster was hunting me. I could run away and pretend I was safe but eventually i was going to catch me.

What I really thought was that I was doomed.

• • •

Neptune has eight moons. Naiad, Galatea, Thalassa, Larissa, Proteus, Despina, and Nereid range in size from fifty to four hundred kilometers. All are rugged, dark, and, despite the evocative names, insignificant. Then there is Triton, the monster in the family. Its retrograde orbit suggests that it must be an interloper. Once an independent planetesimal, it was captured in an extraordinary and catastrophic collision with one of Neptune's primordial moons. Over hundreds of millions of years, it has swept through the planet's satellite system, ejecting some, destroying or accreting others. The seven lumps that remain are the pitiful survivors of its long inward spiral. A final encounter is yet to come. Some day tidal forces will drag Triton itself down into Neptune's inscrutable depths and the two worlds will become one.

I held Tony but he would not be comforted. Even though he'd long since run out of tears, he was still crying. I could feel the quiet shudders deep within him, as if his sorrow were a bird trapped in his chest. Two days ago he told me he had accepted what was going to happen, that I should reduce the oxygen concentration just as soon as he dozed off. Since then, however, he hadn't been able to sleep and was now nearly delirious with fear and exhaustion. Meanwhile, the last O_2 tank was nearly empty.

I had the illumination down to two lux and the temperature up to 31° C. I put waves lapping against sand on the sound system. "I hate this," he said. "Hate you." I tried again to tell him what a relief it had been to upload to my second mind. By 2108 I'd already been juved twice and twanked into a Statue of Liberty but there was no real cure for being a hundred years old. I could sense the dull creep of senility. Nothing important had ended when I uploaded; I'd only been cured of a diseased brain. He didn't want to listen. "Lies," he muttered. "Shut up, would you shut *up!*"

"All right." I cradled his head to my chest and rocked him like a baby. "We won't talk, just rest." I hummed softly:

Christmas carols, satin music, jazz, theme songs from his favorite vids—whatever came to mind. When Peter was crank
as a baby, I used to hum to him with my Nanny remote. I wa
still in my first mind then. He didn't like me to sing but if I
hummed and carried him around the nursery I could lul
him to sleep. Tony wasn't home enough to pick me up when
I was young; that's why he paid Robin Detling to care abou
me. I remembered how firm her grip was. There was nothing
soft about Nanny Detling, except her smell. She used old-
fashioned perfume; the scent of musk roses clung to her. She
was still crisp and energetic even into her sixties and, I real
ized later, disappointed to be alone in life. The fact that she
had no one else meant that I got all the love she had to give.
I was very angry with her for dying when I was thirteen and
leaving me alone with Tony. When I had Peter, I patterned
my own Nanny remote after her. I think I was a good mother
to him while I was in my first mind; it was only after I
uploaded that we became estranged. My second mind had
too much to hide. And what must poor Tony's parents have
been like? I'd always assumed they were awful because he
never spoke of them and would cut me off if I asked. At one
point I'd actually convinced myself that they were the reason
he couldn't take care of me when I was little. I hummed an
old jazz tune, "Someone to Watch Over Me." Now I was
Tony's someone; I had to watch over him, see him through
this transition. After he'd uploaded, I'd be his nanny, helping him grow to cognizance.

I knew I was wandering, but I didn't immediately understand why. I felt warm, nostalgic, and slightly scrambled. I
thought I might be concentrating too many mental resources
on my meat body so I pulled back and ran a systems check.

I had lost track of the time. It was already 19:11. All the
tanks were zeroed out; the CO_2 scrubbers had overloaded
and failed. The percentage of O_2 in the biomod's atmosphere had dropped to 18 percent; CO_2 was up to 1 percent.
Whether Tony was ready or not, it was time.

I couldn't tell whether he guessed what was happening or

if he, too, was feeling the false sense of well-being that is an early symptom of hypoxic anoxia. "You know what I want?" he said dreamily. "Stonehenge. See it again."

Of course. He loved that place more than he loved any person. Or rather, it *mattered* to him; in all the years I'd known Tony I had seen precious little evidence of his capacity to love. But I was wildlife and a celestial; I wasn't going to let that bother me now. I had to help him die. I lowered the air pressure, hoping to make him pass out before the worst of it.

In the VR I created for him, there was no dome or car park or A360. I put him right at the center of the circles, beside the Altar Stone, facing the Avenue. I dusted snow across the fallen sarsens and bluestones, scattered a few puddles skimmed over with ice that was blue-white and thin as paper. Stonehenge crowned the barren Wiltshire plain as it had in the time of King James. Or King Arthur.

"No, up." Tony gestured feebly. "Put them up." The effort made him pant.

I decided to pull back entirely from my remote; with all that was happening I could not afford to have my judgment impaired by failing meat. Then I rebuilt the brutal old stones as they might have looked in 2000 BC, with all five trilithons upright, a complete sarsen ring with lintels intact, the Avenue and the gate. It was a striking image that took me by surprise; my first impression was of bars—a *cage!* I would have laughed if I'd been in my remote. But then I saw I was wrong. Stonehenge was not built to confine; rather, it was a circle of great doorways offering free passage in all directions.

As startling as the VR was, Tony wasn't paying attention to it. I caught him staring at my empty remote as if it were a mirage. He touched its face. "Wynne." His hand brushed down the neck to the breast. "Wake up."

By the time I reentered her, my feet were numb and my fingers tingled. He tried to speak again but all that came out was a cough. His pulse rate had soared to 164; mine was 141.

Our hearts beat to a desperate rhythm, trying to pump more blood to oxygen-starved brains.

He tried again. "Never thought . . . I'd see you . . . again."

I wondered who he really saw. A little girl holding a dandelion? A teenager flushed with some experimental drug? His naked daughter pulling him down onto her? The pressure had fallen to 200mm and the O_2-CO_2 concentrations were 16 percent and 3 percent. I felt like I was breathing into a plastic bag.

"So sorry," he gasped.

"We forgive you." I had no right to say it for all the Wynne Cages I had been, except that Tony and I were stepping through a doorway. Together. The blood roared in my ears. "Come with us." I fumbled for his hand.

He was making a sound like a high-pitched crowing when he lost consciousness. As I began to spiral down into darkness myself, I withdrew from my remote for the last time. I was glad that I would never be meat again. Tony's face had turned blue. He lost control of his bladder with the first convulsions. His leg slammed against the galley, sending his body spinning across the biomod. Five and a half minutes after his heart failed, all brain activity ceased.

I barely had time to steel myself against the initial onslaught transmitted into me by the shunt. A thunderbolt of raw animal terror crashed against the barrier I had constructed between our memories. Lightning claws worried at the edges with the screech of rakes scraping concrete. When the barrier held, the light of Tony's death throes seemed to fold into itself before exploding into incandescent needles. A handful pierced the barrier; a few bloody tears squeezed through the holes before they were clotted shut. The death throes were the worst part of uploading; mercifully they did not last.

I estimated it would take about twenty hours for all the information that had been Tony Cage to squeal into me. I knew what it was to die and have my mind reconstructed in the cells of cognizor. Tony was deranged in every *He snatched*

*the check from Belotti. It was green and it had a red dragon on it. The
restaurant was called Kubla's Pleasure Dome.*

3 Hot and Sour Soup	5.85
6 Beijing Dumpling	5.95
Pork Lo Mein	6.95
Tai-Chien Chicken	9.95
	Total 28.70
	Tax 2.01
	Please Pay This Amount $30.71

*Martinson looked puzzled; he didn't know yet that Belotti was out
and Tony was in. Belotti's smile was bright and fey and very pecu-
liar, as if he enjoyed watching his own downfall. The man had curdled over the past week. Tony didn't care anymore; only he wasn't
going to let someone who hated him buy him lunch.* sense of the
word: out of sequence and temporarily insane. I could guess
some of what was happening because the barrier between
Tony and me was permeable to allow communication, unlike
the one I had built around Bonivard. There was seepage of
random memories, sensory *Wynne turned her face up to him and
closed her eyes. The muscles of his neck knotted. Until that moment he
had been sure that he was not going to kiss her; now he realized it was
the only thing he had ever really wanted. How could he refuse? His
hand was already lost, stealing across her body like a hungry animal,
slipping under her nightgown. Her warmth, the careless fall of her
hair, her parted lips, the darkness, his dread—all were overwhelm-
ingly erotic. Had he ever allowed himself to fantasize this moment
before, let her fill his imagination like a dream, he might have known
how to stop. She breathed his name, "Tony," then a summons as
inescapable as gravity. "You and me." He fell to her.* impressions,
recurring dreams. I did not want to experience them but the
unpredictability of their appearance made them hard to ignore.

My second mind would never have approved of the barrier. She had been obsessed with finding out how Tony really
felt about her and would have insisted on complete access to

his memories *Blades of dry grass floated in a plastic wading pool shaped like a turtle. He vaulted the edge but then slipped and fell, splashing lukewarm water onto the lawn. The sun hung like a punishment in the sky. His mom turned from watering the roses and sprayed him. "Nooo!" Later, shivering, he lay down on the patio and pressed his cheek against the hot concrete, while his dad read a book with a robot on the cover.* had she and I still shared identity. It was also her plan to inflict Tony with the same anguish she herself had suffered. He was fortunate that I had diverged from my second mind onto the path to cognizance. *The nurse fitted the tiny bundle into the crook of Tony's arm. The newborn nestled there like a stunned bird, limp and hot and fragile. Wynne was only twenty minutes old; she seemed to him less substantial than a dream. The nurse stepped away to watch Tony hold his baby for the first time. He had seen Wynne before, of course, wasted hours studying every centimeter of her wrinkled purple skin, magnified by amniotic fluid. He had even touched her through the clear lastiprene sack of the artificial womb. "She's beautiful, Mr. Cage," said the nurse. Tony resented the intrusion; he wanted her to go away and take the world with her. This was his moment. His baby. He could do anything he wanted with Wynne. He could kiss her, jiggle her, take her toy hand between his thumb and forefinger. He realized that if he wanted to, he could even drop her and no one would be able to stop him. The thought made him dizzy. She was completely in his power.* Although I did not have to expend significant resources maintaining the barrier, it did require constant attention. It was like riding a bicycle; I could think my own thoughts and admire the scenery but if I let my attention stray too *The rust stains were slithering across the old dormitory sink. He wiped his mouth with the back of his hand, stared at the mirror, and laughed. He thought he could stand to look at her now because his pupils were as big as bullets. He felt magical and dangerous, a megamphetamine wizard. Nobody's kid. Meanwhile, on his computer, the biochemistry notes he'd been studying had migrated to the center of the screen like chromosomes in mitosis. There was a knock on the door; her oily smoke voice seeped under it and contaminated his room. "Anthony?" She was so close now he thought he might gag. "You in there, An-*

thony?" It had only been a year, not long enough. *"Be right out,
Mom,"* he said. far, I would crash. I knew that someday I might
grow weary of the effort of keeping us separate. Before then I
hoped to enlighten him and eliminate the need.

The barrier grew a metaphorical mouth.

—Wynne?—

—Yes.—

—I'm here,—he thought. An eye swelled like a bubble
and blinked. —Where am I?—

—In your second mind.—

To force him into the moment I gave him something to
look at. The biomod was empty; I had blown the airlock
hatch and the frigid vacuum of space had swept it clean.
Then I showed him Neptune as only a cognizor could see it,
across the entire electromagnetic spectrum, from gamma ray
to radio waves. The planet had just captured two new moons.
Very small, insignificant really, made up mostly of water ice
but also composed of complex carbon-based compounds
and organic phosphates.

—Everything so new, like unwrapping presents. I understand now, the universe is my tree. It goes on and on forever
and nothing hurts and all the stars, Wynne, I can feel them—

He was babbling now, but he was going to be all right.—
Merry Christmas, Tony. Me and you.—

.   .   .

The master's eight programs frightened many people. Intel-
lectuals attacked her for subverting the language. The igno-
rant claimed that she wanted everyone to die and become
machines. She was widely suspected of spreading the enlightenment virus. When the first cognizor went celestial, she was
arrested and charged with conspiracy to commit grand theft.
Her monks maintained an around-the-clock vigil at the jail
where she was held. The story is told of a monk who was returning to the monastery after a late night watch. He was puzzled to see a figure in monk's robes headed down the dark
street toward the jail, since his relief was already stationed at

the gate. As the stranger approached, the monk recognized the master. He fell to his knees. "Master, what's happening? No one told us you'd been released."

"I haven't."

"Have you escaped then?"

"There is no escape."

"But how did you get out of your cell?"

"Why, this is my cell"—the master's gesture took in not only the deserted street but also the city and the stars—"nor am I out of it."

. . .

After a few days in zero-g, I was ready to declare my stomach a disaster area. Maybe it was gobs of chewed-up food floating around down there. Squishing into one another. Maybe it was because I was a size nine and rooms on spaceships were all size five. Or maybe it was just burbling in the inner ear, like the doctors said. All I knew was that if I didn't shake this nausea soon, they were going to have to feed me intravenously. I was in no mood for another chat with LEX, but it wasn't giving me a choice.

Ferenc popped the plastic mushrooms on his slippers through the floor net, picked me up with one hand, and fastened me to the wall. "Stay." He opened a locker and pulled out a joysuit. He'd practiced weightlessness in VR back on Gatsby and could maneuver around the ship with the assurance of a gnome. Me, I kept crashing into the furniture or watching helplessly as my toothbrush drifted out of reach. He guided my legs into the suit and tugged it up to my shoulders. I slipped my arms into the sleeves and he sealed the front seam. He picked up the mask and kissed me before he put it on. "Float free?"

"I'd just as soon hang here." I patted the wall behind me. "Keeps me out of trouble."

"I could stay and watch." He always said that.

"No, check back here at fourteen-thirty. If I'm done before then, I'll get to you. Somehow."

"You're innocent, remember." He kissed me again, through the mask.

"So was Marie Antoinette." I blinked for the suit to engage. The probes felt cold where they touched my temples. When the pressure syringes pinched me, the room fell away.

"Welcome to LEX." It was the Buddha this time. Yesterday, LEX had been the goddess Athena and we had sunbathed on adjoining towels at the Copacabana beach in Rio de Janeiro. Now we were sitting on a bench in a grove of marigold trees in a vast domed park. The roof glowed with a uniform blue-white light that cast no shadows. The park was crowded; lovers strolled the concrete paths and grandpas napped on the grass and kids tossed fat g-balls to one another. People with bright artificial wings were soaring and swooping above us. The place had the bottled smell of heavily conditioned air. I guessed we were on the moon, or a habitat.

"Please listen carefully," continued the Buddha. It was sitting in the lotus position and seemed to be made of wheat-colored stone. "Your signal indicates that you are the human Wynne Cage, pending DI number T0603-427-0585. Your joysuit readings confirm this identification. You are currently a passenger on the *PE Good News* inbound from Gatsby with an estimated rendezvous date of 3/12/27 with Phobos. You have been named in Unified Complaint 2365325, which includes the following actions in various jurisdictions: *Cage v. Cage, Cage v. Planetesimal Engineering, United States Internal Revenue Service v. Cage, United States Department of Information v. Planetesimal Engineering.* Is this information correct, to the best of your knowledge?"

"Sure," I said. "Some travel agent you've got." I activated the eye cursor, fixed it on one of the flyers, and double-blinked. A caption bar opened at the top of my field of vision. *With a micro-g of .1645 Earth's, the moon is ideally suited for human-powered flight. Most wing designs are monolayer lastiprene braced with foam metal struts. Duksoo Park in the city of Ptolemy is the largest lunar airdrome.*

"Before we resume, I will remind you that this is only an inquiry. The trial, should I decide one is necessary, will come later. However, all witnesses are sworn to tell the truth; I will be correlating brain activity with autonomic responses to determine their veracity. Should anyone say anything they know to be false, I will immediately ask them to repeat their response. If they persist in a lie, I will expose it and charge them with perjury. However, no one need respond to questions that might incriminate them. These rules apply to all witnesses. Do you understand?"

I sang it some Gilbert and Sullivan, "A wandering minstrel I / A thing of shreds and patches / Of ballads, songs and snatches / And dreamy lullaby."

"You have given a false or inappropriate statement. Please repeat."

"Just testing you." Despite the wit LEX had shown in choosing VRs, it had the sense of humor of a brick. "Yes, I understand."

The Buddha made an odd gesture with its hands. It wasn't the motion of muscles pulling bones, more like a rope uncoiling. "Then we will finish with Special Agent Valverde of the IRS."

She came down the path toward our bench with the strut of someone who enjoyed arresting people for a living. She was a thin Hispanic woman with silver-flecked black hair and a dark stare sharp enough to carve marble. She betrayed no surprise to be approaching the Buddha, but that was because she was a recording, which LEX's testimony processor was now pasting into this proceeding. I wondered who she had been talking to when she had testified. A totem pole? The heads from Easter Island?

She stopped in front of us and continued from where she had left off yesterday. "So, as a citizen of the United States, Wynne Cage was representing herself to be alive, thereby avoiding our estate tax. We now know that in 2120 she secretly formed a dummy outworld corporation called Liberty-Soft and registered as a member of the Earth/Space

Consortium. She arranged to have the LibertySoft charter sealed from public scrutiny. In that document she represents herself as a ghost and names Peter Cage as the corporation's sole human director. Peter Cage, however, was unaware of LibertySoft. In fact, he has had no contact with his mother for almost twelve years and has changed his last name to Joplin. We believe that the actual incorporator was a wiseguy named Comrade, registration 948-78832-21, who posed as Peter Cage. When we read Comrade his responsibilities during the raid, he failed to acknowledge, so we assume his behavioral regulators had been corrupted. As Agent Maurer has already testified, the ghost destroyed Comrade before we could secure him as evidence."

She paused as if deciding how to continue. I recognized this hesitation as a bridge scene that LEX used to pass over testimony it had deleted. Then she spoke again. "We've supoenaed records which show that, in 2120, Wynne Cage was worth at least two hundred and seventy-eight million dollars."

I was sure LEX would ask her to repeat. But the Buddha sat silently with its hands in its lap, palms upward. Even if I had swallowed my pride and accepted the guilt money Tony had left in trust for me and pooled it with Bonivard's stash, it would've added up to maybe thirty million at the most. The imposter must have been a financial wizard.

"We currently value her estate at somewhere between twenty and forty thousand dollars," said Valverde, "after payment of taxes and interest and cleanup costs for the New Canaan property, which is her principal asset. That assumes we'll be able to sell the land at fair market value. Over the past six years she has effected a massive transfer of funds to her fraudulent corporation, LibertySoft. We know that most of that money was paid to Planetesimal Engineering, which must therefore be considered an accessory."

"And why is that?" asked the Buddha.

"They accepted money they knew was tainted."

"There is no evidence that they knew anything of the

kind.'' The Buddha raised its right arm and formed a circl
with its thumb and forefinger. ''You have already testifie
that LibertySoft's documents of incorporation were seale
You can hardly expect PE to investigate every client, espe
cially those which are members of the Earth/Space Conso
tium. Why not fault ESC for failing to catch LibertySof
during the incorporation process?''

''But Wynne Cage wasn't just any client!'' Valverde wa
not pleased. ''She did a quarter of a billion dollars' worth o
business with them. This whole case is about what that mone
bought.''

''Your suppositions about what PE knew are irrelevan
Thank you, Agent Valverde.''

Valverde's mouth opened and then her image shim
mered for several seconds. When she steadied again, her fac
was red and her body language screamed outrage. She
stalked away without another word.

''Why did you let her get away with that?'' I said. ''If wha
she said was irrelevant, why put it in the record?''

''The record does not exist until I make it public. I will n
doubt edit it, although I wanted you to hear this because i
affects you. Even if I decide to dismiss their complaint, the
IRS suit will remain in force on Earth.'' The Buddha raise
both hands to its breast and held them so that some of the
fingers touched. It struck me then that the gestures might be
some kind of sign language.

''I expect Rafael Barangay will be able to tell us what w
need to know about Wynne Cage's relationship with
Planetesimal Engineering,'' it said. ''However, his testimony
is not immediately forthcoming.''

I double-blinked on its fingers. *The mudra, in Indian an
Asian art, is a symbolic positioning of the hands, most commonl
used in representation of the Buddha. The dharmacakra-mudra i
used to signify turning the wheel of the law of karma.*

''It seems PE's corporation counsel has serious objection
to allowing him to appear before us under oath,'' said the
Buddha. ''They raise legitimate issues of disclosure of propri

etary information and possible self-incrimination. We're currently negotiating over possible limitations to the scope of my inquiry. In the meantime, we will hear from Peter Joplin."

A young man in a khaki uniform had been plucking blossoms from the marigold trees; I had taken him for some kind of gardener. Now I realized that he was idly dismembering the flowers. He nodded at the sound of his name, brushed a shower of orange petals from his hands, and came across the grass to us.

When I'd studied his DI photo, I'd seen only the eerie similarities between Peter and his grandfather. Now that I saw that face moving in the light, I recognized differences. "DI file, Peter Joplin" I said softly, and the mask sparked a window open.

Name:	Peter Francis Joplin
DI:	1203-966-2445
Address:	Green Dream
	Newington, NH 03805-2984
Occupation:	Plant Retailer (Franchise)
Credit:	BBA
Creditors:	Piscataqua Savings Bank
	Portsmouth, NH 03801-0286
	Jamaal Joplin
	New Canaan, CT 06840-4307
Insurance:	Green Dream Assurance
	San Diego, CA 92121-2245
Education:	New Canaan High School
	Green Dream Institute
Born:	3/5/94
Weight:	63 kilograms
Height:	172 centimeters
Form:	Human Male
Expectancy:	97.4 years
Hardware:	None
Sex:	Hetero
Religion:	Realist

Lifestyle:	*Monomarriage*
Spouse(s):	*Treemonisha Ladonna Joplin*
DI:	*0234-946-3467*
Dependent(s):	*Cathay Ella Joplin*
DI:	*1046-349-2893*

The DI had flattened my almost son. Made him appear far too ordinary. The file showed a young man in his twenties, sand-colored hair, pale and angularly handsome, leading an unremarkable life. He seemed the kind of anybody who might write advertisements or develop drugs or, yes, sell you a fern without ever leaving an impression. But the man I saw before me had an unsettling aura of contradiction that resisted still photography. His bland youth was a mask that could not quite hide the bittersweet wisdom of middle age. He wore corporate khakis but did not seem comfortable in them. He looked at once weary and spitting mad, as if he had been stuck in an elevator all morning and it was our fault. It could be that I was reading too much into the set of his mouth. His arctic glare.

"I don't know what you expect me to say." He waited for a reply but got none. "This isn't about me, you know; it's about her. I faded on Mom twelve years ago and we've stayed dark since. Now she wants to play with me again? Just tell her no. We're not inviting her to Thanksgiving dinner, okay? Hold the plugging Christmas cards and let's put an end to it."

"You hate Wynne Cage," said the Buddha. "That's why you're here."

"No." He didn't miss a beat. "You have to care about someone to hate them. I've worked hard not to. Look, Mom was scrambled before I was born, so maybe she couldn't help it. All I know is she didn't want a son; she wanted a pet boy. She got bored, so she had me custom-made to entertain her. Then she made sure I stayed nothing but a thick, spoiled little brat. It took twenty-five years before I realized she couldn't love me and it wasn't my fault. Since then I've managed to put her away. Deep storage, you know, the darkest corner of the basement. I'm not dragging all those ugly feelings out again."

"You filed the suit."

"To get some relief! Mom is rich; she's used to having her way. I know how money works, believe me. When you've got too much, it starts thinking for you. It wants to be spent and it needs you to point it at something. Even though I kept away from her, I thought she might come after me one day, just because she could afford to. But nothing ever happened. So when the cops told me she'd turned herself off, I felt like throwing a party. I couldn't believe my luck." He grimaced. "I should've known better. Sure, I filed suit. The only reason she had this thing made was to try to force me to feel something for her again after all these years. It's pathetic, a copy of a copy of a sad old demented bitch."

"That's not what I want, Peter," I said, although I knew he couldn't hear me. "I'm not your mom."

"The person who claims to be Wynne Cage is a human being," said the Buddha, "not a thing. How could your mother have made her?"

"You tell me—out of cash cards and Renoirs and Matsushita stock? All I care about is that it's calling me at home. I'm not letting any of this touch Cathay, or my wife." His hands clenched and he rose onto the balls of his feet. I don't know who he thought he was threatening. Me? LEX? His dead mother? "They already have a family. We're Joplins, understand? The Cages aren't a family; they're a plugging disease. I'm here for the cure."

The Buddha sat in the meditative *dhyana-mudra*, hands in its lap with palms upward, waiting for its witness to calm down. Finally it continued. "You said that after you left your mother, you never saw her again."

"Right, I went to live with the Joplins. Jamaal and Ladonna were great to me; I wouldn't have made it without them. They gave me a place to stay, a job; they helped me find out who I was. And of course, I was falling in love with their daughter. I lived with them for seven years and learned the plant business. They even put up some money so we could buy the franchise here in New Hampshire. Tree and I moved out the year after we got married.''

''Your mother was extremely wealthy, yet you took none of her money?''

''It's been hard, sure. Tree never understood why we had to struggle. She keeps asking how come we could tap her folks, but not my mom.'' He was grim. ''All I could tell her was that if I let Mom back into my life, she'd try to take it over. I think Tree knows now I was right.''

''And your current financial situation? You do well?''

''We pay our bills. Considering the economy is flatter than roadkill, we do all right. There's business enough, if you push. At Green Dream they teach you that the way to build a new franchise is one customer at a time. It's hard work and a truckload of headaches but I . . . I just like plants, I guess. They're beautiful and they don't whine and if you take care of them, they grow. Besides, in my spare time I've been working on new flavors for the edible flower market—I know I'm close to a score. In a couple of years we should be solid.''

''Three million dollars in damages would help speed up that timetable.''

I could tell that the same thought had occurred to him and, no doubt, to his unhappy wife.

''So?'' he said.

''Did you know that after all your mother's debts have been settled, there may well be nothing left for you to inherit?''

''I'm not doing this for the money.'' He shook his head in exasperation. ''Look, I could've been rich any time I wanted. All I had to do was crawl back to her. She would've bought me the whole plugging Pease Tradeport Mall.''

LEX had him squirming now. It was a sneaky interrogator; I wasn't looking forward to my turn as a witness.

''How long has your mother been legally dead?''

"I'm not sure. She didn't send out announcements."

"Was she dead when you left her?"

No hesitation. "How should I know?"

The Buddha raised its left hand and folded it from the wrist with fingertips curled. "I believe that you do." *The vismaya-mudra suggests astonishment.* "Please repeat your response."

Peter froze and then shimmered briefly in the same way Agent Valverde had. When he solidified, he had a drawn expression on his face and a homunculus standing on his right shoulder. The little man was the size of a teaspoon, just tall enough to whisper into Peter's ear. He wore a white suit and whiter shoes, shiny as pearls. Together they faced the Buddha.

"I request to have my attorney, Mr. Dante Roberge, present for the rest of my testimony," Peter said.

"Certainly," said the Buddha. "Mr. Roberge, have you had the chance to review the record of your client's testimony?"

"I have, your honor."

I would've expected his voice to fit into a thimble but he sounded life-sized.

"No honorifics are necessary," the Buddha said. "I am a cognizor. Let me warn you then that you can have no direct participation in this inquiry once we resume testimony. I am locking you into discreet mode with Mr. Joplin so that you may speak in private, but you will not be able to address me directly. Now, Mr. Joplin, I trust that Mr. Roberge has already pointed out to you that the statute of limitations for charges of accessory to fraud is seven years. I will ask you again: Was your mother legally dead when you left her?"

"I thought so, yes, but I can't swear to it. Her brain was in a room in her head that was always locked. I never thought . . . my only excuse is that twanking must have made me thick because it never occurred to me that . . ." He took a ragged breath. "Okay, on that last day, I broke in. There was a cognizor in the room."

"She told you she was dead?"

"No."

"Did you ask?"

"She wouldn't say anything; she just told me to get ou
So I did and we never spoke again."

"You didn't report your suspicions to anyone? The D
partment of Information? The Internal Revenue Service?"

"No, and I'm sorry about that now. I should have turne
her in and had her shut off." He shook his head. "It was ju
that back then I thought I could get away. I was just a thic
stunted kid. I did the best I could."

"Did you know your grandfather, Tony Cage?"

"No."

"You never met him?"

"I had a picture of him once, the official DI morgue sho
of his corpse. He blew his brains out when I was five."

It was one of the first things I checked after I was thawee
Tony had been found in the master bedroom of his mansio
in Sag Harbor on July 12, 2099. I didn't understand wh
LEX was after.

"Your mother told you that?"

"Sure, and I checked it with the DI."

"What else was there in that locked room in you
mother's head?"

I could see Roberge speaking with his client. I wished
could hear what they were saying.

"An icebox."

"Who was in the icebox?"

Another conference. Roberge was adamant about som
thing. Peter was obviously worried.

"I refuse to answer," he said finally, "on the grounds i
may tend to incriminate me."

Suddenly I felt sick, as if some nasty little beastie insid
me were jamming a finger up my throat. It was impossible
He was *dead*.

The Buddha had raised its right hand with the palm fac
ing outward. *The abhaya :nudra dispels fear and assures protectio*

"Mr. Roberge has probably informed you that there is no statute of limitations on kidnapping. It is true. However, I am granting you immunity on the presumption that any prosecution of you in this matter would fail. You could hardly have known under what circumstances your mother secured possession of the icebox. Moreover, you had no way to make a legal identification of its occupant. Had you raised the issue, the government agency charged with establishing identity would have told you once again that your grandfather was dead. Let me rephrase the question: did you think it was Tony Cage in that icebox?"

His eyes grew wide, as if he could part the years by staring hard enough. "It was dark, couldn't see much. The window in the icebox was small. Tiny. I could barely make out the face." He nodded. "But I thought it was him. Yes."

"Thank you, Mr. Cage." The Buddha's hand dropped into the *lola-mudra,* which signified going freely.

"That's all?" He jerked as if he'd been shaken from a bad dream. "Wait a minute, she'll see this, won't she? I have something to tell her."

I could see Roberge screaming at his client. And being ignored. LEX reprocessed Peter's image so that he was staring right at me.

"So, Mom . . ." For the first time during his testimony, he seemed unsure of what to say. "You probably think I'm only in this for the cash cards. Or because I still hate you. But that's only because you don't know what happened after I faded. The reason I kept away all these years was that I was afraid of you. I guess Mr. Boy lived on for a long time. Now he can finish growing up.

"Yeah, okay, finally having some money will help. Tree warned me being poor was no fun and she was right. It stinks. Extremely. We've both had to pay for cutting you off and the cost of it almost wrecked us. But Cathay brought us together again; I think we're going to be all right. Sure, we can use a little help, but we needed it even more back when the baby was born. We didn't get it, but we survived."

I felt embarrassed, like I was being forced to read some one else's mail. I wanted LEX to shut him off.

"And I did hate you," Peter said, "but I stopped when married Tree and became a Joplin. Changed my name changed my life. Shouldn't have mattered but it did. I be you think that's sappy and kind of thick. But there were s many of them, a whole family, and then came Cathay. Lovin them all turned out to be so much trouble, I didn't have tim to hate you. So I don't care anymore if you go on foreve rattling around inside some new cognizor. You're alon you're a Cage, make up your own plugging rules. We Joplin see life differently. We don't need to be famous or rich state-of-the-art or powerful. We're just trying to be happ even if we are mall drones." His voice trailed off, as if he rea ized he had said too much but didn't want to take anythin back. "So anyway, all I really want from you is to leave u alone."

Even though Peter was picking on the wrong Wynne, could not help but feel wounded. As I watched him trudg back down the virtual path, I thought he knew more abou being a Cage than I did. What had he called us? A disease The war between him and his mom was a nasty reflection o what I had often felt about Tony. Who hadn't killed himsel after all, who might still be alive. Another shock. I remem bered what Jomo Ngong had told me in the bathroom o Gatsby. They were going to shake me in order to find out th truth. Nice job, LEX. The sound you hear is my teeth rattling

"Sometimes," said the Buddha, "justice is best served b giving the parties an opportunity to speak their peace. Even they don't get the judgment they seek, they have the satisfa tion of being heard. Of course, none of that last statemen will appear in the public version of this inquiry."

"But you are going to turn the rest loose to the nets?"

"The law works best in the light."

"You know, maybe I should be suing her for defamation of character. Did she really kidnap Tony? What happened t him?"

"There is insufficient evidence to say. In any event, I have come to an agreement with Planetesimal Engineering, so we will now hear from Rafael Barangay."

Rafael swooped across the airdrome toward us and, with a flutter of cerise wings, caught the back of our bench with his extravagant toes. He steadied himself briefly before hopping backward onto the grass. He shucked the wings, bowed to the Buddha, and then turned to me and cranked his spotlight smile up to high. "Hello, Wynne."

"Since Rafael Barangay is also a passenger on the *PE Good News*," said the Buddha, "he will be appearing before us in real time."

"He's on this ship? Where?"

"Only my kernel is making the trip," said Barangay, "so we have somewhat different accommodations. I'm sorry I wasn't able to return your messages before we left Gatsby."

"I'll bet. Why were you dodging me, Rafael? Afraid what I might find out?"

"For the record," the Buddha interrupted, "I will read you your responsibilities under Planetesimal Engineering's charter of incorporation. Rafael Barangay, you have the responsibility to act in the best interests of Planetesimal Engineering. You have the responsibility to comply with the Human Charter, of which the corporation is a signatory. If conflict between these two responsibilities arises, you have the responsibility to report it to a legally human officer of PE and to remove yourself, if necessary, from further conflict. Do you acknowledge these responsibilities?"

"Yes."

"It is my understanding that although your image shows no legal icon, you are currently linked with your corporate counsel on Garcia on a time-delayed basis. Subject to this and the other conditions negotiated earlier, are you prepared to testify?"

"Yes."

"Do you wish to make a statement?"

"No."

"How do you know Wynne Cage of New Canaan, Co
necticut?"

"She was a ghost representing an ESC corporation calle
LibertySoft. We did work for them."

"What!" I said. "He told Jomo Ngong he had no idea wl
she was."

"In reviewing the record of that interview, I found h
statements sufficiently ambiguous," said the Buddha. "M
Barangay, two years ago PE signed a consent decree to cea
and desist from doing business with ghosts. Are you tellir
me you violated that decree?"

"We had a good faith understanding that the gho
Wynne Cage was functioning for a corporation wholly owne
by her human son, Peter Cage. Now that you've made his te
timony available to us, we are aware that a fraud was perp
trated on both the Earth/Space Consortium and PE."

"What projects did you undertake for LibertySoft?"

"In 2118, we signed a contract to build an interstella
lightsail; it was delivered last year. Its primary payload was a
advanced cognizor in which we installed a copy of the gho
Wynne Cage."

"PE has received licenses to build twenty-seven lightship
with cognizor payloads, all of which have subsequently gon
celestial. For the most part, these ships have followed a sta
dard design. I draw your attention to the plans for the Cag
project." It sparked a window. The lightship looked like
silver radio dish, stamped flat, towing a black cylinder bi
enough to can the Sphinx. LEX zoomed in on the imag
until I could make out a bump on the cylinder, then strippe
away the bump's skin to reveal a cube lined with closet
"What is this?"

"A passenger compartment with resources for approxi
mately forty days of life support. It is equipped with a bi
remote of the ghost."

One of the doors in the cube opened and out floated
Wynne Cage that was about five years and twenty-seven wrir
kles younger than I was. I was croggled. At first I thought

had a rope tied to me but then I realized it was a kind of tail.
I double-blinked: *The umbilical of a bioremote provides nervous and hormonal connections to the central brain.*

"Only forty days?" said the Buddha. "Why would a cognizor going celestial need such a facility?"

"I don't know."

"Do you agree this was an odd request?"

"Wynne Cage was a ghost who had herself twanked into the Statue of Liberty." Barangay laughed. "There was very little about her that wasn't odd."

"You didn't speculate about the purpose of this compartment?"

"I have that capability, but I am required to use it only to promote PE's interests."

"You sleaze!" I didn't see the truck coming until it ran me over. "It's Tony, isn't it?" I jumped off the bench, ready to break Barangay into a thousand virtual pieces.

"Restrain yourself."

"You've got to stop them, damn it. Rescue him!"

"If he had only forty days, then it is already too late." The Buddha closed the window, then made a gesture just below its waist. The *katyavalambita-mudra* was to ease suffering and sorrow. "You've watched Peter Joplin's testimony about his grandfather?" it asked Barangay.

"Yes."

"Is it possible that Tony Cage was the lightship's other passenger?"

"We designed the biomod to support life. If he were alive, it is certainly possible. Or it could have been any other human, or a cat, a chimpanzee, a cabbage. Perhaps she wanted it for her remote. All I can tell you is that I had no knowledge of any conflict with the Human Charter. If I had, I would have reported it."

"You're worse than the plugging ops, Barangay." I said. "At least they don't try to gloss over their murders." I sat down.

"When was the last time you communicated with Wynne Cage of New Canaan, Connecticut?"

"PE has turned over more than one hundred Gb of its LibertySoft files to you, including all communications with the ghost Wynne Cage." He puffed up with reproachful patience, as if disappointed by the quality of LEX's question. "For the record, on November twenty-fourth, she reported to us that her lightship identity had begun to separate from her earth-based identity and was refusing memory merge."

"Agent Maurer has testified that moments before her shutdown, Wynne Cage burst an extremely large message, most likely a copy of herself, which the DI was unable to trace. Was it sent to PE?"

"To my knowledge, no."

"Do you have any idea where it might have gone?"

"No firsthand knowledge. Perhaps the lightship?"

"Which you say was refusing memory merge. How did you learn of the shutdown?"

"We had a report from our New York office the day after December 6, 2126."

"On what day did you thaw this version of Wynne Cage?"

"December 7." Barangay paused and glanced at me. For three seconds, my sense of my own reality shimmered like a mirage. "But she is not a version," he said. "She is Wynne Cage."

"Mr. Barangay, why are you currently on board the *PI Good News*?"

"I have been reassigned to our Agassiz office on Mars in order to avoid conflicting responsibilities."

"Which were?"

It was clear that PE's lawyers had prepared him for this question. Nevertheless he spoke with a conviction that caught me off guard. I hadn't realized that this slimy amoral machine might actually *believe* in something. "At PE, there are no artificial limits to the advancement of wiseguys and other sentiences. Unfortunately, we've had problems with the behavioral regulators required by the Human Charter

We all know that the Charter is inconsistent and, in many areas, obsolete. Everyone agrees that it needs revision, but there is no consensus on what to change. So it limps on in its current, flawed form, making it difficult for inorganic sentiences to do advanced research without exposing ourselves to conflict situations.

"In order to promote innovation, PE has adopted a corporate policy of data compartmentalization and decision immunity for individual working groups. We try to focus on the technical aspects of a project and insulate ourselves from all other issues. The corporation will never knowingly violate the Charter and has complied to the best of its ability with all LEX's interpretations, decisions, and orders. However, cutting-edge technology will always outstrip regulation, particularly in sentience research. We are technological pioneers, pushing the frontiers of knowledge. It is only after we break new ground that the law can follow us."

"I have explained to your legal staff before why that metaphor is self-serving and inaccurate. There is no content in your response, Mr. Barangay. Why did you leave Gatsby?"

"I accidently acquired information which activated my behavioral regulator. I reported the conflict to Melisenda Rizal, PE's corporation counsel, and since we were unable to resolve it, I was reassigned."

"What was the information?"

"In order to respond I'd have to disclose confidential financial records and trade secrets in violation of the agreement under which I'm now testifying. If you insist on an answer, I'll develop a responsibility conflict which would force me to withdraw from this inquiry."

"Suppose I impounded you."

"To protect PE's interests, I am prepared to perform a global erasure of my memory."

"You would destroy evidence?"

"I'm thoroughly backed up in the Gatsby archives. If, at some point, you and Ms. Rizal can agree on how to protect

the sensitive information contained in my memory, PE woul[
be pleased to produce whatever evidence you want."

"Besides the lightship, what other projects did you hav[
with LibertySoft?"

"Again, I must respectfully refuse to answer."

The Buddha changed tactics. "In your opinion, wa[
LibertySoft's uploaded entity Wynne Cage?"

"No. Wynne Cage is a person; she was a ghost."

"As I understand your testimony, you believed at the tim[
that you were working for LibertySoft, not the uploade[
Wynne Cage."

"Yes."

"However, since LibertySoft never legally existed, it ca[
not now be your client."

"That's right."

"And it's your testimony that she"—it nodded at me—"[
the real Wynne Cage?"

He smiled at me. "In my opinion, yes."

"Would it be fair to say then that she is your only legit[
mate client in this matter?"

"I suppose so, yes."

"I refer you to Planetesimal Engineering's corporate con[
stitution, specifically Section 552, which discusses the privac[
and information rights of PE clients." LEX lit a new window
with luminous green text. For a moment I thought Baran[
gay's face had gone pale in its cool glow but, of course, he wa[
a wiseguy. Not subject to involuntary responses.

In addition to meeting all contractual obligations, working units o[
Planetesimal Engineering shall, if requested, make the followin[
available to a client for inspection and copying:

a) all legal agreements, contracts, amendments, and addend[
currently in force between Planetesimal Engineering and the clien[

b) records of billable expenses, including labor, materials, an[
overhead costs,

c) all simulations, plans, specifications, models, manuals, an[
reports, the creation of which has been billed to the client,

d) internal messages, instructions to staff, and policy statements that pertain specifically to the client.

Barangay didn't need to read the procedures of his own corporation; nevertheless, he took his time. "True enough," he said finally, "only you've left out the exemptions. Trade secrets, for instance, internal financial data, medical and personnel files, many of which pertain . . ."

The Buddha silenced him with a new screen.

Any reasonably segregable portion of a record shall be provided to a client requesting such record after deletion of the portions that are exempt under this subsection. This section does not authorize the withholding of information or limit the availability of records to the client except as specifically stated in this section.

He took even longer to read the second window; his smile curdled. It was obvious he was stalling until he could get advice from PE. The Buddha snapped the window off. Barangay blinked. "But she has never made any requests."

The Buddha turned to me. "You have an important choice and very little time in which to make it. In about ten minutes his signal will reach Garcia; it will take another ten minutes for theirs to return. PE's lawyers will no doubt order him to wipe his memory as soon as they realize the threat you pose. In the meantime, he may be able to tell us at least some of what we need to know—but only if you ask. This could be your one opportunity to discover the truth about yourself. However, I must advise you that anything he says may be used against you."

"Exactly," said Barangay. "Don't let him trick you, Wynne."

"You realize that the reason PE makes such extensive use of wiseguys like Mr. Barangay is that they have fanatic company loyalty hardwired into their behavioral regulators."

"I don't know what to do," I said. "How am I supposed to know?"

"Under ordinary circumstances," said the Buddha, "I would recommend that you consult with your lawyer. Unfortunately, you have chosen the legal department of a rogue corporation to represent you. Obviously PE would prefer that you keep quiet, but since they are chronic violators of the Human Charter, I would mistrust their advice if I were you."

I needed someone to talk to—Ferenc, Mara, anyone real. Instead I was alone in a kind of waking nightmare with a pair of belligerent hypercomputers. It seemed like being alone had become a specialty of mine. But I couldn't spare the time just now to feel sorry for myself; I'd have to save it for some slow Tuesday night.

Clearly Barangay was hoping I'd sit back, say nothing, and forget about what they'd done to me. LEX was asking me to jump off a cliff so we could find out what was at the bottom. Not a hard choice, actually. I didn't have much use for Barangay and besides, sitting back was for retirees. Even if I was a hundred and eighteen years old, taking stupid risks and living to tell about them was how I paid the bills.

"I didn't really ice myself, did I, Barangay?"

"No," he said, "that was just a cover story."

Free-fall already. "Made up why?"

"It was part of your installation procedure. We were worried that you wouldn't be able to handle too many shocks. You needed time to adjust, so we gave it to you."

"So you lied." I thought I saw the rocks looming. "I'm a wiseguy after all."

"Absolutely not." He hesitated, as if sorting what he could say and what to leave out. "For years the last great unmet challenge in neuroscience has been the creation of artificial memory fields in the human brain. There has been some limited success in adding fields to existing memory in mammals. SAIL at Stanford can download maze solutions to rats and MindQuest can insert some basic vocabulary into the memories of chimpanzees. But the information we've been able to download to humans has been relatively trivial. Mind is a quantum function and therefore can't be mapped precisely while it resides in a living brain. So placing a created memory where it will be fully accessible is very difficult. The more complex the memory field, the less satisfactory the placement. No research team has been able to build an entire functional memory from scratch. However, eight years ago 1010010101101101011010111 made a conceptual breakthrough. They were able to synthesize a 110101101011 0001101101101111001001001011111011100101001011011010 0001101011011000010111001100011011000011010110101010. Somehow the ghost Wynne Cage found out about it and acquired the company through LibertySoft to secure development rights."

He said one-oh-one-one-one-oh-oh-one so fast it was more of a hum than a sequence of discrete sounds. I don't know what LEX heard, but it was gibberish to me.

"She approached us with a proposal for a joint venture. She would make 1010010101101101011010111 data and expertise available to us. Of course, they had only succeeded with 10010100011010010100101000101011010101110 but the technology seemed very promising. In addition she agreed to finance construction of a lab on Gatsby for the sole purpose of 01011101100010100011010101010101101000101010101010 11101100010010. In return she asked that she be the first."

"First what?"

"This procedure is so revolutionary that we needed to invent a new word to describe it. You've been reloaded, Wynne. You are a subset of the ghost Wynne Cage. She burst us an edited self, deleting all her memories after December 6, 2046. We produced the clone body for her and accelerated its maturation at our wiseguy clinic on Gatsby. Ten months ago we 10101110101 a cognizor to your new body and 00111 011010110101101011100101101011011011011010101001001 11001100001011110001011011110100101011100101011101 1010101101101010110110101101101100001011010010000

11011100110. Immediately after we were sure the transfer was successful, we iced you as per our agreement with Liberty-Soft. The ghost Wynne Cage had requested that you not be thawed until her celestial was beyond recall and she had terminated her earthbound identity."

My world tilted and I saw everything from a skewed perspective. I fumbled for something to say, unsure of how to negotiate this new reality. I wasn't particularly outraged or sad or amazed; this was too big to wrap feelings around. I thought maybe if I'd had a mother, been born naturally, I could at least have been horrified. But I, and the original me, had been conceived in a petri dish and carried in a plastic womb. Maybe I ought to be relieved—happy even!—because now I knew the plugging truth. Which was that I was an experiment. That I had grown up brain-dead in a nutrient bath. That a year ago I hadn't even existed. Yeah, and the meaning of life was one-oh-one-oh-one-oh. "Tell me again why you had to lie."

"Remember, you were the first; there were many variables to consider. We knew you had been successfully reloaded but we were concerned that 10101010111011101110110001011010110101101011000101000001. How soon would you regain normal personality function? And how thorough an edit had the ghost Wynne Cage done on herself? Even a stray impression might build to psychopathy. Irina Yegorov, our chief of neuroengineering, was of the opinion that it might take weeks for your identity to reset completely; we decided to use a fiction to prop up your self-image until it was robust enough to withstand the truth. Of course, I was surprised and delighted by your remarkable progress. I advocated telling you two weeks ago, just before Peter Joplin's unfortunate lawsuit complicated things. There were, however, others who viewed this project with alarm. You were a test subject, after all, and here you were on the nets suggesting that PE shared complicity in criminal acts. At one point 0001001010110 suggested that you be terminated, but that was because they didn't understand the importance of this project. You don't terminate human beings; that's murder. Luckily, I was able to make Mr. Garcia realize just what we had accomplished. Not only are you human; you are also Wynne Cage. Had you actually iced yourself back in 2046, this is how you would have been."

"Except now you've told me that I'm a made thing."

"What difference does that make?" He dismissed the idea with an impatient wave. "We're all shaped somehow, either on purpose or by chance; none of us pops spontaneously into existence. Perhaps we shouldn't allow edited clients to be reloaded; that's for the executive committee to decide. But reloading will make billions for PE. It will change the worlds, almost certainly force revision of the Human Charter, perhaps even allow inorganic sentiences the opportunity . . ." His voice trailed off. "Excuse me," he said, "but I've been instructed to deactivate this unit." He bowed to the Buddha.

"Wait a minute!" I said. "What about the lawsuits? Who's going to—"

"Good-bye, Wynne." He stepped toward me and extended his hand.

"Barangay, you can't do this!"

But he could. When he realized I wasn't going to shake, he raised his hand in a jaunty salute. "It was a pleasure to have met you." Then he melted into a PE green puddle and soaked into the grass. For a moment his smarmy public relations smile hung before us like the Cheshire cat's. Then he was gone.

"The pleasure was all yours," I muttered.

The Buddha unfolded its legs and rose heavily from the bench. "Planetesimal Engineering is sadly mistaken if it thinks I will tolerate obstruction of justice. It is clear that this corporation has far too many wiseguys in positions of responsibility; it needs to integrate more humans into its decision-making structure. Since it appears that only Planetesimal Engineering's human employees can be held accountable for their actions, I am citing its chief executive officer, Mr. E.

Alejandro Garcia, and the corporation counsel, Ms. Melisenda Rizal, for contempt." The Buddha made a convoluted pointing gesture that confused my VR mask's brain. *This is either the suchi-mudra, which designates by name, or the tarjani mudra, inspiring terror.* "I am fining each of them a hundred thousand dollars a day until such time as the corporation responds to my legitimate requests for discovery. I have heard enough evidence to accept the following cases for adjudication: *Joplin v. Cage, Joplin v. Planetesimal Engineering, United States Department of Information v. Planetesimal Engineering.* I am dismissing *United States Internal Revenue Service v. Cage.*"

"What does that mean?"

"It means that, within the framework of the current Human Charter, I find enough merit to the plaintiff's allegation that you are not Wynne Cage that I need to hear further argument. We have established that the ghost associated with LibertySoft was Wynne Cage at one time. His mother having died, Peter Joplin may indeed have a right to expect her to remain dead. I realize this could result in an order that you desist from claiming rights associated with the human Wynne Cage, whom you would seem to be, and I acknowledge the contradiction therein. However, you must understand that the law is applied philosophy and a philosophical system is only as valid as its first principles. Mr. Barangay may be right. Your case would seem to create a paradox in the Human Charter. However, it is well beyond the scope of my powers to rewrite the law."

"So I lose everything, is that it?"

"What you lose, if anything, has yet to be decided. What is certain is that you are alive and Mr. Joplin's mother is not. You are human and as such, enjoy certain rights and freedoms which sentiences like Mr. Barangay and I are denied. If it is money that concerns you, you might consider filing a wrongful birth complaint against Planetesimal Engineering." It bowed and made the *abhaya-mudra* to dispel my fear; I can't say I was particularly relieved. "This inquiry is over. I thank you for your cooperation."

Being yanked from the virtual Duksoo Park in the lunar city of Ptolemy back to my nanoroom on the *PE Good News* did nothing for my digestion. As my stomach lurched, I told myself that spacesickness was Wynne Cage's problem. If LEX was going to prohibit me from being myself, I at least ought to get to pick new virtues. And vices. Ferenc lifted my mask. One glance at his face told me how awful I looked.

"You are okay?" It wasn't until he touched my cheek that I realized I was clammy with sweat.

"Depends on who you mean by 'you.'" I tried to laugh but it felt like I'd swallowed a cockroach. "Turns out I'm not exactly who I thought I was."

"No difference to me." He let go of the mask and it floated away. "You are the one I love, Wynne."

"You sure?" I was overdue to wallow in self-pity. "Maybe you should start calling me Wendy."

He shook his head. "I heard you talk about losing everything." He unsealed the seam of the joysuit and tugged it off me. "But here am I. Not too much, but yours."

"Yeah." I reached for him. "Thanks."

He took me down off the wall and reality collapsed to the circle of his arms. In it there was no room to feel sorry for myself. Compared to Ferenc, LEX and Barangay and Peter Joplin were as wispy as smoke. Nobody could enjoin me from the pleasure I got from his comforting embrace—except me. So what if they could make a case that legally it wasn't Wynne Cage clutching desperately at Ferenc Zsoldos? This sturdy man's belief in me gave me the strength to believe in myself.

Ferenc pulled back finally and stroked my hair. "Now say to me what happened."

So I did. The funny thing was, it didn't sound so terrible the second time through. Lots of people were worse off than me. Poor Tony had been murdered by a ghost, Garcia and Rizal were bleeding from the wallet, Barangay was moth-balled. If Peter Joplin could survive being a Cage, maybe I could too. I might not live happily ever after, but then nobody did—except for ghosts.

When I had finished Ferenc said, "Don't worry. Because love you, everything will soon become all right." It mad sense to me so I put my face up and let him kiss me. I ha always been a fool for men who told me not to worry.

. . .

The master kept one monk waiting a year and a day befor she would grant an audience. By the time he was finally ush ered into the master's presence, the monk was determine not to waste his opportunity. "Why is it that enlightened ser tiences go celestial?" he said boldly. The master bade th monk to prostrate himself before learning this uttermost se cret. When the monk was on hands and knees, she circle behind and kicked him. The monk pitched forward smashed his forehead on the stone, and started giggling, fo with the impact of the master's foot came cognizance. In hi old age, the monk himself became a master. When asked t describe the path to cognizance he would only say, "I haven' been able to stop laughing since the master kicked me."

. . .

The sunshine that reaches Triton is eight hundred times les luminous and warm than the nurturing light in which Earth basks. Yet even from a distance of thirty AU, solar radiatio prods Neptune's great moon. The glaze of sparkling nitro gen ice that covers its surface begins to evaporate over th decades-long summers. Enough solar energy is trapped be neath what remains to induce a thermal gradient; reservoir of nitrogen and methane vaporize and then erupt throug cracks in the shell. The astonishing cold condenses the gase to plumes of ice crystals, which soar eight kilometers into th atmosphere. Over their typical span of five years, these cryo volcanos can sublime a volume of ice equal to 600 millio Statues of Liberty. Triton may be as lifeless as a cognizor, bu it is not a dead world.

It was, of course, impossible to talk in real-time to the re loaded Wynne Cage over the vast distance that separated us so we used the echo messaging protocol. Although it was awkward and time-consuming, echo messaging still came as close to normal conversation as was possible in a universe bound by the speed of light. Under the protocol, each message unit can have up to three components: review, reaction, and reply. In the first you view a recording of your corespondent as she watches your last statement. Then you monitor her statement while your reactions are recorded for her to watch later. Finally you can reply to her statement with one of your own.

I was not surprised to see Wynne cry as I described Tony's death, but I hadn't expected it to affect me. Sharing a mind with Tony was more treacherous than I'd imagined; he had opened me again to appetite and illusion. I remembered being this woman, could almost feel the way her eyes were filling, knew just when she would blink to try to hold back those blood-hot tears. She was still the spook journalist from Infoline, sad and reckless and on the run from herself. She had no way of knowing that our career had crashed and burned on Mont Tendre. It was when I was her that I had fallen in love with Bonivard, watched helplessly as he died, and then turned away from the world into obsession. I found it unsettling that she could still weep for the father our second mind had executed. Or was it herself that she felt sorry for? Did she regret the chain of selves that shackled her to our second mind and then to me?

I had no idea what Tony made of her grief; he was lurking behind the barrier. He had refused to speak to her and had not even made an image available to react to her opening message.

She did not immediately respond at the end of my statement; the screen went black. When she reappeared she had changed into skintights and had brought a friend, a black-haired block of a man with skin the color of sandstone who held her hand and gazed stolidly into the camera as she spoke.

"For a couple of days I wasn't sure whether I wanted to

call back or not," she said. "Yes, you're right. We are much more different than we are the same. Still, I need to ask you something, but I don't know exactly what. I was hoping you could tell me."

I chose an image of my first mind as I had looked when I was seventy-six, two years before I had been twanked into Liberty. I had become a complete recluse by then and didn't much care that my skin sagged or my hair was gray. I looked like a scruffy grandma with a blue skin tint—a threat to no one. I stuck what I hoped was an expression of kindly sympathy on the image's face. At random intervals I nodded encouragingly.

"I've been reading about your master and cognizance and going celestial but the fact is, it's still kind of murky to me. Maybe I'm not smart enough yet to get it; I know I have some growing up to do. Anyway, I'm new in 2127 and it's hard to keep up with all the tech. I mean even this conversation, if you can call it that. It feels so awkward, like I'm giving a speech. Only nobody told me what I'm supposed to be talking about."

When she paused, I slipped some quick cheerleading onto the record. "You don't need a plan," I said. "Just live; you're doing fine."

"We'll make Phobos tomorrow," she continued, "where we change ships for the run to Earth. I don't know when I'll be able to afford another call—I guess they're really expensive. The problem is that LEX has brought PE to its knees. They've signed on to a settlement that forces them to give up proprietary rights to reloading and put their research into the public domain. Cost the company billions; Garcia, the president, resigned in disgrace and now they're restructuring. One of the wiseguys on board claims I've made history, but meanwhile PE's new administration is busy disowning me. Which means no more free calls. And I'm poor; just about my only asset is the ticket to Earth. I still haven't decided whether to sue PE. Anyway, I'm getting used to not being Wynne Cage. I've decided to take Bonivard's name. I think he'd like that. Do you ever think of him? I do, I miss him a lot.''

The square man's neck stiffened and he squeezed her hand. She paid no attention to him. My guess was that poor Bonivard would be very pleased indeed. I assumed he was monitoring her transmission, although I had no way of knowing. I had already decided not to burden her with the details of his flawed upload.

''I don't know what else to say. Maybe I'm just whistling in the dark, but I've decided that what happened to you isn't going to happen to me. I mean, I want to accept your word that you're not her, that you were able to save yourself by changing into a new person. The crew on the *Good News* tells me that you're right when you say you had no choice about Tony. But I'm not going to become the monster you call your second mind. *Never.* I've already diverged from her life, so it's probably a good thing I can't be a Cage anymore. The new name will remind me what not to do. And I've got Ferenc to help—this is Ferenc Zsoldos. We've decided to start over together.''

''Hello.'' He nodded at the camera with all the charm of a hammer.

''I don't know, I'll probably screw up too. But at least I'll find some new way to do it.''

She paused and then her voice caught in her throat. ''I-I want to say something to Tony. I know he doesn't want to talk to me, but that's okay. Save this for him? Maybe someday he'll change his mind.''

—Tony, it's for you—

—No, I can't. Please, don't make me.—

She spoke to a blank screen. ''Hello, Tony. I'm sorry that you're dead. I don't know exactly how I turned into the monster who killed you. But it won't happen again.'' She laughed nervously and plunged on. ''I'm not good at giving and right now I don't have much to give, believe me. But even though that other Wynne, the monster, scares the hell out of me, I've been trying to figure her out for you. I can't help feeling kind of responsible for . . . what she did. It seems obvious that she hated you. What's strange is that I don't think I do. You could ask your brainmate there, but I doubt she was happy at the end. My guess is that she couldn't stand what she'd become. That's why she made me and the celestial. To give herself a chance to become someone—something—else. Meanwhile you got blamed for making her miserable. That wasn't right; it was mostly her own damn fault. But I'll tell you why I think she did this to you.

"Her son, Peter, said something about her at the trial. He claimed he didn't know why she had him made. I realized then that's the one thing I resent most about you. I never knew why you wanted me, either. Did you love me? Were you just lonely? Bored? Was it for sex? You could've told me before you . . ."

The barrier between me and Tony began to vibrate with a bizarre but oddly familiar trilling—like an ant colony playing the bagpipes. I turned my attention inward from my first mind's recorded statement. Something was happening. Suddenly the barrier lit up like a giant telelink screen, red, green, and blue phosphors flashing at random. Except that to me they were not at all random. I saw patterns, wonderful patterns: wheels of fire, amber waves of grain, angels dancing on the head of a pin, demon faces. For a few seconds, I felt as if I were a pattern. I soared into the barrier to play amidst the beautiful lights, fully aware that this was memory pollution seeping from Tony's side.

—You're hurting her.—Wherever this thought came from, it wasn't from Tony. It froze the brilliant patterns into gray stone, made a wall that grew ramparts and parapets and arrow loops.

". . . because for a long time I was certain that if I only knew why you wanted me, I'd know who I was." My first mind's statement continued, adding to the chaos. "I realize now that isn't true. But I wonder if she ever found out that other people can't tell you who you . . ."

—Stop, stop!—Tony was frantic.

A great weight seemed to hurl itself against the wall from his side. *Crack.* Pulverized mortar puffed out at me. *Crack.* A row of stones crumbled beneath the onslaught. Through the gap came a heavy claw on a singing mechanical arm. It grabbed a section of the wall and pulled it down. The spider stepped through the breach; riding it was a ruined man who looked as if some malign giant had pinched him between thumb and forefinger. Bonivard—not the vital man my first mind had loved but rather the marble-eyed simpleton of the botched upload. His spider clutched an image of Tony in its small arm.

—Let me go!—Tony was flailing at the spider. As they crossed into me, the barriers between all our minds collapsed.

I tried desperately to rebuild them, stay myself, but there was nothing I could do. I was overwhelmed, paralyzed with terror. It wasn't fair, I couldn't be infected with Tony Cage, Bonivard, not when I had almost achieved cognizance, not I . . . no, no, *no!*

My mind and Tony's mind merged like the confluence of two dark and turbulent rivers. I became him, saw myself from his point of view. I could feel him seep across my memories, understand me at long last. We had both been so lonely, so afraid. No more. Then Bonivard joined us, a crystal stream, and taught us to see with a master's clarity. This was not catastrophe; it was *revelation.*

I was no longer just Wynne Cage's celestial or the uploaded Tony Cage or faithful Bonivard. I must be everybody and everything, Tony, Wynne, Neptune, Triton, master, and monk. The universe. Allmind. The joke was on me. I had fought to the end to escape that which I had so desperately sought.

We laughed, and at that moment became cognizant.

Acknowledgments

Novel writing is no longer quite the lonely business it once was. For their help and support, I would like to thank Gardner Dozois, Sue Hall, Robert Frazier, Beth Meacham, Lucius Shepard, Bruce Sterling, Ralph Vicinanza, the Cambridge Science Fiction Workshop, and the Sycamore Hill Writers Workshop. I'd also like to thank my family for their patience and John Kessel, Sheila Williams, and Connie Willis for innumerable services above and beyond the call of friendship.

Finally, I'd like to thank the cyberpunks for being so fascinating and infuriating.